NAUGHTIER THAN NICE

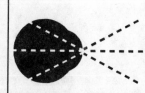

This Large Print Book carries the
Seal of Approval of N.A.V.H.

NAUGHTIER THAN NICE

ERIC JEROME DICKEY

THORNDIKE PRESS
A part of Gale, Cengage Learning

GALE
CENGAGE Learning·

Farmington Hills, Mich • San Francisco • New York • Waterville, Maine
Meriden, Conn • Mason, Ohio • Chicago

GALE
CENGAGE Learning·

LIBRARY OF CONGRESS CATALOGING-IN-PUBLICATION DATA

Dickey, Eric Jerome.
  Naughtier than nice / Eric Dickey. — Large print edition.
    pages cm. — (Thorndike Press large print African-American)
    ISBN 978-1-4104-8403-1 (hardback) — ISBN 1-4104-8403-3 (hardcover)
    1. Large type books. 2. Domestic fiction. I. Title.
PS3554.I319N37 2015b
813'.54—dc23   2015036222

Published in 2015 by arrangement with Dutton, an imprint of Penguin Publishing Group, a division of Penguin Random House LLC

Printed in the United States of America
1 2 3 4 5 6 7 19 18 17 16 15

FOR TOMMIE McBROOM

In this world there are only two tragedies.
One is not getting what one wants, and
the other is getting it.
  — Oscar Wilde, *Lady Windermere's Fan*

We want the ones we can't have, and we
crap all over the ones we can. Rinse and
repeat.
                  — *This Is Where I Leave You*

FOR FRANKIE McBROOM

All you need is to tell the truth. It's always
heartbreaking.
                        — Ethan Hawke

In revenge and in love, women are more barbaric than men.

> — Friedrich Nietzsche,
> *Beyond Good and Evil*

FOR LIVVY MCBROOM-BARRERA

Everything is about sex — except sex.

Sex is about power.

> — House of Cards

Sometimes you have to lose yourself to discover who you are.

> — Paulo Coelho, *Adultery*

THE EVE OF
CHRISTMAS EVE

FRANKIE

Hoodwinked. Bamboozled. Betrayed. My rage was bottomless.

My younger sister Tommie told me that I suffered from dysphoria — a state of feeling unwell — due to overthinking, insomnia, and depression. My middle sister, Livvy, said I was just pissed the fuck off.

I agreed with Livvy. I was pissed off to a level of pissivity previously unknown to womankind.

I scowled at what had been my engagement ring — a two-carat Petra Gems platinum engagement ring — and cursed Franklin Carruthers. It was a ring that looked like the truest of true loves. We'd flown to New Providence Island, leased a suite at Sandals Royal Bahamian Spa, and had a driver take us to John Bull on Bay Street. While the luxury of Gucci, Cartier, Rolex, Bulgari, and Citizen's lines surrounded us, we picked out amazing rings, then set a date and planned a beach wedding in Turks and Caicos. I'd had the ring appraised. Twenty grand. If only love could be appraised to see if it's true or just a chunk of cubic zirconium. After we'd come home from the Bahamas, we had all gone out to a sunset dinner in Marina del Rey, and Franklin eased down on his knees in front of my sisters, Monica, Tony, and Blue. Franklin had asked me to marry him, gave a speech praising me and made it official, slid a ring on my finger knowing bigamy was illegal.

Franklin Carruthers. We used to call ourselves *Frankie and Frankie.* I'd seen a chance Christmastime meeting with a man who had been christened with the male version of my name as a sign. I thought I'd found my knight in shining armor, but he was just another liar wrapped in aluminum foil.

We'd announced to our friends and on social media that we were going to be Mr. and Mrs. Franklin and Frankie Carruthers. I changed my status from SINGLE TO ENGAGED to let other men know they'd missed out on the last single McBroom and to let other women know I'd been bumped up to first class. I had imagined our entire life together, up until the end. The wedding was to be my rebirth. I'd expected both of my sisters to be with me in a thousand photos. Had imagined Tommie, Livvy, and me with big smiles and tears of joy as the McBroom girls stood near the shore and its turquoise water. Life was a false perfect.

We'd become one of those sickening, attention-seeking couples on social media, broadcasting our love for each other at sunrise, having public conversations from the time we left each other to the moment we were back in the same space, tweeting witticisms, and pretty much uploading a new amorous photo every day. We were both entrepreneurs, a power couple living life to the utmost.

We'd taken time from our respective businesses, wanted to be alone, and traveled the world. Our sabbatical from Cali lasted two months. We handled all of our affairs by phone, proxy, e-mail, and fax.

He was going to be my husband, so there were no holds barred.

So many memories were captured in more than ten thousand digital photos.

In Italy, Franklin pulled me to a concealed outdoor location, and as people walked by unaware, that country boy gave cunnilingus like I was better than Momma's baked chicken. My 'Bama man was a wicked double dipper — would feast on me, rock

11

me real good, then, while it was hot, ease down for seconds. After the loving, we rushed by Renaissance and Baroque architecture, laughed as we passed by the world's finest collections of sculptures, carvings, frescoes, and paintings to rejoin the walking tour for the Vatican Museums, the Sistine Chapel, Raphael's Rooms, and St. Peter's Basilica. Having an orgasm, then looking up and seeing incredible frescoes by Michelangelo was like being in God's living room. Photo after photo, my love hangover had me giggling, glowing, before the beautiful *Pietà* sculpture. We tried to behave but acted like out-of-control teenagers with *YOLO* tattooed in invisible ink across our foreheads. The magnificent engagement ring on my hand told me this was the start of perfection.

It hurts to remember how big a fool I was. Two months of traveling, and there was no foreshadowing of what was yet to come. The ones we make love to today will screw us tomorrow.

Before we had taken our vacation, we had gone to see a renowned specialist in Beverly Hills. It blew my mind. We were *trying* to make a baby while we were in Paris, Italy, and Africa. Not an *accidental* baby. An *intentional* baby. I wanted to be pregnant before my middle sister, Livvy, and definitely before our younger sister, Tommie. I was the oldest McBroom sister on this branch and that was my right, to have the first McBroom grandchild. After we had taken our sabbatical and returned home, after we had been greeted by all of our friends and family, we were in my house, in my master bedroom.

The *Titanic* had been unsinkable, the *Hindenburg* indestructible, the Luftwaffe unbeatable.

My relationship with Franklin was supposed to be as unbreakable as the Chicago Bulls during the 1995–1996 season. I'll never forget that night when my romantic illusions came to an end.

FRANKIE

The eve of Christmas Eve. My tree was decorated, presents for all underneath.

We were in the houghmagandy bedroom. We had a room at my home devoted to our passion, a well-appointed room I kept locked. King bed. Armless chair. Bench. Music. Candles. Mints. Water. Wine. Blue Gatorade. Massage oil. Lubes. An assortment of grown-folk toys. Scarves and blindfolds. Chocolates. Wipes. There was a wall of mirrors. I had a journal with my fantasies written down. *Kama Sutra* books. A mini fridge to store cool drinks and fresh fruit. I owned a Sybian. GoPro HERO3 Black Edition to capture memories, or just to play memories while we lounged in bed on a rainy day. We had an amazing sex life and a room dedicated to making love, exploring, having fun, and now to making a baby. If we kept this house, this room would become the baby's room, after it was deep-cleaned.

If they used a blue light on that room it would have glowed and looked like a Jackson Pollock painting.

Santa Claus hat on my head and Argentine wine on my breath, I was on a Liberator pillow, my bottom angled upward at thirty degrees, but at one point it was more like seventy, with me on my shoulders, an angle that caused gravity to pull Franklin's weight down, pulled him deeper inside my love.

He rested on me, at a kinder angle, after his grand finale, winded.

I moaned, sucked his bottom lip, and asked, "Did you find Davy Jones's locker?"

"I was not that deep."

"For the love of sweet black baby Jesus, you were deeper than Obama's speech on racism."

I put butterfly kisses on his lips as I ran my hand through his magnificent dreadlocks.

He moved in and out slowly, kissed me, asked, "Can you feel them?"

"I feel them. Never felt anything like that in my life. You're addictive."

He had gone to Suriname and had *boegroes* surgically inserted under the foreskin of his penis. Round balls rose from his flesh like beads. I felt the rigidity of the beads even when he was flaccid.

15

My cellular rang. It was my sister Tommie's ringtone. I stretched for the phone, couldn't reach it, but he grabbed it, handed it to me, never losing that connection. He kissed my neck and pushed his *boegroes* deeper. I felt the trend in Suriname. I felt what made his wood feel like it was made of steel.

I took a deep breath, tried to sound normal, answered, "What's the problem, Tommie McBroom?"

"Good night, Auntie Frankie."

"Mo, what are you doing up this late?"

"When will I get to see the dress I'm going to wear at your wedding in the Caribbean?"

I laughed. "Is that why you called me?"

"The dress is so beautiful."

"Is that dress on your mind?"

"I just had a dream about it. Only it was black. I don't want to wear a black dress."

"Your dress is white. And it will be the prettiest dress at Auntie's wedding."

"Why are you breathing funny? Are you on the treadmill?"

"Why are you whispering?"

"Momma doesn't know I'm on her iPhone. Our secret, okay? If I use mine, she'll look at the Caller ID, know I was on my phone past my bedtime, and put me on

16

punishment."

"Why are you still awake?"

"The noise woke me up."

"Where is Tommie?"

"She's in the bedroom with Daddy. She's making sounds like her tummy hurts."

"Is the bedroom door closed?"

"Yes."

"Just stay in your room."

"Okay."

"What do you want Santa to bring you for Christmas?"

"Auntie, there is no such thing as Santa Claus."

"If you don't believe in Santa, you're too old to get presents."

"Can we do the name song you taught me?"

I laughed. "Mo Mo bo bo, banana fanna fo fo, me mi mo mo, Mo!"

"Frankie Frankie bo bankie, banana fanna fo fankie, me mi mo mankie, Frankie!"

I said, "Now call Auntie Livvy and do the 'Mahna Mahna' song."

I ended the call and pulled the Santa Claus hat away from my head.

We laughed, talked about how we hoped we'd made a precocious baby like her.

Franklin went to the bathroom to take that post-sex piss and to clean himself. I heard the water come on in the bathtub and I smelled lavender. That meant we'd take a quick shower, clean the sticky stuff from our bodies, sit in the tub a little while, cuddle like that with music playing in the background. We might make love again. Until I was pregnant sex would be fun, but it would also have a purpose.

My cellular rang while a John Handy tune from his album *Hard Work* blanketed us.

Franklin called out, "Is Mo calling again? Does that kid drink coffee all day?"

"Livvy is probably calling me now to curse me out because I had Mo call and wake her up."

Franklin laughed. "Y'all talk all day and call each other all night like you ain't seen each other in weeks. Y'all cuss each other out and ten minutes later y'all are laughing like it never happened."

The ringtone wasn't my sister's ringtone. Then I thought it might have been an old lover from my long-discarded A, B, or C list, and I wanted to answer and tell them merry Christmas, tell them that those wild days were over and their services would no longer be needed. As the phone chimed, I picked it up and looked at the number on the display. It looked like an international phone number.

18

I sucked lime Jell-O from my fingers, then answered in my business voice, hoping nothing had happened with any of my properties. A hysterical bitch was on the other end. I had never heard so much anger. As I sat exposed on ruffled sheets, I found out my fiancé was *already* married. Based on the screams, he had married when he was living in Alabama, several years before he had met me.

I will never forget the look on his face when he left the bathroom laughing, naked, modified cock swinging, and walked toward the king-size bed, his sweet dreadlocks pulled back into a ponytail.

He didn't see the pained expression on my face.

He tossed me a wet towel.

I let it bounce from the bed to the carpeted floor.

I held my Santa Claus hat in my fist, exhaled, tilted my head like the old-school RCA Victor dog, and then asked, "Are you married to a bitch in the military?"

He froze.

My nostrils flared and my left hand became a fist.

He looked at me.

Silence penetrated the room.

Franklin was unable to inhale.

19

He looked at the phone in my hand.

Time stopped moving, folded its arms, leaned against the wall, and waited to see how this was going to turn out for us.

"Yes or fucking no. *Answer me.* Are you married and is the heifer overseas in the military?"

His shoulders tensed; he opened and closed his hands, murmured soft curses, exposed.

That was when I heard them. A lot of people were behind his wife, urging her, cursing me as well, a platoon of fools.

Franklin tried to explain what couldn't be explained to an audience of military wolves.

I slapped him as hard as I could.

He staggered across the room, held his face in disbelief, then snapped at me for striking him.

His wife snapped, threatened to kick my ass for hitting her husband. I told the heifer if she were here I would kick his ass and her ass, then went off on her for having the audacity to get my phone number and call me.

I cursed both of them out, cursed them hard and strong.

I took my cellular, went into the bathroom, locked the door, ended the call with his wife, then didn't answer as Franklin knocked over and over. I stood in the shower, under tepid water, so I couldn't hear a damn thing he said, muffled his lies, shouted for him to get out of my house. He refused to leave.

I called my sisters. Livvy and Tommie hurried over with Tony and Blue — Livvy's husband and Tommie's fiancé. I didn't come out of the bathroom until then, and my sisters were there as I ranted. Franklin was in the living room standing by the Christmas tree, the lights blinking over lie after lie. Mrs. Carruthers called my cellular over and over and over on the eve of Christmas Eve. In front of everyone, I answered.

We all listened to her vile rant with my phone on speaker.

Tommie said, "Franklin, you have a wife and made plans to marry my sister?"

Livvy said, "Woman on the phone, you really need to have some respect for my sister."

Franklin's wife called me all kinds of names, *cunt* being the nicest word to leave her mouth.

Again I hung up on the madwoman and told Franklin to get to stepping and step the hell out of my life. While he was surrounded by my family, while Blue and Tony were in his face and kept him away from me as my sisters hid my gun and grabbed my arms and kept me away from him, while Livvy held one of my arms and Tommie gripped the other, Franklin trembled and tried to plead his case to the jury of his peers.

He said he had been trying to get a divorce for years. No one cared because he had presented himself as being free and single. He had been married and sleeping in my bed like we had already taken vows. He had put an engagement ring on my finger when a wedding ring was already on another woman's hand.

I snapped, "You're a monster, Franklin."

They had all been like brothers, but he couldn't buy empathy from Blue or Tony. My brother-in-law and my future brother-in-law had my back like my blood was their blood, were outraged, like my shame was their shame. Tony picked up belongings that littered the house. I followed Franklin and threw framed photos and F-bombs. I threw his Christmas presents at him. I wanted to throw grenades at him.

My sisters stayed with me, one on each side of me, their turn to be my bookends while waves of agony were drowned first with wine, then with Jack and Coke, my favorite liver killer. The next morning, before the sun came up, I went to my garage and looked at my two rides. I used an Audi for work, but I also rocked a 1968 Pontiac Firebird coupe on most weekends. This had put me in the Firebird mood. To try to clear my head I turned off my phone and rode my muscle car from the southern terminus of the Pacific Coast Highway at I-5 in Dana Point to somewhere up near Ventura. Alone with my thoughts, I was on the road for many hours before I turned around. I gassed up my ride, took to the highway, opened it up, sped down the 101. I found my way back to Los Angeles. Exhausted, numb, I went to Inglewood Park Cemetery and lay down on our parents' graves. They were buried side by side, holding hands in the afterlife, as I had thought it would be with Franklin and me.

I lay between them and whispered, "Mom. Dad. I screwed up. Why can't I do this right? Why can't I have what y'all had?"

Livvy and Tommie knew where I would be, knew where we all went when we were at the bottom of the bottom and could only look up and see darkness. I looked up and they were standing over me.

Tommie said, "Think we can borrow a shovel and dig this funky-breath heifer a grave?"

"There is an open grave about a half mile in. We can stack her like they do at that corrupt cemetery that was in the news for putting one dead body on top of another. What say you?"

"We can bury her there. She looks so damn pathetic."

Breakfast at Tiffany's shades over my eyes, dreadlocks tied to either side like I was Pippi Longstocking wearing an LA Lakers sweat suit, I raised my middle fingers at both of those McBitches.

Livvy's light brown hair was in an Elsa-from-*Frozen* braid. Tommie's hair was all Afro'd up today. Livvy held plastic bags of grilled chicken from El Pollo Loco. Tommie held a tray of soft drinks.

I asked, "What does a sister have to do to have a moment to think by herself?"

I sat up. Soft breeze on a sunny day, the temperature at sixty-seven degrees on Christmas Eve. My sisters, both dressed in sweats, took out paper plates. Then I heard someone calling for her auntie. Mo ran across the graves. I ran toward her, picked her up, and gave her a piggyback ride to the grave site.

I said, "We're a day early. We don't come until Christmas morning."

Tommie said, "We're still coming back

tomorrow."

Livvy said, "I know that's right. Mom and Dad get us two days in a row this time."

We all sat and ate lunch, me, my sisters, my little niece-to-be, with the ghosts of our parents at our side. We didn't talk for a while, not even Mo, not until we started gathering the last of our refuse.

Tommie said, "I can make the phone calls, Frankie."

"Wait until after the first of the year. Let's not mess up Christmas for everyone else because mine got screwed."

Livvy said, "I can help you make the calls, Tommie."

I said, "No e-mails, no tweets, no Facebook. Nothing that can be saved or passed around."

They nodded in agreement.

I shook my head. "It's my mess. Let me pull up my big-girl panties and be responsible."

Mo said, "Auntie, you don't wear panties. You wear a thong if you wear anything at all."

We all laughed and wiped tears from our eyes.

Everyone who had been invited to the Caribbean McBroom-Carruthers wedding had to be uninvited. Explanations, apologies had to be made to those who had scheduled vacations, a reason had to be given, and I didn't try to cover up for his lies or my mistake. I'd been deceived. It was my turn to play the fool. I took the blame, said it was my fault for not doing my due diligence, for not having him fully investigated. I'd entered into a relationship in trust and had exited on the back of a lie.

After the first of the year, Monica came to keep me company and help me take down my Christmas tree. We made brownies and chilled as we watched television. She was worried about me.

"Auntie, why aren't you and Uncle Frankie getting married so I can wear my new dress?"

I looked at her, and her simple words about Franklin made me ache.

The horrible things that adults did had to be explained to children.

"I wanted to dress in white like a princess and be the flower girl at your wedding by the sea."

As she sat between my legs and I French-braided her fine hair I said, "I know, Mo. I know."

Mo had asked me that while we were watching *Even Stevens, Phil of the Future,* and *Kim Possible*. We watched those the way my sisters and I were hooked on Shonda-land on Thursdays. Monica was kicking it with me to give Tommie and Blue a break and some time alone. Maybe it would be the night they smacked it up, flipped it, and finally put a baby in the oven. One like Monica. I'd thought Tommie would be pregnant at least two years ago. Actually I had guessed she was pregnant when they got engaged but was wrong.

Monica said, "Let Mommy wear your wedding dress and we can all still go to the islands and they can get married and you can be the bridesmaid and I can wear my white dress and be a flower girl."

"I was married before, Monica. So I can't be the bridesmaid ever again, thank God."

"I won't tell. You and Mommy can just change places and I can still wear my dress."

"If only life were that easy, little girl."

"Maybe Uncle Frankie will come back and say he's real sorry."

She cried. The kid cried hard. It felt like I had broken a grand promise to her.

Same as I had told everyone I wouldn't get married, now she had to tell all of her friends her truth.

She would not get to be a flower girl. Baby sister Tommie wouldn't get to be a bridesmaid for the last time. In my heart I had wanted to have a kid just like Monica. She was the perfect child.

I needed her company that night. I needed her innocence. Mine was long gone.

He wouldn't leave my mind. I missed Franklin. I missed the life we had been building.

Everywhere we went we had worked out like we were exercise junkies. He had pushed me to the next level. We had planned on running either a half or a full marathon in all fifty states. When the sweating was done we showered together, or bathed together, then massaged each other with oils. We had made love at night on balconies in foreign countries, slept in our birthday suits, limbs intertwined.

I hated him. I missed him. Love had come in a rush, but upon failure, it never left easily.

After I took Mo home, I couldn't sleep. Couldn't eat. Couldn't breathe. Same thoughts on repeat. The relationship had been a farce. I would not become Mrs. Carruthers. I would not become a mother.

To be sure, I went to West Los Angeles Medical to see my ob-gyn, Dr. Debra DuBois.

If I were pregnant by another woman's husband, my life would get real ugly.

TOMMIE

Edgehill Drive was calm with the weekday tranquility of the shrinking middle class.

Monica was at the circular dining table doing homework and I was at the same table rereading a book by Beale Streets. Monica wore jeans and a *Frozen* T-shirt. I wore skinny jeans and a T-shirt that read THE REVOLUTION WILL NOT BE TEXTURIZED. We heard his hoopty pull up in the driveway and then heard the key rattle in the back door. We were all smiles, glad the man of the house was home.

I yelled, "It's unlocked, babe."

Blue walked in carrying his gym bag. Mo jumped up and ran to her dad like she hadn't seen him since President Lincoln had freed the slaves — anything to get away from the drudgery of homework. She thought she was slick. I didn't say anything this time. Blue picked her up, gave her a hug, told her how tall she was getting, teased her about having little mumps on her chest and already needing to wear a starter bra, kissed her cheeks, then put her down. He laughed, came over and kissed me on my lips, slipped me the tongue. This moment felt like a dream, the way I had always imagined our relationship would be.

This moment right here, plus a child or two of our own, would be all I wanted. I wanted to be rich in family and love. Money never meant as much to me as it did to others. We lived in a small three-bedroom home, artistic, colorful, bohemian, a cozy space, so every sound any of us made, especially at night, was loud. I loved it like that. I loved the fact that we shared space day and night, that we were connected.

Blue asked, "How was your day, Tommie?"

"Long. Made us breakfast, dropped Mo off at school, ran the Crenshaw loop with Livvy and Frankie, did some editing, blogged. I worked four hours at the part-time. Picked up Mo. Cooked dinner. Started homework. Kissed you when you came in the door. That pretty much sums up my day."

He sat at the table, picked up where I'd left off, reviewed Mo's homework. English. Math.

I looked over brochures for the LA Marathon, the registration packet, the course map.

I asked, "How was work?"

"Same old. Students never change. Have a lot of papers to grade this weekend. They don't realize that the more homework they have to do, the more work I have to do grading papers."

"You smell fresh."

"Didn't want to come home funky. Showered and changed after the kickboxing class."

"Thought you were doing weights. Wasn't today legs day?"

"Back and shoulders today with Tyrel and Bobby, then ended up in Taj's kickboxing class."

"Taj's class ain't no joke."

"Saw Frankie. She was with Livvy. They were working their core."

"Who else was up there?"

"I saw Beale Streets's girlfriend. Do you remember her from when I took you to his event?"

"Svelte and attractive Nigerian American who has a pretentious Valley Girl accent?"

"Yeah; she was in kickboxing. I think her name is Tanya Obama."

"Tanya *Obayomi*. Was Beale Streets up there with his arm candy?"

"Didn't see him, but that doesn't mean he wasn't there. Just saw Tanya *Obayomi.*"

I felt envious. Blue smiled when he spoke her name.

Blue said, "After dinner, I want to try to write a bit before I go to bed."

"You're back to writing?"

"Wow. I haven't seen that excited smile in a month of Sundays."

"That's great, Blue. What brought this on? Thought you had given up the screenplay."

"I guess seeing Beale Streets, hearing him talk at his event a few months ago, that motivated me. I'm glad I took you to that event at the downtown library so you could hear him, meet him."

"I'm glad you took me too."

"His talk was powerful. Black man adopted by two white parents. Interesting identity struggle."

"It was funny how everyone thought you were his brother or something."

I made Blue a plate, baked chicken and vegetables, became as uxorial to him as my stepmother, Betty Jean, had been to my father, Bernard. Then I took the meal to Blue while he helped Monica with her English. He ate and I took over, helped Mo again, helped her with her math. Soon we sent Monica to take a shower, put her in bed by eight. That was still her appointed bedtime. Put her in bed that early so afterward Blue and I could have some quality time, some adult chill time, before we went to sleep.

I was cleaning up the living room when the phone rang. I looked at the Caller ID. Seeing her name made me frown.

I took a deep breath, forced my lips up into a faux smile, and answered, "Good evening."

Music blasted from a concert as she yelled, "Let me talk to my daughter."

I took another deep breath, and this time, with no smile, I repeated, "Good evening."

"*Look.* Hurry up and put Monica on the phone before Beyoncé finishes her favorite song."

"First things first. Good evening. It's a greeting, Angela. A courtesy between the civilized."

Blue came into the living room. "Who is it?"

"You know who it is, Blue. You can tell by this stiff smile and the tone of my voice."

He reached for the phone. I handed it to him and took three steps back, arms folded.

"What's up, Angela? Well, you know it's past her bedtime. I don't care about the time difference between here and wherever you are right now. Don't go there. What? I know she's your daughter. Do we need to go back to court? Decent hours are business hours, so you need — hold on. Just hold on."

He went to the hallway and called for Monica. She woke up and came to her door, then came down the hallway. He handed her the phone. She started talking, then walked back toward her bedroom.

Blue looked at me, saw me shaking my head, my tongue behind my upper lip.

I said, "You did it again. You gave in to her."

"I don't ever want it to be said that I tried to come between Mo and her mother."

Frustration tightened my throat, burned my eyes. Before Mo could see, I took the book I had been reading, escaped to the bathroom, and locked myself away from the drama. I flipped the novel over and stared at the photo of the writer, Beale Streets. Young face. Pretty eyes. His bio said he had no children.

Back in the living room I put the book down, said, "Blue, I'm going to go by Frankie's."

"What's going on?"

"Grey's Anatomy. Scandal. How to Get Away with Murder."

35

"Last night you went to watch *Empire* with Livvy. Thought you were staying in tonight."

"Changed my mind."

"Why the attitude at such a high altitude all of a sudden?"

Monica came back with the phone in her hand. She had finished her call with her birth mother.

She looked at me and said, "Can I go with you, Mommy?"

"Not tonight. Tomorrow is a school day."

"Can we have a McBroom sleepover tomorrow or Saturday?"

"I will ask your aunties tonight. Now, go back to bed. I need to talk to your father a moment."

"Love you, Mommy."

"I know. Love you too, Mo."

Blue asked, "What am I, chopped liver?"

"Love you too, Daddy. You know I love you more than anything in the world."

I wondered if she felt torn, trying to please one mother too many.

She went back down the hall singing "Single Ladies," dancing and doing hand movements and all.

I told myself that I was overreacting. But I was angry. I felt as if I had no power, as if I weren't being taken seriously. I touched the

36

mark on my face, the mark that was the size of a quarter, where my first boyfriend had burned me. Blue came to me, upset, but only one thing was on my mind.

I said, "Blue, I'm not getting any younger. This uncertainty has left me anxious and scared."

"I know. I can tell that it's always on your mind, Tommie. I see it in your eyes."

"When are we going to talk about it? Our future as a family can't be put on hold indefinitely."

"You're leaving to go kick it with the Mc-Brooms."

"I could stay, if you want to talk about it, see how we can get past this and finally plan for the wedding, because I am tired of people seeing this ring, knowing we're engaged, that we live together, and we haven't circled a date. People think we're going to end up like Frankie and Franklin, that something is wrong, that maybe you have some secret. I'm playing the role of wife and stepmom in public, and then I'm the Shay to your Roc at night. I love you, Blue, and I need to . . . I want us to be on the same page, in agreement. Let's make a plan, see how we can fix this, marry, and become parents, give Mo a little brother or sister before she gets older and the age difference puts them in separate generations."

"Do you think about anything else?"

"You should have talked to me first, and you know that left me feeling like an also-ran."

I had come home one day and found Blue on the sofa, bags of ice between his legs because he had gotten a vasectomy. His unilateral decision had left me in shock and perplexed. I wanted to let it go, but he had done something major and never consulted me. He could get his vasectomy without my consent because we weren't married. From what I had heard, a wife would be asked to sign off on the procedure so the doctor wouldn't end up caught up in a lawsuit; and here in Cali, people sued for everything. Here a wife could sue her husband's mistress to regain community property and win back every dime the old, wrinkled, and racist asshole spent on the affair. No matter how many times we had been together as husband or wife, unless we had been together for seven years and the common-law thing kicked in, I was just a chick living with a dude. He had gotten a vasectomy, and that made me feel like shit. I looked in the mirror and at times I still saw the handprint from that metaphorical slap in my face. I had never told my sisters Blue had cut his nuts. When they asked me if I was pregnant yet, I was too embarrassed to say that rite of passage wasn't a possibility. His sperm was no good.

I was wasting an egg a month.

He whispered, "Are you crying?"

Headache rising, confusion swelling, anger revving up like a deuce, I asked, "What am I to you, Blue? A glorified babysitter? Your wench? I have a ring, but I need you to tell me our mission statement, because I am really, really baffled."

"Grow up, Tommie. Don't talk nonsense and stop acting like a damn child all the time."

Feeling that insult, I pulled away from him, had a smile as twisted as the thoughts that had erupted in my mind, and I grabbed my keys, my purse, my phone, then paused at my front door.

I faced him, said, "Maybe you and Angela should get back together and be a happy family. You and she will always be on Mo's family tree anyway. I'm just a fucking asterisk."

"Stop it, Tommie. You're overreacting."

I repeated the text message Angela had sent to his phone in the middle of the night, when we were in bed together, years ago, after she knew that Blue and I were involved: " *'I'm sorry, I don't care who you're in bed with, you'll always be mine, as I've always been yours. You tell me you're seeing someone. Are you in love with her, do you love her like you used to love me? Remember how we made love in the rain?'* "

"Are you ever going to let that go?"

" *'When you made love to me the last time it was like there was no one else and as if no time had passed. I came so hard, you kissed me so passionately. You will always be the boss of my pussy.'* "

"That was *before* I slept with you, Tommie. We had a moment. I had a lapse in judgment. She brought my daughter back. It was late. I made a mistake. She didn't even spend the night. It lasted no more than five minutes. I came and I felt disgusted with myself. She knows we're done on that level."

"If you dislike her as much as you claim you do, why did you sleep with her again?"

"I guess I needed to unload."

"Wow."

"I gave you the biological man answer. It meant nothing."

"Blue, you had naked pictures of her on your computer."

"I didn't even know those were still there."

"I guess those were to help you on the

nights you manually unload."

"Those are deleted now."

"Have you seen her Facebook page? She posted 'A man would break up with his old bitch for a new bitch . . . just to cheat on his new bitch with his old bitch.' "

"I don't keep track of her personal life. I don't care what she does or writes online."

"Then posts on Twitter, 'Crazy bitches have the best pussy. That's why I'm still fucking my ex.' "

"You and I both know that since we met she has had more exes than we've had hot meals."

"I don't know anything right now. All I know is that since you won't get the vasectomy reversed, I'm not going to march down the aisle. That's nonnegotiable. I guess I'm just where you unload."

He took a breath, rubbed his temples. "Babe, I don't make the kind of money Tony makes."

"And neither did my father, but he worked, sacrificed, and we had a great childhood."

He took a breath. "We need to do the numbers, that's all I am saying. Be logical about this."

"Do the numbers. Sure. You're right. I'm being emotional, not logical."

"We'll talk about it after we've both calmed down. Not after Angela has changed the energy."

"Sure. Let's bow down, then allow her to control when we have our conversations."

"I'm not dodging the issue; it's just that I want to try to write a bit before I go to bed."

"Whatever, Blue. I'm starting to get sick and tired of being sick and tired."

"Whenever Angela calls, we end up having an issue. This is getting old, Tommie."

"Tell her that calling Mo every blue moon and letting her hear her have a good time in a foreign country is not the same as quality time. Remind her that she is Mo's birth mother and not her second cousin twice removed, so she has responsibilities both emotional and financial and Mo should be a priority, not a second thought and not an afterthought, but her first thought and her first course of action. Each time she eats she should want to be sure her daughter has food, and it should be food on the same level, not a Happy Meal from McDonald's. And ask her about the long-overdue child support. Ask the refrigerator; this house needs the money. You are Mo's primary caregiver, not her, so know her role."

Now Blue looked like he had a migraine

plus a side of Ebola with a touch of hemor-rhoids.

He said, "You're right. She's her biologi-cal mother, but you have taken on the role of mother."

"Parity. All I want is *parity* in this relation-ship. I want to be an equal partner and be respected."

"I do respect you, Tommie. There is par-ity."

"I want consistent parity. You're here with me, then you run off and make unilateral decisions, as if we're not a team. It's as if you have a kid and want to cut away my chance to become a mother."

I stepped out through the front door, put a smile on my face, said good-evenings and waved at our neighbors. Vince waved. So did Dana. Their two preteen children called out to me. His oldest daughter, Kwanzaa, from Vince's previous marriage, was there too. I wanted to ask Dana how they made it work. I left home, fled the Leimert Park area, the echo of African drums in the air as the Nubians congregated around the park's fountain to celebrate life, and headed in the direction of Frankie's crib. I had on Old Navy sweats, a wrinkled X-Men T-shirt, trainers. I sent a text message, then deleted it from my history and turned my cellular off. I wasn't planning to go, but the migraine. If I didn't go, I'd lose it tonight.

I looked at my hand; it trembled.

TOMMIE

Feeling conflicted, I drove through the top three richest African American communities: Ladera Heights, Baldwin Hills, and View Park–Windsor Hills. I inhaled the air where family incomes were six or seven figures, where all were seemingly affluent and had created their own black Beverly Hills. The air smelled and tasted the same as the air in my working-class zip code, maybe worse, because smog rose and polluted their gluten-free world the same as it dropped down and polluted mine. Many properties were carved into hillsides and had stunning views of the Pacific Ocean, even though the beach was seven miles away, and ten minutes from Hollywood on a good traffic day.

If Blue and I had that kind of money, if we could live on top of the hill, maybe our situation would be different. If we had money, maybe he wouldn't be afraid. Maybe

I wouldn't be angry. Maybe Mo's mother would become irrelevant. We'd have ninety-nine problems, but needing her financial support wouldn't be one.

She asked, "Do you really think so?"

I looked at the passenger seat and she was here with me. She held a pad and paper.

I said, "It would be nice to live in this affluent African American community."

She scribbled. "This isn't affluent. This doesn't compare to Malibu and Bel Air."

"It's still a nice African American community. Stop writing. Leave me alone for once."

"You have neighborhoods, not communities. A community is more than having a next-door neighbor who looks like you. The African American community is a theoretical construct."

"Here we go again."

"You have to break bread and support each other, shop in black-owned stores to be a community. You drive through the Crenshaw District to get to the mountaintop and most of these people shop on the Westside, or fight traffic north to shop at the Grove, or flee south to their favorite galleria between here and Orange County. They don't drive two minutes away to the Crenshaw District and support black entrepreneurship. My people are afraid of each other and are terrified of their own cousins."

I eased into the parking lot at St. Bernadette Church, then looked around, made sure it was safe before I grabbed my duffel bag, opened it, and looked inside at the wardrobe I had borrowed from Frankie's closet — without her knowing. I wanted to be impressive, the way he was chic and impressive.

"What you're thinking, that isn't the answer."

"No one asked you."

"Blue does his best and you know that."

"But we're not a *community*. Our relationship is just another *neighborhood*. We live together, but he chooses Angela over me, he patronizes her needs, and therefore he is bigoted with his affections. Maybe we need to put a sign out front and do a short sale, because we're losing value every day. We're already upside down and it feels like we're in a hole so deep that when I look up all I see is darkness."

I had changed into a silk trench coat and Louboutin boots. He lived on Kenway, one of the most sought-after streets in View Park. Five bedrooms, six and a half bathrooms, three-car garage. Custom built. Cost

47

way over a million. Open floor plan, more than 5,200 square feet of living space, all situated on a huge lot. Large gourmet kitchen with custom cabinetry. Formal living, formal dining, family room, and game room were just a few of the features of his home.

I punched in the four-digit security code. The mechanical gate swung open. His garage door went up. I passed by the circular driveway, pulled into the garage, turned off my car, then eased out, adjusted my attire, and walked up the five stairs that led to the entrance that opened into the gourmet kitchen.

Before I could put my nervous hand on the doorknob, he opened the door to his home. He saw me and whistled. I blushed and took in his undeniable attractiveness. He was a slender, toned long-distance runner who sported an awesome golden Afro. His hazel eyes, so pretty.

Except for the 1978 Rolex Daytona 6263 on his left arm, he was as naked as my thoughts.

Beale Streets was excited to see me again.

Our lips touched, the gap between right and wrong bridged.

Tongues danced to a jazz tune by Miles Davis that played inside of my head. The kiss was medicinal, as a good kiss should be, and with that kiss he gave me his testosterone, flooded my system with his own desire and therapeutic energy. My brain released chemicals that attacked stress hormones.

Right away my disposition improved. My migraine eased up. Nipples rose. I tingled where I would become moist, and with that soft fire I gasped. I held his pending erection and he mirrored my erotic sounds.

When a woman doesn't feel valued, it makes her susceptible to the charms of other men.

A woman would engage in a short sale and change neighborhoods in hopes of gaining a sense of community.

TOMMIE

After I kissed Beale Streets, I pulled away, looked into his hazel eyes and measured his emotions. They were obvious, yet it was like trying to see music with my eyes. His feelings overwhelmed me in a good way and made it impossible for me to have the ability to see beyond where I was now.

Beale gave me a dozen butterfly kisses and said, "I've missed you, Tommie McBroom."

"How was London? I saw the pictures you took at Leicester Square. How were *The Graham Norton Show, Alan Carr: Chatty Man, HARDtalk,* and the other interviews on shows I've never heard of?"

"I was well received. The series of book signings and lectures was also a success."

"You were on shows that have guests like the Pakistani president, the South African president."

"They also interview Boy George and Richard Dawkins."

He did his Richard Dawkins imperson-
ation and we laughed at his rude boyish-
ness.

They paid him between ten and thirty
thousand dollars to sit on a stage and take
questions for an hour, to tell about being
black and growing up white, about the
eight-million-dollar home his adoptive
parents had on the East Coast, their apartment in Buenos Aires, their flat in London.
They loved to hear him speak in French,
Italian, Spanish, and Russian, or confess his
bardolatry and speak in prose as he playfully acted out parts of Shakespearian plays.
They had made him more qualified to talk
about race in America than men born
decades before him. He existed in a new
class, one rare to a black man from America.
He was the intelligent, well-traveled man I
would want to be if I had been born a man.

I asked, "How were the workouts? You
continue training while you were gone?"

"Time change of eight hours killed me,
but I managed to stay on schedule."

"Me, too. I imagined that you and I were
running at the same time."

"Let me see what you're wearing."

"It's more about what I'm not wearing."

"Even better."

"You want to see, you open the coat. You

unwrap the box."

With him I was the older woman, Mrs. Robinson, the one in charge, and I had grown comfortable being with him, more comfortable than I was with Blue, so with him I acted as if I had no behavior.

Beale Streets smiled. "Lord, have mercy. Never saw you look like this."

We laughed before we kissed again. He led me past sculptures of wood, metal, and marble, beyond high-priced art by Kimberly Chavers and David Lawrence. He had grand bookcases, handmade for a home of this magnitude. One held copies of his works; he had sold their rights in almost fifty languages. His adoptive mother was a writer on the level of Patricia Highsmith, and his adoptive father a man like Steve Jobs. The European half of Beale's apparently mixed heritage, coupled with his upbringing, allowed him to write mainstream characters and no one in the world had complained, especially since his adoptive mother was a mainstream writer. One of her fifty novels was about adopting Beale. The mainstream had embraced him the way a tribe embraced its members, especially with his well-to-do adoptive parents being highly visible. His works had been adapted into films, into Japanese movies, and rock bands had written songs in Japan and Canada based on political themes in his books. Even a Danish band had written songs inspired by two of his characters. All of that, and he was under twenty-five. He was just beginning. He was five years my junior and had achieved more than ten people usually did in a lifetime. For many of us, it is all about where we started. That was Beale's advantage.

Beale Streets led me to the elevator and once again I was deep inside of his world.

We made out as the elevator took us to the top level and passed by a large bedroom that had been converted into an amazing walk-in closet. He put two fingers inside of me while he licked my nipples. When we were upstairs in his master bedroom, I stood in that cavernous suite and looked around before I looked back at him, gazed into his eyes, his pretty eyes, and felt like I was with a man named Christian Black in a novel inside of my head entitled *50 Hues of Houghmagandy.*

I said, "I can only be here a few minutes."

"Don't do me like this, Tommie."

"I'm sorry. Maybe I should leave and come back when I can chill a little longer."

"Leave Blue; come live with me so we won't have to sneak."

"Stop telling me that. If I showed up on your porch with my luggage, you'd freak out."

"Come work for me again. Working at the Apple Store and blogging and editing — you can make much more money if you just work for me. I'm going to option novels, not just mine, but the novels of other writers. I can option novels, own the rights, sell those rights for much more, and I will write a dozen screenplays. I can run my own company out of this house. You can be part of the journey. We can be a team, become a power couple in Hollywood. You could write a movie or create a television series."

"I gave it a lot of thought, actually lost sleep over it, but I can't work for you and sleep with you."

"Why not? I'm not paying you to sleep with me."

"Stop talking business. Show me how much you missed me."

TOMMIE

We traded simultaneous tongue game for throat game. I used to be terrified to put a man's fuck parts in my head close to where my brain resided. I thought that an anxious thrust when he was about to blow could give me irreparable brain damage. I used to worry about hygiene, the scent of urine, and even worse, experiencing the taste of some woman he'd been with before me. It was laborious. So much work and skill and coordination were required. I struggled to inhale and exhale and not choke. He felt good and when it was done, most of the time I felt nothing but a sore mouth. Plus there was also the fear of bodily fluids. Or that he would go to sleep right after, and I'd be sitting there, mouth aching, feeling like a fool.

But I had outgrown all of that under the tutelage of Blue. It was an acquired desire and it had become a fetish. Beale and I only exchanged favors and flavors for a couple of moments.

I became a cowgirl, rode him for as long as it took the second hand to make three cycles around the clock, then I reversed the cowgirl. Soon I leaned forward; he adjusted and was on his knees. He adjusted me, put me on my knees. My face was in the pillow, muffling my harmonic sounds, until he pulled my hair, made me raise my face so he could hear my eloquent moans. There was no child here to hide my sound from. I could be as loud as I pleased, as loud as he made me be loud. He was the dog behind the moaning cat. I was his Calliope in brown skin, his inspiration to endure his own erotic madness. He made lights flash behind my eyes. He made me float. The silk trench coat was pulled up over my backside; the boots were still on my feet. Then I pushed up on my elbows.

She said, "Tommie McBroom. You're here again."

Her voice jolted me.

I looked across the room.

She stared at me.

I stared at her.

Again, as it had been in the car, it was me. It was the therapist who lived inside me. I saw myself across the room. I wore a long black skirt, white blouse with long sleeves. My hair was one color, deep brown, and it was straightened, pressed, pulled back from my face. I looked socially acceptable. I held a legal pad in my left hand, and with my right, I wrote notes about myself to myself, about how I saw myself outside of myself. That version of me stood up, walked over to me, kneeled next to me, and put her lips close to my ear.

She whispered, "Stay on this path and you will suffer. Not only mentally but physically. Irritable bowel syndrome, upset stomach, muscle aches, tension headaches, panic attacks. This is how you medicate yourself, but this could cause you to become infertile, which would be ironic."

I closed my eyes, felt tears coming. That version of me stopped talking. I squeezed my eyes tight, let the tears fall. Each time I'd been with Beale I'd cried afterward. I opened my eyes to see what the therapist who lived within me had to say. She was gone. She had rejoined me. We were one.

Beale playfully nudged me as he asked, "Did you orgasm?"

I playfully bumped him back and nodded. "If that was a song, I'd put it on replay."

"This isn't about sex. This is profound. This is about the chemistry we have, about a love so overpowering that when I can't see you I feel depressed. I was unable to write while I was gone. I couldn't write one decent sentence. You stoke my creative energies. This is about me needing you in my life."

He kissed me. Kissed me. Kissed me. I saw the time. I hadn't planned on being here any more than fifteen minutes. I hadn't come for conversation. Until Mo's mother had called, I hadn't planned on coming at all. I hoped that Blue hadn't called Frankie's crib looking for me. My phone was turned off, so if my sisters had called me, they would've called my house when I didn't answer. Blue could've called my phone to make sure I made it to Frankie's without being jacked or getting into an accident, and when it went to voice mail he would have called Livvy or Frankie's cell phone. I imagined that everyone was in a panic right now, not knowing where I was, calling the LAPD and the sheriff's department, hoping I hadn't been kidnapped, robbed, raped, killed, my body left in a pool of blood in our concrete jungle.

I pushed myself up on my elbows, and in a panicked voice I told Beale, "I need to leave."

He pulled me back to the bed, mounted

me again, put my ankles around his neck, and rubbed the length of his erection where I was most sensitive. He moved up and down, his weight pressing into me. I closed my eyes, wrestled with the good feeling. He made me want more. He made me feel happy.

He said, "I bought you a present from my last trip."

Barely able to breathe, I gazed at him. "Did you?"

"I did."

"Give it to me."

"Next time I see you, you will get your gift."

"That's not fair."

"This isn't fair for me, Tommie."

"I need to go."

"I need to come."

He entered me and every part of me trembled.

My soul quaked.

"You want me to get in trouble."

"I love you, Tommie McBroom."

"You're trying to get me in trouble."

"I love you so fucking much I can't stand not having you."

I put my legs down, pulled him to me, clamped my hand over his mouth, muted his romantic words as I wrapped my legs around his ankles. Then we fought each other, fought each other and laughed when he slipped out of me. I moved and refused to let him back inside, became silly, and he wrestled with me as we laughed. He found his way back inside of me and I stopped fighting, became aroused, and then he was once again powerful between my legs, moving deeper inside of me again.

"Don't come inside of me this time."

"Pearl necklace?"

"Okay."

TOMMIE

Stressed, I turned my cellular on, my heart beating too fast. No one had called me. I exhaled. I double-checked. The borrowed trench coat and high-priced boots were back in my gym bag.

I sped and pulled up in front of Frankie's house in old Ladera. I was going to sneak the gym bag inside but decided to do that later this week. The boots were fine, but the trench coat would need to be dry cleaned first. Might have to dry clean it two or three times. I'd have to sneak it in another time.

After I parked in front, I took in the neighborhood.

A heaviness rose from within.

I felt the pangs of guilt. But I felt guilty for not feeling as guilty as I wanted to feel. I needed to feel vindicated in some immoral, perverted fashion. I didn't want this to be my life.

What Blue had done could be undone.

What I had done in response could never be undone.

The drama with Monica's mother never seemed to end.

Knowing that Blue had taken the possibility of my being a mother away from me, it was as if my insides had been carved out, like I had been given an involuntary hysterectomy. That one act hurt me more than anything disrespectful Angela had ever done. I was angry at Blue and had no love for Angela. That was my mental hurricane. It returned, pulled me back into the storm. I took deep breaths, thought of Beale, of our passion, and smiled. It was enough to move me back into the eye of the storm, enough to allow me to return to being calm enough to shake off the negative energy that tried to cling to me.

When I opened my car door, I noticed a car I didn't recognize parked across the street from Frankie's, in front of the home facing hers. It was a two-door muscle car, the kind Franklin restored, the kind that Frankie had gotten hooked on after she started seeing that married asshole. Whoever it was saw me, and opened their car door, like they'd been waiting on me. Mace was on my keychain and I held it at my side, ready to raise and spray. A woman got out of the car.

European bloodline. Good posture. Wide smile.

She said, "Good evening."

Once I realized she wasn't black or Latina, my body relaxed and I responded with concern, "Everything okay?"

Amazing how we were conditioned. A person saw another's highly favored epidermis and relaxed as if she couldn't be a clear and present danger. I regarded her as if she were Little Red Riding Hood and she was indeed lost in the wrong neighborhood. Her hair was Bonnie Raitt red, but when she stepped closer, the streetlights revealed her keen brows were dark. She wore worn white sweats and worn Nikes.

She said, "These are very nice homes."

I grinned and had to bite my tongue to keep from saying something snarky. People like her were always surprised to see a mostly African American neighborhood in America that didn't look like a war zone. Nobody was hanging out on corners; no loud music was blasting to disturb the calm.

She asked, "You're from here?"

"From LA? Yeah. You?"

"I was born in Intercourse, Pennsylvania."

"That place is real?"

"It's real."

"Saw the name on *The Cleveland Show* and on *Ellen.*"

"It's a respectable place with honest and dedicated people. My relatives work at the Military Edged Weaponry Museum."

I looked to my left when someone came running up the street. It was another white chick, one who was blond and in her teens. She ran track at a private school in Brentwood. Her Swedish mother had married a brother and moved into the area last year. She was a regular Forrest Gump and ran like the wind, her ponytail long, below the middle of her back. She had headphones on, her big dog at her side trying to keep up with her pace. There were plastic bags in her hand so she could scoop after her companion pooped. As she passed the redhead, the blond spoke, did that same thing that black people in odd environments do.

The jogging girl tried to stop to have a conversation.

She asked the stranger, "New to the neighborhood? I've seen you parked over there quite a few times."

The other woman said, "I'm looking for a home."

"To rent or buy?"

The teenager's dog wanted to keep going,

so after a couple of seconds of being tugged, she resumed her fast-paced run. The red-head eased back inside of her muscle car.

Her muscle car had two doors, so that told me she didn't have a family, didn't have kids. Needed four doors for kids.

And not many mothers would rock a car like that.

When she pulled away I saw that her car had Texas license plates, but that didn't stick in my mind. What was humorous and made me shake my head was that the girl who had been running had seen me many times over the last few years and had never once said hello or waved a greeting in my direction.

I had always felt like that girl looked down on me the way some of the EBTers — people who used WIC and EBT to get by — disrespected the immigrant Vietnamese women who squatted at their toes to give them pedicures. EBTers had an air of superiority and acted like they had royal blood, like they were the queens when they had a little change in their pockets.

Everyone needs to feel superior to someone.

TOMMIE

I used my key and went inside Frankie's two-level crib. I turned the beeping alarm off.

Frankie called out, "Tommie McBroom?"

"It's me. Put your gun away, Quick Draw McGraw. I see Baba Looey is already here."

Livvy called out, "You're late."

"Was busy."

"Blue was putting a pole in the hole?"

"You got jokes."

Frankie snapped. "Be quiet, both of you."

I turned the alarm back on, set it on STAY, the way Frankie kept it when she was home.

Livvy was lounging in sweats, socks and trainers off. She was on the L-shaped sofa, empty plate in front of her, glass of Argentine wine in her hand. I kicked my trainers off, went across the cool room to the kitchen, made myself a plate of grilled white corn, asparagus, sweet potatoes, salad, grilled salmon, and baked chicken, then sat between her and Frankie. While I ate, I held my plate in my lap, then leaned back against Frankie while I put my feet across Livvy's thighs. I was starved. Beyond hungry. Nervous hunger.

I told Livvy, "Nice bracelet on your right ankle."

"A bracelet on an ankle is called an anklet, like a bracelet around your neck is called a necklace. Pretty clever, huh?"

"Whatever. That anklet is new?"

"Bought it when I was in Paris with Tony."

"Tony bought it for you?"

"Bought it for myself. Is there an issue?"

"You know, on the right ankle it means you're married but available, still looking, and you're still down for whatever."

"Does it?"

"Swingers wear those; that's what I heard. Yours has an Eiffel Tower on it. That's a sexual position, you know that?"

"Tommie, I wear it because it makes me feel pretty."

"On the left ankle it means you're not available."

Frankie snapped, "Don't come in here talking about nothing but the show. One more word about a damn anklet and I will go Huck on you two. Now shut up, McBitches."

Simultaneously, we showed Frankie our stiff middle fingers.

We fell into fan mode, talked to the television, high-fived each other, oohed and ahhed. When there was a commercial break, Livvy picked up her cellular to call Tony. Frankie paused the show and left to go potty. I took my empty plate to the kitchen, rinsed it off, and put it in the dishwasher. Had a surreal sensation regarding Beale Streets. Imagined I felt him draining out of me. But it was nothing. I touched my neck, expected to feel the pearl necklace he had created, but there was nothing. Nothing to worry about. I called Blue from Frankie's house phone, did that to create the illusion that I had been with my sisters since I'd left home angry; had a jovial tone to maintain the illusion we had fostered, then asked him to take the turkey bacon out of the freezer so I could make that for breakfast in the morning.

I asked, "Who is that I hear talking in the background?"

"Tony's on Skype with Livvy. I see you on his oversize and overpriced iPhone."

"Hey, don't knock the iPhone. That's putting food on our table."

Nervous that Livvy would say something to Tony, and Tony would mention it to Blue, and then Blue would ask about my missing hour, I waved at Livvy's phone as she passed by.

I said, "Thought you were going to write until you went to bed."

"I was. Then the doorbell rang and Tony was here holding a six-pack of Corona."

"I see. Well, that was the coincidence of all coincidences."

"I live in a House of Estrogen. You and Monica wear me down with that female energy. I need some man time."

"Sorry to interrupt the bromance. I hear Livvy in the other room laughing and talking to her husband."

"They act like newlyweds. I guess Paris was their second second honeymoon."

"Must be nice to be that happy after being together for over ten years. She's thirty-five and has been with Tony since she was twenty-two, I think. When she was my age they had been married for years. I can't even remember them not being married. I can't remember her life before Tony."

He asked, "How soon before you get back home?"

"Don't wait up."

Blue said, "Wake me when you get in."

"Just get your sleep. We'll add this to the long list of unresolved things to talk about."

69

I ended the call, took a few breaths, felt Beale inside of me, went back to the sofa with my sisters.

Livvy asked me, "How are things with Blue?"

"Perfect. Everything okay over in the Barrera household?"

"Everything is great."

Frankie asked, "How was that trip to Paris?"

"After Tony's medical convention ended, we had fun. You see the pictures I posted?"

"Did he put some salsa in that taco and finally knock you up?"

Livvy laughed. "Do you see how much wine I'm drinking?"

Frankie asked, "When y'all going to make that blacktino baby so it can go through some of the racism that you and Tony have had to put up with since y'all decided to defect on y'all's cultures?"

Livvy gave Frankie two middle fingers, then looked at me as she laughed, said, "You go first, Tommie. Have that baby. I need to focus on getting this business going. This spa is my newborn."

Frankie's phone blew up, "Always and Forever" ringtone, and that killed that conversation.

She grabbed her phone and answered like

70

a whip, "Stop calling this number."

Livvy asked, "Is that that Franklin Carruthers?"

Frankie hung up the phone and nodded.

I asked, "When did that cheating . . . when did he start back up calling?"

"I can handle it."

Livvy asked, "Did he ever stop?"

Frankie snapped, "I can handle it."

She was rattled. An emotional mess. Destroyed hopes swam in her eyes.

Frankie massaged her temples. Livvy and I moved closer to her, waited, watched her.

After a few ragged breaths Frankie said, "We were all supposed to be in the islands this week."

I massaged her foot. "We can get through this."

Livvy rubbed Frankie's shoulders, said, "I know this isn't an easy week for any of us, Frankie."

Once upon a time, after Tony had strayed, it had been Frankie and I trying to console Livvy.

I felt the betrayal Franklin had brought into our world; it resonated. The negative emotion was so powerful that I felt what Blue would feel. I felt the anxiety that I had felt because Blue had exercised his rights as a wise yet paranoid man. I remembered the angst in Beale Streets's voice and eyes.

Thirty seconds later my older sister's phone rang again. "Always and Forever" ringtone.

Livvy grabbed the phone and answered, "Motherfucker, stop calling my sister."

I cosigned with a harsh bark: "Don't you get it? You are persona non grata, asshole."

Frankie growled and grabbed the phone, hung up on Franklin, and cursed, now too upset to watch television.

Livvy wiped tears from her eyes.

I wiped a whole set of tears from my eyes too.

"Franklin had my nose and soul wide open. Never had been that happy. I had a nice diamond ring and a box of chocolate-covered deception to go with a mountain of lies. His wife received the same."

I said, "All that deception, all of this stalking, and he has a wife overseas in the military?"

"I even had my chocolate star bleached, because he asked me to."

Livvy snapped, "You did what to your which, Frankie?"

She realized what she'd said, grunted, gave a fake smile. "Sure is nice weather outside tonight."

I said, "You don't say you bleached your

72

booty hole, then go on talking about the weather."

Livvy laughed. "It's not a *hole,* Tommie. It's a *valve.*"

"Not the way she uses it."

Frankie snapped, "Go to hell, Tommie."

Livvy said, "We will revisit the anal bleaching, Frankie."

I said, "And no, I do not need to see it, but you can Instagram a picture."

Frankie cringed. "He had me good. He was trying to get me pregnant. So glad it didn't happen. I'd be pregnant with the baby of a man who is married to a deranged bitch in the military."

"I've been the fool before. And this too shall pass, just like my humiliation did."

"Shut up, Livvy. This is my two-minute pity party. You had yours a long time ago."

"Can't believe you went to someone else's spa and paid for them to bleach your valve."

I sang, "Frankie, since you bleached your booty valve, when you poot, does it smell like Clorox?"

We laughed until our bellies ached, then we had to sip wine and calm down.

It gradually evolved from hard laughter to extreme silence.

Frankie stared at her three-bedroom home, her once-again bachelorette pad. Her glower became a scowl, a glare of disdain, until her bottom lip trembled. She took another handful of deep breaths.

We tried to console her, but that was like staring into the abyss.

Frankie shouted, "My hair. My goddamn hair."

Livvy asked, "What about your hair?"

"He's in my dreadlocks."

I asked, "Franklin is in your hair?"

"I can feel him in my dreadlocks. His smell is in my dreadlocks. We're connected."

I said, "I'll wash your locks for you."

Big sister said, "He has dreadlocks. I have dreadlocks. People still look at my hair and associate me with him. To them I'm still part of *Frankie and Frankie.* We're going to do one better."

Frankie went to the bedroom and came back with two pairs of scissors and a garbage can.

She said, "Cut him out of my hair."

I said, "You'll look like you have cancer."

"Then cut it all except for the new growth."

Livvy shook her head. "Then you will look like a lesbian."

"Cut my goddamn dreadlocks, McBitches."

LIVVY

One hour later. Manhattan Beach, California. Crisp late-night air came off the Pacific Ocean. After Livvy had kissed her sisters and left Frankie's home, instead of heading toward her own, she had driven to Highland Avenue. She had returned to her own never-ending memory. She had done that many nights, driven to Manhattan Beach and parked where it had happened, searched for him — for her too.

She remembered the rented apartment that used to be their love nest. Near the sand dunes, two minutes from the ocean. The asking price for the rental had been $1,120 a month back then, long ago yet like yesterday, when Cliff and Janine ruled mornings on KJLH. It had been leased for six months. She closed her eyes, remembered kiwis and mangoes, colorful pillows, remembered Norah Jones and Sarah Vaughan CDs. She remembered being Bird.

She remembered flying. She remembered Carpe. She remembered Panther. Her senses flooded with memories. The slow, heavy breathing. The feel of her skin while her lover was inside her. Then the girl he brought. Two mouths on her. In that small apartment.

Her cellular rang. It was Tony. She answered. He was back home, asked her where she was.

"I'm on Sepulveda, Tony. I stopped by my business."

She told him she loved him and hung up the phone. She didn't want to leave. She wanted to go up to the door, knock, have it open, and be back in time. She put her hand on the car door, was going to go knock on that door, wanted to see who lived there, if he was there, if Panther was still his lover.

Livvy's phone buzzed and she cursed.

Now it was a text message from Tony.

She rubbed her temples, touched the right side of her head where she had just shaved away her hair. Drastic change. She started her SUV and made a U-turn, headed toward home. She drove slower than the flow of traffic, ignored all who sped around her, horns blowing, middle fingers extended.

When she made it home she pulled into her driveway, turned the engine off. She sat in silence. She remembered what she could not forget. She remembered the worst of times, the best of times.

TOMMIE

After Frankie's, I didn't want to go back to my world. Feeling a little lightheaded from the wine, I went back to Beale's home. I wanted him to see me. Maybe I wanted to make sure Tanya Obayomi wasn't there. I was being careless. I didn't check to see if I was being followed. I felt entitled to his space.

He said, "Your hair. Wow. You shaved one side of your head."

"My older sister cut most of hers off, so I let her cut down the left side of mine."

"Looks awesome. Funky. When a woman changes her hair, she's going through some things. She's crying out for help. She wants to change her life. You know I'm here for you, Tommie."

"Wanted you to see it before I went home. Wanted you to see it first. Now I'm leaving."

"Come in."

"No sex."

"No problem."

"Promise?"

We held hands, talked, strolled to his gourmet kitchen, took fruits and vegetables from his Sub-Zero refrigerator: apples, cucumbers, carrots, celery, kale, oranges, parsley, and lemon. He washed the fruit. I chopped up the vegetables before I went to his pantry and took out honey while he opened a cabinet to get his Jack LaLanne juicer. We did juice shots. Sat on bar stools. I had come back this time not out of anger but out of desire and curiosity. This had been an act of foolishness and free will. I was in love with Beale. In that moment, with wine in my blood and residual orgasm in my system, I felt like I was madly in love with him. I wished I had met him first. I could walk away from Blue. I could do this. But I had to shake it off. Then we cleaned up the kitchen, washed the juicer, held hands, and went to the basement, the man cave filled with neon lights, a popcorn machine, a treadmill, a Bowflex Tread-Climber, a pool table, a half dozen big-screen televisions, pinball machines, and a weight room that had both machine and free weights. One of the televisions was on. A commercial for Franklin's car restoration

businesses. That was a big deal in Southern
Cali. Rebuilding homes and restoring cars,
and Frankie and Franklin were killing it in
both fields, raking in money hand over fist.
You had to have a new car to get the girl to
come to your crib in Cali. The only thing
sexier than a brand-new car was one from
back in the day that had been restored with
all of the original parts. A restored car cost
more than a new car, made no economic
sense, but that was the thing in car country.
People shipped their cars to Franklin from
all over the United States. That's how big
his business had gotten in the last two years.
He'd restored a car for Hollywood actress
Regina Baptiste's husband. It was publicized
when she did an interview on *The Tonight
Show,* and due to the Baptiste Bump, as
they called it, his local business took off.
Franklin appeared in all of his commercials
the same way Frankie was on billboards.
Frankie's ads were humble; Franklin's were
full of braggadocio. I could see now what I
hadn't seen back then, that grandiose sense
of self-importance, his excessive self-
admiration, his sense of power and arrogant
behavior. It all came off as if he were making fun of himself, but that was the real him.
Frankie's Auto Restorations, shops from the
Bay to San Diego, and he had a half dozen

car washes and repair shops that worked with all major insurance companies. He was becoming a local celebrity, like car salesman Cal Worthington had done back in the eighties. All he had to do was eat a bug as a gimmick and get some adorable pet as a mascot and continue with his 'Bama shtick. I picked up the remote and turned the television off, gave my tipsy attention to Beale Streets's pretty eyes. We played a game of Ms. Pac-Man. We were both competitive. I won, and then we rode the elevator to the top. My eyes went to the bed. He had changed the come-stained sheets, made the bed with fresh linen that had a thread count higher than my SAT score, and sprayed the room with a fresh scent. My aroma was gone, as was all evidence. It was as if I'd never been there that evening. I didn't say anything. We climbed on his freshly made bed. I played with his kinky hair for a while; he gave me a smooth back rub. I'd been there thirty-seven minutes. That was thirty-seven minutes too long.

I thought about Monica. Imagined her waking up without my being there.

I said, "I need to leave before I get too comfortable."

"Tell me the real reason you came back."

"You don't tell a woman you bought her a

present and expect her to be able to sleep, do you?"

"You still have to wait."

"Five more minutes."

"Ten."

He pulled my sweats down to my ankles, put a pillow underneath my butt, and went down on me again. I shouldn't have let him do that, like this was his, but I did let him do that like he was mine. Why I felt the way I felt at this moment, this sensation, was an enigma, a mystery as deep as the Atlantic.

His cellular rang, a ringtone that made his tongue stroke falter, pulled me out of heaven.

I opened my eyes. "Tanya Obayomi is calling you. That Drake song is her ringtone. She's not coming over, is she?"

He pushed me back down. "I'm only sleeping with you, Tommie."

"I'm more concerned with who you're staying awake with than whom you're sleeping with."

His tongue hit a new rhythm, a strong beat, like the drumbeat to "High on the Ceiling."

First there were lights behind my eyes, then gradually colors returned, deep variations in and subtle gradations of light and shade, as if the world had become a chiaroscuro painted by Rembrandt.

When I was done, as I twitched and came down from the high, he rested his face on my thighs.

I looked around. This lifestyle, this silence, this level of tranquility, could become addictive.

Monica would love it here. I imagined her running up the stairs from the basement to the bedroom, then riding the elevator back down and playing the pinball and video games until I yelled for her to quit.

Five precocious children could live in this home and rarely be in the same room.

I sat up, tugged my sweats up, but he pulled me back to the bed, made me chill out a moment.

I asked, "You've been all over the world. What's your favorite place?"

"You're my favorite place. You're the place I want to be. Right here."

"How many girls have you been with?"

"Many girls, but you are the first woman."

"You're my third adventure into premarital sex."

"Do you feel as if you've lost part of yourself by being with me?"

"I haven't gained anything."

"But? Feels like there is a *but* to that statement."

"I knew that if we kept being alone, with this energy between us, this chemistry, it might happen."

"When did you start to feel that way?"

"At Eso Won. That night. You invited me to Starbucks after your event. I actually went with you. I followed your driver and went to Starbucks on Crenshaw and Thirty-Ninth. You had a very sexy female driver."

"She had an amazing smile. The chauffeur named Panther was driving me that night."

"She waited in the town car for you. She saw the engagement ring on my finger. She smiled. Women know these things. She knew that it was more than us just getting coffee. I sat out in public with you like it was no big deal. It was a big deal. Since I had been with Blue, I'd never been anywhere with a man in a way that could be misconstrued as being a date. We were a half mile from my home. Was terrified I'd see one of Blue's and my friends."

"I couldn't tell. You were talking in a very distant way, were very professional."

His phone rang again. Tanya Obayomi. He ignored the summons, then moved closer to me.

Beale asked, "What are you thinking?"

"Asking myself what it is I like about you,

84

what attracted me to you."

"And the answer is?"

"Same as everyone else. I love your work, respect your artistry, and you have told me time and time again that you love and respect my poetry. You give me inspiration as only another artist can."

"You have become my muse as much as I have been your muse."

"That's part of the reason this sort of thing became possible."

"I still wonder how this happened, Tommie McBroom."

"You needed someone you could trust as a beta reader with your unpublished work."

"I'm just as surprised as you at what has transpired. For me, this was a miracle."

"I told you I could do both, edit and read."

"I needed to be able to trust you. People have betrayed me, backstabbed me before."

"And I had no problem signing a confidentiality agreement. You asked me my fee and I told you it was standard rate but negotiable. I thought you would lowball me, tell me I should be happy to work for you. I needed the money but didn't want to admit how badly we needed that money in our household."

"I paid you top rate, plus thirty percent. Will still pay you top rate if you come work for me again."

"I was really flattered, and nervous, hoped what I did was to your liking and up to your standard. I wanted to impress you with my work. It was a professional relationship. Putting money on the table made fantasies dissipate. It did change the fabric of our friendship. We would text, but not as often as before, and we never talked every day, only when there was an issue. Sometimes a week or two would go by before you had something for me to read and edit. You e-mailed me the work. I e-mailed it back with notes and opinions. If it was needed, after Blue had left for work and I dropped Mo off at school, we met at Starbucks to discuss the work in person. You gave me a check. A handshake. A smile good-bye."

He took ice in his mouth, kissed me up and down my spine as he asked, "Then what?"

I closed my eyes, arched my back, said, "I took the check to your bank, cashed it, and went home with two bags of food, or paid a bill, or paid some unexpected fee at Mo's school. I was contributing to my household on a higher level that made me proud. So far as you and I, it was an honest relationship."

"Was it honest? Did Blue know you were

working for me part-time?"

"Blue had no idea, but it was honest in the sense that if he found out, it would be no big deal. I have many jobs and would say that was just added to the list. I could look him in his eyes and say there was no affair going on. But it changed. Blue's baby momma went on another rampage regarding custody issues. She hadn't called her child in three months, nor sent a dime to support her child, and she was making demands. It was too much. I was unhappy at home and just wanted a place to sit and not feel stressed. You told me I could sit in a room at your home. You had plenty of space. You lived in your office. Your televisions, your computers, sofa, and bed were all in that one gigantic room. I could use the rest of the house as if I were at a bed-and-breakfast, or at Barnes and Noble, with the library you had."

He turned me over, took more ice, sucked my left nipple, said, "Keep talking."

I moaned. "You were in one room. I was in another wing. This big house. You were so far away I couldn't hear you or tell that you were there. I was happy to be around you, happy being in your space."

"Why were you hiding on the other side of the house? Felt like you were miles away."

"You were in one room. I picked another in the far reaches, afraid to be close to you, alone with you in the same room, in your creative space. So close, yet so far, yet able to tell Blue, if needed, we were never in the same area."

He licked my nipples. "That was professional."

"I blogged, posted my YouTube videos about hair and being a stepmommy and made my political statements in the form of haikus, worked at the Apple Store with the techno-maniacs, and worked for you. We needed the money. Children are expensive. They never stop growing and never stop eating."

"You worked. I paid you each time. I didn't 1099 you. Didn't increase your taxes."

I rubbed his wild hair. "I bought Mo more clothes, used coupons and bought more food."

"You're the coupon queen."

"Never pay for what you can get for free or at a discount. Learned that from Momma, and thanks to her I am the queen of coupons and sales; I can make one hundred dollars stretch like two thousand."

"For a while, while I was working on that

project, I was able to see you almost every day."

"I told myself I was providing for my family while you and I were rooms away from each other, sending text messages, messages that would make anyone who read them think we were miles, cities, states, maybe even countries away. I was alone with a man in a home that had many luxurious beds and I felt like I could trust you. You gave me compliments but never overdid it, knew where the line was drawn."

He moved down to my belly, more ice kisses on my warm skin. "I know. I had to respect you."

I clenched the covers, shivered, caught my breath, felt so damn alive.

I whispered, "It made me want to be around you more and more. Each day the line that had been drawn moved. Soon I worked from the bedroom next to your office. I needed to be around positivity. That made me want to find a way to see you on the days I had other obligations."

"I thought about you night and day, Tommie. Looked forward to you being here."

"That time I needed to be alone with me, it turned into time I needed to be alone with you. I stopped resting in another part of your home and began lounging on the big chair in your office."

"It surprised me when you came into my office and chilled out on the big red chair."

"You would write. I would read. We never disturbed each other."

He pushed my legs open, said, "In silence. Occasionally making eye contact."

I shivered again, anticipating. "I would stare and imagine reading naked."

"I would have written naked if you had asked."

"I wanted to fellate you while you wrote."

He said, "And while you read, I wanted to give you cunnilingus like you'd never experienced. I was dying to use my mouth, to taste you, to know your saccharine flavor and use my tongue with the intent of making you come. I wanted to lick your pussy and suck your cunt until you went mad. I wanted to be more personal than sex, than normal penetration, wanted to hold your ass in the palms of my hands and with this tongue show you just how much you meant to me, show you exactly how I felt. I wanted to penetrate you with my tongue so badly. When you left, I masturbated while imagining I was doing that."

"Damn, Beale. Damn."

"Surprised?"

"I imagined younger girly girls like Tanya Obayomi were your style."

"I assumed you only liked older men."

"I like maturity in a man. I like a man who knows how to be responsible. You handle your business and that's a turn-on. You have a lot, but you don't seem to waste a lot. *Right there. Right there.*"

I grabbed the sheets, back arched like a bridge to my own orgasm.

He made me need to come, then slowed down, backed away, teased me, nibbled my thighs, ran his fingers across my skin. Beale relaxed with his head on my thigh. His bushy hair tickled my flesh.

He asked, "When did you think this might be possible?"

"One day I was here working for you. Will never forget that day. The way you came up behind as I was reading those loose pages, your work in progress, the way you stood behind me, barely breathing, gazing at me, and I knew you were entranced. Your energy was in the red, the same level as mine."

"You were dressed up, had on sweet perfume. You were irresistible."

"I told you that I was dressed up, told you that I had my hair done and face made up because I had been hanging with Frankie, but in reality I had dressed sexy for you. I didn't see Frankie that day. Everything I had on was brand new, including the perfume. I had a new hairstyle, just for you."

"You did that for me? You came to work dressed up like that for me?"

"I needed you to notice me the way I had noticed you. I wanted that visceral reaction from you. I wanted that smile. I wanted to know you wanted me the way I had started fantasizing about you."

"You wanted to become involved with me."

"I didn't think it would go beyond flirting."

"You wanted more than that."

"Maybe."

"Why?"

"I don't know. I tried to analyze, but there was no clear reason, other than my anger."

"Being with a man a little bit younger, is this your way of going back in time, going back to the moments before you met Blue? Maybe I represent that other life you never had a chance to live."

"Don't stop licking me, but please stop analyzing me."

"Licking you like this seems to be what makes you tell me the truth."

"It makes me weak. Makes me confess."

"Am I your time machine?"

"Hadn't analyzed that either, but isn't that always why the more mature seek out youth?"

"Why did you want to make me your H. G. Wells and get into the metaphorical time machine only once, Tommie?"

"I would move on after the kiss. I would have made myself available, but the kiss, it would have been your idea, or it would seem like it to me. I would enjoy it; then when it went too far I might jack you off, maybe make you come in order to get you to chill out, as a therapeutic way of bringing you down from your high and stopping it before it went too far, then express my confusion, wash my hands and remind you I was engaged and petting wasn't right. It would be my guilt, my issue to deal with. Had no idea. It might have even become our wink, the thing we never addressed, our secret, nervous smile."

"You were so sexy. When I came up behind you, when I put my hand on your waist, when I whispered I was crazy about you, I expected you to have a fit, or run and tell Blue."

"We arrived at that moment. I'd made myself available. You'd confessed. I had to decide where I wanted it to go."

"You have no idea how scared I was, how

I felt like I had blown it with you."

"Beale, we'd had weeks of silent foreplay. The energy, the tension, had built up inside me."

He nodded. "I know. It had built up inside me as well. It was torture, madness made of fire."

"I was scared. I knew I was about to lose control."

"Tommie, I wanted you. I was tired of waiting to be with you again. I needed you."

"I was lost in your pretty eyes. Looking in your eyes was like traveling to a new world. I wanted to know what it was like to go there. I took a breath, closed my eyes, trembled, and eased my body back into yours, put my butt against your groin, took another breath, and moved against you."

"That was your answer."

"Yes, that was my answer."

"You moved your ass around and around in subtle motions. Had no idea you could move so deftly. You are so . . . dignified . . . great posture . . . articulate . . . had no idea you could be that sensual."

"I felt you grow. Tingles shot through every part of my body. Tiny explosions."

"I had an erection and you kept rubbing that sweet ass against me."

"I ain't gonna lie. It felt wrong, but it felt

good. Teasing, foreplay, that wrong felt so good. I wanted to stop it right away, but I wanted you to stop it for me. I didn't know how to halt the momentum. It was as if desire had taken on a life of its own, like I was no longer in control. How did it make you feel?"

He said, "I put my lips on your skin. Couldn't believe I was actually touching you like that."

"You trembled too. I'd never seen that side of you. So passionate. You looked so vulnerable."

"I'd only seen the public and professional side of you, not the sensual side."

"How did I look to you? In that moment what did you see on my face?"

He whispered, "You were a tigress and a lamb all at once."

"We all become someone else when aroused. A woman can't be a lady while aroused. We want to be aroused so we can take the weight of being a gentlewoman from our shoulders and be liberated."

He said, "That first kiss will always be remembered."

"You kissed me like you were famished, not a sloppy kiss, but an intense kiss, intense and controlled. You fought to maintain control, and then your hands rubbed my back, went down across my ass, and came up, went to my breasts. My breasts felt like they'd doubled in size. My nipples were hard."

"I touched your breasts and you moaned and began to shake like you were coming."

"I was floating. You kissed me and squeezed my breasts and I was squeezing my thighs together, struggling with the wicked heat. I was surprised you could make me feel that way, make me that hot."

"You told me to fuck you."

"I told you to fuck me?"

"You told me to fuck you in the most sensual, erotic, melodic, horny tone I had ever heard."

"All I remember is you pulling my pants down, then having trouble getting them over my ass."

"Tight jeans on that rotund, robust, ridiculous ass. You have no idea how that aroused me."

"I stood in front of you in high heels, my pants at my ankles, my breasts out of my bra, lipstick smudged, my hair in a state of madness, the breeze from your air conditioner tickling my exposed vagina and ass. You undid your pants, rushed them down, and just like that you pushed me up against the wall."

"I held you up and you wrapped your legs around me."

"That was after I kicked one leg out of my pants."

"Yeah, your pants were still trapped on one leg."

"You held me up and worked your way inside me."

"And as soon as I was inside you, when I was all the way inside, remember what happened?"

"I was starting to lose control, was coming, and my phone rang. Blue's ringtone. I was terrified. I thought he knew, that he had sensed someone had invaded me. Then I dropped my feet to the floor, stumbled, and you slipped out of me."

"No, you pushed me out of you, away from you. You freaked out, shoved me across the room."

"I was scared. Saw my life flash before my eyes."

"You sounded so calm when you talked to Blue. You became someone else. I got to see who you were when you were with him. I got to see Tommie McBroom the frustrated fiancée, the faux mother."

"I was terrified until I realized Blue was calm, that he had no idea where I was. He was just calling to check on me. We call each

97

other a dozen times a day just to chat. We still do that. We talk a lot."

"You told him you were about to go to Walmart and buy paper towels."

"Told him a lie. Told him I loved him."

"You know that is the lie of all lies."

"I told him I loved him, then ended the call and faced you, naked from the waist down."

Beale chuckled. "Awkward moment."

I chuckled too. "Very awkward moment, Beale."

"I didn't know what we would do after that."

"You shuffled back toward me."

"I almost tripped on my pants."

"You had a fire in your eyes, a fire that intimidated me."

"You bunny hopped back toward me and I rushed back toward you, let my pants drag, and met you halfway."

"That next kiss."

"Yeah, that was something else."

"You sucked my breasts and put your fingers back inside of me."

"You sucked my neck while you stroked me."

"You fingered me and I could hear how wet I was."

"I was so hard that I felt embarrassed."

"Feeling how hard you were, that made me so wet."

"You made me want to come."

"You fingered me and we kissed and kissed and kissed while I masturbated you."

He said, "I couldn't stand being jacked off, and I wanted to get back inside you. Wanted to hide my erection inside of you so you couldn't see what you were doing to me."

"You slipped back inside of me, went inside effortlessly, all of you went inside of me, and the shock made my knees go weak. I couldn't stand up anymore. All I could do was hold on. You caught me, eased me down to the floor, to the carpet, opened my legs, kissed me, put it deep inside me again."

"It was so wild."

I whispered, "It was animalistic."

"I have never had sex like that. No woman has ever made me feel the way you do."

"Never in my life. It was like I had been possessed by the spirits of Venus, Tiacapan, and Tlaco."

"You were acting weird when you left. Your face was red, your eyes were on the ground, and you were crying."

"I'd cheated on Blue. I was ashamed. I couldn't look at you. I didn't know how to leave, and I didn't know how to go home. I knew Blue would see the betrayal on my face or find a new mark on my skin."

"The first time, when we were done, you were a mess. It was like I had done something wrong. Wondered if I had forced myself on you, or if you had only done that because you didn't know how to say no, or were afraid to say no; I was terrified of what would happen if you had seen it that way."

"There was a big knot in my stomach. It was like pain and sorrow had mixed up inside of me, and I cried, but when I was home I threw up. I felt like I'd done the stupidest thing in the world. I kept asking myself how I had put myself in that position, how I'd allowed that to happen. Moths were in my body eating my insides and I wanted to scream and tell someone. I wanted to talk to . . . to somebody about it."

"A big knot was in my stomach as well. I thought back on what had happened, wished I could change it. I was unable to sleep. There was a pain in my body, a sharp guilt stabbing me, and a fire in my mind. I wanted to apologize but was afraid to call you. I expected the police to show up at my door."

"I had no idea."

"But we had done what we had done, and

that could not be undone."

"I analyzed it, tried to be all intellectual about what had happened."

"What was your conclusion?"

"It had been what I had to do, what my body craved. Maybe it was a psychological need manifested in a physiological way. I knew that Blue's sperm were pointless. Maybe my body craved a man who was fertile. Maybe I desired a man whose sperm were powerful, felt like the sperm of a real man. Maybe my body can tell the difference."

"We went bareback."

"Like husband and wife."

"I came inside of you."

"Why did you?"

"You didn't tell me to pull out."

"We had no control, were at top speed on black ice."

"That part of you wrapped around that part of me, you have no idea how I felt when you let me come inside of you."

"That was dangerous."

"I know."

"That scared me more than you will ever know."

"Had me concerned as well."

"You saw that in my face, in my body language."

"I saw regret. There was regret. You left without saying good-bye. You just dressed and all but ran out of my house."

"I felt like if I had left your house and gone to church to get baptized and wash away my new sins, the water would have burned away all of my skin, scorched my flesh. I had been with another man. A younger man had made me come. You are so much younger than Blue. That was on my mind too. There are more than two decades between your ages."

"I know. I have thought about that as well."

"You're barely younger than I am. We're pretty much of the same generation, but it felt like I had robbed the cradle. I was bent out of shape, needed to get back to my world, and by the time I picked up Mo, I was faking the funk."

"Holy water would have set you on fire? You were that miserable?"

"I couldn't think straight for a couple of days. I couldn't do anything right."

"I didn't think I would ever see you again."

"I wasn't going to see you again. I wanted to erase you from my mind."

He said, "You could've let it stop there, but you came back ten days later."

"I know. I counted the days."

"That surprised me."

"I didn't plan to come back. The next time, it was after another argument with Blue's ex-bitch baby momma, another bad night with Blue because of her. Again I was seething because she had intruded into my happy world, had chipped away at what was left of my happy place, and I was acting out, being rebellious, saying fuck it, fuck Blue, and fuck the bitch he had fucked ten years ago and had a baby with."

"My churchgoing friend, I have never heard you talk about anyone like that."

"She stokes the devil inside of me."

He asked, "How do you feel after you have been with me now? I've always wanted to know."

"It amazes me how life goes back to being typical after I leave, as if it never happened. I go back home, back to my life, back to cooking, washing dishes, blogging, taking care of Mo and Blue. It's like I'm in a movie and I'm moving from one surreal dimension to another, knowing both worlds could collide."

"No guilt when you leave me? You should feel guilty that you are leaving me."

"Each time I leave you, I shower again, take a long shower, and at night I am in bed with Blue."

103

"Had hoped that things were so bad in your home that you'd stopped sleeping together."

"We've never stopped."

"Hurts me to hear that. Hurts knowing that while I'm alone at night, you're with him."

"You need to know that so you can understand your position in my life."

"You go back to your world, to your small house and the large problems."

"I leave this world and follow the yellow brick road back home to Blue and Mo."

"To dysfunction and misery."

"I could say that the first time with you was an accident, could be the woman and blame you, say you seduced me, claim you had power over me and took advantage of that power; I could be a typical woman and take on the role of naive girl once again. I could play that worn-out card many women play."

"The second time, what was that encounter, in your eyes?"

"The second was where my part of the sin began because I chose to come back."

"The third time?"

"The third time, when we undressed, laughing, reading, that was as intentional as an affair can ever get. When we were done,

I lay across your bed as if it were my bed, walked around your home as if it were my home, moved from room to room in peace, went downstairs and played on the pinball machine, went to the kitchen and made a snack, then went back to reading your work as I strolled naked."

He whispered, "The fourth time?"

"The fourth time, like the third, I didn't pretend that I was interested in reading."

"You barely made it through the front door."

"You took me on the carpet in your hallway, then on the stairs."

"I don't remember what I did, Tommie; I just know we started downstairs, then we were on the elevator riding up to the bedroom. We rocked the elevator so hard, I thought it was about to break."

"The fifth time I wore new lingerie, tied you to a chair, blindfolded you."

He said, "The sixth time we were in my Jacuzzi."

"The seventh was in the living room on the sofa."

"Now eight."

"This is the eighth time I've been with you."

He asked, "How many times have you been with Blue?"

"Enough to make being with you eight times seem as insignificant as a dime in a pile of C-notes."

"What are we doing here, Tommie?"

I paused, felt the weight of his desire. "I don't know what we're doing. Hoped you knew."

"I want more than revenge sex when you're angry at him. I want you here because you want me."

"I met Blue before you."

"So what?"

"His roots are deeper."

"I can go deeper. I can find a space not even you know exists."

"Stop being jealous. Grow up. Stop being childish."

Beale mounted me, put my ankles around his neck, struggled to make the dead rise, but he was a young man, could rearm the sailor quicker than Blue. Youth had advantages. Half-erect, Beale rushed inside me. He began to move, rose and dipped, took it round and round, stirred and stroked.

I sang, *You are my secret. As long as you are unknown, I have dignity.*

He stroked harder.

I moved up and down, became his roller coaster.

I moaned more improvised poetry, the

rhythm of five-seven-five. He stroked in the rhythm of his own haiku, five hard, seven deep, five intense. He stroked. My spoken word rode on my every moan. We were in a battle. Five-seven-five for each five-seven-five. As my poetry elevated, he was reduced to grunts. Strokes and grunts. Like a man gone mad.

When he realized I could do this all night, that I could exchange the beauty, art, and rhythmic qualities of our beautiful tongue for his every stroke, that I could five-seven-five as long as he could five-seven-five, when he realized that his strokes made me come as he tried not to orgasm, he knew he could not win at this, knew that he could never win at this, not with me.

He barked, "Stop reciting haikus and just tell me you love me."

I ended a haiku, the most vulgar I'd ever recited, then laughed between shudders. "Make me stop."

"Say you love me."

"Make me, make me, make me if you're man enough."

"If I'm man enough?"

"You heard me. Make me tell you that I love you."

He pulled me at my waist, pulled me up into him, made me feel his frustration swell, found a strong rhythm, yanked me into him over and over. I let my arms fall to my sides, hands in fists, didn't help him. I was so wet, anticipating each thrust. He hit my hallelujah. I bit my lips and tried to be quiet, to not make a sound, to make him feel like he was less of a man than Blue. He did his best to make me loud. He rocked the bed. Tried to break the bed. Tried to fuck me in half so he could fuck both halves back whole. He held my waist and gave it to me like that, no holding back, made the bed walk across the wooden floor with each stroke. Teeth clenched, hands in fists, eyes closed, I refused to surrender. Then I looked up at Beale's pretty eyes as he looked down on me. He frowned the deepest, most desperate heartbroken frown I'd ever seen in my life. Beale growled, sweated, held me tighter.

His phone rang again. It was that familiar Drake ringtone.

I felt her pain. I felt her unhappiness. I felt her energy.

Tanya Obayomi was determined to reclaim what she had lost.

I wondered how many times Beale had been with her.

How many ways.

I had no right to be jealous.

Yet I was.
I had no right to sleep with Beale.
Yet I did.

TOMMIE

The gas needle was getting close to E and I had to take Monica to school early in the morning, when traffic was mad and it would be impossible to get in and out of a gas station with ease, so I rode back over the hill to La Brea and Slauson to get gas. When I pulled in, the red sports car pulled in behind me. The same white woman I had seen before. She didn't look at me, just got out of her car, opened her gas cap, swiped her card, and started filling up, same as I was doing. Music poured from her car. Stevie Nicks ended a tune and Pearl Jam started the next one. I took out my phone, wondered if I should call home, wondered if I'd messed up. My heart beat hard. My head ached again. I sent Blue a text; told him that I had just left Frankie's crib, said we'd had an interesting evening and that I was stopping to get gas and groceries.

I went to the trunk of my car, opened it,

looked at the box with the T-shirts from around the world, at the trinkets, at all the sweet little gifts Beale had bought me, things I couldn't take inside my home without an explanation. He had also bought me a pair of cowboy boots, a pair I had wanted for so long. They were sexy, not corny, and would look great with skinny jeans, or with jean shorts and a sexy T-shirt.

I closed my trunk and the woman behind me said, "Pardon me. Your face looks familiar."

"We saw each other a little while ago. You were looking for a house."

"That was you?"

I almost said that she probably thought all black people looked alike, but I didn't go there. I knew that wasn't true. I knew that many people had problems identifying people outside of their own assigned races. I couldn't distinguish between Vietnamese, Korean, and Chinese on my best day.

She asked, "Are you Frankie McBroom?"

"Do I know you?"

"When I was in that area, the young girl with the dog, I saw her again. She stopped running to chat. I asked her to recommend a real estate agent. She told me that I had been in front of Frankie McBroom's home, and she was the person to know if I wanted to buy property in the area."

"I'm Tommie. Frankie is my sister. We were in front of her home when I met you. Could've introduced you to her, if I had known."

"She has a nice home. How would I get in contact with your sister?"

"What's your name?"

"Rosemary Paige."

Her name, its rhythm, for some reason, reminded me of Rosa Parks.

Again, coupled with her congenial tone, there was some level of trust.

I said, "Hold on for a moment, Rosemary Paige."

I reached into my purse and gave her one of Frankie's business cards.

She read the info, nodded twice, then asked, "You're in real estate too?"

"Nah. I work at the Apple Store in Manhattan Beach, but I do other things. Creative things."

"I see you're married."

"Engaged."

"Congratulations."

"Thanks."

"One more thing. Do you know a mechanic?"

"What's the issue?"

"Gas gauge is malfunctioning. It stopped

working about two months ago."

"Dangerous to ride around like that."

"I know. Not an easy fix. They will have to take out the gas tank to address the issue."

"I wouldn't know what to do if mine didn't work. Triple A would be my best friend."

"I know the range I can go on a tank. Until I get it fixed, I count the miles and remind myself to fill up. Almost forgot this time. See how much gas I had to get? I must've been driving on fumes."

Her pump clicked. I checked mine. I had it on the notch for the slowest setting and hadn't realized the mistake. She opened the trunk of her car and took out a red gas can, started filling that up.

I said, "That's smart."

"I've learned."

"You've run out of gas, I take it?"

"No fun running out of gas in the middle of nowhere on I-10 in the middle of the night."

I leaned against my car, looked at my engagement ring until I noticed Rosemary Paige was still watching me. Her interest made me wonder if she was hitting on me. Wouldn't have been the first time a woman checked me out and offered to buy me a cup of coffee or take me to dinner.

I felt uneasy.

She motioned at the back window on my car and said, "I see a twenty-six point two sticker in your back window."

"I've earned a few."

"You're a marathoner."

"Oh, yeah."

"I run too. Training for an ultra."

"That's awesome."

She nodded. "Frankie is a runner as well?"

"Both of my sisters are, but running is Frankie's religion."

"You have a sticker for Turning Point."

I smiled. "Private school. My nine-year-old daughter goes to school there."

"Turning Point."

"It's a concept. Two words say so much."

She said, "I understand. Powerful concept. The point of a major decision. Some days it feels like I'm at my turning point. I know I'm almost there. At the point at which a very significant change occurs."

"Yeah. I guess I'm almost there too, almost at a very decisive moment in my life."

"Whatever you decide to do, you have to have the guts to follow through."

"It's not always that easy, especially when things . . . things aren't always so clear."

"Life is not about doing what's easy; it's

about doing what needs to be done. I've never taken the easy route in life."

I checked my phone to see if Blue had messaged me back. He hadn't. I opened my purse and pulled out a few coupons, began to read the expiration dates. The click told me my car had finally filled. I was trying not to freak out, but I needed to be back home. This juggling act was maddening.

Rosemary Paige put her extra can of gas in the trunk of her car; then, as she stood with one foot in her car, she said my name, called for my attention again, then smiled and told me, "Well, Tommie, thanks for the information. First thing tomorrow, I will find Frankie McBroom. Can't wait to meet her."

TOMMIE

When I eased through my front door, our alarm countdown commenced. I put down two bags of groceries and then turned it off, reset it to STAY mode. I expected Blue to be up waiting for me, but he wasn't in the living room watching television and I didn't see any lights on in the kitchen. I hurried and put the groceries away, put the four empty beer cans that he and Tony had left on the counter into the trash, and wiped down the table. I kicked my trainers off, stripped naked, and stuffed everything that smelled of wrongdoing into the hamper, then went to the bathroom and turned on the shower. Exhausted with this game, I stood underneath the warm water a long time before the bathroom door opened.

Mo staggered and rubbed her eyes, nodded, and went to go potty. When she was done, she washed her hands, then dried them on a paper towel before tossing it into the small trash can.

She yawned. "Good night, Mommy Mommy bo bommy."

Body covered in mango-scented soap, I said, "Good night, Mo Mo bo bo."

She pulled the bathroom door halfway shut behind her. Again everything was quiet. A moment later there was a tap on the door. It scared me. The door opened all the way again. It was Blue. Gray boxers and wrinkled white T-shirt that read RESPECT THE LOCALS: REGENERATION NOT GENTRIFICATION. White low-rise socks. He'd had more than a couple of beers — I could tell by his stance and the twinkle in his eye. His energy was strong. His desire, his need, obvious.

I wanted to bang my head against the wall.

He stepped in from the dark hallway and said, "You're back late tonight."

"Frankie had a breakdown. We had to be her bookends."

He opened the door to the shower, looked at me.

He said, "Your hair."

"You should see what's left of Frankie's and Livvy's."

"Not even going to ask. I called Frankie. She said you were gone. I knew you'd cut your hair. Wanted to see."

"Ran a couple of errands. Went grocery

117

shopping on the Westside, then had almost made it home and saw that I needed gas, and had to turn around and go back up the hill to Shell."

I arranged the events of the evening to fit my needs. Truth and lies danced in the pale moonlight. I faced him, smiling, nervous, fingerprints from my transgression fresh on my skin.

Blue hummed, looked at me the way a man does a woman, asked, "Want some company?"

That simple question spoke of his desire to have me, to reconcile by intimacy. I almost told him to leave me alone. Almost confessed that I had been with Beale. I wanted to reject him. One simple act of rejection could change the dynamic of a relationship. One rejection could put us on the path of becoming ex-lovers. One rejection could give me back my freedom. I felt like I was evolving, becoming more in sync with Beale, losing synchronicity with Blue. Both hurt like hell. I imagined Beale, then I thought about Mo not being in my life and burst into tears. Had to let the water hit my face to hide my conflicted feelings.

Blue asked, "You okay?"

"Just thinking about the way Frankie broke down crying. She had a horrible breakup."

"I'm sorry for the way things went earlier."

"What's the solution? How do we fix it, Blue?"

"You have to understand that I'm a guy surrounded by girls and women, and no matter how I try to keep things smooth . . . don't know what to do at times. I get over-whelmed."

"No problem. I'm over it. I'm sorry for my behavior as well. I should back off and let you and Angela handle your business. I really shouldn't be this involved. You're the adults."

"Don't do that, Tommie. Don't put a wall up like that. I spoke to Angela. She gets the point. She says she'll do better."

"No problem."

Being with Beale had felt real when I was there, felt false when I was away.

But each time being with Beale felt less false. And being here was feeling less real.

Blue said, "You look like you're in a zone."

"Thinking about . . . I guess . . . right now . . . turning point . . . that's on my mind."

"Everything okay at school with Monica? Did I miss something?"

"Nothing happened at school. Come here, Blue. I can't stand us being like this. Get in

119

with me. I miss you."

Blue saw me as being unpredictable, as being irrational. All that I did was inspired and made sense to me. I was at a turning point, at my decisive moment. Whatever I decided, I would need the guts to follow through. Rosemary Paige's profound words lived inside of me, tried to give me clarity.

He asked, "Are you sure?"

With the hand that wore my engagement ring, I motioned for Blue to join me.

I didn't want us to be like Frankie and Frankie. I needed us to be like Livvy and Tony.

Blue stripped, came into the shower with me, wanted me as Beale had wanted me.

The therapist reappeared, was seated on the toilet, watching, pen in hand, scribbling.

LIVVY

After leaving Frankie's home, she needed to decompress. She needed to destress.

Olivia McBroom-Barrera was dressed in a lipstick-red, deep-V bow-tied backless party mini, one of those skintight numbers that she couldn't put on without inhaling. It molded to the shape of her body as if it were a new layer of designer epidermis. Drink in hand, she glanced down at her Lucite and leather T-strap Manolo Blahniks. Those shoes were an emotional favorite. She inhaled and her mind retrieved the sight, sound, smell, feel, and taste of so many memories. She inhaled and loved the scent of the new perfume on her skin. Hair light brown with highlights, down over her shoulders, now shaven on the right side. Silver jewelry. Men stole glances at her as if she were a queen sitting in the nude. Tipsy. She was at Bar Nineteen 12 in the Beverly Hills Hotel. Swank. Comfy chairs. Sofas. A DJ was in the back playing house. The bar was private, exclusive, but very chill, very elegant. Expensive. Food cost about forty dollars a bite. Her husband, Antonio, was next to her, his hand in hers. She leaned over and kissed him. Then they sat back, cuddled, and watched the pretentious party.

"Tony?"

"Yeah, babe."

"I bet that table of women with fake faces will spend over five thousand on drinks."

"Nine hundred dollars a glass. They'll spend ten thousand before the night ends."

Her cellular buzzed. She looked down and saw a message from her sister Tommie.

Just showered. Checked on Frankie. Checking to make sure you made it home.

Tell Blue g'night. Tell Monica her favorite auntie said g'night.

Livvy put her Samsung away, slid it back inside her clutch, smiling, thinking about her sister Tommie and her great love affair with her fiancé, Blue. Tommie had returned to university, obtained her degree, all while running a household, working, blogging, and being a mother in training. It was an enviable relationship. Her baby sister had grown into being a responsible woman, and one day soon the wedding bells would ring. Maybe Tommie would be the first Mc-Broom to have a child. Livvy had wanted to have a baby a decade ago, but now she wasn't so sure. Just then she saw Tony's attention was fixed somewhere else, on someone else, on a beautiful Indian woman who bore a resemblance to the actress Mindy Kaling. Deep brown skin, curvy. Designer clothing. Well put together. She sat at the bar alone. A moment later a tall European man, a Brad Pitt, entered the bar, went to her, kissed her.

Livvy nudged Tony. "Mind paying attention to the sexy bitch sitting next to you?"

"You were distracted. Was that work?"

She removed her phone from her clutch, let him read the exchange, satisfied his jealousy, then kissed him gently. He kissed her neck, sucked her lip, spoke to her in Spanish. She sucked his tongue, spoke to him in Spanish; they made out like newlyweds. Married ten years. Not easy years at all.

She remembered how her marriage had been from the start. Tony kissed her and she remembered the night she first met him. It was at a Halloween party. She was twenty-two, young, naive, insecure, and arrogant. It had been a random meeting at a costume party in Ladera Heights. He was dressed as Dracula. She was the devil in a bustier, leather pants, and six-inch heels. They had slow danced. He had kissed her just like this, with passion that came from his soul.

When the kiss ended, there was a change. She saw her husband glance at another woman at the end of the bar. High-end little black dress paired with expensive pink suede ankle boots with metallic gold accents. The heels were by Miu Miu. The woman was alone in a bar where sexiness and the need to play with strangers hovered in the air the way smog did over Los Angeles. The woman yielded a furtive glance, then a flirtatious smile, before she turned away. She sipped her drink and toyed with her necklace, legs bouncing with hidden urges, and she looked at Tony again. She twirled her long black hair. She was seeking a man, but she was sitting at the bar, buying her own drink, for now, maybe to keep a well-dressed stranger from slipping her Rohypnol. There were a lot of misogynistic and opportunistic assholes in Los Angeles, vile men waiting to slip a woman whatever was the latest Mickey Finn, so a woman partying alone had to be careful from which fountain she drank.

Olivia felt that the woman wished that Tony were here alone. The flirty woman couldn't sit still, couldn't stop staring, was restless. Tony couldn't stop stealing glances either. Olivia was a woman and a woman knew the desires of other women. Olivia said nothing about Tony and his wandering eyes.

Tony traced his finger up and down her thigh as he asked, "Livvy, did you ever see him again?"

"Did I ever see who again, Tony?"

"The mystery guy you had your little affair with."

"He doesn't contact me, never has since it ended, if that's what you're worried about."

"If he walked in and shook my hand, I'd never know it was him."

"Your indiscretion changed me. How it was presented. The shock of it. How I was demeaned."

"You're changing the subject."

"The subject has never changed, Tony. It's been the same subject since it happened."

"What do we have to do to get past that?"

"I don't know. I'm trying. I really am trying."

"He changed you from the nice Olivia Lynette McBroom I married to the naughty woman you are now. It's not the sex. It was

125

the change. It was a change no one has seen, only me, behind closed doors."

"It was an awakening, both from him and from you."

"And now you've modified and funkafied your hair. Like a sudden makeover. Women do that to announce a change."

"Is this about my hair? My side-shaved, swept-to-the-side funky hairstyle too much for you? We can get you a Mohawk."

"It looks too damn sexy. That hair and that hot dress make you look seven years younger. Every man here watched your ass as you walked by like they were following a bouncing ball to keep up with the rhythm of a love song."

"I have a nice ass."

"That nice ass is married to me."

"You can't stop people from looking."

"Well, I don't like it when you smile back at them."

"It's for you, Tony. Tonight, this is for you."

"Tonight?"

"Tomorrow will be a brand-new day."

They sipped their drinks. Livvy thought about her mother. She thought about when the widow Mrs. Wimberley met Mr. Mc-Broom and married. She thought about the type of love her mother had had, the type found in romance books. Then she thought about her own marriage, what it had become.

Heavy in heart but light in tone, Livvy asked her husband, "Did you enjoy Paris?"

"I'd never seen that side of you before."

She said, "Everything changes. People change in time. Or when traumatized."

"Are you comfortable here? Should we go back to marriage counseling?"

"It's not ideal, but I'm not uncomfortable. I was uncomfortable for a long time. Was hard to make love to you for a long time. It's better now. Everyone goes through something that changes them forever."

Olivia glanced at the girl at the end of the bar. The eye contact, the blatant rousing of sexual interest, the repeated stolen glances, the way she sat with her back straight due to being excited, the way she positioned herself so she could continue watching Tony from the corner of her eye, the smile whenever Tony smiled in her direction, the blush that came after — Livvy watched every response, even noticed when Tony tried not to look that way too long to keep from coming off as being perverted.

It was like Morse code, as if sensual messages were being sent back and forth.

Same as it had happened in Paris. Just like

127

it had happened in Canada.

Olivia said, "The way the two of you are carrying on right in front of me, this is insulting."

Tony sipped his drink. "What are you talking about?"

The girl had been admiring Tony too long.

Livvy put her Hardy Perfection cognac sidecar down.

She stood, adjusted her dress, pursed her lips.

Livvy stared across the room at her rival.

Livvy picked up her drink again, frowned as she began her well-paced sashay directly toward the overly flirty, svelte Asian woman sitting at the bar.

LIVVY

Livvy knew the woman saw her coming across the room, could tell by the way she adjusted herself on her bar stool, turned her back to Livvy and Tony, then raised her drink and sipped.

Olivia stood next to the woman, stared at her drink. Crème de la crème slurper, served in a Waterford crystal goblet, made with Bacardi Reserva Limitada, D'Ussé VSOP cognac, Neveux Artisan Creamery organic honey, English lavender, split-bean Tahitian vanilla ice cream, and Ghirardelli chocolate caramel fudge, garnished with edible gold flakes and a Swarovski Nirvana Montana blue-crystal ring, accompanied with a selection of truffles on a sterling silver truffle tree. Olivia hadn't had one of those since Paris. The drink was beautiful, sexy. If a man tasted that good, she would stay intoxicated. The woman shifted in her discomfort, faced Olivia. She leaned away and gave uneasy eye contact.

The Asian woman was at least six feet tall in her bare feet, with long, sexy legs. She wore five-inch heels. Her body was toned like she was Diana of Themyscira, daughter of Hippolyta. Olivia was five foot five and wore five-inch heels, still no match for the woman's height.

In a hard, unpleasant tone, Olivia said, "Happy New Year."

The woman evaluated Olivia from head to breasts, then from breasts to her shoes, then asked, "Is there a problem?"

Olivia posted up and evaluated the woman the same way, maintained eye contact, counted to five, then reached and took one of the woman's truffles, bit into it, chewed, then said, "You tell me. Is there a problem? Am I in the way tonight?"

"You're American."

"Did you expect my husband to show up alone?"

"I have no idea what you're talking about."

"Are you his mistress? Is this a game you're playing?"

"I am afraid I must invite you to leave my space immediately."

Olivia wasn't afraid.

She had played basketball, and most of her opponents had been taller. She had had to prove herself and go up against many women and many men since she'd been born. Same for Tommie and Frankie. The entire McBroom family had had to fight many outsiders to gain their respect.

Olivia took another truffle and gave her a daring glare.

The woman said, "That was rude. Have I unintentionally done something to offend you?"

"You were staring at my husband. That was rude. You've admired him the last twenty minutes."

"I'm sorry, but I felt him undressing me with his eyes."

"He was."

"I'm flattered."

"Do you want to meet?"

"I'm sorry?"

"Is he your fantasy? Are you looking for an adventure?"

"Are you asking me if I want to meet your husband?"

"If you want company, my husband and I would love for you to join us and share a drink."

"This is an unexpected twist."

"Why did you think I came over here, if not for that?"

"I assumed I'd committed lèse-majesté, if

that is the mot juste, and you'd left your king and your slice of sovereign land and come to throw your drink in my bloody face. You looked very angry."

"Not angry. Since you're eye-banging him, in my face, then looking at me, sizing me up as well, I wanted to extend the proper invitation to sit with us, come meet us, have a drink, make new friends."

"You're beautiful as well. He's a lucky man. You're lucky to have a man who loves you like that."

"Thank you. You're in a crowded bar and don't seem to be enjoying yourself."

"This pretentious place is interesting. It's like you either belong here or they look down their noses at you and shake their heads and roll their bloody eyes. Everyone is obsessed with their modified looks. So much Botox. I am out of my element. With her maturity, I doubt if Julia Roberts would get noticed here in Miley Cyrus–ville. But the hostesses are rude, and that makes me feel like I'm at home in the UK."

"Love your accent. Your dry humor is cute."

"If only I could have majored in sarcasm at university."

"You're British?"

"I'm Chinese with a little Japanese in my

blood. Born in Wales. Grew up in Aberystwyth. Lived in Cardiff and Swansea as well. Went to university in Bangor. Wales is in England to the west. Irish Sea to the north. You hear Wales in every syllable I speak, and that makes it hard for Americans to understand me. The bloody accents here are horrific. I understand the words separately, but put together they make no sense. Women make all statements sound like questions. I am in a room of inebriated caricatures."

"Waiting on someone? I should have asked you that before offering our company."

She bit into a truffle. "No. I am traveling alone. My first time to the United States."

"You're staring at me again."

"I'm amazed by your skin. Not a single blemish. It's like staring at a pretty doll's face."

"Thank you. I'm in skin care. Have my own business."

"Impressive. One look at you and I'll bet the clients are banging at the door each morning."

"My husband, he's a well-respected doctor."

"You're really husband and wife?"

Olivia sipped her exotic drink, bit into her

sensual chocolate truffle. "Married ten years."

"You've survived the seven-year itch."

"What's your occupation?"

"I'm also a doctor."

"Really? Where?"

"At London Bridge Hospital."

"Your area?"

"Cardiology and cardiac electrophysiology."

"That's impressive, but you're in a part of the world where few actually have a heart."

"So it seems. They are killing children in Gaza, but here, every dull conversation in this bar is about fantasizing about being a movie star. Everyone here loves to talk about themselves. They're dropping so many names ten street sweepers will have to work overtime to clean up afterward. I'm becoming underwhelmed by the arrogance, sense of superiority, self-importance, and entitlement."

"What brings you to Sunset Boulevard?"

"Here on what I guess I would classify as a last-minute holiday from London."

"Here to take advantage of the weak dollar and the men's weakness for Asian women."

She smiled. "Since there is no visa required for entry, and I didn't fancy returning to Anguilla, Barbados, or Turks and Caicos — not this time — I decided to take an eleven-hour flight from Heathrow to LAX and see this part of the world. Other than on television and in movies, I had never seen up close what the former Brits in this part of the world did after they defected from the UK. So far, not impressed. Horrible architecture. Compared to Paris, everything looks like it was designed by a two-year-old."

"I sense a heartbreak. Am I wrong?"

"I found myself suddenly single and decided I needed to get away from everything familiar."

Olivia whispered, "Are you a woman betrayed? Have you been cheated on?"

"I have been cheated on. I found out he had a mistress and an outside child. Had to escape. And now I am a heart specialist who has a broken heart that she has no idea how to fix. Oh, the irony."

"I had to escape once upon a time. It was the worst yet most intoxicating time of my life."

"How do I go from this being the worst era of my bloody life to its also being the most exciting?"

Livvy said, "And where are my manners? We never properly introduced ourselves."

"My name is Ashley Li."

"I'm Olivia."

"*Olivia* is Latin, means a symbol of peace. I need peace. Maybe this is a positive sign."

"I know you. You're a beautiful bird who's lost her wings."

Ashley Li sipped her drink. "What is your husband's name?"

"Antonio Barrera."

"He's Latin. Antonio. In his language his name means 'beyond praise.' 'Highly praise-worthy.' "

"And what does your name mean?"

"*Ashley* normally means 'one who lives in the ash tree grove,' but tonight, as I sit in a classy bar in Beverly Hills and finish my second Velvet Goldmine, an amazing drink that costs five hundred American dollars, my name means 'woman from Wales who came to North America in need of peace and praise.' "

"Trust me and my husband with your wounded heart tonight; you can have peace and praise."

"To be honest, I'm not into anything like that. To be honest again, I've never done anything like this. I've never gone to a fancy *pub* like this hoping for . . . whatever usually happens at fancy pubs like this to happen to me."

"You're hoping someone sees your long legs, your sweet hairstyle, realizes you're wearing fuck-me boots because you crave a wicked night to take away the angst inside, to give you the acceptance you desire, to praise you the way you deserve and make you come the night away so you can forget the asshole who has done you wrong. You want to escape that memory and get away from everything negative you left on the other side of the pond. You're sitting here drinking your liquid courage, and if someone doesn't make a move, you will get the nerve to because you want to get laid for the sake of getting laid, for the sake of making a statement to yourself, and because you refuse to sleep alone because now you know the man you loved was off fucking some other woman while you worked your ass off. He made a fool of you. He humiliated you. You know what you need. You know what you want."

Her breath caught in her chest, and her voice softened. "Yes. I wanted that, all of that, tonight."

"Then I will leave you to your chances. I'm sorry to hear about your heartbreak, and I do hope that you enjoy your night and find peace during your stay here in the Americas. I'll go back to my husband."

"Wait, Olivia."

"Olivia Barrera. People call me Livvy. Shall we part ways now?"

"Don't leave so bloody soon, Livvy, unless the offer you were extending was rubbish."

"You're not ready for this level of entertainment."

"Let the alcohol take hold and I will be ready for anything that doesn't include a pokey or a cheese-eating surrender monkey. I don't want to just say yes like I've lost the plot or I'm a slag. I am a lady."

"Tell me what you want, the pace you prefer, and I will try to make it happen."

"I don't want to spend the evening sitting in a bloody American bar tipsy and alone."

"If you fancy company, lounge with us. We can chill, drink, and chat. You and Antonio are both doctors. He's a vascular surgeon, so both of you are intellectuals and in fields that are highly regarded and respected. I can see that you're professional and girly with a love for fine drinks and expensive shoes. I feel your pain, so I'm sure a particular type of friendship with us will be very easy."

She laughed. "God, if I keep staring at you I think I will develop my first girl crush."

"It's the alcohol. That's why wannabe

starlets are in the bathroom doing lines and making out."

"When a woman is betrayed by a man, when she becomes the cuckquean, sometimes she feels more comfortable around a woman. It will be impossible for me to trust another man for a long time."

"When I was where you are, it was a hard choice, but I preferred to make him the cuckolded too. I refused to stand in the arena of cuckoldry alone. He had secrets, so I created another life for a while."

"Does he know?"

"He knows some. Not the guy's name. Has no idea where we met to have our sexual encounters. He knows enough to make him jealous, enough to lose sleep at night over not being satisfied with the incompleteness of my answers to his questions. Enough to not take me for granted anymore."

Olivia put her nails on Ashley's skin, moved them up and down, slowly scratching an invisible itch. Ashley Li closed her eyes and moaned. A moment later she opened her eyes, evaluated Olivia, then reached to her, touched her face, her perfect skin, wiped a bit of chocolate from the corner of her lip, then put her finger inside her own mouth, tasted chocolate, hummed like the flavor was new and exhilarating.

Olivia said, "Say yes and walk from here to there. Or say no and I'll walk alone."

"I'm but one word away. One word and about six meters away from being naughty, or a two-letter word away from being alone tonight, in America, with thoughts of an unworthy man across the pond."

As an old lover had once murmured to her, Olivia whispered to Ashley, "Yes or no, baby?"

"I've never done a threesome. I've been interested but never have."

"So you're interested?"

"I've been interested from the start, just too nervous to get up from this bloody bar stool. I have to remind myself that I am far away from my family, from my sisters and brothers, from my colleagues."

"No one will know but us. We're professionals and have the same concerns with discretion. I have sisters, two sisters, and family, so I understand the powerful need to keep parts of our lives private."

"I will need another drink."

"No problem."

"Tonight I can stop being the doctor."

"You're on holiday. Make it a holiday to remember."

"I can also stop being the boring, well-behaved daughter."

"Let us welcome Union Jack to the land of Old Glory red, white, and blue."

"Yes, Olivia Barrera. Yes. My answer is yes."

Ashley Li gathered her clutch, adjusted her form-fitting dress, signed off on her drinks, then winked and waved good-bye to the gay bartender. Ashley stood up. So tall. Towered over Olivia. Livvy adjusted her red dress, one that kept easing up toward her waist; gauged her level of tipsiness; and walked next to Ashley, taking slow steps by Hollywood-heads chatting. They navigated through the crowd. Livvy guided the tall Asian woman with the Welsh accent toward her smiling husband.

LIVVY

The next night was a light-jacket-and-scarf night, the temperature right at sixty-five.

Olivia was a mile from Tommie's home, in the tree-lined streets of Leimert Park. Where most of the homes were of the Mediterranean or Spanish colonial revival type, built back in the forties, some as early as the twenties. One square mile of affluent blacks and hipsters whose African art and music were being invaded by a slow-moving redevelopment that could cause the area to revert to the demographics it had boasted before the white flight in the fifties, before the flood in Baldwin Hills, when it was an area of European immigrants. It could go back to what it had been before the change of hands and the rise in crime, before the riots had done their damage, before the Northridge earthquake.

This area was where Frankie had made the lion's share of her money. Leimert Park ranked in the top twenty-five areas in the United States for home-flipping profitability. For a woman like Frankie, there was gold in these streets. Zip code 90008, where ten thousand people lived in each square mile, had been Frankie's jackpot for the last two decades and had bought her success and a house on the hill.

Livvy had always been motivated by her older sister's entrepreneurship.

She rushed from the parking meter in front of the bookstore, crossed Degnan Boulevard, passed by the Afrocentric shops in the African Village Marketplace, and made it to World Stage. She was there for a spoken-word event. She made it inside and sat in the back just in time. Tommie was being introduced. Her younger sister looked super hot. She'd stopped by Livvy's earlier and borrowed jewelry, then had run by Frankie's and borrowed a pair of Louboutins. High heels transformed the body language and attitude of a woman, and Tommie had been renovated. She matched the shoes with skinny jeans, her face with very little makeup. This was a crowd where most women were not afraid to show their true beauty and natural faces. Her younger sister took to the stage and stood before the microphone. She witnessed a different version of Tommie. This was her church, her people, her choir, her pulpit, her peers.

Tommie said, "I will start with a couple of haikus relevant to this generation."

Integration failed. / Black brown children everywhere. / Killed, not protected.
Ferguson, realize. / The sixties never left us. / Old mind-set, new gun.

The Nubians clapped like Sister Thunder and Brother Earthquake having a mutual orgasm.

I'm Tommie McBroom. / Sharp mind with dangerous curves. / Tall drink of water.
GPS goes boom / When McBroom enters a room. / Good poon-tang sensor.

The brothers yelled out a churchlike *amen* to that, sounded like a room of deacons at a revival of the loins. Tommie acted like a shy little girl. The men laughed harder. With it on a sensual level, with her voice like top-shelf bourbon on a cold night, men shifted in their seats, flirted with smiles.

Her jeans were tight and her heels were high, made her legs look super long, and the McButt had been given more McBubble. Livvy glanced at the men. Their GPS systems had definitely been activated.

Tommie continued to perform her haikus, introduced one she had written for Blue.

A woman has needs; / no longer chaste,
    unbroken; / virtuous days gone.
Met a strong brother. / Single dad,
    responsible. / My second lover.
My first orgasm. / It was better than
    cocaine. / Hooked on a grown man.
Ankles on his neck. / Doors to my church
    wide open. / I become his choir.
Kisses silence moans. / Hot like sun in
    Africa. / Middle passage throbs.

A woman with an Angela Davis/Pam Grier Afro responded, "Hello. G'wan, girl."

Livvy felt her face redden, uncomfortable with the topic. Tommie spoke of sex aloud and in public, but women understood the journey and applauded. Brothers snapped fingers and licked lips.

Two souls now conjoined. / Inches away
    from my heart. / I love him inside.
The things he taught me, / hard to find that
    perfect fit, / my sweet chocolate.
Bodies turn around, / teach me sixty-eight
    plus one. / God I love his math.
My man love so good, / if he wanted a sex
    change, / I'd get me one too.

Sisters howled, then stood and applauded like Tommie was their newly elected Nubian queen.

Tommie did a silly, Shakespearian curtsy, made funny faces like she was Carol Burnett or Lucille Ball.

Beale Streets, the writer who had introduced her, Tommie hugged him and kissed his cheek.

She left the small stage floating, laughing, blushing, putting on the innocent McBroom face, biting the corner of her lip, high-fiving a couple of sisters along the way, an instant celebrity.

Outside, Livvy told her baby sister that she had rocked World Stage, then, without judgment regarding her choice of material, without frowning on her theme for the night, asked her how it felt.

"The attention felt good. Being around my peers, around poets and writers, always feels good."

Livvy said, "You were performing and I checked out the brothers checking you out."

"They probably liked Frankie's overpriced shoes."

"Not even. Your jeans are so tight I can almost see the lining in your pocketbook."

"Mine are not tighter than your skintight,

painted-on skinny jeans, so back down, Livvy."

"You are a different person onstage. You were always good but have gotten so much better."

Tommie grinned. "I needed this. This is my me-time. It was a much-needed natural high."

"Where's Frankie?"

"You know she's not skipping the gym."

Livvy said, "She ran with me this morning."

"And she is doing three classes tonight."

"Her ass is going to fall out."

Tommie said, "She's single again so she's burning off that extra energy at the gym."

"She's afraid she'll gain weight and become Fat Frankie again if she ever eases up."

"She's always overcompensated for her insecurities."

A brother stopped and hit on Tommie despite seeing her engagement ring. He complimented her haiku, the one she had penned for Blue. His conversation was transparent, made it obvious that he took her sexual haiku to mean she was down for whatever. Even when they claimed they were enlightened, men were still men. A woman expressed her sensuality and brothers thought it was open season on clit.

Livvy said nothing. This was Tommie's world, a world Livvy rarely visited, and it was an artistic world that didn't really interest her. Tommie politely turned the brother down, but he was persistent, upped his game, offered to take her to dinner, offered to take his queen shopping, said he admired her because she was not your typical sister. Again, Tommie showed him her engagement ring and in a firm tone asked him to refrain from being disrespectful, or she would call her man and have him come kick his ass.

He grumbled, "Bourgeois-ass big-booty black bitches in subfuscous wardrobes treating a UCLA-educated Nubian like they bowels don't move. I was just giving you superfluous bitches some accolades and offering a modicum of my time so we *Africans* could get to know each other better. Fuck y'all."

He strutted away; went to a parking meter; unchained his bicycle, one barely big enough for a ten-year-old; climbed on; and pedaled off into the darkness. As a poet inside the venue did a piece pondering whether God created man or if man created God, Livvy and Tommie laughed until they cried.

Livvy cackled. "*Subfuscous* clothing?

148

What the hell is *subfuscous* clothing?"

Tommie wiped tears of laughter from her eyes. "Just means dark. We both have on dark clothes."

"Why in the hell didn't he just say that? This is why I don't get along with *subfuscous* poets."

"He was pissed. I was about to break out my mace and paint his eyeballs."

Livvy said, "And he claims he went to UCLA?"

"Had to be University of Compton, Left on Alameda."

A girl with a deep-brown complexion came up from the parking area near Eso Won. She wore silver jewelry and was dressed in all white, the contrast between her epidermis and clothing amazing. Large, trendy black-framed glasses, probably for form over function, gave her the randy-librarian appeal.

Tommie shifted on her heels, looked surprised, and said, "Hey, Tanya."

Couture head to toe, sugarplum lipstick that accentuated the magnificence of brown skin, the thin-yet-shapely girl paused, looked back, saw Tommie, looked her up and down, then said, "Excuse me?"

"You're Tanya Obayomi, right?"

"I am she and she is me."

"I'm Tommie McBroom."

"Tommie McBroom? Do I know you? You say my name as if we are acquaintances."

"We met at Beale Streets's event that was downtown at the main library."

"Right. *You're* Tommie McBroom. You are she and she is you. You're Blue's fiancée, right?"

"Yeah. You remember Blue, but you've forgotten about me?"

"Blue and I work out together at the same gym."

"He told me he saw you up there."

"We've kicked it and worked out together quite a few times."

"Really?"

"After we did weights, I talked him into doing Taj's class with me."

"Cool." Tommie's nostrils flared as she paused. "You came to see Beale Streets?"

She grinned at Tommie. "Even if you weren't performing, you'd be here like his number one fan."

Tommie asked, "What does that mean?"

"When Beale Streets performs, you're in the front row, or invited to be on the same stage."

"Thought you didn't know me."

"You're dressed up tonight. Didn't recognize you. You almost look like a model to-night."

"Been this tall since I was sixteen and it's the same face I've had since I met you the first time."

"You look very nice for a change."

"Thanks for the backhanded compli-ment."

"You've been inspired. Not surprised. Beale is good at giving inspiration."

Tanya Obayomi then introduced herself to Livvy, was surprised to find out she and Tommie were sisters, Livvy at five foot five and Tommie five inches taller being only part of the reason. There was energy. Livvy felt her energy, a sensual attraction to the girl; that tingly feeling rarely came from another woman, and never from one so young. Tanya Obayomi evaluated Livvy. Livvy asked Tanya who she was, since she'd never met her, since she couldn't break her stare. Tanya Obayomi let Livvy know that she was twenty-one, working on her master's at USC, then let it be known that she had been dating the brilliant Beale Streets up until recently; said they were on a break. With that, she sashayed toward World Stage, hand fluffing her elegant hair, high heels clicking on forty-year-old concrete as her exaggerated walk took her toward the crowd.

Livvy asked, "What the hell was that about, Tommie?"

"You're nobody if you don't have a hater who thinks she's the next Azealia Banks."

"Sounded personal; she made it a point to let you know she worked out with Blue."

"Jealousy is a disease and I hope she gets well soon."

"It was hard to tell who was jealous of whom."

"Oh, that jealousy is running in this direction. She ain't got nothing I want."

Tanya Obayomi stood at the doorway, listened, but didn't go inside the crowded venue.

Livvy said, "She's stunning, but she has ruined her natural beauty by trying to be perfect. I can see what using the wrong products has done to her epidermis. I would love to work on her skin."

"She's all right. She's not all that, Livvy."

"Too bad Hollywood and too many black men love dark-skinned black women in theory but hardly ever in practice. Just like some African Americans love Africa in theory but rarely in practice."

"She's beautiful. I get it. Whoopty-whoop."

"Beauty is in the eye of the beholder, but first those eyes have to be opened."

"Stop staring at that heifer. Let it go, Livvy."

"I'm stuck on what she said. She *works out* with Blue. They *kick it.* That was a public service announcement. Was that one of those euphemism things? Did you see how she was looking at you?"

"That will be addressed as soon as I get home."

"Somebody's jealous. Both of you were catty."

"Whatever. She's hating because when I perform I blow up the room."

"Same way you blow up a bathroom."

Beale Streets was on the stage. Tanya Obayomi stayed at the door, watching him perform.

When he finished one piece of work, everyone applauded again. Then came the interruption. Tanya Obayomi banged on the door with her fist, a frenzied, possessed beat in the rhythm of a heartbroken drum, and when she had everyone's attention she began to sing. She sang and beat her emotions into the wall, disrupted the night with a voice as powerful as that of the late Whitney Houston, her frenetic song tragic, about how she was all cried out, but yet she had

153

another sad love song to sing as she tried to figure out how she was supposed to live without him, and even if she couldn't make him love her the way she loved him, she wished she could have one more night for him to unbreak her heart and make her feel immortal, a night to make her fly without wings before they sent in the clowns. She dropped down on her knees as she banged the door like it was her drum, and when she stood again, blood made a scarlet river from her kneecaps down her shins. Traffic had stopped in the middle of the boulevard.

Livvy held Tommie's hand, held it tight, entranced, disturbed, unable to breathe.

Tanya Obayomi limped away but stumbled, legs wobbling, and she held the stucco wall, grimaced with the pain in her heart. She took a step, then looked down at the open wounds on both knees, each bleeding like a heart that had been stabbed. She sang her heartbroken chorus one more time. Her public disgrace done, her societal opprobrium was fresher than doughnuts at Krispy Kreme when the HOT NOW light is on. Her eyes were filled with tears. Her heels clicked as she limped down her Boulevard of Broken Souls in silence. Hearts began to beat. The wind blew. Traffic began to move again. The world resumed spinning. Someone clapped; then someone else joined in; then someone else.

Behind that performance erupted the applause of all applauses, an earthquake caused by hand claps. Beale Streets came to the door of the venue, pushed through the crowd, and looked outside.

As Tanya Obayomi limped by, Livvy took a step toward her and asked, "Do you need help?"

The girl waved a hand, the sign of the heartbroken saying they'll be fine one way or another.

Livvy related. When she had found out about Tony's affair, that was how she had felt, the agony, only there was no song. All she had heard was the rhythm of the pain that had been within.

Then she realized what it had been about the girl. She reminded Livvy of Panther. The enviable complexion. The physical attributes. And now Tanya Obayomi was as heartbroken as Panther had been the last time Livvy had seen her, when Panther begged her to comfort her and Livvy had been cold and rejected her. Livvy had been in pain too. It had been the best of times, and it had been the worst of times.

Tommie's voice shook and her breathing was labored as she asked, "Ready to go?"

"You don't want to go back inside and catch the rest of the performance?"

"I'm done. I'm ready to leave now. Tanya has changed the energy around here, the same way Mo's mother changes the vibe in my house. I mean, who does crap like that? Is her life a musical?"

Then came another interruption.

Livvy said, "Franklin Carruthers is coming toward us."

"You're joking, right?"

His muscle car eased from the direction of Eso Won. Livvy saw that he had seen them. He passed them, signaled to turn left, but that section was now blocked off to allow pedestrians to meander the way people strolled the promenade in Santa Monica. Franklin turned around and this time, since he was closer to where they were, he stopped, rolled down his window, and called out to them, his face one big smile, like on his bullshit commercials.

He said, "Hey, Livvy. Long time no see, Tommie. I've really missed you guys."

Livvy said nothing, stared at him, her expression of disgust carved in stone.

Tommie exploded, "How's your wife, Franklin? How's that bitch doing, asshole?"

Franklin drove away, tooted his horn as a good-bye.

Livvy asked, "Tommie, we leaving or what?"

"Let that asshole get out of my zip code first. I run into him before I get to my car, I swear to God I'll catch a case."

"We'll catch two cases."

Loud applause came from World Stage.

Livvy followed Tommie's anxious walk back to stand in the door and watch Beale Streets. It was like watching a young preacher and his soul-filled congregation.

Livvy said, "Those hazel eyes have these Afrocentric sisters' panties as wet as the Nile River."

"Be quiet so I can hear Beale Streets."

After listening, Livvy whispered, "Wow. I never knew that America wasn't a true democracy but was a polyarchy."

"Hush. This next piece about Africans in Israel is deep."

Minutes later Livvy said, "He's profound and has humor, charm, and poise. Handsome. No wonder that girl lost her mind."

"Quiet, Livvy. This is his closing. Show some respect and learn something about the world."

When his presentation was done, after he had informed, entertained, outraged, and enamored all, they stayed outside. The audience filed out of World Stage, brought conversation to the pavement in Leimert Park. Beautiful sisters whispered, both young and old enough to be Beale Streets's mother, said they imagined him, their young, prosperous, and sexy cunning linguist, engaged in cunnilingus.

What Tanya Obayomi had done seemed to have made him that much more desirable. He'd done something right to make her act like that. He'd done something right, left, and center.

Young black men stopped near them and soon it was a group conversation, one that echoed the theme of many of the poets. The killing of unarmed black men was once again the hot topic, talk of how history repeats again and again, and never in favor of the black man. They talked about how white artists were appropriating black culture the same way Elvis and the Rolling Stones had become rich from the black man's blues. Everything was stolen, even dreams. Beale Streets emerged from World Stage. Straight-leg jeans, striped shirt, bow tie, awesome blue wing-tip shoes. His Afro was wild, untamed, very flattering. In that moment Livvy wanted to touch his mane; it was rebellious, heritage proud, and sexy. Beale Streets looked toward her and Tommie, nodded, then went back inside World Stage.

Livvy said, "His name is Beale Streets. Is he from Memphis?"

"He's never been to Memphis. He told me that he'd never been there, but his adoptive parents were blues fans. They met on Beale Street when they were both attending college at the University of Memphis. Their surname is Streets. The father had changed his name to Streets to avoid stigma and xenophobia. A foreigner with a name hard to pronounce in America is the same as a black woman having LaKisa or LaQuinisha across the top of her résumé. Name too Jewish, name too black, name too Mexican, and if you have a Muslim name you're the most fucked of the fucked. You're still prejudged, or judged, by your name. Anyway. He changed it to Streets and doors opened and I guess America liked him more. They have an interesting story as well. When he was adopted, they gave him the name Beale."

"What was his name before it was Beale?"

"Never asked him."

Livvy shrugged. "Whatever. Beale Streets. His name is weird. That's like me living on Crenshaw Boulevard and naming my kid Crenshaw Boulevard. Who does that?"

"Let it go."

"Whatever. It's weird. That's all I'm saying."

Tommie called home, told Blue she was with Livvy before Monica got on the phone.

Tommie said, "We're going to kick it a bit. Go to bed, little girl. Okay. Hold on."

At that moment Livvy's phone buzzed. It was a text message from Dr. Ashley.

She had sent her a smiley face, nothing more.

Livvy sent her a smiley face in return. She tingled. She grinned.

She glanced down at her right ankle, at her anklet.

She glanced at the symbol.

Tommie handed her phone to Livvy. Monica wanted to say hello, asked her auntie Livvy to sing the name song; then Livvy gave the phone back to Tommie. What Tommie had, that was the way Livvy had always wanted her life to be with Tony. The youngest McBroom had the best relationship.

TOMMIE

Driving fast, I turned down Grayburn Avenue, one street before Edgehill Drive, where I lived.

Beale Streets's SUV was already pulled to the side of the road, parked in the middle of the block on that residential strip. I parked behind him, then hurried and got in his ride on the passenger side. I had stopped to make out with him, to steal a good-night kiss, then run home. That was the plan. Our lips touched before there was a chance to say hello, and right away, things escalated. Music played low. World music. Songs by the artist named Sampha. As the songs "Too Much" and "Happens" played, we kissed.

Seamlessly, we evolved from kissing to petting. He pulled up my top, unsnapped my bra, and sucked my breasts. I unzipped his pants and masturbated him. He tried to put his hands in my pants, but my skinny jeans were too tight. I let my seat back and pulled my pants down below my knees so I could open my legs. He fingered me, massaged me. He let his seat back. I slid off my borrowed Louboutins and climbed over to his side, my borrowed jewelry jingling with every movement. There wasn't enough room. The steering wheel was pressed against my back and would leave a mark, so we played Twister. I moved and he pried himself from underneath me before climbing over the gearshift, bumping the rearview mirror along the way. We were laughing until he was in the passenger seat. He pushed the seat as far back as it could go, made it as horizontal as possible, and I took a deep breath, took in the neighborhood, let two cars go by, their headlights in our faces, before I found the nerve and climbed over. I sat on him so I could see the neighborhood, so I could see trouble, because it was the hour of carjackings and robberies. It was also the prime time for police harassment, when videos could only capture the shadows of abuse. Moving like a Kizomba dancer, I rode him facing the windshield; my hands gripped the dash for support, and I felt him grow inside me as I continued to watch the neighborhood. It was too hard to focus, plus I couldn't move the way I wanted to, so it frustrated me, and I didn't want another car to come down Grayburn. What we were doing would be too damn obvious. I crawled across the armrest into the backseat. Beale followed me. Another car passed by and we froze. I hoped it was no one who would recognize my ride, then come to see if I was having car problems. I hoped no one had called the police. Whoever it was pulled into the house two driveways away. Beale sat up and I straddled him, kissed him, sucked his tongue, and had more room to go up and down, not much, but enough to feel the length of what was inside me. The SUV rocked. I tried to rock it until it flipped. Wasn't easy doing it inside a vehicle. I still needed more room. I had to get off him so he could reach and let both front seats all the way forward. That was better. We had more room. Then he rocked it man-on-top. It was so damn good. I fantasized while he grunted and went deep. I imagined us being outside in the cool night air, him going down on me while I sat on the hood and rested my legs on his shoulders, the angle of the SUV's hood and gravity pulling me down on his tongue. Imagined leaning over the hood and him taking me from behind, inhaling fresh air at the same time. Imagined sucking him while he drove down Sunset Boulevard, the bright lights falling across my back as I gave his appendage an eye-watering massage.

My first words to him were when I whispered my mantra, "Don't come inside me."

When we were done, I expected to look up and see LAPD outside our fogged-over window. No one was there. I cleaned myself with wipes before I pulled my pants back up. Beale pulled his back on, then leaned forward and hit the power switch to let the windows down a bit. It had become stuffy and the windows were steamed over. We sat there a moment, winded by our quickie, panting in a post-orgasmic haze. We hadn't planned on having a Roc and Shay moment on the side of the road, hadn't imagined us doing anything in my zip code.

With the windows up, it had felt like the greenhouse effect. I was hot, sweaty, uncomfortable, could smell his cologne mixed with my perfume. That scared me. I needed to cool off before I drove to my home.

I had left Livvy fifteen minutes ago. She should just have been getting home. If I went by her house to take a shower, she'd ask questions. I would have to creep home, get to the bathroom. I was tripping, hoping Blue was in bed, sleeping.

Beale said, "Monica's mom piss you off again?"

164

"Tanya Obayomi pissed me off."

"Is that the only reason you chose to abuse me on the side of the road?"

"That thing that Tanya Obayomi did . . . how everyone applauded for her like they wanted you to run out and catch her and kiss her like she was the woman of your dreams, that left me a little irritated."

"It mattered to you. You're jealous. That means you're in love with me."

"I'm catching feelings."

"The more you're in love with me, the less you will be with Blue. I need you to forget that he exists."

"You want Blue to become insignificant and I want Tanya to leave the West Coast and go back to the coast of West Africa. Let her go to the motherland and sing background for Tiwa Savage, or work on her own thing. She's trying to be Tiwa any-damn-way, from head to freakin' toe. She probably wakes up singing 'Folarin.' Keep that heifer out of my space."

"Wow, Tommie. All I can say is . . . wow."

"I know I have no right to feel that way, that it's hypocritical, and I know it sounds mean, but it's how I feel."

"Blue will become insignificant. He will be outside your door singing and you'll ignore him."

"And Monica? Since you can see my future so clearly, please tell me, what will become of Monica, O ye Ghost of Christmas Yet to Come? Will she be fine or is there a crutch sitting in the corner?"

"The moment you have your own child, the love you have for her, that obsession, it will go away and you will refocus. You will love your child and wonder how you ever loved another woman's child."

"You're speaking on things beyond the realm of your understanding."

Beale let his window down some more and said, "I'm going to kick it at Club Mapona tonight."

I fanned myself, made the cool breeze chill the sweat droplets before I responded, "For real?"

"I want you to go with me. That would be so fleek, me and you walking into the club together."

"I can't go and hang out in Hollywood with you. I can sneak and meet you at Runyon to work out, or go catch lunch with you at Islands, or connect with you far away in Santa Monica to have coffee, but I can't go out with you on a date at night in Hollywood, not when I have a family at home."

"Want to take you. I need you to find a

way to go out with me. I need you to find a way for me to introduce you to the people I know, so they will know that the anonymous woman I talk about really exists."

"You tell your friends about me?"

"I tell them about you and they think you are a figment of my imagination."

I was flattered. I smiled and bit the corner of my lip, entranced by his eyes the same way Livvy and Frankie were entranced by shoes, purses, and hairstyles. He'd become my secret, my fetish.

He said, "Have to say this, because this is on my mind right now, and we're always honest with each other. You did the piece you wrote for Blue. Don't ever perform that in front of me again."

"Why are you tripping, Beale? I have done that piece in front of you at least ten times before."

"And each time I have hated it. It's not your best work. It's the equivalent of rap music when I know you're capable of a piece that rivals Beethoven. What you did only appeals to the base senses."

"Did you miss the standing ovation?"

"You're better than that old piece of work."

"Not every piece will be like Maya or Toni or Chimamanda."

"I need you to write about me, about us. I want people to be envious and applaud what we have."

"Be professional when it comes to our work, Beale."

"I am being professional."

"Intellect without emotional maturity is pointless."

"You don't think I'm emotionally mature? I'm not the one living a lie, Tommie."

His phone chimed. Someone had sent him a text message. He didn't look at the phone. I was so close I would have been able to read the screen. There was no time for extreme jealousy, not tonight.

I said, "I have to go."

"Talk to you tomorrow."

We kissed good-bye. It was one of those kisses almost impossible to pull away from.

My bones would not be able to support being two women for much longer.

TOMMIE

I pulled up in front of my home and my wayward thoughts went back to my fiancé. To my family. I smiled at our home, but it was a heavy smile. I sat in the car for a few minutes. I was disappointed with myself, guilty for enjoying myself without them. Felt bad for not wanting to come back to this home tonight. I had been with Blue awhile. We talked a lot, but it was for the sake of talking; there was no new information, so the conversations with Beale felt different, felt inspired. With Blue, most talk had become about the business of the relationship, the business of caring for Mo, the business of dealing with her mother, the business of trying to survive from week to week. How this started with Beale had been through simple words, through chat, and it had been refreshing having a light conversation with a stranger. That spark created a flame. It had felt wonderful to be away from all the things I carried.

I showered, then checked on Monica, saw she was out cold, before I eased into bed with Blue.

He asked, "How was World Stage tonight?"

I jumped. "You're awake."

"Was up writing. Worked on my screenplay about an hour. Was tempted to go over to Vince's and Dana's and see if their daughter Kwanzaa could stay here with Mo while I went to watch you perform."

"That would have been a nice surprise, to look in the crowd and see your face."

"Was writing and waiting on you. Never saw you dress up like that for poetry in the hood."

"Can't be sweats and trainers all the time. Have to represent my family when I leave the house."

"I watched you get ready to leave. You changed clothes a half dozen times, put your hair in just as many styles, then put on a brand of perfume I'd never smelled on you before."

"I knew Livvy was going to be dressed up."

"You were nervous before you hurried out of here, kept redoing your hair. I saw you putting on makeup. You were being so persnickety. Your energy was so different before you left. Mo noticed it too."

I said, "I ran into your friend Tanya Obayomi tonight."

"My friend?"

"She made a point to tell me that y'all kick it and work out together. What's that all about?"

"She doesn't work out with me. Me and the homies were pushing weights and she joined in. I asked her a few questions about Beale Streets. His background is very interesting, that's all."

"She sees it differently. She makes it sound like you were on a hot date."

"Come work out with me, if you want. You have a membership. I have nothing to hide."

He asked me if I was sleepy. I wanted to say I was exhausted, but I shook my head no and once again became an eccedentesiast — a master at hiding my misery and pain behind a fake smile.

He pulled my *Walking Dead* T-shirt over my head, pulled my bottoms away from me. He was ravenous, wanted to go down on me, but I took a deep breath, felt the pain from my heart being torn, being broken and rebroken, and told myself that I never knew when the last time we touched, the last time we made love, would be the last time. I felt

171

the clock counting down between us. His soldiers had no weapons. Each time we were intimate began to feel like it might be the last time. As I had done to Beale, I masturbated Blue, didn't want to play the Honey to his Mr. Marcus and fellate, just wanted to use the rhythm of my hand, discharge his angst in two or three moments, and relieve myself of what felt like a burden, but he wanted more. He moved my hand away. He was a man and wanted to make love like adults, not like randy teenagers parked on the side of the road. I tried to go down on Blue, changed my mind about playing the role of Honey, didn't want him inside of me, but he pulled my mouth to his.

He asked, "Have I been neglecting you?"

I didn't reply. We kissed, a shallow kiss, a kind kiss, a kiss that checked the reservoir of love, then stopped and stared at each other in uncertainty, wide awake, inhaling, exhaling, pondering.

He said, "Put on a pair of heels. Put on the ones you wore tonight."

I eased my feet back into my shoes, then searched for music on my phone, Sampha on my mind, played the song "Without," danced the erotic way the girl in the British singer's video danced, danced with emotion, feeling myself. I danced feeling Beale.

I couldn't deny the place I existed, the between, this dimly lit place in between here and there. I had created my own purgatory.

Blue had enough of being teased and pulled me to him, kissed up and down my legs, made me tingle. I pulled his mouth to mine, sucked his tongue, opened my legs, and encouraged him to rest between my heated thighs. I pulled his T-shirt away from him. He stood and pulled his boxers off, his power strong, then eased the door closed before he came back to the bed and found his place between my thighs. He licked the curve of my lips. He sucked my bottom lip gently. He sucked my tongue.

There was no way to avoid what was next, what was inevitable on this night.

We kissed and he wiggled until he was on my opening, until he was on my slickness, until that part of him was wiggling and sliding inside of me. It hurt. It felt like my vagina refused him, had closed. Blue moistened his fingers, moistened me, found the right angle, made me open up, and went deep.

He whispered, "Something wrong?"

"I'm fine."

"This is like the first time we made love. You're closing up on me. You're tense."

Blue handled me, increased the depth, and

increased the frequency of his thrusts. I wondered how many people had affairs and had to go home and make love once again to keep the peace.

Outside of myself I sat across the room and watched Blue and the version of me that was more complex than any person I had ever encountered, watched a damaged woman who was struggling not to come unhinged, not to yell for Blue to stop making her feel so good so she could break down and confess her moral dilemma. I wrote in pristine handwriting, turned page after page, stayed outside of myself and analyzed myself on a profound level, until orgasm tickled me once again, until it made it hard to write.

Orgasm rose and I rejoined myself, became his fiancée, his future wife, a childless woman.

We found a good rhythm.

Blue rose up on his knees. He was over me, on all fours, and I held on to him, was suspended, hanging down from his body as I moved against him. Our bed rocked, squeaked. He massaged my spot. I pulled my lips in as I always do, tried to bite my arm to muffle my sounds, but it was overwhelming, at an enormous level, and I became vocal. So did Blue. He moaned like an old man singing an ancient hymn during vacation Bible school. He put it on me good, stroked Beale out of my head, and when I surrendered to his loving, it was so damn wonderful. A thousand times Blue told me he loved me. I wondered if love would be enough. I wanted a future, not promises. I cried. I cried a thousand tears. Tears had a purpose; they were designed to force a body to cool down when emotions became extreme, be it happiness or sadness. I cried. I cried. I cried. So much guilt rose. So much sadness. Part of me wished I had stayed in that SUV with Beale, had gone to Hollywood, and had turned my back on this world. I could've followed him and had all the things that I wished for. It hurt to love Blue, but I did love him. Blue was on me, his weight like that of the world, a man whose great-great-grandfather was a slave while my great-great-great-grandfather suffered the same at the hands of European-born Christians. We had a connection deeper than I would ever be able to understand. I cried guilt and passion and love and desire, I cried for all the foolish, maybe archaic things I wanted for me in this life. His hunger for me was out of hibernation. Blue reignited my hunger for him. I was starved to have what we used to have.

In the beginning I had only wanted him. I wanted us to be a family. I wanted to have his children.

Then my mind completed that circle of thoughts, took me back to the start.

That was no longer possible. We could not share DNA and create a new branch.

I returned to the source of our problem, to the moment I had felt betrayed. He would orgasm and it would have power, would leave his body at twenty miles per hour, but would not be strong enough to crack a soft and fertile egg. I held him, put my fingernails in his flesh, almost told him to stop, stop, stop. In that moaning moment, I detached myself from myself again and studied myself once again. I was here with Blue, but I was also seated across the room, dressed in a business suit, hair pulled back, low heels on my feet, glasses on the bridge of my nose, as I held a legal pad and wrote notes, scrutinized what was in front of me. I watched her experience the weakness that penetration brings. Mouth opened, she gazed toward me. As the small bedroom heated from passion, I analyzed the good girl forced to turn bad.

I said, "Blue is filled with envy that has manifested itself as passion and creativity tonight."

She panted, "Okay. Okay. Okay."

"He is giving it to you the way a jealous man fucks his most prized possession."

"Oh God. Oh God. Oh God."

"Do you think he knows? I think he does. His expression says he feels things are different."

"About to come."

"Don't come for him. Only come for Beale. Only for Beale. We only come for Beale."

Soon I had to squeeze my legs together. The heat spread and desire awakened between my thighs. I watched them in a seductive war, one both physical and of the wills. So much determination on both parts. So much desperation. He held her hair, forced her to kiss him while he stroked. I scribbled as fast as I could, my handwriting rapidly becoming illegible, scribbled notes until I had to drop the pen and pull my glasses away, until I had to forcefully open my blouse, until I could no longer breathe. I squeezed my thighs and slid from the chair to the floor, trembled as I crawled back to the bed, moaned as I crawled and rejoined the version of me on the bed, was unable to remain separated from the version of me with Blue. He lifted me, carried me across the room, sat me on the dresser, took me that way, made the dresser tap into the wall, made things tumble to the floor. Borrowed shoes fell from my feet as he carried me back to the bed. He put me on all fours. Again I fought the overwhelming need to orgasm, the need Blue had created. Coming would make me feel unfaithful to the man I was cheating with. Still, as he gave me measured strokes, as he danced inside of me, my reluctance to orgasm was weakened by his conviction, and I surrendered. It was an orgasm that put light where there had been darkness. I felt intoxicated and enamored and my orgasm created rainbows as I danced with stardust.

I said his name over and over. "Blue, Blue, oh, Blue. Oh Blue, Blue, Blue."

Blue grunted. Grunted. He grew inside of me. He was at the point where he needed to come. He was powerful. It was one of those sessions where you weren't sure what was going to break first, the bed or someone's back. What surrendered first was the footboard. The bed came loose and slid forward. We slid that way, but Blue didn't stop, didn't pause, just took me missionary, found his position and kept on doing the damn thing. That angle made him go that much deeper, surprisingly deeper, and made his madness feel so damn sweet. The footboard had detached from the bed and he kept going until the headboard collapsed. Inhaling and exhaling heat, I clamped my hand over my mouth, but I had already waked the sleeping gods and shook all devils. He was trying to give me death by orgasm. I said his name over and over, as if that was the only word left in my vocabulary. There were three faint taps on the door. There was a pause. There were three more distant taps. *Mommy. Daddy.* There was the voice of an angel tickling my ears while I was drunk on the sense of infinity. *Mommy.* The cherub sounded like she was a thousand million bazillion gazillion miles away.

Mo had come to the door and knocked. Her knocks went unheeded. Monica went away and we assumed she had gone back to her bedroom. Mo hurried to the kitchen and found the keys to the lock on the bedroom door. When I was facedown, butt up, biting pillow, gripping sheets, and Blue was dominating me Froggy style, when I was in a position where his weight made it impossible for me to move, the bedroom door opened. Blue was at his moment, singing his song of orgasm. I called out his name and Blue mistook my saying his name as my urging him to finish. I became a bronco. Blue took it to another level, shocked me, made my love come down hard and fast, made me feel three degrees of glory. Before I could raise my head and sever myself from my unwanted rapture, before I could break from the powerful rapture that held me in bondage, as I trembled and cried, Monica turned on the lights. Everyone screamed, shrieked, or cursed. Monica witnessed the two-headed beast. The four eyes of the butt-naked, growling, moaning two-headed beast looked up from a bed that had been rocked until it came apart and saw her. Monica fled the room in wide-eyed terror, bumped into the wall, fell down, got back up running, screaming like a child in a Grimm Brothers' fairy tale, one where the beast devoured the grandmother and the child before being killed by being split open with the ax of the huntsman. We scrambled to get to our feet, both of us freaking out. We looked at the room, a room that looked like it had been hit by an isolated earthquake, then engaged in rock-paper-scissors to see who had to check on Mo.

FRANKIE

Cutting Franklin's essence out of my hair wasn't enough.

During the days around Valentine's Day, Franklin stopped by my office, left candy, left flowers, and the receptionist made it known he was not welcome on my property and no gifts would be accepted on his behalf. Posting his photo in color and the size of legal paper helped. His face was circled in red with a slash across the center. SOME THINGS CAN'T BE RESTORED, NOT EVEN BY THE KING OF ~~RESTORATION~~ PRE-VARICATION was written across the bottom in a bold, large font.

The only Franklin I wanted in my office was on a hundred-dollar bill.

Franklin Carruthers didn't like his photo being on the door, and he ripped it down.

He snapped, told them to tell me that he loathed me for doing that, but he also still loved me and would never stop trying to get me back. He ripped the second down, and when a third photo with the "no Franklin" symbol and the same slogan was put up, he didn't hesitate to rip that one down too.

I had a hundred of those fliers made.

I was tempted to hire people to put them on car windows at his business, to put them on street poles and in the public park near his home, but I didn't go there. I didn't let my anger get the best and make a fool of me. I didn't do anything that could cause a lawsuit against me. My revenge was moving on.

But he refused to move on.

After that, the bastard stopped by my home, rang the doorbell forty-eleven times. I didn't answer. I hid inside of my own damn home, in the dark, armed. I heard him rip the "no Franklin" photo from the front door and ball it up. He cursed under his breath, and then I heard him take out keys. My heart tried to break out of my chest. His key no longer fit the locks. All had been changed the day after I kicked him out.

He went to the garage and punched in the code to open the double doors, but that code had been changed. He checked the windows again. I should've called the police then. In the end I would wish I had dialed

911 two times over. Two hours later, he drove away. Two hours after that he came back.

He called. My phone had only been on ten minutes. I stared at my phone in silent horror, hoping it would stop ringing, shouted when I realized he wasn't going to stop calling, so I answered, panting.

He asked, "Where are you?"

"It's Valentine's Day and I'm at my new boyfriend's phat-ass crib in Bel Air, boo."

"You have a boyfriend?"

"Look, boo. We were in the middle of doing some serious thangs, and you know Valentine's Day is also known as Mandatory Blow Job Day, so I won't try to talk with my mouth full. Stop disturbing us."

I hung up on him. He crept to the front of my home, tried to peep in the windows.

All the lights were off and I went from room to room as he moved around my home.

None of my windows were unlocked. That asshole was actually trying to get inside.

One of my neighbor's friends, Billie, passed by rocking her yellow Ducati. She slowed down, then turned around, came back to the front of my house, called out to Franklin, asked him what he was doing. Franklin marched back to his car. He picked up his cellular, dialed, and my phone rang again. I rejected the call. My house phone rang. I went and unplugged the phone. The girl on the yellow Ducati sat there on her motorcycle, not leaving. Billie took a photo of Franklin's license plates. She yelled at him, her cellular in her hand, threatened to punch in the number to the police. Franklin flipped her off and pulled away. She sat there five more minutes before she left too.

I would have to thank Billie for that. I would have to bake her a cake. Franklin was gone, but I sat for three hours, jumping at every sound, unnerved like I was living in a Stephen King horror novel.

I hoped that telling him I was seeing somebody else would make him back off.

I hoped he'd tell his wife that I had a new man and she would back off as well.

But the calls from Mrs. Carruthers continued.

Franklin kept stopping by my home.

I slept with one eye open, gun by my side, its safety off.

FRANKIE

Half a handful of days eased by and it felt like things had calmed down.

Feeling that it was finally over, I dropped my guard.

I'd gone to the gym after being at work all day, had worked my core and pushed weights with Livvy, Tony, and Blue, then hopped into Taj's class. When I made it home, the alarm wasn't on. I figured I had neglected to turn it on when I had rushed out to the office that morning, and I had come home that night both tired and in a hurry to get showered and eat. When I stepped out of the shower, I noticed things had been rearranged. Perfumes and makeup that were on the counter, everything had a different configuration. But I still didn't give it much thought. As I sat on the edge of the bed putting lotion on my skin, I glanced over at the dresser. Not one drawer was completely closed. I paused. The closet door was ajar. I stood up, pulled the towel around me, and felt like I was coming out of a trance into reality. I always kept my closets well organized, everything on wooden hangers, clothes arranged by style and mood, by professionalism and play. Now it was totally disorganized, half the items on the floor.

I reached under my mattress and pulled out my .380.

It was like that all over the house. Nothing was missing but things had been moved. A chair had been left out at the dining room table. A glass was in the sink. The glass was clean.

I checked the houghmagandy room, but the door was still locked, so I didn't go inside.

I went to my office and my laptop was on. I thought I had left it on standby or turned off, not on.

Since she had the codes, I called the housekeeper, asked Lupe, *"¿Viniste aquí a mi casa hoy?"*

"No, Frankie. *Voy a tu casa pasado mañana. ¿Hay algún problema?"*

Lupe hadn't been to my home. I told her all was cool, then let her go.

Nothing was missing. I went to the alarm system and played back the video feed from the DVR.

After I had left this morning, it had malfunctioned, or so it seemed. The last footage was of me leaving my home. Then the feed went dead. I reset it and it came back on.

I turned the alarm on, was tempted to spend time in the houghmagandy room, but went to bed.

When I woke up the next morning, I met Livvy for a short run, then went back home, again in a hurry to shower so I could leave by eight and beat traffic. As I stood in the kitchen hurrying to eat boiled eggs and turkey bacon, I felt a breeze, a rush of fresh air. That breeze inside of my home paused me again. All of my windows were always closed. I stood still, alarms going off in my head.

I followed the breeze. The front door was wide open. Panic rose. First I spied outside, then I closed the door before I considered checking behind me. I jumped. Nothing was there but my shadow. I took slow steps and inspected the living room, crept across the carpet, walked the tile into the kitchen.

I reached to the butcher's block to grab a knife, but the block had been moved to the opposite counter. Either my mind was playing tricks on me, or things had been moved again; everything was in a slightly different configuration, only by a foot here and a foot there, just enough to make it seem like I was flying over the cuckoo's nest when I called the sheriff's department to have them send someone out.

The cops walked the house while I stood out front, barefoot, cellular phone in hand.

When they said all was clear I went back inside and we walked room to room.

One of the cops just happened to be from our running group.

She asked, "Anything missing, Frankie?"

"Nothing that I can see, Officer Becky."

"Maybe they thought you were gone and when you came back, they left before you saw them."

"Someone was definitely here."

"Check your cameras."

Again I went to the DVR attached to the alarm system.

Again it wasn't on. The only footage was when I had turned it back on last night.

It had been turned on for about an hour, and then it went off again.

Becky said, "Malfunction?"

"Never had a problem with it before."

"Well, call your alarm company and have them come check it out."

Officer Becky walked the house with me, showed me she had gone into each closet, covered every nook and cranny, then checked the backyard before she reviewed things I could do better to help prevent a break-in, but I had pretty much covered it all. Nothing could be upgraded. All windows were locked and there were beams to keep the windows from being opened if they were broken, plus the alarm had glass-break sensors, so if glass were shattered, the sound would alert the alarm company and law enforcement would be dispatched. I wanted them to fingerprint my house, but that was a different part of the sheriff's department.

Officer Becky said, "I can make sure a patrol stops by here for the next few days."

"I would appreciate that."

"Here's the number to request fingerprinting, but the kind of paint you have on your walls is rich folks' paint, Frankie. That high-end paint doesn't keep fingerprints. You need cheap paint for that."

"The drawers on my bedroom furniture were opened. So were my closets."

"You might catch a print there. I think they were in the house, taking inventory of what to steal, and you came back home and caught them off guard. You had workers here doing your renovation, and a lot of those guys will come back and break in. They did the work and know your house better than you do. They'll leave a window open and then come back and rob you blind. Be glad it didn't turn out badly."

I called and they said it would take five days to schedule someone to come out to fingerprint, like I was supposed to walk around my house and keep my hands in my pockets until then. I inhaled, cursed under my breath as I exhaled, then said never mind, especially since Lupe was coming to clean.

I left home feeling as if I had been violated. I had changed all the locks and codes, so Franklin couldn't have gotten in. But where there was a will, there was a way for the determined.

I was about to send him a text, but that would've meant I had caved in to the madness, plus Tommie called. They had called from school to say Mo was sick. She had a runny nose and a cough, and when a kid had two symptoms, they had to go back home. Tommie wanted to know my schedule. I picked up Mo, took her to my agency, gave her some kiddie medicine, and let her rest on the sofa in my office while I made a few calls and rearranged my day. I passed on a couple of things to other workers, rescheduled a few things, then left the office early. We stopped by Toys "R" Us to get her a new doll to keep her company, and then I took her back to my house. When I pulled up inside my garage, Erica Stockwell — a twentyish girl who lived across the street with her mom and stepdad — was pulling up in her secondhand Toyota, her friends Destiny Jones and Kwanzaa Brown with her. USC students. Kwanzaa lived across the street from Tommie. Erica Stockwell said she hadn't seen anything strange but would look over the DVR feed to their security system and let me know if she saw something of concern. I thanked her, then went inside. I fed Mo and put her to bed. She loved my bed because it was king size and like a playground, but her little ass wanted to hang out and play like a Mc-Broom. We went to the kitchen and I broke out the Borax, cornstarch, and glue. We made bouncing balls. We made homemade lava lamps by filling a vase with cooking oil and adding some water, a few drops of color, and some Alka-Seltzer, and watched the bubble of carbon dioxide gas float to the top. She thought that was awesome.

I smiled but felt a little sad. I would have been a great mommy. I really would have.

Monica was there until late afternoon, and the time flew.

Blue called. "Hey, how's my little girl?"

"She's great. I think she had a twenty-four-hour bug."

"Let me talk to Tommie."

"She's not here."

"She told me she was there with you guys."

"She's not; call her."

"Her cellular is off."

"Maybe she was on the way and her phone died. You know how she is."

"Okay. Well, she said she was there with Mo and you."

"I'll have her call you when she gets here."

"No, it's fine. Let me talk to Monica."

She talked to her dad for two seconds, then hung up and went back to being a scientist. Tommie showed up almost two hours later, but we didn't notice the time. I think both of us had forgotten that Blue had called. It seemed so irrelevant. Tommie was always late. The moment she picked up Mo, I changed and headed to the gym, met with Livvy, and on machines side by side, we ran the treadmills for ten miles.

When I made it home late that evening, nothing was out of place.

I had become paranoid to the point of taking photos of each room before I left home, even if I was leaving for ten minutes, then comparing them when I returned.

I still slept with the door to my bedroom locked, the gun on my nightstand, ready to burn.

The next morning, after I showered, I opened my lingerie drawer.

My heart tried to break out of my chest and all I could say over and over was the word *no.*

Some of my panties and bras were missing. Tommie would borrow things from time to time, but a woman never put her sweet spot in another woman's lingerie. I picked up the phone to call the police but knew that would sound stupid, the idea that there was an underwear bandit in the area, so I hung up.

The next few nights I left all the lights on in the house, had the inside lit up like high noon.

I slept dressed, gun at the ready, wishing someone would come inside of my home, pretty much praying that they would violate my space again.

FRANKIE

There was a day of silence, of peace, and I thought that maybe the stalking had ended. Then Franklin resumed his calling. He sent text message after text message.

Hey, Frankie.

Dafuq you want, Franklin?

Wow. You actually replied.

You have my ear. Now dafuq you want?

When can I see you?

When hell freezes over and heaven falls to the earth in flames.

Did you come by my home?

Of course not. I don't go to married men's homes.

You left one of your toys here at my house. The nine-inch-long Jack Rabbit.

I left quite a few things there. Add it all to your next garage sale.

The reason I messaged is because I just walked in and saw it on my bed. I know I didn't leave it there when I went to work. Are you sure you didn't come by and do your thing with it?

Don't be disgusting.

Should I drop it off at your office?

Hell no.

What should I do with your toy?

Sit on it and do a 360 while you scream GO 'BAMA.

As I dealt with his aggravating texts, my phone started to send alert after alert after alert, all for e-mails from a government address that ended in something like afghan-

.swa.army.mil and said its geographical location was in the heart of the Middle East. She had used at least a dozen e-mail addresses. As I had a pointless, immature text war with Franklin, Mrs. Carruthers continued her harassment. It was too much. It was as if they were teaming up to try to drive me crazy.

I threw my phone on the bed, actually slammed it down on the mattress.

Then I cried. I sat alone, in my home that had no love, no husband, no child, and I wept.

It felt silly, and I felt like a fool, but I wept for a child that wouldn't be born.

When I got in bed, the moment my face touched the pillow I jumped back up and turned on the lights. I thought that my pillow smelled like a light-scented cologne. The scent was faint, but it was there. I was in my bedroom with the bedroom door locked. I went to my bathroom and lifted the toilet seat — something a woman rarely did if she wasn't cleaning the commode. I checked for pee stains on the rim. Wanted to see if a man had been here, if he had found a way to sneak inside my home.

Lights came on outside. The motion detector had been activated. My heart raced and it felt like I was looking at the world through a narrow tunnel. I hurried to get my gun from its hiding place. Stumbled. Cursed. Then I changed the flat-screen television anchored to the wall over the dresser to the mode where I could look at the security cameras. No one was outside, at least not in the range or view of a camera.

LA had a leash law, so no stray dogs were on any streets, but there were a few random cats.

I texted Livvy and she responded, said she was home.

I texted Tommie and she told me she hadn't been by my house today and was home in bed.

I wasn't delusional, even though I walked from room to room with all the lights on and my gun in hand, the end that shoots the bullets leading the way.

I was about to call 911 again, but I didn't want to become the paranoid woman.

I walked like a burglar might be there. Nothing was missing, but when I went back to my bedroom I saw something hanging on the back of my closet door that I had walked by and not noticed. It was a blue dress, short and sexy. I stopped. Stared at the dress. Throat dry. Heart pounding.

I had left that dress at Franklin's house. It

had been a gift from him.

Inside the closet were the heels that had been paired with that dress.

Then I noticed most things in my walk-in closet were off, rearranged, out of place. Someone had been in here and gone through my clothing, unfolded things and tossed them in a pile on the floor.

I walked around again, hand trembling, too scared to blink, jerking left and right. It felt as if Franklin were there. I noticed something else. I had a portable record player. A Jay Z album was on the turntable. I hadn't listened to Jay Z spit about his ninety-nine problems in years. I had been listening to Amy Winehouse. It was as if I had been in a dream and was waking. I looked at my home differently.

My house was clean. That was the problem. It was too damn clean.

I remembered that when I had left this morning, I had made a quick breakfast, had cut fruit, then had left everything unwashed and in the sink. Now I saw that all of those dishes had been washed by hand and left on a dish rack. I knew that I hadn't washed the dishes and wiped down the counters. I don't hand-wash dishes and leave them out. I wash and put them in the dishwasher to dry, same as Momma used to make us do.

Water saved was money saved.

I ran back to my bedroom. It took me a moment, but I realized the sheets on the bed were different. They were mine, but those were not the sheets I'd woken up on this morning. The corners were tucked, but I didn't make my bed that way. The ones from last night, I found in the washing machine. I didn't put those there. There was another thing. In my master bedroom, I looked in the corner nearest the closet. I had ordered twenty pairs of shoes from ShoeDazzle and they had been delivered two days ago. They were still in the colorful pink or brown-and-black boxes. I had stacked those shoeboxes in two stacks, by the color of the boxes, and the ones in the larger boxes were on the bottom. That arrangement had been changed. At first I was sure that Tommie had come here and tried all of my shoes on. She would do that. She might even sneak and borrow a pair. None of the shoes were missing, but each pair had been moved from its original box and put in the wrong box. I called Tommie. She had no idea I had new shoes. She hadn't been inside of my bedroom. She hadn't been to my home in a week. Two seconds later I was in the bathroom checking my medicine cabinet. Three of my birth control pills had been popped out of their packet. Then I looked behind me, saw there was a dirt ring around the bathtub. Someone had been here, lounged here, touched my belongings, and taken a bath.

I suffocated as the room spun in circles.

I went to the door that led to the houghmagandy room. It was locked, but I used the key, undid the two dead bolts, held my breath as I opened the door, and turned the lights on. For the first twenty blinks the room looked normal. It was hard to tell, but one of the drawers seemed to be slightly ajar. Nothing was missing. Everything appeared to be as it had been left the last time I'd come inside.

I wanted to call the police again, but they'd ask if anything had been stolen, and I would say nothing, only that dishes had been washed, the bed made up, and a dress I had left at my ex's house was once again in my closet. Just thinking that out loud made me feel like I was becoming a crazy catless cat lady.

Outside I heard a car start and pull away. It roared away like a muscle car. It was Franklin. I ran out the front door, but it was too late to see anything but fading tail-lights. I went back inside, checked my house again. I had to make sure a rattlesnake hadn't been left underneath my bed. Made sure all the windows were locked. A couple of hours later, still on edge, my cellular rang and I jumped.

Someone had broken into my office on Sepulveda. I dressed and made it there in fifteen minutes. The Westchester police were already there. Someone had dumped bags of fertilizer over every desk, every computer, and thrown the same shit at the walls. The cameras at the office had been disabled.

There was no evidence. They said it was probably young kids and this was a prank.

Hours later, after I had called a professional crew to come clean up the office, after I dealt with that bullshit, I went home. The level of anger and disgust I felt made me want to go nuclear.

The moment I stepped back inside of my home, I walked into more madness and confusion.

My living room furniture had been rearranged.

Pictures had been taken off the walls and left on the floor.

Televisions had been left on, each on a different station, the volumes at their maximum.

My second car, it was in the garage, the engine running, garage filled with poisoned

201

air. Deadly carbon monoxide had been let into the house because the door to the garage had been opened wide.

Now I was terrified to the point of hardly being able to dial three digits.

Again I was outside until the police arrived. They told me that Franklin was still in San Diego. In a frantic tone I told them that there had been enough time for him to drive to LA, break into my home, and be back in San Diego. He would need only five hours to go round-trip, less if he took the toll road.

People had been with him all day. Other businessmen vouched for him.

My mind wasn't playing tricks on me. I told them I had heard his car speed away earlier.

The problem was I hadn't seen his car. They told me it could've been anyone's car I heard.

They refused to believe Franklin had filled my home with poisonous gas. He was the liar. He was the one rejected. I was no longer safe inside of my home. My dream home had become a nightmare.

FRANKIE

I moved within two weeks, changed homes, relocated to a larger, more modern home in View Park. It was a short sale due to divorce and pending bankruptcy. Tommie sold my old furniture online. I started over. The living room was decorated with family photos; the largest photo was of the McBroom daughters and our parents, that one over two decades old. The four-thousand-square-foot home had plantation shutters on all the windows, so no one could see inside. I had two dead bolts on all entry doors and burglar bars installed in the floors, the New York–style that lifted up and fit snug under the doorknob, making it impossible to kick a front door down. My alarm was set so all lights would flash and the house would scream loud enough to wake everything living and dead from my home to Denver, Colorado.

I could breathe again; I felt safe.

There was nothing there to remind me of Franklin.

Another week went by.

Another Sunday morning came and we continued training for the race.

By six fifteen, the parking lot on the Bank of America side of the Baldwin Hills Crenshaw mall was filled with cars. We were adults, but we were men and women, and more than a few relationships or affairs had taken place out here. People run together for hours, talk for hours, and become intimate in that way. Eventually many fall into bed, despite wedding rings or other promises. A lot of good-looking men were there, but I had avoided that trap. Those men were typical men, flirting with the younger, flat-bellied sisters in colorful spandex and runner's ponytails. Most of the sisters wore black girls run! T-shirts. Tommie and Livvy moved from person to person, hugging and chatting, all smiles. I had ridden with Tommie, and I did the same, acted like there were no demons battling for first place inside my head. I pretended that two hundred calls hadn't come from Mrs. Crazy in the last twenty-four hours.

A handsome brother came over and stopped near me. He had on black running shorts and a yellow T with the timely phrase I CAN'T BREATHE in bloodred letters. I'd never seen him before.

We made eye contact.

He grinned at me like he knew me, waved, came in my direction.

That scared me.

He said, "Didn't you used to have dread-locks?"

I adjusted the scarf over my head and nod-ded. "Yeah. I did."

"Wow. This is a trip. It is you."

"Well, I'm usually me. So yeah, from my perspective, it's me."

"Nice to finally run into you again."

"Sorry, but I think you have me confused with someone else."

"Weren't you at the Peachtree Road Race in ATL the last Fourth of July?"

"Yeah, well, I went with most of the people out here today. We pretty much took over a Delta flight. Hold on. There were over fifty thousand people out in that wretched slave-heat and humidity. You actu-ally noticed me down there?"

"You were with that sister over there. There were three of you, actually."

"That tall sister is my youngest sister. The shorter sister near her is our middle sister."

"I think all three of you were arguing."

"That's how we communicate."

"I'm Daniel Madison."

I told him my full name, then asked, "How did you end up out here with us today?"

He had heard about our group and joined online. There were more than a few African American running groups in Los Angeles. He tried to chat, but I wasn't down with being über polite that early in the morning, and just as I was about to excuse myself from the lollygagging, Franklin called.

I answered as I walked away from the weekend warriors.

Franklin asked, "Who is that guy you're talking to? Is that the new boyfriend?"

I hung up and looked around. Then I saw his car. He was exiting the parking lot, headed out on Crenshaw, in the direction of I-10. He had been sitting there and waiting for me to show up.

He had wanted to get a glimpse of me.

He had wanted to get under my skin.

Daniel grinned at me. He was near Dr. Shelby, Dr. Debra, and a few others who'd run these hills with us this season. Daniel had a nice chest and arms, was toned, under six feet tall, and sounded like Harvard and all things successful. He looked like a brand-new heartbreak waiting to happen. It was still too soon. I was a woman with the needs of a woman, but I was still nursing an open wound. I moved my eyes away from him and jogged over to Tommie. She was on the phone being flirtatious.

I said, "Tell Blue I said good morning."

"I'm not talking to Blue."

"Who is that?"

"Do you mind?"

She walked away.

At six forty we headed out to Crenshaw Boulevard, prepared for the start of a twenty-mile run. We were going to run Inglewood 10, an all-hill route. That was the first ten miles. After that, the rest of the run would be flat. We'd get back here, and the people who wanted to go on for the second half of the workout would keep moving from Crenshaw and King toward Rodeo Road, run the next five miles through Culver, then turn around and head back to the mall's parking lot. The last five miles was no joke. I used to always break down on that strip. I refused to be broken. Today would be like living in hell. But hell was nothing new to me. I'd been burned many times.

Daniel jogged from the back of the pack, caught up, walked next to me, and started another conversation.

He asked, "Mind if I run with you?"

"I don't need a babysitter."

"I don't know the course."

"I'm training with my sisters, not here to be hit on."

Daniel walked near me to the starting point at the Macy's. I stopped with my sisters and our crowd. He kept going toward the faster runners. We stood there, getting our last-minute stretches in. I glanced to my right, looked in the parking lot at Macy's. Franklin's muscle car was there. I couldn't see him, but he was there. His energy contaminated my soul. He was watching, today the gentle stalker.

I jogged up to the front of the pack and told Daniel, "Hey, why don't you run with me today."

"Are you sure?"

"Yeah. I'm sure."

Tommie and Livvy took off with the rest of the group, at least fifty of us out there now. Daniel and I started and trailed them. We didn't talk much. Hard to chat and run ten miles of hills. The last ten miles were a bitch. As I ran with him, I saw Franklin six times, parked at different locations on the course.

I had a tendency to break away from the pack, and he'd hoped to catch me running by myself. For the next three and a half hours, I was with Daniel, ran with him from beginning to end.

When we were done with the grueling run, as some of us sat on the asphalt parking lot while others sat in lawn chairs, we all sipped water and ate fruit. We cooled down and waited for the slower runners to make it back. Franklin was parked on the other side of Crenshaw Boulevard, in front of a strip of apartment buildings, his eyes on me. If he wanted to watch, let him watch. I cranked up the smile and gave Daniel as much attention as he could bear. I touched him a lot, laughed a lot, held his arm a lot, and when he sat on his lawn chair, I pulled mine up and took his feet in my lap, massaged them. Then he massaged mine. He rubbed my aching feet and woke up something I needed to stay asleep. Soon I heard Franklin's ride speeding away. He zoomed down Crenshaw, enraged.

I asked Daniel, "You have schoolboy crushes on many women?"

"Not in a long, long time."

"When was the last?"

"Years ago I used to live out in the Inland Empire. Over a decade ago."

"Just checking."

He asked, "You ever had a crush on

someone so strong you thought it would never end?"

"I did. Once upon a time I did. I fell in love with this guy and thought he was the one for me."

"Was he a runner too?"

"Yeah, but he's not part of this group. I don't date people in my group, but a lot of the other women here probably will. Lot of intelligent, educated, pretty women out here. Welcome to the group."

I broke away from Daniel then, rubbed my temples, went and mingled with the rest of the crew.

Twenty minutes later, as a few more from the group came in exhausted from the long run, a red muscle car pulled into the parking lot. It was a sweet number. A red-haired, well-tanned white woman got out. She smiled, waved, and called my sisters' names. Livvy and Tommie waved, then went to her. She wore runner's gear, skin salty from a workout. Tommie came back over to where I was.

I asked, "Who is she?"

"Rosemary Paige. She said she just did the Culver City stairs forty times."

"Damn. Look at her legs and abs. Friend of yours?"

"She is looking for a house in this area. I

had given her your business card a while back."

"Introduce me. I have three nice properties ready to hit the market within the next two weeks."

Right about then Livvy and the woman walked over, casually speaking to Daniel as they passed.

He looked back, checked out her ass, but didn't linger and become lewd.

Livvy said, "Frankie, this is Rosemary Paige from Pennsylvania by way of Texas."

She nodded. "So you're the famous Frankie McBroom your sisters keep talking about."

I said, "I hear you're looking for property in the area."

"Let me text you my cell phone number, Frankie. What's your cell number?"

Without thinking about it, my mind on my money, I told her.

She said, "Tommie told me that you live in the old Ladera area."

"Did. I moved closer to this side of town."

"Baldwin Hills?"

"Other side of Stocker in View Park."

"I would love to see your area too."

"Houses in that area start at about three-quarters of a million, and on that level you'll need to get preapproved before we start looking at properties. That way you don't waste your time looking beyond your preapproved loan amount and I don't waste mine burning up my gas."

After we exchanged information, Rosemary Paige put her phone away.

"I'll be in touch, Frankie McBroom."

Ten seconds after that, she was in her car, taking to the boulevard. As soon as my potential client mixed with the big-city madness on the 'Shaw, my phone buzzed. I opened it. Attached was a video. We were in Africa. The video was from Franklin. We were making love. That confirmed he'd stolen the GoPro.

Teeth clenched tight, I refused to let him defeat me.

I frowned back toward Crenshaw; expected to see Franklin had resumed stalking me. He wasn't there, but I knew he wasn't far. Daniel was still checking me out. I went over to him.

I asked, "So, when are we going to go out on a coffee date and see what kind of vibe we have?"

"You're hot and cold, you know that?"

"I'm hot, that's why you can't keep your eyes off me. You're pretty hot yourself, Daniel. If you want to get cleaned up and get a twenty-minute chat with the girl you have a crush on, I might be game."

"Twenty minutes?"

"As long as it takes to sip a cup of tea is all the time I need to see what you're about. No need to waste a half hour. One hot cup of tea is all it takes to see if you're real or a bullshitter like the rest."

"You do keep it real."

"My time is limited, and time is money. You want to play a game, flirt, flatter, work your way up to a horizontal workout, no clothes, no Nikes, only confidence and condoms required. I know the objective."

"Damn. You are up front."

"Too old for games, unless it's Scrabble or Jenga. So listen, I love a handsome, fit, professional man. It's great for my ego. You know what you want — at least you think you do. Let me break it down. I'm the new stimulant in your life. You're chasing what interests you. We've seen each other in our running gear, and this is sexy because we give off that energy, and not only that, but we've seen each other a yard of spandex from being naked, and I can see what you're working with, more or less, and it hangs like it's more than less. You can ogle me and see what I'm working with, see my curves, see how I work hard to make this frame look better than a twenty-year-old track star's, see how my nipples stand, and might catch me with a bit of camel toe before things get adjusted, but that's how it is out here, and outside of a carnal fantasy, be sure you can handle this route. The marathon is much easier to handle than I am."

"That sounded like flirting. I thought you said no flirting, Frankie McBroom."

I maintained an irritated grin. "Did you really see me when I ran in ATL?"

"I really did."

"And you've wanted to meet me since last July?"

"Yeah, I have. But I assumed you lived in ATL. Hope it doesn't sound crazy, but after ATL, you were on my mind for a very long time. That same weekend, I was at Taki Japanese Steakhouse and saw someone who looked like you and broke my neck to get to her, only to embarrass myself. Thought I saw you at Czar Ice Bar, at Gladys Knight's Chicken and Waffles, even thought I saw you walking down Peachtree. Looked for you all over ATL. Then I ran into you in LA. I ran into the woman who had caught my eye, captured me, and she had no idea. So finding you, running with you, this is a fantasy come true for me."

"Wow. Not sure if I should be flattered or concerned."

"I would say I'd hope you'd be flattered, but you said no flirting."

"Good point. We really shouldn't be flirting. This has gone too far as it is."

"Were we flirting? My bad. If I was flirting, I both digress and apologize."

"Well, it was nice meeting you. Thanks for getting me through this grueling run."

"So no coffee date at some place where we can sit down and not flirt again?"

"No coffee date. Blame it on the pain. That long speech about no games and yada yada yada — I get delirious and talk crazy after a long run. Let's pretend I never said any of that. I embarrassed myself."

"I loved it. We are too mature for games. I like Scrabble, and if you were my woman, we'd do shots and play strip Jenga while talking about the top philosophers of ancient Greece."

"Strip Jenga? You're a pervert."

"Don't steal my ideas. I bet you will drive to Toys 'R' Us as soon as you leave here."

"Whatever. You need to run to Big 5 and get to the men's department."

"Yeah, I'll buy a better jockstrap because I didn't intend to display that much information."

"That's why I wanted you to run in front

of me most of the run. It's a bit distracting."

"I was trying to run behind you. Much
better view."

"Well, when I was behind you, it was
definitely motivating."

"Now who's the pervert?"

We laughed. He was humorous and had
made me laugh on a dark day. Laughter
does things to people. He was articulate,
professional. Had something that Franklin
lacked. He was an upgrade.

But then again, everyone was an upgrade
compared to Franklin and his lies. Too bad
I was out of the dating game. For good. I
was done. Franklin had burned me and left
me burned out.

Celibacy and me had become a team. But
that didn't mean I couldn't flirt every now
and then. Flirting was positive, made me
feel good about myself, and therefore it was
good for my mental well-being.

Toes tender, butt aching, I limped away,
moved through the exhausted finishers
before I glanced back. Daniel watched me
like I was an empress dressed to the nines,
smelling of the sweetest perfume.

While I gave Monica a piggyback ride,
Livvy tickled her and Tommie yelled for us
to all stop before we dropped her daughter.

I checked out Daniel again, imagined sensual things. I had been alone since two days before last Christmas, and I think I was at my celibacy limit. He had given me attention this morning and that slumbering part of me had been shaken ever so gently. I needed affection that wasn't self-imposed. Masturbation sucked unless I was being sucked while I masturbated. I did what I had to do, praised myself often, but self-love was getting old. I needed a new lover. Someone like Daniel.

I imagined him on top of me. I imagined being occupied.

I imagined taking a few minutes and forgetting everything that was troubling me.

Then I had flashbacks of Franklin. Of that last night. Of that phone call from his wife.

I needed to move on. It was as if Franklin was still controlling my sex life.

Each day I didn't date, each night I didn't have a new lover, each time I ignored a call from someone I used to know or love, it felt like I was trying to remain in the same state I'd been left in by Franklin, as if part of me wanted us to reconcile as lovers. I did look at the engagement ring from time to time, and my emotions remained heavy. My heart didn't want him, and my mind was in agreement.

I eyed Daniel until he felt my energy and looked in my direction.

He nodded at me.

I nodded at him.

FRANKIE

I asked Daniel, "Did you have any problem finding my home?"

"Used my GPS."

"Yeah. I'll bet you did."

Daniel drove to my new residence, picked me up, brought me flowers, opened the car door for me, the whole nine. Seeing me in makeup, a red dress, and six-inch fuck-me pumps did a number on him. After dinner, we went to the club Savoy in Inglewood, mixed with the locals and threw down some dancehall on reggae night. We had a private booth, and after we had danced like maniacs and finished a bottle of wine, we left the club and went in search of a late-night meal. We grubbed at an all-night diner-style restaurant in Marina del Rey, then we walked in the chilly air. He held my hand. Soon Daniel pulled me close, came into my personal space. I didn't push him away. We started kissing while standing between parked cars.

I wanted to be kissed, wanted to allow my sensual self to come out to play, but had to cut it short for fear of revealing too much about that part of me too soon. Ten years ago, things would've been different. This would've been instant love, just add the magic stick and stir, stir, stir until we were at the altar.

He drove me home and walked me to my front door.

The lights around my house came on. That meant neighbors could see us. We stood on my porch, chatting, until the lights went off again. In the darkness, he pulled me to him again. We kissed until the good girl inside of me almost lost a battle with the bad girl. I almost invited him inside for a warm shower and a late-night McSnack, then I'd toss him a granola bar, and walk him to his car, blow him kisses as he drove away.

All I wanted were the kisses.

I tried to convince myself that kisses were all I needed.

Even the strongest of the strong felt lonely at times.

Being stimulated, aroused, and alone was not fun. Most nights I woke up restless and in need. But I wanted emotional as well as physical intimacy. I wanted depth as well as something moving deep. I wanted a man to tell me he loved me. I wanted to tell him the same. I wanted what I thought I had had with Franklin. Maybe that life wasn't meant for me.

But a girl could dream. A girl could kiss and dream.

We ended a series of lip sucking, sensual kisses. It was hard to let go, but I eased away from him far enough to see what I had felt rub against me, saw that his pants were protruding, showing me he wore boxers, not briefs. I saw the outline of what wanted to be inside of this fire, then Daniel and I made eye contact, held it, stared at each other. Oxytocin was flooding our systems and increasing desire and sexual arousal. Oxytocin made lust feel like love.

Oxytocin made you want to have an orgasm.

Too bad we had just met.

Too bad this was a first date.

I needed to come. He had exacerbated that need. This extreme need to orgasm was his fault. I should make him responsible, make him fix what he had done, and fix it good.

But it was time for us to part ways, not my legs.

I thanked him for the evening, eased into our farewell.

In the soft voice of a gentleman he asked, "Think we can go out again at some point?"

Tingling, my tone sugary, I said, "Maybe. Tonight was wonderful. I needed a night like tonight. After my last relationship, guess I've locked myself inside. We'll have to see. I broke my rule. I'm not comfortable mixing a relationship with the group I hang out with. This is nice, but I don't need my business in the streets, not like everyone else's is."

"Then I won't hang out with the group. I've only been there once."

"That's not the issue. I'm just not ready for anything right now."

We kissed until it became a little too hot for comfort, until I pulled away, barely able to breathe. I stared at his lips, at his pretty mouth, felt his longing as he tried to control his breathing. Instead of going inside, I succumbed. I gave him another sensual kiss on his mouth, a slow kiss, then kissed him again and dragged my nails across his skin. I wanted him in two orifices, three if I had another glass of wine. My senses were overaroused and I wanted to feed the fetish before I lost my mind. The world felt so dreamy. He could be a brand-new day, a new partner, a new man, a new experience, a new era.

Or just the next mistake dressed up like a gentleman. Shards of glass from broken dreams piled at my feet. I felt the burns from the fires before him. Once bitten, twice shy, as Momma used to say. The trance broke, sanity returned.

I whispered, "Good night, Daniel Madison."

We kissed a couple more times, then he eased away. He thanked me for spending the evening with him, thanked me for allowing him to take me on a date, told me I was twice as amazing as he had imagined me to be, kissed my lips a final time, and gave me a gentle hug, then left, happiness in his pants still protruding, all but skipping like a schoolboy.

I had talked a lot of smack, but I was scared. I hadn't had sex since that horrible night with Franklin, since the breakup. My mind said it never wanted to have sex again, but I was so damn wet now. Nipples were still hard. Being with a man, at this point, would be more symbolic than a quest for new love. I was a grown woman. If I wanted some, I should get some and be done with it. It didn't have to be serious, about marriage, about love, about a new relationship, just about achieving orgasm. I was tempted to call him, tell him to come back.

I held my phone, pulled up his name, but didn't make that call. He was overly infatuated. That was a red flag.

I undressed, showered, walked nude down the hallway, took the two orange keys and went to my locked bedroom, to the new and improved houghmagandy room. There was no knob on this side of the door, only two dead bolts.

I opened a drawer on a nightstand, teased my fingers over a variety of dildos, Rabbits, chocolate-hued penises with veins. I even had two pink ones. One I called Fitz; the other was named Jake. Fitz and Jake combined were only half the size of the chocolate dildo. That one had been named Idris.

I opened the closet and pulled out a vinyl record, Coltrane, *A Love Supreme,* put that on the portable record player. I dimmed the lights. As music played, I rode Sybian. I let it Idris my Elba while the projector lit up the wall with sensual videos of men orally pleasing women, the volume muted. While I engaged my carnal senses, I fantasized about doing a Morris on a sexy man's Chestnuts. It was a sweet torture. It was intimacy without heartbreak. When that side of the album ended, I put on Carlos Santana, let the vibes from his guitar stimulate me, let them ride my every fiber. Then I picked a clit stimulator and relaxed on the king bed, remembered the Bajan twins in Cancún, let wicked fantasies take me where I needed to go that night, and while Santana and India Arie sang their duet, while the guitar proved it could gently weep, I wept gently. I hummed. I needed to calm the fire. I need to ride and sing away my blues.

The next morning my phone buzzed before the sun had come up. I pushed Jake and Fitz to the side, let Idris fall to the floor, and grabbed my phone. It was another text message from Franklin.

Last night you looked good in red. You've cut your locks and moved on like we didn't matter. I'm not giving up on us, Frankie. And another thing. I didn't like the way that punk was looking at your ass.

After that message came a photo of Daniel and me laughing and dancing at the Savoy.

TOMMIE

Beale called me. He had just made it back to LAX, was in his chauffeured car, was being driven home, and wanted me to meet him. Beale asked me to meet him for ten minutes, and I did, was with him long enough to have coitus in his foyer. I had an orgasm; he pulled out of me, had his, and spewed on the carpeted floor. I pulled my dress down, kissed him, jumped back in my ride, sped away like I'd robbed a bank and gotten away clean. Exhilarated. I picked up Mo and we went by Livvy's half-million-dollar spa for manicures and pedicures. Days later Beale made love to me in his shower. Two days after that, he smacked it up, flipped it, and rubbed it down in his giant bathtub, water splashing everywhere. I moaned and told him what to do to me. He visited me at the Apple Store. He took me to lunch, then we did it in the back of his SUV at the mall, people walking by unaware that we were getting down like getting down had an expiration date. The next day, after I dropped Mo off at school, I stopped by his house and we did it again. As soon as I walked in, we got busy on the carpeted stairs at his place, didn't quite make it to the bedroom before we had gone buck wild while we were half-dressed, his pants down at his knees, me with only one leg out of my skinny jeans. Sunday I sat in the living room with Mo and Blue and we watched *Black-ish.* By Wednesday I was restless. I told Blue I was going to watch *Empire* with Livvy. I made a detour by Beale's first. The next evening I told Blue I was going to go by Frankie's, again for *Scandal* and *How to Get Away with Murder* night with the McBrooms. Again I stopped by Beale's home. We were naked on his pool table. We left a sex stain the size of a quarter on the woven wool. Two days later we were in his spacious laundry room, him stroking me as I sat on top of the washer as it hit spin cycle. I had never behaved this way. Beale was turning me out, changing me from quiet and calm Tommie McBroom to Freaky by Noon Mc-Broom. The sex was bombastic, but the emotional connection had solidified.

Emotions redefined right and wrong. We adjusted our morals toward that with which we agreed. We revised our values the way conquerors have down through history.

After a while, even the truth was nothing more than a lie told over and over.

I needed to get away from the lies. With Blue, it had become a house of lies.

I needed to be free, needed to feather my nest with the truth as I knew it.

Cuddled next to Beale, I said, "I might move in with you."

"When?"

"I'm writing Blue a good-bye letter."

"Really? Why?"

"So he will know how I feel, why I left, why I couldn't stay any longer. Plus I need to see the words, the emotions in black and white. I need to see what I feel on paper. I might leave him and come to you, but I am not leaving him for you. I need him to understand that I am leaving for me."

"How soon will you give him the letter?"

"I might need some space before I officially move in with you."

"I can get you an apartment, for the sake of having one, but you can move in, unofficially."

"Okay. That might work."

"How soon, Tommie?"

"Soon. We're breaking up in slow motion, but we are easing in that direction. We are closer to the end than we are to where we started now. Closer to the end, but not close enough to end it all."

"I feel like I'm a hummingbird, watching you move lethargically."

"We're in the same home, but I can feel the distance between us, like we're two icebergs moving in opposite directions; the love that is . . . or was between us . . . is gradually melting with each passing day."

"Can't say I am sorry to hear that. My only regret is that it's not ending faster."

"I will have to tell Monica. I will have to tell our friends, will have to tell my sisters. Will have to work out how we will handle the house. I have put all of my savings into our investment, and so has Blue. I don't want to have either one of us ending up with bad credit. I don't want him to end up without a home. We have a charge card we use for house emergencies. And there is the matter of Monica and school."

"You make it sound like you're getting a divorce."

"That's the hardest part. Breaking up gives more pain to the mind than breaking a leg gives to the body, and that pain won't end nearly as fast. It can damage you in ways unseen and in ways that never heal."

"You're not the child's mother."

"Telling her I'll be going away will be hard. It will be like divorce. It will be like death."

"She'll forget about you, as my mother forgot about me."

"I don't want her to forget about me. A mother never forgets about her child, Beale."

"When you have your own, your focus will change, and you'll forget about her."

"I'll never forget about her."

"She will become less important."

"I might not be her birth mother, but I will always be her earth mother."

"Will he let you see her after you leave?"

"I know he won't. Like you said, she's not my daughter. She's a branch of his family tree, not mine. I need to look for my own legacy. I feel like that's my duty, being my father's only child. Some women don't want to have a child, and I support them. But I am not one of those women."

"You want me to know that."

"Yes. I don't want to make the same mistake twice."

"We could have a child nine months from today, if you want to go for it."

"Slow your roll."

We played video games in his basement, got into an argument, and he decided I needed to be disciplined. Beale bared his teeth and pulled me to him, forced me to bend across his lap. He held me down, smacked my ass with his open palm. He gave me lashes like he was the director at a school.

He raised his hand high and smacked my ass again, again, and again.

The pain spread across my bottom, the heat tremendous.

Nostrils flared, teeth bared, I said, "Harder."

He hit my bottom a dozen times. Each time I grabbed at the air, refused to scream.

I crawled from his lap and lay on the carpeted floor. I lay there in pain.

I massaged my throat, coughed, and said, "So it's like that, Beale Streets."

"Are you angry?"

I grinned. "I kinda liked that. That was different. I am so turned on right now."

Beale touched me between my legs, massaged my wetness, then bent one leg and sucked my toes. Eyes closed, I squirmed. When I jerked and opened my eyes again, he smiled at me, kissed, licked from my foot up my leg. Across my calf muscle. Nibbled my inner thigh. His nose grazed my sex over and over. Then I felt his tongue. I let out a long winding sound of absolute surrender.

He went down, licked me down low, and I felt like I was floating so high.

He said, "Let's go upstairs and get in the bed."

"If you want me upstairs on your bed, you'll have to pick me up and carry me to the bed."

"You think I can't do that? You think I'm not strong enough to carry you upstairs?"

"And you can't use the elevator."

"What do I win if I manage to do that?"

"You can do anything you want to do to me for ten minutes."

"Anything?"

"Anything. Including that."

He picked me up, adjusted my weight, and carried me. I pretended I was dead. I closed my eyes and became dead weight in his arms. He transported me from the basement to his master bedroom.

He eased me down on the bed and I didn't move. Pretended not to be alive, except for the shallow breathing. After he put me on the bed, he positioned me, had me how he wanted me.

The next day, I was back at his home, and I was there the day after the next day, for an hour before I went to work. He made me breakfast. I was back the day after that day, for only twenty minutes. I was going to see him almost every afternoon. I lived to be naked with him. On my back. Legs open. Blindfolded. He had me for lunch. He made his tongue move north, south, east, and west, then deeper and deeper. I couldn't handle it and pulled him up to me, made him stop eating the cake like Anna Mae, and pulled him on top of me. He kissed me and I wrapped my legs around him, put my hands at the small of his back to urge him toward me. We came together. After we showered, he led me into his master bedroom and took me into an empty closet that was the size of a living room in a regular home.

He said, "This is a large closet, Tommie."

"This is the size of my first apartment on Fairfax right below Slauson."

"I bought this home hoping that I would meet the woman of my dreams."

"Tanya? You bought this mansion for you and Tanya?"

"She wasn't the woman of my dreams. She was the bronze, when I want the gold."

"Okay. She didn't pass probation. She was a temp but never went full-time."

"You are the gold. When you move in with me, this will be your closet."

I stood in the closet, speechless, imagining that space filled with clothing and shoes.

He said, "This can be your home. Our home. You can change my house into a home."

"Don't say things like that. Don't gas me up, Beale."

"You think I'm joking?"

"I think you're full of shit."

He took my palm, opened it, and dropped in a golden key, the key to his front door.

"Whenever you're ready to leave the nightmare, Tommie, all of your dreams can come true."

"You're serious."

"I have to speak at Princeton and Yale. I'll be gone ten days. Use this like it's your home."

"For real?"

"I want you to come here, eat, relax, get in bed, masturbate, think of me while you come."

"You are for real."

"If you moved all you own in here while I'm gone, I would love that."

I paused. Felt emotional. Words escaped from my lips: "I love you, Beale."

"I know you do, Tommie. It was love at first sight for you as it was love at first sight for me."

Tears in my eyes, I went down on my

knees, took him in my hands, told him I loved him over and over. I suckled him. My tempo was without pause, increasing, his length and girth above average.

"You are wicked, Tommie McBroom."

I took out a Fruit Roll-Up, did that thing, took him close to nirvana, but didn't make him lose control. I climbed on top of him, mounted him, leaned forward, let it hurt so good, and when I couldn't hold out, rocked him slowly, slowly, slowly.

I whispered, "That's my closet."

"That's your closet."

"And I have my own key to the castle."

"You have your own key."

"You want me here."

"I want you here."

"You want me to be your queen."

"You are my queen."

"Just give me some time to get things sorted."

"Ride me like that, baby. Just like that. Just. Like. That."

I left Beale, went and picked Mo up from her private school, walked in a daze, hardly spoke to any of the other parents, that golden key inside of my jeans pocket as I drove us to our quaint home.

Mo asked, "Why are you so quiet,

Mommy?"

"Just thinking, Mo. Mommy's thinking about things."

"About what things?"

" 'Which things,' not 'what things.' "

"About which things?"

"Just thinking about things that adults think about."

"What kind of things?"

"About the things I want for me."

"What things do you want?"

"You know I love you with all of my heart, Mo? You know that, right?"

"I know."

"I need to stop worrying about making other people happy and focus on my own happiness."

Blue came home from the gym. We kissed. I helped Mo with her homework.

Blue asked me about dinner. I hadn't cooked. I didn't care.

Blue said, "Want me to run out and get Chinese food from Yee's?"

Monica said, "I want chicken."

"I'll run and grab something from El Pollo Loco."

He left and came back in twenty minutes.

We sat as a family, ate grilled chicken dinners.

Blue asked, "Everything okay?"

As I picked at my food, I nodded that I was fine.

Mo said, "Mommy is sad. She's been sad since she came to get me from school."

"What's wrong, Tommie?"

"Nothing, Blue. Nothing."

Mo showered. Blue showered. I showered. Blue went to bed.

Everything was by the numbers. There was no excitement. Only predictability.

I sat on the sofa, in the dark, holding a novel by Beale Streets, thinking about a better world.

In the middle of the night Blue woke me up. The book was on the floor.

He moved it to the side and asked, "Coming to bed?"

"I'll sleep out here."

"Something happen?"

"No. Nothing happened. Nothing has happened and nothing is going to happen."

He asked, "Want to talk?"

"No."

"We have things that need to be resolved."

"No means no, Blue. Not tonight. Not now. Nothing will have changed tomorrow."

"Did the vasectomy . . . did my exercising my rights as a man . . . is that when everything changed?"

"Good night, Blue. I'm trying to be polite,

so just say good night and let that be a wrap."

"Why does a woman get pissed when a man does the equivalent of what she has the right to do? Have you consulted me on your every decision? Do you ask me if I mind whether or not you take birth control? When you get pregnant, however you choose to handle it will be your right. Where is my say-so in the matter?"

"Angela really messed you up in the head. You should talk to someone about that."

"This doesn't have a damn thing to do with Angela, and don't patronize me, Tommie."

"On that note, from the passenger, the bill maker who you can only see as being just another baby maker, the one incapable of taking control, the immature one you use to unload, good night."

He pushed the palms of his hands against his eyes, took deep breaths.

"Honest, I didn't do it to hurt you, Tommie. Never wanted to hurt us. Love you. We say hurtful things to the ones we love the most. When we're frustrated, that's who we hurt. I'm sorry for that."

I said nothing. Apologies without actions were just another Easter speech.

He turned, went back to the bedroom.

This was our first night sleeping apart.

This was my first night not wanting his touch.

When I woke up again, Mo was on the sofa with me, snoring, her warmth blending with mine.

FRANKIE

Saturday morning.

My group of between twenty and thirty weekend warriors had a run at five A.M. We did a short run that day. Our crew was mostly African American, most transplants from all over the country who had come to California in search of their own form of gold, but we were an international bunch, a few whites and Indians and people with their roots from south of the border in our mix, this being our version of being progressive. During the afternoon we were all poolside at a barbecue at the home of CEO Tyrel Williams and his wife, Dr. Shelby Williams. It was a casual get-together for both adults and children.

The men were on the other side of the pool, laughing and talking man talk, and the women congregated like we were at a book club meeting, only we had profound and at times divisive conversations on the

Michael Brown verdict, racial profiling, how some felt the Democratic Party was as beneficial for black people as the GOP had been for rednecks trapped in trailer parks. The hot issue was the Metro on Crenshaw, how that would change our neighborhoods. The property values would go up, but the culture would evolve. Capitalism. Religion. Politics. We were a group of learned women and all knew how to debate and agree to disagree on many relevant issues. We did a great job getting down to the nitty-gritty and if we had been in a film, we would've passed the Bechdel test with flying colors.

Soon the karaoke machine was out and we were all having an impromptu concert, and everybody was as competitive on the microphone as they were running on the pavement. Livvy, Tommie, and I were on the small, colorful backyard stage and we gloriously butchered two En Vogue numbers. Passionately but off-key, we begged the men to hold on to our love, then gave them something they could feel. Tommie pulled Blue up and was freaky dancing all up on him. Mo ran from over by the pool and tried to join in. Everybody cracked up. Mo stole the show, then ran back to dive into the pool.

Blue threw Tommie into the pool. Tony

241

was pulling at Livvy, trying to do the same. She went in, but she pulled Tony with her. Daniel wasn't there. I almost wished he had shown up. I was in the mood for both fun and the company of a gentleman. I guess he was out in the Inland Empire.

I ran and did a cannonball and splashed water on everyone I could.

When I resurfaced, I saw Rosemary Paige standing near the edge of the pool wearing a fuchsia two-piece. We waved at each other. I guess she was becoming part of our circle. I swam to the edge of the pool and reached out to shake her hand. As we shook, I got a firm grip on her wrist and pulled her in. She smiled at me after she wiped the water from her face and unclogged her ears.

We swam four laps together, racing. I was faster than she was in the water.

She floated on her back as she asked, "When can you and I get together?"

"I'll text you. Would love to show you a property or two before they are snatched up."

"Text me your new home address. I will make sure I call before I stop by."

"Sure, no problem. You can ride around and look at the homes, see if any fit your needs."

Monica came over and I introduced Rosemary Paige to the precocious kid. Rosemary Paige swam a couple more laps before leaving the pool. Dr. Shelby handed her a towel and she dried off. When I looked around she was already gone. I hoped she wasn't mad because I pulled her into the water.

Blue swam up next to me. "Who was that?"

"Tommie's friend from somewhere."

"Tommie has a lot of new friends lately."

I jumped on Blue, dunked him, and held him down. He flipped me and we wrestled until he broke free and swam away. I joined in with everyone else and swam and played pool games. Mo rode Tommie's shoulders and had the happiest face on the planet. Her hair was braided on both sides, the top loose, so she looked like she had a Mc-Broom Mohawk. A moment later, Monica was on Tommie's shoulders while Tommie balanced both of them on Blue's shoulders. We applauded the family pyramid.

All were yukking it up.

My phone was off to the side, and I could see it vibrating on the glass bistro table. It was one of those assholes. It was Franklin or his crazy wife. No one knew that the threats, everything, had escalated.

LIVVY

Soon she and Tony were showered, changed, and back in Beverly Hills, this time dressed work casual. They picked up Dr. Ashley. She had returned to the States in order to hang out with her American friends again. They went to a concert at the Dolby Theatre, then walked Hollywood Boulevard before going back to Dr. Ashley's celebrity-filled hotel, back to the bar where food cost twenty dollars a bite, the same DJ again playing house music. In a room filled with also-rans and hangers-on, they flirted unabashedly as they danced. Livvy looked at her husband, at Dr. Ashley. Both smiled broad smiles. The time had come to move the party. They headed toward the elevators, with drinks, smiles, and laughs.

Livvy saw that Dr. Ashley was as excited as she was nervous. It was her fourth time being with them. It reminded Livvy of how she had felt years ago, the time she was going to the hotel with her lover in San Diego. Recently, when she had gone to the door of her former love nest in Manhattan Beach, she found a Greek man now lived there along with his lover — a black man — and two small dogs. They had no idea who Carpe was. They invited her in, offered her tea. She sat with them awhile, told them her story. They had cried.

Ashley Li asked Livvy, "What are the rules this time, Livvy?"

Livvy snapped out of her trance. "There are no rules this time, Dr. Ashley."

"You're generous with your husband."

"And Dr. Antonio Barrera has learned to be generous with his wife."

"I've missed both of you. This experience has changed my life, for the better."

"This has helped me, helped us, more than you will ever know."

"That's what doctors are for. I'm here to help your heart heal."

Ashley Li kissed Olivia. Tony's hands found their way to Olivia's breasts.

Olivia kissed Tony as Ashley toyed with Olivia's nipples.

Livvy put her hand in the small of Tony's back, eased him toward their companion.

As they made out, Livvy glanced down at her Blahniks.

She stared at the shoes her lover Carpe had bought her during her heated days with him.

TOMMIE

After I left the pool party, I went home with Blue and Mo. Mo got in the shower with me so I could wash her hair; I gave her nine French braids going back toward her neck, then read her a story about princesses, one where I did voices and acted out all of the characters, before I put her in bed. I told Blue I needed to work a couple of hours, said I was going to take my laptop and drive to Starbucks on Sepulveda. I packed up and talked to Blue on Skype as I drove, kept him on my phone as I ordered a green tea and a muffin. I set up my computer and blew him kisses, told him I'd be back home in a couple of hours and to text me if he needed anything. He told me he loved me. I told him I loved him.

I ended the call, packed up my belongings, and headed to my car.

Soon I was punching the code into the gate at Beale Streets's mansion.

As I pulled into his garage I realized I wasn't there because Angela had pissed me off. I was there because I wanted to be there, because I couldn't stay away. It had become about desire, no longer about anger. We were no longer at eight times. We were beyond twenty. This affair had taken on its own life.

I parked in my designated spot in his garage, used my key to enter. The alarm started to count down. It was on the HOME setting to disable all motion detectors when Beale was here. If a window or door opened, the alarm was activated. The home was so large, someone could be in the basement of this mansion and if Beale was upstairs working or sleeping, he'd have no idea he had an intruder. I put in the four-digit code, stopped the countdown, then reset the alarm, put the code in again, set it back to the HOME setting. I hadn't called. I no longer had to call before I came over. I just came over like this was my Shangri-La.

Here nothing went wrong. Here I didn't age. Here I was in utopia, had access to an earthly paradise. I went to the kitchen, made a three-course meal. Tilapia. Mixed veg. Mashed potatoes.

I hummed as I took the elevator up, went to his office. He was at his desk, working.

He whispered, "Hey, baby."

"How was your day?"

"It just got better."

"Come eat."

I kissed him and took his hand, had him come downstairs. We sat at the dining room table, had dinner like we were a family. Not long after, we were almost naked, on the living room floor, my feet on his chest as he sucked my toes and eased inside me as far as he could, then stroked me in slow motion.

Minutes after that, we staggered to the elevator, went upstairs, and fell across the bed.

TOMMIE

Over Beale's sound system, throughout his home I could hear the clear, soulful voice of Tink singing she wanted someone to treat her like she was somebody. After a few minutes of being intimate, I rested my head on Beale's chest. I hummed and hand-combed my wild hair as I looked at the time, saw I had at least another free hour. I checked my cellular, returned text messages to Livvy and Frankie, sent a flirty message to Blue, told him the writing was flowing and to check on Mo, then rose long enough to kiss Beale, shared his taste with him as he had shared my taste with me, then rested my head on his chest again, my hand automatically reaching for his penis. He was still hard. I think he took Viagra for kicks. Virile men took that blue pill the same way weight lifters took steroids. They didn't need to but loved the advantage, the results, and the ability to be super in bed. I wondered if Viagra caused cancer too.

We got up, naked, walked to the bathroom, washed up.

I asked, "How old was your birth mother?"

"Very young. Looks like she was in middle school when she was carrying me."

"Middle school? Are you sure? She could be as young as thirty-seven. In LA forty is the new thirty, so if she's in shape, you and your mother could look like siblings more than like mother and son."

"That's the only thing I am sure of. I am trying to obtain the sealed documents. I'm very close to finding her. I can feel it. My adoptive parents don't support my doing this, but they understand. My identifying so strongly with this part of my heritage, it has left them both perplexed and disappointed. They think it is a horrible investment to buy a home this size in a black neighborhood. They say I am a fool for having the best house in the area. It will be impossible to sell, unless I find another fool."

"Maybe you shouldn't go down that road. Maybe your adoptive parents are right."

"Every child who has been abandoned wants to know why. We send probes into the universe because on the most basic level we want to know who we are. We want to know our parents. We want to trace our heritage back to the start, back to the big bang, back to God. We want to find God to ask why he created us and abandoned us. Why did he forsake us? Were we not good enough to keep?"

"Wow. Never thought about it like that."

"I tend to overthink things."

"Your adoptive family has money. You could kick back, live the life of the rich, chill out day and night in Argentina or live in another country. Why do you work so hard, the way you do?"

"I want to be seen. I want to be found. I want to be famous so my mother can see me, so my father can see me, and they will have to know it's me and that I am here. I tell my story so they can hear and put two and two together, so they can come out of hiding. They know I am closing in on them."

"You want them to acknowledge you."

"They created me; they owe me at least that much."

"What if they are dead?"

"That's the only thing that would stop me, but still I would seek out relatives. I need to look into their face, see the eyes, not only of people who have my complexion but who look like me, who hold a strong resemblance to me. I was the odd one in every photo my adoptive parents took. I was the odd one. I was the one asked to play any black character in any play that had a black character. I was the one they looked to in February, as if I were the expert on that month and the history of my unknown people."

"You're right. I had parents. Wonderful parents. I can't relate to that part of you that's missing."

We left the bedroom, then he led me to the elevator. He pushed the button for the basement level, then cornered me, kissed me. The elevator stopped and we stepped into the room filled with pinball machines, video games, a pool table, all the accoutrements of a well-appointed man cave.

I sat at the Ms. Pac-Man machine. He played some sort of shoot-'em-up game next to me.

After I lost, I stood behind Beale, sucked his ear as he shot *Walking Dead* zombies.

Beale asked, "Do your sisters know about us?"

"No one knows about us. Keep it that way if you know what's good for you."

"Frankie has no idea? You don't girl-talk and talk about the sex?"

"You wouldn't try and hit on Frankie just to piss me off, would you?"

He gave up on killing the zombies, picked me up, carried me to the pool table, laid me down gently, went down south, found that space where my legs meet, and filled my emptiness with his tongue.

I pushed his head away, sat up, panicked, said, "I think I hear my phone ringing."

I ran, bypassed the elevator, and when I made it back upstairs, I saw I had more than a dozen text messages. Blue had called four times back to back. So had Livvy. So had Frankie.

I said, "Something's happened. Something bad has happened. I have to go."

Beale was right there, had followed me. "I'm not letting you leave."

"Everyone is calling me. Something is going on."

"You promised me two hours."

I snapped, "Damn it, I have to go."

He grabbed my clothes and I freaked out. I screamed at him, felt my heart about to burst in my chest. He took my clothes and ran into the bathroom, locked the door. I banged on the door. My cellular rang, Blue's ringtone. That made me fall apart. I banged on the door harder. Then I tried to kick it open, only managed to hurt my foot. My phone rang. It was an old-school Sister Sledge song. "We Are Family."

And just like that I was overwhelmed with shortness of breath, had a racing heart.

Trembling. Shaking. Could barely swallow, felt like I was choking. I was out of my body floating above myself.

He made me wait twenty minutes. Blue kept calling, but I couldn't answer my phone, not here.

Beale opened the door and tossed me my clothes. There was no time to fight. I rushed to get my clothes back on, then growled and pushed his big screen over, let it crash to the floor.

I threw his golden key back at him. I cursed and told him this shit was over.

I screamed, "That was immature, Beale. That was so fucking immature."

I ran out of his home, backed out of his garage, scared that Blue would be on the other side of Beale's gate waiting on me. Wondered if my phone had given up my longitude and latitude. The gate opened on an empty avenue. I sped through the gate, went to the top of Kenway, then pulled over at Valley Ridge, not knowing whom to call first, not knowing if my world had fallen apart, wishing I had never met Beale Streets. I called Blue. I called and hoped Monica was okay. He answered on the first ring.

When I made it to the Fais Do-Do on West Adams, the police and a fire truck were outside; so was a small crowd. Blue was there, Mo standing next to him. Blue looked at my hair, at my clothes, then Monica came over to me, put her arms around my legs. Frankie had on red high heels and a short black dress that had Saturday-night cleavage, her new hairstyle as popping. She was ranting, furious. The flashing lights, being out at an adult place — it was a different world for Mo. Livvy and Tony pulled up ten minutes later. Frankie had been sneaky and gone out with Daniel, went to see Sy Smith perform at the club named after a Cajun party. While Frankie was inside, someone had broken the windows out of her Audi, poured cheap red, yellow, and blue paint over the interior, then dumped what looked like two gallons of battery acid all over everything from the hood to the trunk.

Someone said the damage would be at least thirty thousand dollars.

TOMMIE

Frankie's car had to be towed. It was left in front of a repair shop on La Brea and Florence. It would have to be left there until her State Farm people could send someone to look at it. It was easy to see that the car was totaled. Frankie had told the police she had no idea why her car had been targeted. She had been at the club only twenty minutes, so that made it seem like whoever did it did it the moment she went inside of the club. LA was a city where if someone felt like you had cut in front of their car while you were driving, they would become offended, speed up, honk their horns, then pull up next to you and wave a loaded handgun at you while cursing you out. Or wait for you to park and fuck up your car. This was the kind of madness they would do, then run like a bitch-baby. Two hours later we were all back home. Livvy and Tony had dropped Frankie off at home. Blue put Mo back in bed,

257

stayed with her until she went to sleep. She had seen things I wished she hadn't seen, Frankie being hysterical in her hoochie-momma dress at the top of the list.

Blue asked, "Sure you don't want to pack a bag and go spend the night at Frankie's?"

"I'll check on her in the morning. Why did you ask me that? That was random."

"This would be a good opportunity for you to leave and not come back until the morning."

"What do you mean? I've rarely *not* spent the night at home, and when I did, Mo was with me."

"Just thought you might want to go stay with your sister, be gone from here for the night."

"Why would I want to be gone from here for the night?"

"You would have to tell me. I have no idea. But this is your chance to get away, alone."

Blue showered. I showered when he was done. We dressed for bed. He wore boxers. I wore a Superman T-shirt, no panties. I dressed the way I usually did on Saturday nights.

He was in bed, on his side, near the wall, his back to me. He had never turned his back to me.

I asked, "Sleep?"

In a dark tone he asked, "Where were you tonight, Tommie?"

"Starbucks. We were on Skype. Did you forget? We talked until I started to work."

"An hour later, when Frankie called here, I couldn't reach you. She couldn't reach you."

"My phone was on silent while I tried to focus on my work. Is that a crime?"

"After Frankie called, I called your cellular five or six times. No answer. Then I was worried something had happened to you. That's why I called Starbucks. They said you weren't there."

"I was there. Maybe I had gone to the bathroom. Maybe the worker had cataracts."

"Why are there condoms in your car?"

"Condoms?"

"Why do you have condoms in the pocket of the jacket that's hidden in the bag in your car?"

"That jacket is Frankie's jacket. Those condoms are her condoms."

"Are you seeing someone, Tommie?"

"The condoms were in there already when I borrowed the jacket, and she has no idea I borrowed it. I took it from her closet to wear if you and me went out, or if Monica was gone for the night I was going to wear that and the shoes and surprise you and I never checked the goddamn pockets. Glad you did."

"You have an answer for everything."

"Are we ever going to talk about you getting the vasectomy reversed? When will you have an answer for that? We really don't have much to talk about. I'm not going to keep shacking up, not going to keep living in *concubinage.* If we're not going to get it reversed so we can get married and start a family, I might as well move out and let you and Monica keep the house and then I can just get my own apartment."

"This is what you asked for, for us to live together. You asked for this house, not me."

"That was when I thought you had ambition, Blue."

"I was doing fine, Tommie. Before I met you, before you came into Mo's life, we were fine. I take care of my daughter. That's where my ambition, where my energy, is focused. Tell me what you have added to my life. Tell me what value you have, besides being here, becoming a burden, and complaining day after day about something. Every time you complain, you suck the damn oxygen out of my lungs."

"Damn, Blue."

"Don't mess with me, Tommie. I deal with

emotional and financial pressures every day, and I never say a goddamn word. Most men would have sent their child to live with a relative, or would have given her to her mother, but I did what I had to do. Don't try to make it seem like I have no damn ambition. I'm not Tony, don't make money like Franklin, but you ain't no Livvy and you damn sure ain't no Frankie."

"I'm sorry I said that, Blue."

"Don't insult me, Tommie. I have put three meals a day on the table and kept a roof over Monica's head and I have done that without fail. There are many days that I would rather be doing something else, and there are days where I wish . . . I didn't have . . . I wish I didn't have this responsibility. I want to go skiing, I want to sleep in on Saturdays and Sundays, but those days are long gone. I want to have a day of peace and no one giving me stress or needing me for nothing. There are days I feel *stuck,* when I feel *depressed,* when I feel *trapped,* when I wish I were free to hang out like Mo's mother hangs out, when I wish I had my weekends to myself and could stop being an adult and could've kept pursuing my screenwriting. I feel lost at times too, but I am here, and I am doing what I am supposed to do to make sure that little girl will one day be able to do better. Ambition? My ambition is to make sure Monica will be able to do the things I will never be able to do. She will be able to see the world the way Frankie has, will travel like Livvy and Tony have, and I will cherish every postcard she sends me. Ambition. My ambition is in front of your face, Tommie. Until you can do better than what I do, don't insult me. A black man puts everything on hold to take care of his seed, and you tell me I have no ambition? Do you know how many shitty jobs I have taken, how many hours I work to make sure my daughter will have a better life?"

Seconds passed. The tension was like a fire, filled the room with invisible smoke.

He grabbed a pillow, then stopped at the hall closet long enough to yank down a blanket.

He marched into the living room, settled on the oversize, secondhand sofa.

My heart ached. I looked for the therapist, but she had left me to face this moment alone.

I went down the hallway, checked on Mo before I took cautious steps to the front of the house.

I stood in the door frame, gazed through the darkness at him as I shifted foot to foot.

Silence stood between us as tears rained down my face.

I said, "I didn't mean it. I swear on my parents' graves I wish I had never said that."

"I have never once said anything about leaving. I have never vanished during the day or at night. You know where I am at all times. I don't delete text messages from my phone. Don't drag it out. Leave."

I stood over Blue. I bumped him with my knee. Blue moved over and I made myself comfortable on the sofa, in his arms. A moment later, Monica ran into the living room and saw us on the sofa. She stood in front of us. I heard her crying. I couldn't see her clearly, but I heard her labored breathing.

I asked, "What's wrong, Mo?"

"Mommy, I had a nightmare about Auntie Frankie. I saw her car on fire."

Blue said, "Oh, no. Sorry I woke you and took you down there, Monica, but I didn't have another choice. Auntie Frankie called and she was upset, so we needed to be there for her right then."

I said, "It was just a dream."

"Can I call her to make sure she's okay?"

"We'll call her first thing in the morning."

"In my dream Uncle Franklin was in the car with her."

Blue said, "He's not your uncle anymore.

When people go away, when they pretend to be something but are really something else, when they lie, you're nothing to them, so they are nothing to you. He was a liar. He broke Auntie's heart. Never care about someone who breaks your heart."

His words were to her, but I felt like they were directed at me.

Blue and I moved over, made room for her to climb up.

I wrapped my arms around her. She was my life vest. She was my child.

Soon the phone rang again. It was Livvy calling this time. She and Tony were heading over to Sepulveda in Westchester. Someone had broken out the window at Frankie's real estate business.

I said, "You're joking."

In a worried tone Livvy asked, "What the hell is going on?"

"I have no idea."

Blue leapt to his feet, hurried and dressed, grabbed his keys, and went to help my sister. I called Frankie's number, but it went straight to voice mail. She had to be on the other line with the police.

I called Livvy back, but she didn't answer either. I kept the phone in my hand.

Monica and I stayed on the sofa, waiting

to hear what the damn problem was this time.

Blue's rage-filled monologue, the confession of his angst, it echoed, resounded inside of me.

I whispered, "Ambition."

TOMMIE

Two hours later, Blue came back home.

I heard his car pull up, saw the lights come on inside. He searched the house, didn't see me, then came to the back door, saw the light was on in the backyard. I was out on Mo's swing set, on the end swing, slowly moving back and forth, the metal chain creaking with each movement, needing some WD-40 to remove the unwanted friction. If only all friction could be fixed so easily. He came out and sat in the swing on the other end, left a space between us. He started swinging, added creaky sounds to mine.

I asked, "What happened to the drama queen this time?"

"Someone had thrown a cinder block through her business window."

"Same night her car was messed up."

"She's tight-lipped. Says it's two random events. Same night. Hours apart."

"Franklin?"

"Hope not. He's up in the Bay. But he's not that kind of guy. He's all mouth."

"Do you talk to him?"

"He calls to check in from time to time. He misses Monica."

"He misses kicking it with you and Tony and watching the games all day on Sundays."

"That too. We had become a band of brothers; now he is kicked out of the brotherhood. He misses hanging with us."

"Don't talk to him. Don't *ever* let Monica talk to him. He betrayed us all."

"He just wanted to know if I thought he had a chance with Frankie."

I took a deep breath, nostrils flaring. "Thanks for being there for my sister."

"No problem. She's my sister. Same as Livvy. We're all family."

Friction. Friction. Friction.

Then the sound stopped when we ceased moving.

We sat still, the cool breeze covering us. Police helicopters appeared in the distance. They were on the hunt for someone in the vicinity of Rodeo Road and MLK.

I said, "I hope another black man doesn't get gunned down. In the old days, in the Westerns, you never shot a man in the back.

Anyone who shot a man in the back was a coward. If a cop shoots a citizen in the back like that, if he shoots a man in the back then lies about it, that cop is worse than a coward."

"It's open season on black people, and too many of the cowards have badges and guns. We're paying for our own murders with our tax dollars."

"This has been going on since before Rodney King."

Blue said, "This season of hate and disrespect started in 1619. That's how long the black man has been mistreated in this country, since the first slave ship landed here."

"Now it's something new on video every damn day."

"Same problem every day; it's exhausting. That's why black people are suffering from racial fatigue syndrome."

"When anything goes on too long, it wears you down. Nobody wants to have to deal with negativity day after day."

"I agree. Negativity can change your spirit."

"It wears you down because you can't see it ending."

"Again, I agree."

We were no longer talking about cops and

racism. The conversation had evolved and the negativity we were addressing was our own. Being with Blue used to feel perfect.

He asked me what I was thinking. I said what was on my mind. I didn't hide my true feelings. We were beyond that now.

He said, "Being with you used to feel perfect, Tommie."

"Used to."

"Used to."

We watched the sky, stared up at the helicopter like it was our own problems circling us, chasing us, and trying to shine its light down on us. There was no escaping where we were.

Blue asked, "What do you want to do now, Tommie?"

"I don't know."

"You're at a fork in the road."

I whispered, " 'Two roads diverged in a yellow wood.' "

"And I have to let you know, you can't travel both. I won't tolerate it. Don't test me."

"And don't test me. Neither can you, Blue. You can't travel both. I know you love me, but I need more. You can't expect me to be a wife and to never be able to be a mother. I won't tolerate that either."

He said, "I know you won't. You

shouldn't."

"If I am to be your wife, I have to fully be your wife."

" 'If.' Everything is 'if' now. Condoms are in your car, and now we are at the 'if' part. Those condoms have been in your car awhile. I keep waiting for the day one goes missing."

"You've been spying on me."

"Not spying. Just losing trust. Am I wrong, Tommie?"

I wiped tears from my eyes.

Blue sighed, his hands opening and closing on the chains supporting his swing.

He paused, whispered, "I wish I had met you before I met Angela."

"Everything would have been perfect."

"Not perfect. Just would have had different issues."

"True. There will always be issues."

"If I had met you before Angela, I wouldn't have Mo."

"Who are we without Mo between us? Who would we be then? Would we have connected?"

"You're my heartbeat, Tommie."

"Don't make me cry. How can you do that? Make me so angry I can't breathe, then say one sentence and make me cry?"

"You do the same to me."

"You're my heartbeat."

"You're my heart. You made this cold soul warm again. I don't know how I existed before I met you. Don't know how I will after."

"You made me forget this burn on my face. You made me forget my heart was ever broken."

"You are my heartbeat and the beat is getting slower. I have to prepare for it to stop."

I heard an angelic voice at the back door. "Mommy?"

Blue and I jumped, surprised the cherub of the house was awake and on night patrol.

Blue asked, "Why does she always call out for you first?"

"Girl power. Stop hating, Blue."

Blue called out, "Go back to bed, Monica."

"You're back home, Daddy?"

"I'm home, Monica. Why are you up?"

"Is Mommy gone to help Auntie Frankie?"

I called out, "Come here, Monica."

"I can come outside when it's dark?"

"Yeah. You can this time."

"Are any bears or rattlesnakes or ugly people out there?"

"Bears are in the forest and rattlesnakes are in the mountains." I chuckled. "Come here."

Monica came outside, paused, then went back inside, ran to her bedroom to get her trainers.

Blue looked at me. "She has to be up early for school."

I said, "It's about memories. When she's older, she will remember being on a swing with her dad in the middle of the night while the rest of the world was sleeping. She'll remember you being a fun dad."

"You remember your dad being a fun dad?"

"I remember back rides and going to movies and him picking me up from school every day. I remember being jealous when he started giving Frankie and Livvy rides on my favorite back too. I had to share my father's back with them."

"Weren't Livvy and Frankie too old for back rides?"

"You're never too old for back rides, Blue. I still like back rides. You haven't given me a back ride in a long time."

"Didn't know you wanted a back ride."

"I shouldn't have to ask. Mo shouldn't have to ask."

"I'm not much of a fun dad, am I? I work too much. I worry too much. I get too serious. I've done it all wrong."

"You're a good man, Blue. You're one of

the best."

"But am I fun? Does Monica like being around me, or does she tolerate me? Would she rather be with her mother? She's a girl and maybe I'm wrong for fighting to have custody. Maybe I did this wrong."

"If she were with her mother she'd go wild. You'd end up watching Hannah Montana change into Miley Cyrus in your own home, under your own roof, one bottle of Patrón and a blunt at a time."

"She always does what you say and ignores me or asks you for the last word on an issue."

"I'm closer to her age. It's like we're sisters and you're always acting like you're our father."

"Jokes, always jokes."

"You are more fun when I show you how to be more fun."

Mo came outside, looked around for bears, then ran to us and climbed into the other swing.

She said, "Don't argue. Don't fight. People who love each other aren't supposed to fight."

I said, "We weren't fighting."

"You were fighting in my dream. I woke up to tell you to stop fighting and go to sleep."

Blue said, "She's a McBroom."

"Yeah. She is. My mother had dreams and visions and saw crazy things in her head too."

"Mommy, Daddy, swing higher. Make your feet touch the stars like this."

"Mo —"

"Blue, be the fun dad. Just do it. Learn from her as we teach her."

A second police helicopter light disrupted the desert city's darkness a few blocks away. They were in the direction of Slauson. At the same time police sirens also lit up Crenshaw Boulevard. The constant din in this EBT-accepted area reminded me that I wasn't inside a swank house on the hill where no sound penetrated the walls. Blue, Mo, and I, we sat in the swings. Ours was a used swing set we had bought on Craigslist after we'd moved in. We went back and forth, made creak after creak, each time sounding squeakier, louder. They laughed, Blue and Monica, father and daughter, tried to outdo each other. Mo was very competitive. Mo called for me to try to beat her to the stars. I accepted the challenge and joined in on the competition, went higher and higher, higher and higher.

Our feet touched the stars, tickled constellations.

We made our little backyard our own private Disneyland. Tonight, in the middle of the night, this was better than being in a private booth at Nic's Beverly Hills, a Sofitel luxury hotel, or having dinner at a top-of-the-line restaurant like Mastro's.

Throat tightened. Face warm. More tears fell from my face. They couldn't see me cry, but I cried.

As we talked and laughed, I knew I would always remember that moment. That moment right there; if I could have put time in a bottle, I would have saved that moment. I didn't want it to end. I wanted to swing forever.

It would be hard to leave there. But I knew that I had to go. It was already written.

Blue had to do what was best for him, and I had to do what was best for me. My money had all been invested in this house, in this family. I needed to be able to take care of myself when I walked out of that door. I needed to be independent.

It became clear to me then. I needed to stop spending my money on another woman's child so I could save enough money to start over. I had to prepare myself to move on.

LIVVY

Livvy's Spa was as amazing as one built on the deep-blue waters of Lake Mohonk.

When Olivia McBroom-Barrera walked through the back entrance, loyal clients were waiting for facials, manis, pedis, and exotic massages; a few movie stars also waited to get waxed and pampered.

There was a call from a celebrity in Hollywood, one who didn't want their name given out.

That was not unusual. The word was out. They had heard of Livvy's Spa, or Livvy Barrera, and wanted her to come to their home to massage, wax, and vajazzle them for their husband's birthday.

It was last minute, an emergency, and the client would have to pay a ridiculous fee for Livvy to go to the edges of Beverly Hills. To ensure it was legit, the session was paid for in advance by telephone. The celebrity was sending a chauffeur to pick up Livvy and whomever she needed to aid in the service. Livvy packed her products, took her two top estheticians, and within minutes a driver was in the lobby waiting. Tall, dark-skinned, well-built man, bald, wore glasses, had to be in his forties.

"They call me Driver," was all he said before he handed Livvy documents to sign.

It was a nondisclosure agreement. NDAs were common in Hollywood. Livvy wouldn't be able to say she had the unknown celebrity as a client, not unless the client wanted it known.

Her two employees signed the same papers.

Once her bags were loaded and they were in the backseat of the town car, as the chauffeur eased into traffic on Sepulveda and headed north, the curiosity got the best of Livvy.

She asked, "May I ask who the client is?"

"Regina Baptiste."

Her employees gasped. Livvy was stunned.

The chauffeur nodded and said no more.

Again her heart raced. Regina Baptiste was the top actress in Hollywood, if not in the world.

Regina Baptiste turned out to be one of the nicest people Livvy had met in her career.

She allowed Livvy and her two workers to take after-treatment photos and said she could post them on social media. Regina Baptiste tweeted. She also told Livvy she wanted to use Livvy's Spa twice a month, and when she was on location shooting, she wanted to be able to have an esthetician on set.

It was part of her contract, and the studios paid ridiculous money to keep her happy.

Dressed in green Nike sweats, a pink wife-beater, and white sandals, hair pulled into a simple ponytail, Regina Baptiste said, "My driver had to take my husband to a meeting at Sony. Another chauffeur will arrive any moment to take you back. I hope the delay is not too much of an inconvenience."

Livvy said, "Not at all. We are more than happy to be of service to you, Ms. Baptiste."

No one complained about being delayed in the lap of luxury.

They all sat out by the pool as a server brought them drinks. Best happy hour ever.

They were told their new driver had arrived. They thanked Regina Baptiste for her generosity and hospitality, gathered their bags, and with broad smiles and tipsy strolls headed to the stretch limo.

Their new driver stood there, holding the car door open, a smile on her face.

A beautiful brown-skinned woman.

A face that Livvy had thought she'd never see again.

Livvy lost her smile.

The chauffeur looked at Livvy, and for a moment she lost her professional smile as well.

One of her estheticians took her elbow. "Olivia? You okay?"

She chuckled. "I'm fine. It's the wine."

Livvy faced her driver, unblinking, in shock, looked at her face, her eyes.

She said, "Panther. It's you. It's really you."

Equally surprised, the chauffeur responded, "Bird."

"Olivia. My name is Olivia. People call me Livvy."

"Never knew your name. Only knew you as Bird. The woman betrayed."

They stood motionless for a moment, then Olivia nodded, eased inside of the limousine.

Her workers were ecstatic, talked all the way back to Westchester. Livvy spent the entire ride in silence, the partition up, the driver on the other side on her mind. It was Panther. She was a few years older, her hair had changed, she was more fit, but it was the woman Livvy had searched for.

For years Livvy had wanted to see Panther, had tried in vain to find her.

Now that she had found her, she didn't know what to do, what to say.

Livvy was terrified.

When they arrived at Livvy's Spa, the limo took them to the back entrance.

Livvy instructed her estheticians to take their bags inside. Then she stood at the front of the limo, arms folded, facing Panther. She faced a curvaceous woman she had spent time with, but never alone. They had always made love with Carpe as the focal point, as part of a three-headed beast.

Livvy said, "Very small world, Panther. Is that what I should call you?"

She nodded. "Livvy's Spa."

"I'm the owner."

"Your surname on the paperwork is Barrera. I had assumed I was picking up a Latina."

"My husband is Latin. Barrera is my married name."

"Worked it out after . . . after that thing with Carpe?"

"Still trying. Hasn't been as easy as I would have hoped. We're different now."

She nodded. "This was awkward. That caught me off guard, seeing you at the mansion."

Livvy said, "Had no idea you were still in Los Angeles. You said you were going back to Atlanta."

"Was. Never left. Still here. This Southern girl is still here."

Livvy said, "What we had, sorry it ended the way it did."

"Well, Bird, I said horrible, vile things."

"You did."

"Might have thrown something at you. I apologize for that. I used to drive by there, then slow down and reminisce."

"Really?"

"It was good for a while."

"It was fun. I enjoyed what we had."

"I hated the way we ended things, those final words."

"I didn't mean to be, but I was so angry at you for a long time."

"It was a hard time for both of us. Glad you're doing okay for yourself."

Livvy said, "You're rocking a fitted suit and now you work for this limo company."

"No, I am part owner with the guy I see. We have a few employees. Funny, Dante was supposed to come pick you up, but he was caught in traffic after an Oceanside run, so I picked up the job."

Livvy said, "Congratulations on the business, on the new life, on everything. You have a business and I have a business and I guess our businesses have brought us back together. Well, two-thirds of us."

Then came the silence, the kind that buffered the start of what she really wanted to ask.

Panther beat Livvy to the question that was burning inside of her.

Panther asked, "Did Carpe come back to you before . . . were you with him again before . . . ?"

"He never contacted me. To be honest, I've looked for him. Did you keep in touch with him?"

"Oh, my God. You have no idea. I assumed you knew."

"What?"

"He's dead."

Livvy paused and her heart raced; she felt her brain start to short-circuit, felt the need to sit down, the need to scream, but she took deep breaths.

Panther said, "Sorry to drop it on you like that, Bird."

"Dead? I don't understand. How could that happen?"

"He was killed, Bird. He was in the islands with his wife when it happened."

"Carpe is dead?"

"Maybe two years ago. Could be three

years. It hit me hard too. Hit me real hard."

The moment Panther said that, tears fell from her eyes, same as she had cried back then.

Livvy was rocked to the core, her shoulders slumped, and she shut down. She had never had a lover die before. But that was inevitable. Death was inevitable for us all, and she knew that.

Livvy whispered, "He's dead. Are you . . . sure? I mean, are you really sure?"

Panther trembled, pulled her full lips in, twisted them, nodded. Leftover love was in her bloodstream. Emotions had risen, lodged in her throat. She was unable to speak.

Livvy said, "I went by there, the place we had. I would park out front."

"It's destroyed now. Someone threw a poor man's grenade through the front window."

"Are you serious? When?"

"Happened not too long ago. They think it was a hate crime."

"Seems like it was just a few days ago . . . I went there . . . looking for. . . . I knocked on the door."

"People assumed they had been attacked because they were gay."

"I met the guys. I told them that I used to

283

lease that apartment. They were kind, invited me in for herbal tea. I told them about us. I told them that me and Carpe . . . and you . . . we were there before them."

"Why did you knock on the door? Why did you go back there after the way you left me?"

Livvy asked Panther, "Why do you go to that area, then slow down when you pass by there?"

They held eye contact.

Livvy saw the memories in Panther's eyes.

Livvy said, "Carpe changed me. You changed me. I wish I had never left. I've missed you."

Panther shook her head as if those days were behind her, then eased into the stretch limo. She drove away. Livvy stood in the parking lot, motionless, cars hitting speed bumps as they passed, the echo of planes floating into LAX, horns blowing, music blasting, the din of traffic coming from all directions.

Panther left her now as abruptly as she had left Panther back then. Livvy was stunned. On the heels of Panther's departure, Frankie exited the back door to her real estate business, her office being in the same block-long structure on Sepulveda Boulevard near LAX. Frankie's company was only two businesses away from Livvy's spa. Teary-eyed, Livvy wanted to avoid her sister, but she had been seen. Frankie called her name and headed her way, jogged that way in a hurry. Something was wrong. She could tell. Livvy wiped her eyes, wiped away tears, shock, and memories. She knew whatever was going on with Frankie, it had to do with her ex Franklin. That jerk had become the thorn in everyone's side. Livvy had never liked that bastard from the get-go.

Frankie said, "There is a long line out in front of your spa."

"What do you mean? Traffic is backed up? It's always bumper-to-bumper."

"No, *people.* There is a long line of women fighting to get inside your spa."

"You're joking, right?"

"It looks like Black Friday at Walmart at your front door."

When they stepped inside Livvy's Spa, one of the receptionists came to her in a hurry. Livvy could hear the rumble in her usually peaceful place. She felt a new energy. She felt the anxiety.

Since they had posted the selfie with Regina Baptiste, it had hit Instagram, had been given likes on Facebook, and been retweeted thousands of times. Due to that one photo, the phones had been on fire. They accepted walk-ins, and the waiting area was filled with customers. Some waved platinum cards.

Frankie stepped forward, helped get people calmed down and organized.

Livvy had one thought. The man she had longed for day and night, the man she had pined for for years, was no more. And there was no one she could call to confess her pain, no way she could grieve out loud. He was no longer among the living. And no one had notified her of his passing. She had been nothing to him. He had meant too much to her.

Livvy greeted her customers with smiles, then excused herself to one of the bathrooms, locked the door, bit into her hand, felt a pounding chest pain, had difficulty breathing, had feelings of unreality, an extreme level of fear and detachment from herself, then bit harder, almost hard enough to draw blood.

Soon she was able to control her breathing.

Then another wave hit her.

She shivered, grieved as tears fell from her closed eyes across her fist.

She was free.

The apartment was destroyed.

Carpe was dead.

Panther wanted nothing to do with her.

It was done.

Finally Livvy was free.

But this did not feel like freedom.

Tears fell, created a torrent as she bounced her leg and shook her head over and over.

Not everyone wanted freedom.

Not everyone knew what to do when they had been released.

FRANKIE

The madness continued.

At seven thirty in the morning, after putting in my required roadwork with Tommie and Livvy before the sun came up, as rush hour was changing into the hours of road rage, I had parked in the expansive lot behind my real estate company. There was no street parking on Sepulveda until after the road rage ended. Dressed in business attire, I was channeling the stylish and forever-iconic Diahann Carroll, yet behind my good-morning grin I was nervous, so nervous I almost dropped the venti latte from Starbucks I carried in my right hand. I looked across the lot at the other businesses, felt like I had been followed. But these days it always felt like I was being followed. Paranoia. Before I went through the rear entrance of my office, I looked at my new car. My new Maserati. My Audi had been totaled, the check written expeditiously by

State Farm, and then within forty-eight hours I had bought my GranTurismo. I picked up my new hoopty at a police auction for the price of a five-year-old Toyota Corolla. I could sell it for twice what I bought it for within a matter of hours. I never paid top dollar for anything, except for love. Took that philosophy from that handbook of the rich. One of the guys in our running group was a top cop and had hooked me up. As I rolled the streets of LA in my new ride my message was this: You can't stop me from rising to the top. Burn it, I'll get a better one. But to be on the safe side, I had parked directly in front of the business's security cameras. I wasn't stupid. I had too many haters living in my world. Mrs. Crazy Carruthers sent e-mails over and over. The bitch wouldn't dial back the crazy.

Franklin claimed that he had nothing to do with what had happened to my car.

He said he had nothing to do with the window at my office being bricked the same night.

After I had called Franklin and made harsh accusations, he took that as a sign, as a ray of hope.

I told him, "Hope is the worst evil of all because it prolongs the torment."

"I'm not giving up, Frankie."

My voice weakened, splintered, and I could barely say, "Leave me alone, Franklin."

"Look at that engagement ring, put it back on, and tell me you don't want us back together."

I hung up on him, wiped my eyes, took a dozen deep breaths, screamed into a pillow, hollered out my pent-up madness until my throat was raw, then I shivered and turned off my phone.

I still didn't want my family involved, but I wanted this fixed. Desperate, I made a few calls, asked around. One of my trustworthy neighbors, one who was also my business adviser and my accountant, Geneviève Forbes, gave me a name and a number. It was for a man known only as Driver.

I took the number and put it on my refrigerator.

That night, at home, I sat in my Batgirl pajamas and gazed at the engagement ring.

I gazed at it as my cellular rang once again with Franklin's romantic ringtone.

I answered, "Why do you keep calling?"

"I want to see you, Frankie."

"Ride a drone to the Middle East and see your wife."

"I love you and will do anything to make

290

this work. Just tell me what to do."

"You made me the clown."

"I'm sorry for what I did, for how you found out, but I'm dying without you, Frankie."

"Obviously you're not dying fast enough. Try cyanide. Heard it works wonders."

"I miss loving you. I miss making love to you. I miss all that we were building."

"You should be incarcerated for what you did."

"Tell me that you don't miss us. Tell me that what we have ain't real."

Then I took the long pause, was consumed by an emotional lull, by memories.

In a soft whisper he repeated, "Tell me you don't miss us. Not the sex. Bowling, doing karaoke, snow skiing, sitting on the sofa looking at Netflix, meeting for lunch, doing long runs together."

It felt like this was the part where the heartbroken woman missed a bad love and, despite his lies and deception, fell prey to her own emotions, took him back in her bed, allowed the poison to be the cure.

He repeated, "Tell me that you don't love me as much as I love you. Tell me that you don't miss the good you felt with me. Those months we were together, they made the rest of the world irrelevant."

I didn't say anything, just stared at the ring as if it held the answer to my dilemma.

He repeated, "Tell me that you don't miss me, Frankie."

"I can't tell you that."

"Tell me that you have stopped loving me."

I paused, struggled, and finally admitted, "I can't tell you that and say it's the truth."

"If you love me, then there is hope. Then we can fix this thing and get back on track."

Now I hated that I had relaxed, surrendered to love, and now he had that power.

I said, "No, you can't come see me. If my sisters found out you came here . . . you can't."

"Tell me where you live and I can park out front. Or I will park a block or two away."

"I can't have you in my neighborhood. You're not welcome in my world anymore."

Hearing his voice made it seem like we'd been together only yesterday.

In a pained Southern accent he said, "Then come see me. Not seeing you is hard."

"I'm not coming to your home."

"Then meet me somewhere. Just you and me. No one will have to know but us."

This was the part when a strong woman said she was done, then crumbled and crept back. I looked at my nightstand, at the engagement ring, the diamond I had dreamed he'd leave on my finger. I placed my hand over my flat belly, where I had wanted to house the next-generation Mc-Broom child.

He whispered, "We left love locks all over the world."

I wiped liquid weakness from my eyes, said, "Yeah. We left at least fifty locks in fifty places."

"The cultural things we did in the motherland. You know we have a spiritual connection."

"It was amazing. It was like our souls had returned home, had left all the ism in the USA behind, and we had arrived where we were loved and cherished, not chastised and ridiculed."

Memories, like quicksand, pulled me under.

The first night in Africa, he gave me thirteen orgasms in one session. He gave me thirteen orgasms in the motherland, at an oceanfront villa in Zanzibar. Never in my life had I felt that way. I cried for an hour, cried for every soul lost during the Middle Passage. I cried and he held me and

rocked me like I was his soul mate. We saw
the sun come up over the motherland.
Intimacy had felt so spiritual. A new record.
That was how my body responded to his,
by achieving orgasm over and over and over.

Those moments and many others spent in
the sun were impossible to forget. You could
melt pearls in vinegar, but memories were
stubborn. Even when Enlightenment and
Hate arrived, Love refused to leave the
building. Franklin had taken me to the *motherland.* We had made passionate love in
Africa. We had left inscribed padlocks all
over the world. It wasn't easy to bury the
memory of your best friend.

Frankie loves Frankie.

The engagement ring sparkled. I went to
the closet, sighed at the mind-blowing Stephen Yearick and YSA Makino 2666 wedding dress, ran my fingers over the incredible Vera Wang I would have worn to the
reception. I would have married him.

I had wanted to make an *intentional* baby
with him. I had tried to make a baby with
him.

This was unfair. This was hell. This was
worse than my first divorce. My first marriage had been a rebellious, youthful mistake, for independence, to act grown, to
have sex, not for love. Franklin had stimu-

294

lated me in a thousand different ways and in many places, physical and geographical.

I asked, "What happened to my car, to my business? Was that your jealousy at play?"

"I'm jealous, not going to lie, but I don't roll like that, Frankie. You know better. That guy you were with, maybe it was because of him. Maybe whoever he's seeing didn't like the idea of him going out with you and attacked your car."

"Why would they attack my car and not his car?"

"It wasn't me, Frankie."

"It was you and I know it was you."

"I love you too much to do that."

"*Love?* You have no idea what love is. I know *love* and *lie* start with the same letter, but they are not synonyms Franklin. You're a liar and the truth does not live inside of you."

"I love you, Frankie. You know I love you."

I ached.

Fissures spread across my soul with each breath.

Franklin said, "Come see me. I need to see you."

I took a deep breath, then whispered, "You're right."

"And I know you still love me too."

"I need to see you. I'll come see you."

I sat on the bed, head throbbing, massaging my temples.

Nobody likes to be bamboozled, led astray.

I picked up my small gun, and after I made sure the clip was loaded, I made a phone call.

FRANKIE

From the front seat of the town car my chauffeur asked, "You okay back there, Miss McBroom?"

I snapped out of my trance, said, "Please, call me Frankie."

"I prefer to call you Miss McBroom."

"I'm as fine as I'm going to be until this is resolved with Franklin Carruthers."

The desert air was crisp, the air conditioner was set at seventy-two degrees, but my palms sweated. As I was driven away from View Park, I evaluated myself. Should've worn a coat, but I didn't have on any heavy clothing, just a pair of skinny jeans, an LA Marathon T, a thin hoodie, and trainers.

I didn't want to put on makeup or dress up and give him the wrong impression. A woman wears a dress, short or long, and a man thinks he's going to be able to raise it up and pull her panties to the side.

This was a reunion, but there would be no uniting.

I held my small purse close to me. I was discontent, had been stalked and demoralized for too damn long. I had contacted a car service used by the movie stars, made what was known as a Dark Call.

That Dark Call connected me to a man known simply as Driver.

Soon Driver eased into the center lane, then turned left from Jefferson Boulevard onto Hetzler and cruised up the snaking hill to Baldwin Hills Scenic Overlook. The park was closed, but the heavy metal barrier that swung across and stopped traffic from going up to the top after-hours had been left open. We passed by a handful of homes situated halfway up the four-hundred-foot hill, all of those cribs on the left. Nothing but darkness was in front of us for the rest of the climb. The night was unsettling. In the distance was a view toward Santa Monica and the lights and traffic on streets and freeways.

I asked, "What would you do, Driver? In this situation? But you're a guy. It's different for men."

"I'm six foot two, two hundred pounds, dark as an open road; people say that I have about as much fat on my body as a sea otter, so not many cross me, and those who have crossed me once have never crossed me twice. I'm paid to be nice and act accordingly. At times I'm paid to be mean. But crazy is crazy, and despite my build and size, once upon a time, a long time ago, I did have a situation like this."

"You had a stalker?"

"Let's focus on you, Miss McBroom. Headlights are coming our way. It's showtime."

My cellular rang and I jumped. It was Livvy calling. My headache magnified.

Driver said, "Ignore that call. Focus on the moment."

"Call ignored. I'm focused."

"Does your enemy have a gun, a rifle, any type of weapon you know about?"

"Not to my knowledge."

"Why are you carrying a gun if there isn't that level of concern?"

"How did you know I have a gun?"

"You're angry and the way you keep touching your purse tells me that something extra is inside. Miss McBroom, don't play me. A breach in trust will create a breach in confidentiality."

"I want to protect myself. I want to scare that fucker the way he has scared me."

"Ever shot a man? Even when it felt justified, have you ever pulled the trigger and killed a man?"

"Have you?"

"Certain questions only go in one direction, Miss McBroom. Have you ever shot or killed someone?"

"No. I have never shot anybody."

"If you think he has a weapon, we leave. You're afraid, and that's fine. If you are afraid and have that gun, you will make a major mistake. If we go to the next phase, you leave your gun on the backseat."

"Fine. I'll hand it to you."

"No you won't. My fingerprints will not be on your weapon, no matter what happens. If a weapon is involved and he gets shot, this meeting will look like a setup. You think the police will see it your way, but you're not a white woman in America, and dying your hair Marilyn Monroe blond wouldn't help."

"*He's* the one stalking me. *He's* the villain. I'm not going to run from him."

"I'm taking the kerchief from my suit pocket, so hand me the clip, drop it in the kerchief. I will lock your things in the glove box. If the police happen to pull up behind us, there is no law against a black woman having a registered and unloaded .380, and it could be from when she had contemplated

300

going to the gun range on Florence earlier in the day."

"Take it. That's the clip. Franklin is getting out of his car."

"Drop your gun in the slot behind my seat, business end pointing down."

"Business end?"

"The part of a weapon that does the damage. The barrel of the gun, point that toward the ground."

"Okay. Business end is down. Dagnamit. My phone is ringing again. One of my sisters is probably —"

"That's me calling you. I want you to recognize the number I'm using. I'm going to ring your phone when time is up. Hate to do this, because this triangulates you by the cell towers, meaning you can be placed here. So let's hope it goes smoothly."

"You can be placed here too, Driver."

"My phone is a throwaway, untraceable. As far as I'm concerned, I'm on the other side of town, listening to the blues and sipping on Jack and Coke."

"Understood. Wish you had let me keep my gun and given me a throwaway. All I want to do is shoot him twice and start singing 'He had it coming.' I'll even crank up 'Cell Block Tango' and dance like Mýa while I scream the tune."

"No need to bust a cap and make it a Broadway musical. Don't get nervous. I'm looking out for you."

"I'm used to being independent; reaching out for assistance, asking for help — this is hard."

"Should Franklin Carruthers be allowed to touch you?"

Memories came in a flash. I answered, "No. Never again."

"You hesitated. Are you sure?"

"Yes. I don't want his hands, not one finger, to touch me ever again."

"He will be advised."

FRANKIE

Driver opened the car door, eased out one solid muscle at a time. In his black suit, with his midnight complexion, he was ominous. He glowered toward Franklin Carruthers. Franklin started coming his way but stopped. Unmoving, Driver let seconds pass, measured the threat, and came to a conclusion before he opened my door. I did as he told me, stood next to the car and waited in the chilling breeze, the desert's dry air like naked ice on my skin. Driver adjusted his gloves, headed toward Franklin, marched at an unrushed, antagonistic pace, his wing-tip shoes crunching over gravel, those dark hands in black leather mitts that now looked like fighting gloves, hands in fists that looked like iron boulders ready to demolish a building made of lies and disrespect.

Franklin's anxious-yet-troubled voice came through my phone. "Who are you?"

"If I wanted you to know who I am, I would have introduced myself. All you need to know is this, Carruthers: Miss McBroom is under my watch. Here are the ground rules for the way this meeting will go."

Franklin grunted, listened to the rules. A weekend warrior faced a real warrior.

Driver stepped back and reached inside his pocket. Franklin jumped back and his hands went up. He expected a gun. Driver pulled out a cellular, took a dozen photos of Franklin, flashes like lightning. Franklin didn't make a move. No backchat. He didn't tug on Superman's cape.

Driver patted Franklin down, made sure he was unarmed, then took a half dozen steps backward before he turned, came back across the lot, walked up to me as if he had been civilized from the womb.

"If you want me to monitor the conversation, Miss McBroom, leave the phone on."

"I will turn the phone off, Driver. It might get too personal."

"Three minutes start when you're six feet from him."

"Six feet."

"Don't get any closer to Carruthers than a dead man in his grave is to the people still living."

FRANKIE

I took slow steps, moved across the lot, and confronted Franklin. As I moved closer, as my heart raced, the way he stood, Franklin Carruthers was just as handsome as he had been the day I had met him, still had a body that looked like it was chiseled from stone, and his dreadlocks were as perfect now as they had been then, only down the middle of his back. I remembered that first moment I looked up and saw him in my field of vision, still remembered the jeans, a T-shirt that had 205 across the front, and a silver earring dangling from his ear. That day he had on running shoes. He was pretty much dressed the same way.

He was angry to the fiftieth power. Then he had a clear view of me, of the new me.

This relationship hadn't been about sex. He wasn't just a random guy I had used as a booty call, or vice versa. This relationship had been about love. Now it was about betrayal and heartbreak. You break up with someone, and they know too many of your goddamn secrets to make you feel safe.

He frowned and said, "What's this all about, Frankie? Who is that guy?"

"What he is to me, that's none of your business."

"You had him search me? Do you think I'd harm you?"

I said, "Catch."

He saw the small box I tossed toward him. He caught the package, opened it. Inside was the engagement ring he'd given me. I wished I could throw all of the memories back to him, every last one. I wished I could give him back every kiss, hug, laugh, smile, and lie. Wished I hadn't been so gullible.

He said, "I want you to keep this. This will blow over and you'll want to have it on your finger."

"Three minutes, Franklin. Then I start to sing 'Auld Lang Syne' as I moonwalk back to my ride."

"Can't believe you cut your dreadlocks."

"Two minutes, fifty-seven seconds, Franklin."

He dropped the ring into his shirt pocket, nodded. "So, now I'm back to being Franklin."

"I wanted to see you and tell you face-to-face, for the last time, that this shit is done."

"*We're not done.* I love you too much not to find a way to make this work. You are extraordinary. Do you not understand that? How can I be with you and then go back to dancing with ordinary women?"

"*We're done.* It was all one big lie."

"If I had told you everything at the start, would you have wanted to know me? To travel with me? Or would you have seen me as a loser?"

"I would not have seen you as a liar. When a woman sees a man as a liar, then he is a loser."

"I love you, Frankie."

I took a deep breath, my voice unsteady. "If you love me so damn much, why did you lie?"

"Fear of losing someone makes you afraid of being judged by the truth."

"Here is my truth. Take me out of your love triangle. I am no longer your damn sidepiece."

"You were never my sidepiece. I never had sex with her while I was with you."

"*While I was with you.* Of course not. It's impossible for one dick to fill two orifices at the same time. *While you weren't with me,* who knows what the hell you was doing or whose orifice you filled."

307

"Did you hear what I just told you? I haven't slept with her in two years."

"Don't contact me ever again, and advise your bitch to do the same. I had printed the book of e-mails to show you, but I left them on my dining room table. The bitch has sent me over five hundred messages. I have never responded."

"I'm sorry. I'm two hundred levels of sorry, and I hope you find it in your heart to forgive me. I will do whatever it takes to make this relationship work, Frankie. Just tell me what to do to get you back."

"Today the bitch went too far and made negative comments about Monica being bi-racial."

"She said something offensive about Monica?"

"That bitch's disgusting comments about Mo being biracial was what led me here, Franklin."

"Did you tell Blue and Tommie?"

"No. Your wife is overseas and I'm telling you to contact the military, speak to her commanding officer, write a letter to the president, do whatever you have to do to make her cease and desist. You caused this drama. I don't need my family tripping over this bull. Man up and squash it."

"Ignore her. With any luck, she'll finally

get what's coming to her while she's overseas."

"You played me. You got me in bed. You
won. If it makes you happy, I will make you
a plaque and give you a trophy to honor the
way you got over on me. I will take out a
full-page ad in the *Times* and say I should
have known better and acknowledge that
you won the get-the-pussy game you
played."

"*This wasn't a game.* I met you. I fell in
love. I am *not* going to lose you over this
shit."

"Stop texting, stop calling me, stop sending e-mails, or I will take this to the police,
Franklin."

He paused, stunned. "Wow. The police.
Because I love you and send you love letters?"

"Look up *stalker* in the dictionary and you
will see you and your wife's wedding photo."

"You'd go to the police and say I'm a
stalker? You know what that would do to my
business?"

"I should've done that from day one. I
will go file a report tonight if I have to."

"Sure you want to do that, Frankie? I've
worked hard to get where I am. Don't go
and lie."

"I just need you to leave me and my family the fuck alone."

"You have sent me a lot of mail too. I guess you've been stalking me as well."

"I sent you mail when we were together, before I found out about the secret wife. I have not sent you one letter, other than the cease-and-desist e-mail from months ago, which you obviously ignored."

"When we were happy, you sent me a lot of mail. Lots of photos to get me through the night."

"Oh, what, now that your feelings are hurt and the rejection has set in, a little black-mail?"

"I have the photos we never wanted any-one to see but us. I have more than that."

"You stole the GoPro from my bedroom. That didn't belong to you."

"Yeah, I have it. Was wondering if you had missed it and why you hadn't called for it."

"You stole it. You broke into my house and stole it."

"I took it the last night I was at your house. When you locked yourself in the bathroom, I put it in my car. I wasn't going to leave that with you, not with you being angry. You could have blackmailed me."

"I want it back."

"Would be a shame if everything on the GoPro, if all of those hours of you and me traveling the world and making love in those foreign countries, if that intense night with us in Africa, ended up online."

"I have personal things that you sent me as well, Franklin. I'm sure everyone would love to see a picture of your dick and see how you had it altered in South America. Your dick is ugly, by the way."

"You didn't complain when it was inside you."

"It will never win a Pretty Dick contest, that's for damn sure."

He nodded. "You're a tough one. You fight. You are like no other woman I've ever met."

"Thought you were different. I was in love with you. Felt comfortable with you. Trusted you."

"Frankie, I can't get you out of my system, and I know you feel the same way."

"Have you tried three or four coffee enemas back-to-back? Worked for me. Got rid of candida, flushed out parasites, and finally detoxified feelings for your lying ass out of my system at the same time."

My phone rang. I looked down at the number and pushed ignore, then waved at Driver.

I said, "I'm not stupid. I know what's going on. How much money will it take to end this? How much do I have to pay you to have you return my stolen GoPro? Tell me your price, Franklin."

"Don't make me laugh. I don't need your money. I've never wanted your money."

"How much to have my life back? How much to be able to sleep at night? Give me a number."

"Don't forget all we did together, all the conversations we had as we stood over your mother and father's grave site. You took me to meet them. I stood there at your side when you told your mother you had finally found your Bernard. Your and Livvy's mom met Tommie's dad, and y'all became Mc-Brooms."

"Leave my parents out of this. Don't you *dare* speak their names."

"I went to Inglewood Cemetery to see them today."

"You went to my parents' grave site?"

"I did. I took lunch and sat down with Mister Bernard Lee and Miss Betty Jean McBroom. I told them the whole story. I told them the truth. I told them I had married the wrong woman a few years ago and had been trying to get that undone. I told them that I love you, Frankie. Then I fell to my knees and asked them to please forgive me, and to ask you to do the same. See the grass stains on my pants?"

"You have the audacity to take this shit to my parents' grave site?"

Angry beyond belief, I reached into my purse, but what I was reaching for wasn't there.

Driver was right. I would have started shooting and this would have ended up on *Snapped*.

My phone rang again. Driver. He'd called a moment ago, was calling again.

I stormed away, city lights in the distance, trainers crunching dirt and gravel.

Franklin shouted, "Where are you going?"

I stopped walking, turned hard enough to make dust rise from my feet, and yelled, "Make Mrs. Carruthers stand down. You'd better do the same. I've had enough. This ends now."

"So it's like that? After all we did, after my confession, you just walk away from me?"

I marched back toward him, my finger pointing toward his face, jabbing the air for emphasis. "You should have been honest when you first met me. You should've spoken to me, said you were married, and kept on stepping when I told you I had too much integrity to deal with a married man. I have too much dignity for this shit. You had many

313

chances to tell me that before we were intimate."

"The Bajan twins. You were with two men at the same goddamn time. One was married. Where was all of that integrity then, Frankie McBroom? Stop acting like you're a brand-new virgin or some shit."

Again I turned around, again I stormed away, middle fingers saluting his arrogance. "Fuck you, Franklin. Fucking fuck you, you lying fucker."

Gravel crunched as he followed. "Walk away from me, Frankie McBroom. . . . I love you, but you will regret it."

Rage made me turn around again. I went and stopped six feet from him and spoke to him in a harsh whisper. "You know what? I don't care. If you're going to post it, tweet it, put it on a Goodyear balloon, hire a skywriter, go by the Junior Blind of America and pay to have it cast in braille, do what you have to do. The world has seen where Dwyane Wades, they know where Meagan keeps her Goods, so if you want to add me to the list, do what you fucking have to do. Just remember that when you do, I have money, I know attorneys, I have resources, and more importantly I have Blue and Tony. Plus I can take this down to the hood level if need be. I have Ray-Ray and a lot of crazy

Crip- and Blood-worshipping relatives on the Eastside, and I will call them from the top of this hill and put a contract out on your pathetic ass."

"Is that a threat, Frankie?"

"I am tired of this. I'll do whatever I have to do to show you that I am the wrong sister to fuck with."

"Is that how it's going to be, Frankie?"

I walked away again, for the last time. "This is how you made it, Franklin. All you had to do was leave me alone. This is the war you started."

"War? We're going to become enemies now?"

"We've been enemies ever since my phone rang and your wife was on the other end, you moron. You created all of this mess. You have my secrets. Whoopty-motherfucking-do. I have yours too, you ugly-dick sonofa-bitch. Remember that when all of this comes back at you. *I'm done being nice.*"

Franklin ran behind me. He was too close.

I cringed when I felt his hand touch my shoulder. I yelled for him to get his hand off me. He broke the law that had been laid down. That was when circumstances became inflamed to a point where control was lost and the excrement made physical contact with a hydroelectric-powered oscil-

315

lating air current distribution device. In other words, Franklin put his paws on me and that was when the shit hit the goddamn fan.

Driver moved so fast he passed me like he was part of the chilly night breeze. He was ready to kick ass and take names.

FRANKIE

By the time I looked back, Franklin was on the ground, on the gravel, cursing. Driver was over him, gloved fists doubled, leg cocked back like he was about to kick a game-winning field goal, prepared to kick Franklin in his ribs, his head, in whatever part of his body was uncovered. I thought Driver was bluffing, but I realized he wasn't the kind of man who bluffed. He kicked Franklin hard. I couldn't stop the first kick. I didn't want to stop the first kick. Or the second. The third kick was hard enough to send Franklin back to Alabama.

Driver spat to the left of Franklin, then said, "Franklin, stay down until we leave. Do not follow us. Do not contact Miss Mc-Broom. Do not fool yourself — and there are two ways to be a fool. One is to believe what isn't true, and the other is to refuse to believe what is true. This is true. Next time you go down, you'll be six feet under the people already six feet under."

Franklin's ego pulled him up to his knees. He was going after Driver. He yelled that he was going to kick some ass. That primal growl — one that sounded like the gruff noises weight lifters made when they had lifted three times their weight — its coarseness scared me and I turned and raced toward the car.

There were grunts like a man had become a punching bag. When I made it to the car I looked back into the darkness. It was quiet now. Driver marched toward me. When he was closer I saw he was undamaged, but his suit coat was ripped. Franklin was on the ground again. This time he was holding his bloodied nose. He tried to get up, looked as steady as a newborn deer. He collapsed. He tried again and made it to his feet. He bent over, let his blood drain into the dirt to make mud as red as Georgia clay.

Driver said, "Miss McBroom, you will receive an invoice for the suit."

"For the repairs?"

"No, for a new suit. This one is ruined and officially yours."

Driver helped me ease into the backseat. Within a second, he was in the front. He did a three-point turn and headed down the winding road named Hetzler. All of a sudden the street name looked too much like *helter-skelter.* Confused. Disorderly. On edge, shaking, headlights brightened the back of my head, and my heart wanted to explode as I looked behind us. Franklin flashed his lights, sped up behind us, revved his engine like he was going to force us off the side of the cliff and make us crash on the houses below. Driver slowed down, dared him to try. Then Driver stopped at an angle that didn't leave enough room for Franklin to pass us on either side of the two-lane road to darkness. Headlights flashed. I looked at Driver's reflection and saw the kind of anger I had never seen on the face of a man.

Driver got out of the car and faced Franklin's car before he popped the trunk. He took out a sledgehammer, and like John Henry, he raised it up and brought it down on the hood of Franklin's car.

I screamed.

The short-handle sledgehammer came down again.

I screamed again.

Franklin threw his car in reverse, his tires screeching across the blacktop. He became a coward and ran the fuck away.

Driver put the sledgehammer in the car, on the passenger seat, then he eased back in and put the car in drive. He crept down the hill, did no more than five miles an hour for the remainder of the descent. That was the longest ride I'd ever experienced. When we made it to Jefferson, Driver turned left.

Franklin sped, exited the snaking hill, his car now a one-eyed wreck. My ambitious stalker turned left too. He followed us down the four lane, high-traffic street until we passed Crystal Rose, flashed his surviving headlight, but at Duquesne Avenue, Franklin made an abrupt, screeching right, sped toward Washington Boulevard.

Driver said, "The road he turned on, the Culver City Police Department is about a half mile up."

"I don't want the police in my business."

Driver said, "No police involvement means there is something you don't want exposed. Everyone who has been intimate leaves something behind they don't want the world to know, especially women."

"Well, Driver, this is where I stop answering questions."

"I wasn't going to ask for any specifics, was just offering my summary. If he has something to lose, that changes things, tells me how far things can go on this end to resolve things on that end."

"I don't want it to get out of control.

More important than it all, I have sisters and I don't want them to know. I'm the oldest. I'm supposed to be the example. I'm not supposed to be doing stupid shit."

Driver said, "More tissue is in the center console."

"I need another box, yeah. Sorry for breaking down like this."

"I will circle the neighboring cities. No extra charge. Clock is off. The wind-down is on me."

Trembling, I asked, "Think he's going to CCPD?"

Driver shook his head. "He knows better."

"He crossed the line with me."

"With me too. Two things you never touch: a man's woman and a man's ride. But you would know better than I do if he's the type of man who will run to Johnny Law."

"He's done things he doesn't want exposed."

"So he's done things that have left him vulnerable."

I wanted to keep it to myself, but I told Driver that my car had been given an acid bath, told him about my business being bricked.

He said, "You left a lot out of the equation. If he's that kind of a man, that changes everything, Miss McBroom."

"Who does this shit?"

"There are two types of love: The kind where you love someone and all you want for them is the best. Then there is the selfish kind, where you'll stop at nothing to have them for yourself. Some men will destroy a woman if he can't have her, same thing some women will do to a man if she can't have her way. You have to deal with crazy in a special kind of way."

He drove me through Culver City, took the long route toward Loyola Marymount, then back toward Inglewood, stayed under the speed limit, let traffic rush by, gave me time to think, to ask myself how in the world I ended up here.

Again my cellular buzzed. My nerves were on fire until I saw it was a text message from Livvy. She was still up. Palms dank, hands trembling, I ignored the message, but two minutes later, when I wasn't crying as much, I tried to call Livvy back. I had to keep up the façade of normalcy. Olivia didn't answer. It was almost ten. Tommie was probably in bed, in mommy mode, with Mo crawling between her and Blue. Livvy's married ass was probably in bed, sleeping naked with Tony on love-stained sheets.

I leaned my head against the window as

the county of Los Angeles went by, tears falling.

Driver asked, "You okay back there?"

"I have to be up by five to pick up my youngest sister before sunrise. We're running the marathon in the morning."

"I'll get you back to your home right away."

"I'm not ready to go home to bad memories. I doubt if I'll be able to sleep after a night like this."

"Tell me where you want to go from here, Miss McBroom."

"I really feel like going to a dive bar and getting wasted with a bunch of losers."

"Heard of a hole-in-the-wall juke joint in South Central called Backbiters and Syndicators?"

"Never have. What's the crowd like in that zip code?"

"People like me go there, occasionally people like you."

"Heartbroken?"

"Just broken."

TOMMIE

Blue and I jerked awake when his iPhone rang. It was Angela's ringtone. It was way past late and Monica's mother was calling his cell phone. I pulled the covers back, was going to go for his phone, but Blue answered. On my back, eyes closed, ears open, I listened. He frowned, said a few words to her, groaned, cursed, and hung up. He didn't look at me, sat staring at the wall, grinding his teeth. He stood and picked up his pants.

I asked, "Where are you going this time of the night?"

He said, "Mo's mother has a little issue right now."

"What's going on?"

"She had too much to drink and needs a ride home."

"Then she should call a taxi or Uber, not you."

"She went to some Beyoncé tribute thing

at Savoy in Inglewood. Dangerous area. Taxis and Ubers don't go there."

"Her being too drunk to drive is *not your problem.*"

"Tommie, please don't start. We were doing so well the last couple of days."

"She calls. You jump. I don't like how that makes me feel, Blue."

"You don't like it and I don't like it, but part of being an adult is *doing shit we don't like.*"

I snapped back at him, *"She's not a child."*

"No *she's not a child,* but if Angela were Frankie, or Livvy, wouldn't you want someone to make sure they got home okay? Doing what's right doesn't mean doing what's comfortable. Didn't I just run to try to help Frankie when someone poured battery acid all over her car? Don't I help your sisters all times of the day or night, and never once have I complained about it being inconvenient?"

"Stop enabling her. Stop giving in to her."

Blue sighed, pulled on distressed jeans and a T-shirt, and grabbed a jacket, his decision made.

While I stood with my arms folded across my breasts, he walked out the door. His car started. Headlights came on. His car pulled away. I didn't know how to deal with this. I didn't have the tools.

I went to the bedroom, put my hand on my Bible, cried out to the Lord in my trouble, begged him to deliver me from this ongoing distress, to make the storm be still, for the waves of the sea to be hushed.

I went and checked on Mo.

She woke up. "Mommy?"

I said, "Scoot over, Mo."

She did. I eased into her twin bed with her.

My phone hummed with a text from Livvy.

Change of plans. See you at Marker 20.
Thought you were going to meet us at Marker 13?
Dead tired, just showered, crawling in bed now.
Can I call you before you go to sleep?

There was no response. I called her anyway, and it went to her voice mail right away. Her phone was off. Wasn't going to wake Frankie. I had to handle my troubles myself. My cellular rang and I jumped. Blue's ringtone. I let it go to voice mail. I left Mo's bedroom and went back to mine, sat on the bed, mumbling.

Minutes later I heard noises at the front

door. Blue was back sooner than I expected.

He yelled my name in a piercing and angst-filled way that sent a chill down my spine.

I hurried down the hallway and saw that he was soaking wet. He wasn't alone. He held his drunken ex in his strong arms. He'd brought her into my house. He'd brought the devil into my home.

TOMMIE

Blue held Mo's mother in his arms like she was an unconscious rag doll, her suntanned skin sticking to his buttery complexion, both soaking wet, rain dripping from both of them, her face nestled in his neck, her arms around his shoulders, one of his hands holding her back and the other holding her juicy booty to keep her from falling and crashing to the floor. She was so inebriated he had to carry her like a bag of groceries. My nostrils flared and I lost the ability to breathe. She didn't have on a bra, and her breasts had fallen out. Pink nipples stared at me. No shoes were on her feet. Her blond hair was shaved on one side, just like mine was shaved, only the rest of hers was in a Sons of Liberty Mohawk painted with streaks of purple and pink and red. I stared at the caricature he held in his bulging arms. He held her tight, with concern. It looked like they'd married and he was carrying her across the threshold.

Blue said, "It was worse than I expected."

"Blue, you can't just bring her here . . . into my home . . . not like that."

"I tried to call you four times to see if this was okay."

"You were supposed to take that Beyoncé chaser to her apartment in Carson."

"She's too drunk. Could barely get her in my car without dropping her on her head."

"Why didn't you leave Angela at that motel on Slauson between La Brea and Overhill?"

"She could pass out and choke to death on her own puke. I can't pull up at a motel, get a room, and drop off a drunken woman, then speed away. Since I picked her up, by law, now I'm responsible."

"You're responsible for the irresponsible, and bring her here so I can be responsible for her irresponsible ass too?"

"Make this easier for me, Tommie. I don't like this situation any more than you do."

"I asked you not to go get her. I asked you not to get involved. This is on you, Blue."

"Let's not do this. What's done is done and I could really use your help right now."

"Look at this. I'll bet you wish you had gotten that vasectomy a lot earlier now."

Monica's bedroom door opened; I heard her feet sticking to the wooden floor as she came out of her room. I called for her to go back to her room, but that only made her that much more curious.

Then Mo was there, wearing her pink Supergirl pajamas, golden hair in a sweet ponytail.

A look of horror and confusion covered her face, like a kid having a bad dream.

Monica began to weep. "Mom?"

At the same time her drunken mother and I answered, "Yes?"

Monica was looking at Angela, not at me. It was wrong, maybe inaccurate, but in that moment, I felt demoted, like I was about to be dismissed. I had become redundant in the home I'd created.

Blue carried her into the bathroom, sat her down in the shower, turned on the cold water. Angela shrieked and squealed and kicked like she was in the ocean drowning while surrounded by sharks. I wished he had poured bleach and peroxide all over her. Mo held on to me and cried like a newborn.

Just like that I was no longer the important mother in the house. The vampire wore pink lipstick. So did Blue's left cheek. I eased away from the situation, left them in the bathroom, went to the bedroom.

If I stayed, I would lose it. I went and grabbed my prepacked bag. Pulled on tennis shoes.

Blue spoke in a stressed whisper, asked, "What are you doing?"

"She calls, you jump and do what she asks like she's your wife. You don't listen to me. What I say, what I want, becomes irrelevant the moment you hear her voice. You've never broken up."

"You're really going to leave?"

"Why in the world would you bring her here?"

"Daddy! Come quick! My mother fell down and bumped her head."

"Thomasina, if you're going to act immature, if you're leaving, then just shut up and go."

"Angela is drunk, half-dead, and puking, calling in the middle of the night while I'm here taking care of her daughter; you've brought her to my zip code, to the place where I pay half of the damn mortgage without fail, and I'm the one immature in the middle of all of this fucking bullshit?"

"You know I'm as tired of this as anyone in this house."

"This is my last night here. When I leave, I ain't coming back."

"Are you serious?"

"As serious as three new condoms in a borrowed coat in my damn used car. Maybe when I make it back home, the coat pocket will be empty this time. Maybe it should have been empty a long time ago."

He reached for me and I raised both of my palms, didn't want him to touch me.

I said, "I am through with you. I am done with this drama. Mo has her momma so she'll be cool. I am going to move on and have my own family. I know someone who loves me more than this shit."

"So you're seeing someone?"

The sounds of a violent regurgitation echoed, followed by powerful pleas to God.

I said, "Go check on your woman, Blue. Run to your baby momma, like you always do."

I went down the hallway, followed Mo's crying. She became hysterical. She held her mother's hand and cried. The woman lay halfway in and out of the bathroom. Angela managed to raise her head and look up at me with pathetic eyes. Then I looked at Mo, wanted to pull her away, but I knew she'd never abandon her true mother. So I watched her sitting with her mother, saw her tears, and saw her suffering. Mo looked at an enraged version of me. This night would change how she saw me. This night would change me. This night changed everything. I stepped over the sloppiness in the hallway. I stepped over the mess and looked back, let my mind photograph the moment.

Beale Streets was right. This was someone else's family. I had been the maid, the babysitter, the concubine, the fool who had spent her time and last dime taking care of another woman's parental obligation. There were no refunds for this selflessness, and the time lost couldn't be retrieved.

I had no blood ties, so I had no business being there.

This was not my family. This was not my reunion.

Blue asked, "Where are you going?"

"Don't worry about it."

Monica screamed for me. For the first time I snapped at her and told her to stop calling me her mother. I told her that I wasn't her mother. Her mother was there. I told Monica to go to her mother. I was done with her. I was done pretending. She had her mother. She had her father. She had her family.

I didn't have a damn thing to show for all the years I'd been with them.

I might have been the queen for a while, but she'd been the pope all along.

Seconds later I was out the door, driving away in the rain, fighting a migraine.

I pulled over to the side of the road after I had passed Valley Ridge, turned on my flashers, throat tight and tears falling. I wasn't married to Blue, but I thought that I had just broken up with the love of my life. Wanted to rip my heart out. It hurt like divorce. It hurt like the death of someone you loved more than life. I wasn't sure if we had just divorced. I wasn't sure at all. But what we had was dead. Tonight, it died. It hurt. A sudden hollow ache in my chest gave me unimaginable agony. I wanted to cut myself. I wanted to take too many pills. I knew a broken heart would heal; it would heal like the mark on my face. I knew I could survive, but it still hurt like hell.

Frankie

Backbiters and Syndicators was the dive bar of all dive bars. Wooden bar stools, pool tables, dartboards, and a room of disgruntled men and women who looked like they were on their third strike. Not even Gugu Mbatha-Raw walking by naked could have made the bad-tempered smile in a den where the only din was the moans and groans of people like Bobby "Blue" Bland, B. B. King, and John Lee Hooker. I loved the crummy place. Hound Dog Taylor groaned and I made Driver stand and do a mild boogie with me to the beat. He was more comfortable swinging a sledgehammer than dancing. Soon we went back to our crummy bar stools.

I shifted and said, "You responded to my Dark Call very quickly."

"You had perfect timing. I'd ended a job about two blocks from you when your request came in."

"I'm curious. Can you say what kind of job it was, or is that confidential?"

"It was a regular job. It's on the books. Drove this writer named Beale Streets to a private event in Hollywood Hills."

"My younger sister's fiancé is a big fan of the guy."

"He lives on Kenway Avenue."

Driver's phone buzzed. He turned away, checked the text message before he thumbed one back.

I asked, "The woman in your life?"

He nodded. "She's just finishing her night. She's had a long day today."

"What does she do?"

"We're equal partners in this business. There are six of us in total; four are part-time."

"I guess you'll take that sledgehammer home and Idris her Elba to put her to sleep."

"Idris her Elba. Never heard it put that way."

"Any woman who can get a man like you to Idris her Elba is lucky, especially if she can get him to Shemar her some Moore after she does a Morris on his Chestnuts."

"Idris, Shemar, and Morris."

"My fantasies run deep."

He looked at me, licked his lips, then looked away as he said, "I have a good

336

woman. And as far as I know, she's done me no wrong, so I try not to bring her no harm. But I'm still a man. I'm human. I'm virile. Every day I fight that desire to know another woman."

Driver stood up. It was time to leave the land of the brokenhearted losers. He helped me from my crummy bar stool, then led me through the bottom-feeders to the front of the dive bar.

Rain was falling.

He took his coat off, draped it over my shoulders, led me back to the town car, eased me into the backseat, then slid into the front. I was inside of his coat wondering what he would be like inside me.

We were silent until we made it to the edges of View Park.

He asked, "You okay back there, Miss Mc-Broom?"

"I'm hating that I ever met Franklin Carruthers and wishing I had met someone else, or just had met nobody at all. Being alone left me lonely at times but never left me feeling disrupted like this."

"One day you will have the right man, someone who makes you feel good both day and night."

"You're a cool guy. You're sexy. Wish I had met you that day, instead of Franklin."

"Back then meeting me might've been another dumb move for you."

"What if I found you tempting, Driver?"

"That's your pain talking. Give it a deaf ear."

"What's talking to you, Driver? What pain do you have? I saw you check me out. I went to the ladies' room and saw your reflection in the mirror over the bar. You were definitely checking me out."

"I should walk you to your door."

"Would you like to come inside?"

"Come inside?"

"Yes, would you like to come inside?"

He looked at me in his rearview. I stared at the reflection of his eyes. We held each other's gazes.

I bit my bottom lip, bounced my leg, then took a breath and whispered, "I bet you can Idris a woman's Elba real good. Bet a lot of women have done a Shemar on your Moore after they did a nice, slow Morris on your Chestnuts. Some nights, when I'm this stressed, I need a few minutes of *Idris*ing, *Shemar*ing, and *Morris*ing to be able to sleep."

He asked, "Is this one of those nights, Miss McBroom?"

"This has become one of those nights."

"You sure you want me to come inside?"

"Yeah, I'm sure as night is dark."

LIVVY

Beep-beep-beep. There was a *beep-beep-beep.*

Livvy opened her eyes. She pulled the bed covers back, struggled to sit up, the Lucite and leather T-strap Manolo Blahniks on her feet, always on her feet when she was in this mode. She listened and imagined she heard a door open and close.

A light from the kitchen fell across six bare legs and blurred her vision. It was a queen bed that was in the guest room situated just beyond their kitchen. There was a soft humming, the sound of their newest Roomba, another vacuum-cleaning robot, making it to this part of the home.

Two bottles of wine were on the nightstand. Three glasses. Dr. Ashley was in their bed, next to her, between her and Tony.

Roomba assaulted the door frame, bumped, then spun, redirected itself, and entered the guest bedroom. Livvy scowled at the time. Then she frowned at the irritating light that came from the kitchen.

Something about the light wasn't right. She had heard *beep-beep-beep.* And the kitchen light was on. And the bedroom door was open. Livvy had turned off that light when they brought phase two of their debauched night to this bed. Tony had closed the door to keep Roomba from coming inside. No lights were left on when they had entered the home. She untangled herself from warm arms and legs, eased from the bed, cleared her throat, hand-combed her hair, moved away from Tony and the Welsh woman, pulled on Tony's dress shirt, and went to the door frame, leaned forward, listened for an intruder. No phone was in the guest bedroom. She had left her cellular in her clutch, and her purse was in the living area. Maybe. She sensed someone's presence. Someone's energy was in her home. She smelled apples and raisins. A fourth person was there. Her heart beat fast. She went to the edge of the bed, whispered Tony's name, and shook him lightly. He didn't awaken. She didn't want to alarm their guest.

Livvy tiptoed across the kitchen floor, took steps over the trail of clothing they had left from the dining room to the bedroom door when they had entered the home, hurrying to again become naked and have adult fun. Water stuck to the bottoms of her shoes. Water. Parts of the floor were damp. The storm didn't start until after they were home, until after three bodies had become one and moans from a black woman, an Asian woman, and a Latin man filled the room as Roomba moved back and forth like an anxious pet begging to be fed. Another sound came from the kitchen. The electric teakettle was on, hot water bubbling, a tin of rooibos tea open; a bottle of honey with the top taken off, a tall cup, and a spoon waited next to all of that. The kettle had been left on the wrong setting, had been left on BOIL, for cooking or making soup, and not on AUTO, for making tea. Livvy turned it off. She turned up the lights. Nothing was missing. No one jumped out with a gun. No one was there, but someone had come in from the rain. Damp footprints were in the foyer, and the water in that area told Livvy that whoever had come inside had taken off their shoes. Burglars never removed shoes, none she had ever heard of anyway. Someone had come into her home, gone to the kitchen to make themselves tea, had selected African tea from the ten types of tea in the pantry, chosen the tea that was fragrant to the nose and pleasing to the palate. As they took out cups and honey, they had heard a noise, then come to the bedroom door, looked in on professionals in a ménage à trois, then abandoned their tea, had left in a hurry. Livvy looked behind her, and her heart skipped a beat when she saw a figure in the bedroom doorway. The Welsh woman was there, naked except for a brand-new anklet on her left ankle, smiling like she had discovered a new world. Naked she was svelte, but not skinny, had a modest ass, nice breasts, was model-tall and -fit, but not as intimidating without her heels on, especially when Livvy had her guest walk her home barefoot. Livvy always wore her Blahniks when she was with Tony and Dr. Ashley. Livvy always put on the shoes that had been given to her by a lover who was suddenly, by her emotional frame of reference, no longer among the living. Like the anklet, the shoes signified something greater, something powerful, something spiritual.

She was the only one who knew the significance of the Blahniks. When they were in Paris, when this part of her was finally revealed, when the itch had become too powerful, Tony realized that whenever she wore them, she was in a special mood, to

343

not ask questions, and it would be a special night.

Naughtiness in her inebriated eyes, Dr. Ashley held a pink vibrator in her hand, a Mahana waterproof toy that had been her gift to Livvy, as the anklet the doctor wore had been Livvy's gift to her. They wore identical anklets.

Each anklet had a trinket depicting the Eiffel Tower, their favorite position, the position taught to Livvy by Panther and Carpe.

Livvy had taught Tony and Ashley the proper way to construct the Eiffel Tower, their version with two women — instead of two men — forming the tower by holding hands over the women they pleased. Tony had placed Ashley on her back, then Livvy had sat on Ashley's face, and while Ashley savored Livvy, with a mouth filled with moans, Livvy shivered and held Tony's hands, her fingers clasped between his as she rode the tongue and lips of the Asian woman from Wales. At times Livvy had leaned forward, had ridden Ashley's tongue as she had kissed her husband with passion. Livvy had been a good student. In the past it had been Carpe moving between Panther's dark thighs as Panther gave Livvy's anxious sex her Atlanta-born tongue, a tongue that made Livvy writhe and hold on strong to her lover's powerful hands. Each time, at some point, she leaned forward, rode toward orgasm as she kissed the man they had called Carpe. Eventually she and Panther had changed places. They had taught her how to please a woman and a man all at once. Livvy had become the road over which they had traveled. It had all come to an end. An abrupt end. An unwanted end.

Livvy sighed herself free of the past; nervous, concerned; wondered what position they were in when the bedroom door was eased open.

Someone had seen Livvy, Tony, and Ashley in their heated moment. Someone had seen their Eiffel Tower.

Dr. Ashley said, "With what I have learned to do, I'm becoming a regular Abi Titmuss."

Dr. Ashley sat Livvy on the arm of the sofa, parted her legs, journeyed south. With lips, tongue, and toy, Dr. Ashley continued giving Livvy her carnal therapy. Livvy held the Welsh woman's hair, wiggled, moaned, then she heard a sound, movement across the carpet, footsteps that came their way at a measured pace. Ashley Li stayed on task as Livvy gazed around the room. She expected to see the person who had entered her home to make tea, only Tony was there, standing in the bedroom door, watching. Livvy realized what she was doing; this was a reconstruction of the past. She had become Panther. She controlled this as Carpe had controlled her. She was the leader. She was the one who set boundaries. Tony had become Carpe. Dr. Ashley was hurt, in need, as Livvy had been. Dr. Ashley was the woman betrayed. Livvy moaned again. Tonight she had given Dr. Ashley to Tony, then refused to allow her husband to penetrate her, had used Ashley Li as her proxy. Livvy knew Tony wanted his wife, was dying to have Livvy, *only* her. This pleased him physically, but it didn't make him happy on an emotional or a spiritual level. In Livvy's mind, lust never won over love. She believed that lust could evolve and become what felt like love. And maybe lust needed love as much as love needed lust. She was convinced that for her, this was lust.

Dr. Ashley had become pure, unadulterated lust. But Livvy could tell the woman from abroad was falling in love with her American hosts. She recognized the signs. It was the same as when Livvy had evolved from being in lust and had unexpectedly fallen in love with Carpe and Panther.

As Ashley made the toy hum between

Livvy's legs, Livvy observed Tony. Powerful, yet powerless, and in love. As she was licked and fluttered, tasted like she was communion wine, as the vibrator forced her to hold Ashley's head to maintain her balance, Livvy watched Tony suffer to have her affections.

She had to remember why she had left the bedroom.

They were not alone.

Then she looked across the room; regarded the damp floor, the boiling water, smelled the fruity scent of rooibos tea. The *beep-beep-beep* was made whenever a door opened or closed. That warning, that alert, had been drowned in alcohol, a trio of rising orgasms, and a trifecta of sumptuous moans.

Livvy glanced toward Roomba, wondered if she was being watched, and through the alcohol-induced fog she remembered when she'd heard the beep. They were in the throes, so far gone that she had thought it was an alert from her phone, and the intrusion was dismissed. The first *beep-beep-beep* was when someone entered. She and Ashley were like this, a version of this only, or maybe it had been the reverse, but she knew that Tony was included, his eyes on Livvy as he was connected with one of Ashley's orifices. The combinations and permutations of a three-headed beast seemed endless. Livvy was sure the first series of beeps was when someone entered, and the last *beep-beep-beep* when they had left. A Welsh-born tongue went deep and made her stop thinking, made her back arch.

Livvy shut her eyes, moaned, "Tony, baby . . . take her . . . from behind . . . while she . . . she . . ."

Tony did as instructed. Ashley Li lost her power, submitted to Tony's Latin wickedness, her moans sharp, childlike, her words curt and arriving between suffocating pants, her erotic, dirty talk in a foreign language. She looked as if she felt so good she was going to lose consciousness.

Tony was a Latin man, a Latin lover to the bone.

Ashley lost her place, and Livvy eased from the moment, walked away, glanced back at them, left them to their passion. She went upstairs, stood in the window, looked out at the street.

Carpe was dead.

Soon Tony came upstairs, knocked on the door, then walked into the bedroom, sweat on his skin, the smell of perfumes, cologne, and unadulterated sex on his flesh.

Livvy whispered, "Someone saw us in bed."

"What do you mean?"

"Someone was here."

"In our home?"

"They came in and made tea."

He asked, "You didn't make that tea?"

"No. I know you didn't. I know Ashley didn't."

"Had to be someone from your family."

She nodded.

Tony cursed. "What do we do?"

Livvy said, "Go back to our guest."

"You're not worried?"

"What's done is done."

"What do you want to do?"

"Don't be rude. Keep Dr. Ashley company."

"Is that what you want?"

"She really likes you, Tony."

"Is that an issue?"

"Not at all. You and Ashley, you are good together."

"What does that mean?"

"Means, if you want to go to London and spend some time, I won't argue. I haven't been easy to get along with. If you left and decided to not come back, I would understand."

"Is that what you want?"

She paused. "I want to be who I was before all of this; I want to be naïve again, but a river's current goes in one direction."

"A river's water flows from a higher elevation to a lower one. So, yes, it goes in one direction, from a high point to a low point, in the strictest sense."

"We are being pulled to a low point."

"Not necessarily. I'm waiting for it to go back the other way. A river can never flow in both directions at once, but it can change its course."

Livvy shook her head. "The way the water flows is beyond the control of the river. Water is just water. It goes where gravity takes it. Fighting gravity is foolish."

"You could say that. But other factors control a river's flow, external factors, gravity, physics."

Livvy whispered, "It can be forced in the opposite direction."

"I guess you can say I caused the earthquake that changed the course of our river, but every earthquake has to end."

Again, Carpe was on her mind as she asked, "What happens when the force . . . ceases to exist . . . is gone?"

"It will eventually go back to normal."

"How long does that take?"

"Depends on the level of force."

She repeated, "When the force ceases to be, how long before the river adjusts its direction?"

"You've changed, Livvy."

"When you had your affair, before you were served the paternity papers in front of my friends and family, didn't you feel changed? You created the earthquake. Your affair was the earthquake that caused our river to change its direction. We are living in its never-ending aftershock. Each time we try to change, the memories resurface, and those are the quakes that keep the river running in the wrong direction."

"Livvy, I thought you were over all of that when you came back home. You cried, we cried, and you said you forgave me."

"I did forgive you, but that doesn't mean I can go back to being the same person. You can't go back to being the same."

"I know."

"Not for the pregnancy, I never would have known."

"I can't do this over and over. What I did was wrong, selfish, but at the same time it forced me to realize how much I loved you. I would not go through this, would not tolerate this, if not for love. The back of love can only bear so much."

"Go back downstairs. Kiss Ashley Li's

sweet spot for me. Condoms are on the nightstand. They are optional. Go have fun, Tony."

"She would prefer to be in bed with you more than with me. Being with a woman is new for her, and she enjoys it."

"We always enjoy what's new."

"You enjoy her as much as she enjoys you."

"Go be with her and let me breathe."

"I had no idea you could be that way with a woman."

"I never thought you'd cheat on me."

"Touché."

In a kind tone, Livvy said, "Sleep downstairs with her."

"You want me with her while you shut me out of our bed?"

"That's what I want tonight, Tony."

He made a fist, like he wanted to strike the wall a dozen times. "What are we doing here, Livvy?"

"What do you mean?"

"Do you still need me in your life? Should I have moved on back when . . . when it happened?"

She stood motionless, whispered, "I need both of you."

"For how long?"

"Until I don't need both of you anymore."

"I don't understand this."

"You shouldn't try, Tony. But if you can't handle it, if I come back home one day and you're not here, if you've decided to go spend time in London, I will understand."

"The wine is talking for you."

"Maybe."

"Look, get some rest."

"I don't want to go, but I have to get up early."

"I'll wake you in a few hours."

"I doubt if I will sleep tonight. Enjoy yourself."

"I love you."

"I know."

He went to Livvy, pulled her to him to kiss, but she put the palms of her hands on his chest, refused to let him.

He retreated from their master bedroom, a stranger in his own world, in his own home.

Olivia stayed in the window, her gaze fixed toward faded memories in Manhattan Beach.

She whispered, "He's gone. Carpe is dead. The force is gone. Yet the course of the river is still reversed."

Their upstairs Roomba whirred, bumped into her leg, then easily moved on with its life. Soon she heard the doctors downstairs, first laughing, having fun, then there was silence, followed by sounds of passion. Livvy closed her bedroom door, then sat in an oversize chair with her knees pulled up to her chest, staring at her Blahniks, her only remaining gift from her deceased lover, her eyes on her precious heels while toying with her anklet. She focused on the anklet, turning the symbol around and around in one direction, and then became the force that caused it to switch its course. She did that over and over.

FRANKIE

If my gun had been in my hand I would've shot that intruder on the spot. When I stepped inside my crib, I saw the silhouette and almost jumped out of my thong as I fumbled to get my gun, then bumbled and dropped the damn thing. I picked it up as fast as I could and was ready to scream and pull the trigger.

It looked like Franklin Carruthers was inside of my home.

But it wasn't Franklin. I lowered the gun and took my finger off the trigger.

Tommie was chilling at my informal dining room table, dressed like a bum, in a zone, writing frantically by the light from her cellular. She had scared me and had no idea how much.

Two red roses and a half-empty bottle of blue Gatorade were on the table in front of her.

She jumped to her feet, took off her

baseball cap, yanked away her Dr. Dre headphones, and fell into fight-or-flight mode when the front door closed hard. Eyes wide and enlarged by fear, she was a Margaret Keane painting come to life. Her mouth dropped open.

Then my eyes widened and my mouth dropped open.

I had rushed out and left the thick binder notebook with all of the logs of harassment from Franklin and the foul e-mails from his lunatic wife on the dining room table. Those were supposed to stay hidden. I freaked out, was ready to become defensive and embarrassed because Tommie's body language told me something was wrong. She turned off her phone, put her writings away in a hurry.

I turned the lights on low, then cleared my throat and asked, "What are you doing here?"

"Want to tell me what's going on, or has every McBroom gone crazy tonight?"

I exhaled and inhaled a few times. She was here like she had already found out about my being stalked, about the lunatic mentioning Mo, and had thrown on the first thing in reach and stormed over.

I asked, "Is Livvy here with you?"

"Livvy and Tony are in bed eating Chinese food."

I hurried to the bay window, waved, and Driver pulled away, windshield wipers on high. I was glad Driver hadn't come in for that drink. Would've made a fool of myself. But I had been a worse fool.

Tommie put her headphones on the table by the two roses. "Frankie? What's going on?"

I snapped, "I just walked in the friggin' door. Give me a moment. Let me take a breath."

Tommie said, "Frankie, where are you coming from?"

"Don't start a question-asking party, unless you plan on answering a lot of questions."

I went to the dining area. Her face looked fatter, swollen, skin reddened.

I asked, "Why do you have that nasty bag on top of my table?"

"You scared me when you came in the front door like that."

"Your car isn't out front in my driveway."

"It was raining, so I parked in the garage."

"Isn't your hoopty leaking oil?"

"I put cardboard under the engine."

I went toward her and picked up her pages and a novel she had on the table, a worn one by Beale Streets, shoved it all inside her gym bag. I didn't ask, just rubbed the top of her head, then saw the notebook I was concerned with hadn't been opened. Or if it had been opened, it had been closed and put back in the exact spot I had left it in when I walked out with Driver. I was about to show those messages to him when he picked me up, then had changed my mind.

I asked, "Why didn't you check the small bedroom? You know where I sleep most nights. I'm not seeing anybody new and I haven't dated for a while. That empty bed would've told you I wasn't home."

"But you told me you were home, Frankie. Why would I think you had left when you told me you were in bed? I saw the small bed empty, and assumed you were in the big bedroom doing Jell-O tricks, and I didn't need to see more shit that will rearrange my brain any more than it's been rearranged already."

"You will never let me live that down. It was Jell-O. Get over it."

"There are things a woman should never see her sister doing with Jell-O."

"That's why people should call before they pop up at someone's home."

"Look, I don't want to argue."

"What were you doing?"

"Was trying to sit here and write a letter."

I wiped rain from Driver's damaged Italian suit coat, draped it across the back of a dining room chair, kicked my trainers off, let them rest on the tile floor, did all that before I put my gun and purse on the dining table, let the gun stay alert on top of that notebook. I yawned my way back to Tommie, took a deep breath, and put my arms around her. She twisted her lips, and the tears eased down her cheeks.

She asked, "Why do you have your gun with you?"

"This is LA. Everybody has a gun with them; most people have two."

"What's going on, Frankie?"

"What's the issue that has you here in the middle of the night?"

"Why aren't you in bed like you told me you were?"

"Let's focus on you, Tommie."

"I can't do anything right. Went by Livvy's first. Walked in and they were in the middle of the middle, so that's why I was scared to go to your big bedroom; didn't want to be pissed off and traumatized three times in one night. This has got to be the worst night of my friggin' life. I mean, the worst night."

"You walked in on Livvy and Tony?"

"I walked in on them big-time. They're nasty."

"What did you see?"

"Must be in the air. Everything is out of alignment."

I said, "You're tired and sound like you're delirious."

"And in a mood. Actually I'm in so many moods. They're all spinning like the Wheel of Fortune. I need the wheel in my mind to stop going around and around and settle on one emotion."

I took her hand, led her to the big purple sofa, and pulled a yellow blanket over us.

She said, "Daddy and Momma made this relationship crap look so damn easy."

"Yeah. They did. I think they did a good job of hiding the rough parts from us."

"Where are you coming from this time of the morning, Frankie?"

I took a breath and exhaled. "I had a meeting with Franklin Carruthers."

"Frankie . . . no . . . *no*. Tell me you're not sleeping with that loser."

"I wanted him to look me in my eyes and tell me he had nothing to do with what happened to my car, to the window at my business. I had to look in his face to see if he was the one doing all of this crap."

"How did it go?"

"I gave Franklin his ring back."

"Two things a woman never gives back: shoes, lingerie, and the ring."

"Three things."

"Okay, three things. But that list needs to be amended to include a bunch more stuff."

"Now he has no reason whatsoever to contact me."

"That ring was the ring of all rings, Frankie. Superheroes don't have rings that nice."

"I returned his ring and gave him a few harsh words. I've had enough of him and his wife."

"What does that mean? What did his wife do?"

I almost told her all about Franklin and the stalking, needed to purge and confess. I would tell them all after it was over. No point in having everyone stressed.

Blue called her over and over, his ringtone Erykah Badu's "Love of My Life." Tommie didn't answer. Each time he called, Tommie cursed and shook her head. That wasn't like her. She used to turn cartwheels and do somersaults whenever he called. But her phone rang again and it wasn't Blue's ringtone. Tommie jumped up and took that call, went to the far reaches of the house, smiling, laughing, flirting. She was talking to a random guy. She had become a big ball of sunshine as soon as he called.

Tommie had left her gym bag in the dining room, so I just happened to go in that direction, then happened to peek inside to see what she was writing so intently when I had come home, hoping that she hadn't cracked open my notebook and seen the love letters from Franklin and the threats from his wife.

She had written a string of nonsensical phrases, like esoteric poetry gibberish at spoken word.

I fucking hate him. / The night as dark as
    my thoughts. / Wanted to scream, rant.
Desired a true friend. / Wanted you to
    console me. / Tears fall like hot rain.
You answered door nude. / Eloquent
    silence, kisses. / Then echoed passion.
You slid deep inside. / I tell you this now is
    yours. / No longer felt Blue.

Tommie snapped, *"What the hell are you doing, Frankie?"*

I jumped, turned around, saw Tommie standing there, body wet, towel around her.

I said, "Was about to bring you your gym bag so you can hurry and get ready, and your papers somehow accidentally fell out and I just picked them up and was putting them back inside of your bag."

She marched to the table and snatched her papers from my hand, shoved them back in her bag, then cursed and pushed me. I grunted and pushed her back. She pushed me again. I pushed her.

I asked, "What is that?"

She yelled, "Nosy-ass bitch. Can't nobody stand a nosy-ass bitch. Livvy is sneaky and freaky and your ass is nosy and nasty. Both of y'all need Jesus the way Fat Joe needs Jenny Craig."

"Why are you so defensive? What's going on?"

"Why do you have a book of love letters from Franklin? What's up with that?"

That paused me. "You went through my binder?"

"I was looking for paper to write my thoughts on, saw the notebook, opened it, and *accidentally* found a lot of love letters, and they're all disgusting, like you were reading all of it this afternoon, reminiscing about Jell-O and God knows what else, got hot and bothered, then went to see him."

"I went to give him his ring back. He has something that belongs to me as well."

"I'm not stupid, Frankie. You lied and said you were in bed hours ago and come in wearing straight-up booty-call clothes. You'd better not ever see that asshole again, or I will kick his ass."

I yelled, "And don't leave your Gatorade and those cheap 7-Eleven roses on my damn table."

She stormed back to the edge of the dining room. "What are you screaming about, Frankie?"

"Get your mess. Leave your house messy, but don't come to mine and make it a pigpen."

"You know I don't like red roses. They are cliché and for losers. Sent only in apology. That's not my Gatorade. Frankie, you know I don't drink that sugar water, so quit playing with my head."

She marched down the hallway, pissed, agitated, cursing me out with every step.

I stared at the roses, at the Gatorade, heart racing. Then once again I had that old feeling of dread, of being violated, and I looked at my home in a different way. Again things had been moved. Art that had been on the wall in the living room was now in the dining room. The dish drain was upside down and had been moved to the opposite side of the sink. Drawers had been opened and not closed all the way.

This couldn't be happening again, not

here, not in my new home.

I went to the kitchen. A bar of soap had been put in the microwave and cooked until it made a soufflé. I went to the foyer. Red ink had been added to the water in all of my fresh-cut flowers.

Tommie didn't do that. Tommie would never do that.

She had no reason to destroy my sanity.

Since the first round of stalking, so I would know I hadn't lost my mind, I had taken photos of my home, of how things had been placed. I broke out my cellular, looked at the photos. Things had been moved, only the change wasn't as drastic as before. Some items only by six or seven inches, but many small things had been moved. In my office, cups of pens had simply been turned around. I went to every door, checked to make sure all were locked. I double-checked the alarm system. I went into the garage. I had done this as an exercise every night. I picked up my gun, jogged from room to room. In the master bedroom, I turned on the eighty-inch television, switched to security mode, and rewound the feed on the DVR. There was very little traffic up here on the hill after dark, but it looked like the same car passed by my house four times in six minutes.

There were dozens of houses on this strip of Olympiad, so that car could've been passing anyone's house over and over. The car never slowed down in the view of my cameras, so I wrote that off as someone lost, or just cruising and looking for a place to have sex on the side of the road. Nothing else suspicious had happened since I had met with Driver.

I exhaled. Had going through my head Franklin drinking blue Gatorade countless times.

Flowers didn't magically appear in a house, not even if you watered the carpet with Perrier.

The fax machine rang and I jumped.

I went to see what came through in the thick of the night.

It was the image of a smiley face. Its eyes were poked out.

I recognized the number on the fax machine. It was the number to the fax machines at my office on Sepulveda.

That was impossible. No burglar alarm had been detected.

Hand shaking, eyes welling with tears of anger, I stared at a half-empty bottle of Gatorade and cheap red roses. But it was when I went to my master bedroom that I knew Franklin had been here.

The evidence was on top of the bed, waiting on me, staring at me. The nine-inch-long Jack Rabbit I had left at Franklin's home was in the center of my bed. An ass print was on the end of the bed.

He had sat there, after Driver had kicked his ass, angry, waiting on me to come back home.

I hyperventilated, had to sit down, had to wait for my life to stop spinning like it had done before. Soon the world moved in slow motion; I felt like I was swimming in oil as I picked up my phone.

I called the man who is six foot two, two hundred pounds, dark as an open road. A giggling woman answered his phone, changed her tone and became professional, and said the business's name. She had a Southern voice. That caught me off guard.

In a rushed tone I said, "Good evening."

"It's more like morning now. So good morning."

"Good morning. This is Miss Frankie Mc-Broom. Is Driver available?"

"Miss McBroom, this is Driver's partner."

"Is this Mrs. Driver?"

"Panther."

"Panther?"

"If you're wondering, I took my nickname from the Clark Atlanta University roaring

Panthers."

"I'm sorry to disturb you, but could you tell Driver that I seem to have a situation with my stalker?"

"We were just getting in the shower."

"I think my stalker has been inside of my home tonight."

"Is he still inside of your home?"

"God, I hope not. My sister is here and I hope he's not in my home hiding."

"Let me get Driver for you, Miss Mc-Broom. In the meantime, I suggest both of you wait outside."

FRANKIE

Soon Driver was back at my home.

Panther was with him.

Both wore suits.

Our introduction was brief and very professional, head nods and no handshakes. She smelled nice. Despite all that was going on, I noticed that she smelled as nice as she looked.

Driver smelled fresh and had on a different suit. His disposition was as it had been before we went to see Franklin. With them there, and since I had my gun and made Tommie wait with me in the garage, I had to explain what was going on. I told Tommie that I thought someone had broken in before she had come over.

I said to everyone, "The roses and Gatorade weren't here when I left home to go have that quick meeting with Franklin."

Tommie said, "Who breaks into someone's house and leaves roses and Gatorade?"

"I'm trying to find out."

"Has he broken into your house before?"

"He broke into the old house, Tommie."

"Is that why you just up and moved all of a sudden?"

"Yes, that's why I moved. I'm not going to lie."

"Is that why you have so much security here?"

"Tommie, give us a moment. Let me handle this. Driver, Panther, please come with me."

Driver said, "You said he left something on your bed?"

"Something that had been left at his home before we broke up."

Driver came into the office and looked at the DVR feed. He saw something that I hadn't seen. The video had been tampered with. The recording was continuous, not motion activated, and there was a huge time gap. Two hours of feed were missing. Between the time that Driver had picked me up and when Tommie had arrived, the video had been deleted, the system had been manipulated, and most of what I was looking at was from the night before. He said that the system hadn't been manipulated remotely.

Driver said, "Your stalker was inside of

your home."

"You're joking, right?"

"He had to have been right here. He came in, came here, and manipulated the footage."

"Can I prove that to the police?"

"Nope. You sure can't. Gatorade. Flowers. And the toy. He sat and waited for you this time."

"Why would he do that?"

Panther said, "Miss McBroom, I think the vibrator speaks for itself."

I shook my head. "No, not that."

Panther said, "One can only assume."

Driver said, "There was a confrontation and it didn't work out in his favor. His car was smashed. He was pissed tonight. He would take it to the next level."

She said, "He felt humiliated and the next move could have been to humiliate you."

I asked, "Isn't that evidence, the tape being erased?"

Driver said, "No evidence is not evidence, even though we know it is evidence of tampering. You can't prove anything without any evidence. Gatorade and flowers. You said the toy was yours, but you left it at his house. A pen was moved. A painting was moved. It's circumstantial. As far as they know you have a malfunction with the camera, or erased the feed yourself, and the rest of your complaints about your house being redecorated probably wouldn't get more than a yawn from any police officer at this hour."

"So tonight, Franklin sat in my bedroom and waited for me and had the vibrator in his hand?"

"While I drove you around, Miss Mc-Broom, my bet is that he came here."

"He knows where I live."

"It's escalated, Miss McBroom. It always escalates. Especially after a confrontation like the one you had with him tonight."

"I've looked, but please check to make sure he's not hiding in my home. I'm going to call him and have a few more words."

"Don't contact him. He wants a reaction. Just keep a record of when he calls, of his messages, and save all you can. With that notebook you have a great case, Miss Mc-Broom. I recommend going to the authorities at this point, especially with what he did tonight. I think sexual assault is his intention."

Panther said, "Sexual assault is about power, Miss McBroom."

"He'd assault me with my own vibrator? Who does crap like that?"

Driver said, "Where I went on vacation,

Miss McBroom, I was around men who did things far worse than that. He was angry. He tried to run us off the road. If I hadn't been with you, he might have assaulted you."

"Who leaves a vibrator in a woman's bed?"

"Now is a good time to take all you have to the police."

"I can't. This is embarrassing, but I can't."

"What does he have on you, Miss Mc-Broom?"

"It's silly."

"Nothing is silly at this point."

"There was a GoPro recorder. We used to record private moments."

"Say no more. And he has it."

"He stole it when we broke up."

"Anything posted anywhere?"

"Not to my knowledge. Where would I check?"

"There are twenty-six million porn sites in the world."

Panther said, "Sorry to hear that, Miss McBroom. There are some vile people out there."

Panther and Driver checked the house, the backyard.

I checked the windows and doors again.

When we made our way back to the front of the house, I saw Tommie was standing up. The heavy notebook of e-mails and threats was in her hand, and she had read beyond the love letters this time. While I had been with Driver and Panther she had read what I didn't want anyone else to read.

She said, "His wife has been e-mailing you for months and threatening you like this?"

"She's sent a few e-mails."

"A few? Don't minimize this shit, Frankie. It makes it seem like you're protecting Franklin, and I know you better not be protecting him. His wife is in Afghanistan sending threats on the government's dime."

I showed the notebook to Driver and Panther; I let them see Mrs. Carruthers's text and e-mail rants.

Panther asked, "Do you mind if we take a few pages of this? Would love to trace the e-mail addresses. From what I can see, most were from overseas, but the e-mail addresses seem off."

I said, "I have it all saved on my hard drive and the cloud. Take the entire notebook."

Driver said, "Some of these look like library e-mail addresses. A library in Texas."

"She has an accomplice stationed down there? Is this a team effort?"

"Wouldn't doubt it. If she's e-mailing this much, she's probably not doing it alone."

"I hadn't noticed or checked for consistency in the messages, so far as writing style. At some point I just stopped reading most of the madness and saved and printed and added to the collection."

Panther regarded the damaged suit coat as it rested on the back of the chair.

She glanced at me, proffered a questionable smile, then stood by Driver.

Driver said nothing, remained professional.

As soon as Driver and Panther left my home, veins popping in my neck, I called Franklin.

He snapped at me. "I'm being treated for a concussion in the emergency room at Kaiser on Cadillac."

"Is this the part where you want me to sound concerned and ask why?"

"You set me up tonight."

"How do you figure that? You called me, you wanted to meet, and I went to meet you."

"You had your gorilla in a suit attack me for no reason."

"Oh, he had a reason. How did you like that sledgehammer?"

"You're paying to repair my car, Frankie."

"Fix it your damn self. You're the King of Restoration. Restore that shit and call it a wrap."

"This hospital bill is yours too. So will be the lawsuit that follows."

"That's a punk move. I'm fighting back now, Franklin, and now you want to go to court?"

He barked, "Jesus. It was you, wasn't it, Frankie? Is that what this call is about? You're calling me, recording me, making accusations to make it seem like I'm a burglar? Why are you setting me up?"

"I'm not playing this game. I will have you arrested for breaking and entering. I hope there is a way to charge you for leaving flowers too. Did you think leaving roses would make me feel better?"

"Roses? The two red roses I bought for you? You have them? How did that happen?"

"At least you admit to knowing about the roses you broke in and left here at my home. Who does shit like that? Why would you break into my home and wait in my bedroom for me to come home?"

"The roses should be in my kitchen right where I left them. They can't be at your house. I haven't been back home since I came to see you, since you had your gorilla attack me. Goddamn thug in a suit."

"Your roses are in my kitchen, and don't try and pretend you've lost your memory."

"You have the roses. Oh. I see. You're

recording this and trying to set me up. This is unreal."

"Step in my house one more time and I will shoot you in the heart, Franklin. I will not hesitate to shoot you and break into a happy dance. Heed my warning; hear the seriousness in my voice."

"Why did you bring your underwear to my house if you didn't want to get back together?"

"Are you mad? If anyone is recording anyone, it's you trying to make it sound like I'm the one stalking you. I have all the e-mails. You stole my underwear. Who does that?"

When I hung up, Tommie was staring at me, head tilted, mouth open, like I was a loon.

"Franklin broke into your house, stole your underwear, and left the flowers and the Gatorade?"

I nodded.

She asked, "Was he here watching me? While I sat here with my headphones on, while I was focused on what I was writing, was he in this house watching me? Could he have attacked me?"

"He came for me, not for you."

"I felt someone's energy. I assumed you were home. I thought I heard the toilet flush and that's why when I looked up and saw you at the front door I jumped like that. Then I assumed I hadn't heard the toilet flush. I had my headphones on and he could have stood over me with a knife and stabbed me."

"Calm down, Tommie. He's not here. He says he's at Kaiser with a concussion."

"Now you tell me that he says he's at Kaiser because he has a little headache?"

"He's trying to establish an alibi, Tommie, that's all. I've seen this on a dozen television shows."

"I'm telling Livvy right now. I'm calling her . . . eating Chinese food and getting in-dickgestion will have to wait."

"Let her sleep and let me tell her. Let me tell her and the rest of the family after the race is done."

Her phone rang again. Blue's ringtone. She didn't answer but hearing his ringtone wrecked her.

I asked, "What's the issue that has you hiding at my house in the middle of the night?"

Tommie told me about Blue, Angela, the phone call, her being fall-down-and-pissy drunk. She ranted for ten minutes.

I said, "Please tell me Mo didn't see her mother like that."

"They can have each other. I can have another man by the time I finish this race. I can snap my fingers and have a life better than this, with no baby-momma drama, with no disrespect."

"Never leave a bitch in your house. The queen *never* leaves the castle for some bitch. *Never."*

"But what pisses me off is that I don't understand why he gave that *slunt* a baby. Since he's already had a baby with her, he's not sure if he wants to have another one at all. I guess I'm not good enough. That's how that makes me feel. If we're going to be together, we should be a real family at some point, and not wait until my eggs are old or his sperm has to shuffle out of his dick using a damn walker."

"Well, I love you with Blue, think you should be with a man like him, Tommie, but if it's that bad, don't be ashamed to admit it like I was ashamed to admit my one and only marriage was a trip to hell. Break up with him, move on, get a new boyfriend, or have no boyfriend. Just make sure you're happy."

"Blue and I are done, Frankie. He knows we're done. Monica knows it too. This time tomorrow, I'll have a new home, new address, new zip code, new loves, and a much better future."

"Stop talking crazy, Tommie."

"We'll see who's talking crazy. This is my last night crying over Blue."

Gun in hand, I put my arms around her, rocked her. My alarm buzzed and I squeezed the trigger on the gun. Thank God the safety was on. We had both jumped. It was time to rush and go to the race.

I hurried and showered, grabbed my bag. Tommie was in the living room, pacing. When I passed the new and improved houghmagandy room I heard a faint noise. Something electric was alive. I opened the door and went in, still nervous. The noise came from one of the drawers. Buzzing, buzzing, buzzing.

Both dead bolts had been locked, so I had assumed Franklin hadn't infiltrated my houghmagandy room. I was wrong. He had been in there, touched my things, and then locked the doors again when he left. I knew because Fitz, Jake, and Idris were turned on; the trio danced side by side and sang in harmony.

FRANKIE

By eight in the morning, Dodger Stadium was a madhouse of music and half-naked weekend road warriors. Despite the rainy weather, more than a few people wore outrageous costumes that made this yearly event look like Bay to Breakers and Halloween combined. I adjusted my cheap, disposable rain poncho, then looked down at the plastic bags covering my Nikes. Needed to keep my feet dry. My Lycra shorts stopped midthigh, so my legs were getting cold. I bounced up and down on my toes to keep the body warm and circulation going. Tommie was next to me covered in black garbage bags. She had a finger up to her left ear to muffle the noise, her cell phone up to the right, arguing and breaking up with Blue one curse at a time. Roses and faxes were on my mind, as were Fitz, Jake, and Idris. So were a totaled Audi and a broken storefront window. That stolen Go-

Pro was on my mind too. In the back of my mind I was waiting on Franklin to let his anger get the best of him and post what we had done when we were on the road to marriage; expected to see a very personal part of my existence on as many websites as would allow, then to have people recognize me before I had any idea what was going on.

He hated me now. I could feel that.

I hated him. He knew that.

On little sleep and a small cup of green tea, I faked the funk and kept it moving.

The guy I'd met not long ago, Daniel, pushed his way through the crowd. He was on his cellular.

When he was near me he put his phone away and said, "Long time no see, Frankie McBroom."

"We really have to stop meeting like this."

"I called you a few times."

"Meant to call you back."

"Did the police find out who that hater was who poured acid on your car?"

I shook my head before I changed the topic. "Which group are you in, the seven-minute-milers?"

He nodded. "If you want, maybe we can chat after the race, Frankie McBroom."

"After the race, Daniel, the only thing I

will chat with is a sports drink and Tylenol."

"You're a hard one to read. Even when we were at Sy's performance, it was hard to read you. You were jamming, dancing, but your body language was telling me not to try and get too close."

"We kissed on the date before that one. I think we got ahead of ourselves."

"I wasn't going to bring that up. We kissed on the first date, after we had talked about childhoods, favorite sports teams, music we liked, music we hated, religion, politics, and how you valued your family and friends, how you want to have kids one day. We kissed. Then you went cold on the second."

"What happened at Sy's shindig, my totaled car, well, I guess I have a few unresolved issues, without getting specific. And because of that, I guess it's a bad time to try and get serious with me."

"We can be friends."

"Bad time to look for a good time too. Despite how that kiss went, and it was a very nice tongue dance, I'm not emotionally available or physically willing to do anything that goes beyond my front porch."

"You're cute, and I am interested in you, but you're not the only girl in town."

I laughed a little. "Nice meeting you, Daniel."

"Look for you after the race?"

"Sure. If my car has been set on fire, I might need you to give us a ride home."

We laughed at my tragedy. I didn't think it was funny, it was too soon, but I laughed to keep from crying. He finally eased his plastic-covered body away from mine. His plastic crinkled against mine. All of the wet plastic rubbing plastic sounded like lubricated condoms rubbing up against each other.

He glanced back, smiled with his eyes, gave me the thumbs-up as a sign of encouragement.

I motioned and said, "Daniel. Yo. Come back here a second. Come back. Hurry."

He did. My plastic rubbed against his as I kissed him on the lips, then encouraged him closer, tongued him for two seconds. A few people around us applauded. The world loved romance.

I said, "That's all I wanted to say."

"Wow."

As the crowd rumbled and rain fell on plastic coverings, I wished him both speed and luck.

He smiled with his heart, looked surprised, then backed away, pretty much floated away.

Celebrities were on a stand making announcements, cheering us idiots on, telling us we could do it, and thousands of colorful umbrellas filled the sidelines. Nothing in the world was like this moment.

I took my mind off Daniel, same for Driver, roses, forgot Franklin and happy faces on faxes, forgot his wife, and took in the crowd up there at Echo Park, the weather, focused on my purpose for being there. I wasn't going to let someone scare me into abandoning my own goddamn life and personal goals.

Tommie snapped, told Blue to get their house disinfected. She had been too preoccupied to notice Daniel. She told him that she was coming to get all of her things, as much as she could, when the race was done, ended her blasted call, cursed, put her phone on its shoulder strap, shook her head, scowled up at the dark sky. I felt the same way. This was a bad day to have problems at home.

My phone buzzed. I touched the answer button on the earphones.

"Miss McBroom?"

"Driver? You're going to have to speak up. Real rambunctious out here."

"Mrs. Carruthers left Afghanistan. My contact said she finished up her last tour and ended up in North Carolina after a little time was spent at Walter Reed. After that she was at a base in Texas."

"Was?"

Driver said, "She went AWOL."

"What does that mean?"

"It means she's absent without leave."

"I know, but what does that have to do with me? What does it mean in that sense?"

"It has to do with Franklin, as far as I can tell. A service member cannot be served for divorce while they are in the Middle East, but the process can begin. Franklin started the process three or four years ago, but it's not like it is for civilians, and the courts will not give an unfair advantage to a spouse whose partner is deployed and can't show up for the proceedings. Back in World War II a lot of women divorced their husbands while they were in combat. A lot of Dear John letters were sent out, but they passed a law that shut that down. A distraught soldier with a gun might not be a reliable soldier."

"He tried to divorce her before he met me."

Driver said, "Seems that way."

"Not because of me."

"Maybe he assumed it had been processed, then found out it wasn't."

I said, "He knew he was still married. He didn't dispute it when she called."

"He had plenty of time away from her. Basically, it was like he wasn't married."

I said, "So he had time to gallivant around the world and plan a wedding."

"Easy to do when the wife is away dodging bombs."

"Well, she dropped a bomb on me, that's for sure."

Driver said, "His divorce was in limbo, his marriage was in suspended animation, and the paperwork could not be finalized until she returned and was served properly.

"I'm surprised she made it out of there alive.

"When Mrs. Carruthers made it back on American soil, before she could slip away, this time they caught up with her and she was served with divorce papers."

"Come home from war, get slapped with divorce papers."

"I assume she didn't take too kindly to that."

"I guess that was right after she found out he was engaged to me. She was hit with one thing after the next."

"So, if that was the case, she'd think the divorce was all about you. If a man is trying to divorce, and the current wife finds out he's about to remarry, the one put out to pasture would see it that way."

I said, "You were right."

"About what, Miss McBroom?"

"I should have contacted the police a long time ago."

"We can do that now."

"After the race."

"Call me when you're finished."

"What about my home?"

"Panther will sit in front of your house until you return."

"How long has Mrs. Carruthers been AWOL? She's ruining her life, wrecking her career over Franklin?"

"Not sure exactly, but it's been at least a couple of weeks."

"What's her first name? I've never heard him say her first name."

"Her name is Phyllis R. Carruthers."

"Do you have her maiden name?"

"I'll work on that right now. Panther is on the phone with my contact."

"Okay, but don't do anything to get the information that can have you arrested."

"Just letting you know. I'm using a hacker, so all of this information does not come cheap."

I took a deep breath and looked around at thousands of women who could be my enemy.

I asked, "Can you get a photo of Mrs.

Phyllis Carruthers?"

"Will see what I can do."

"Get it and text it to me."

We ended the call just as Rosemary Paige came up behind me. She had on bright pink spandex shorts and a sports bra under a bright yellow poncho. She was dressed minimalist, like a true runner.

She said, "Frankie McBroom."

"Hey, you. You ready to do this?"

My new friend waved at Tommie. "Frankie, I'm going to wiggle by and move up a section."

"Have a good run, Rosemary Paige. Represent the women and beat the Kenyans."

"See you when you're done, Frankie. Will look for you at the finish line."

"I didn't get your preapproval letter."

"I thought that it was sent to your office two days ago."

"It could be there but was overlooked. Things have been hectic in my world."

She hugged me, kissed me on my cheek, then wiggled her way through the rain and the crowd.

The gun went off and I jerked like I'd been shot. The skies opened up like a mortal wound.

The storm grew and the crowd roared

loud, long, and strong. It was the beginning of the end.

FRANKIE

At mile nine we were at Barnsdall Art Park. A group came up behind me on my right, their crowd about ten runners deep, moving like warriors going to rescue the three hundred missing girls in Nigeria.

I said, "Tommie. That guy with the wild Afro who passed by, is that Beale Streets?"

Tommie sped up, ran by guys wearing Elvis Presley costumes, a barefoot Mexican carrying his country's flag, a fat Batman, and another woman with more muscles than any man I had ever dated.

That was when I saw Franklin Carruthers. He was in the crowd of cheering spectators, dressed in Levi's, a cap, and a T-shirt. His face held damage from being struck by Driver last night.

He didn't run the race that day, but he was there. Tommie didn't notice.

I made a call as I ran, again to Driver, told him I had seen Franklin Carruthers.

He said, "Keep your eye out for him. Call me back the moment you have an issue."

I sped up, paced myself four steps behind Tommie. She ran with Beale Streets. He grinned at Tommie as sweat rolled over his smooth complexion like liquid sugar. People recognized him. The young man whom women on the sidelines were trying to get a photo of, he ignored the crowd, only eyed my sister. Tommie had on spandex shorts and a sports bra. I was dressed the same way now. The T-shirts and gloves we had had on at the start of the race had been tossed to the side of the road miles ago.

Tommie told Beale Streets, "Get back on pace, babe."

"I'll look for you when we're done."

Beale Streets and his running crew grabbed cups of water from the outstretched arms of the volunteers, sipped, and poured the rest over their heads. Beale Streets and his partners eased away.

The fear caused by seeing Franklin rose and mixed with a rush of adrenaline.

Tommie said, "Slow down, Frankie. Fall back to our pace."

"Beale Streets. What's that guy to you, Tommie?"

"Stop talking. Save your energy. We lost twenty seconds on the last mile."

"You're seeing Beale Streets, and don't tell me you're not seeing him."

"It's because of Angela. I hooked up with him because of Angela."

"I'm sorry, did Mo's mother hold you down and stuff another man's magic stick inside you?"

"Being with Blue has been one long mind-fuck, so don't mind me if I fuck someone else."

"Let me send you back to therapy, Tommie. I'm serious. You're angry. I am very worried."

"Frankie, enough trying to fix me. Besides, there ain't nothing you can do anyway."

"You left Angela at your house throwing up and you don't know how to deal with a woman who acts like that. I would've come to your crib and handled that nonsense like I was Olivia Pope."

"She's nothing to me. Angela is nothing. Will deal with it and Blue when the race is done."

"We should all deal with it."

"It's my problem."

"This is a family issue."

Tommie said, "Since this is family, let's call a meeting and deal with Franklin. Deal with that first."

"Don't tell Livvy about Franklin. Let me

tell her."

"Livvy has her own concerns. Livvy and Tony . . . they have issues on a grand scale. I will never, ever sleep in that bed in their guest room again. I will never be able to look at them the same way. Gross. There are things a woman should never see her sister doing while getting other things done to her."

"What did you see at Livvy's this morning?"

"So you did sleep with Franklin last night, or this morning, or whenever you saw him?"

"Hell no, and answer my question and tell me what you saw at Livvy's house."

"How did he get into your house? Why do you have that man and woman in black suits coming by like they work for the Men in Black? Who steals drawers to sniff but leaves flowers and Gatorade?"

"What in the name of Saint Peter and Mother Teresa did you see at Livvy's house?"

FRANKIE

At the twentieth mile marker we saw Livvy. In the heat of the day, our middle sister called out to us.

She was posted near the water station. Middle sister Livvy hopped into the race. The unshaved part of her mane was pulled back into a healthy ponytail. Her bright yellow running shorts and green T-shirt were fresh and drier than Las Vegas.

Livvy said, "I've seen a lot of people from our group. Probably forty people at least."

Frankie asked, "Who were the last ones to go by before we got here?"

"Dr. Debra and Dr. Shelby are going to finish at about three hours and a half."

"We'll never catch them. They will have bragging rights this year."

Tommie panted, "Why in the hell . . . do we . . . keep . . . doing this shit . . . year . . . after . . . goddamn year? I'm never doing this again. Never. How did I let you talk me into running in the damn rain?"

Livvy said, "Focus, baby sister. You're almost home."

Tommie went on and on: "We're not getting paid. We're tearing down our bodies. *We're morons.*"

Livvy was just getting warmed up and Tommie and I had entered the Zone of the Suffering. Every part of my body ached from pounding the pavement the last 105,000 feet. Muscles and mind cried in agony. Legs were on fire. Arms were anvils. Sweat ran from the top of my scalp to the arches of my feet. Tommie looked worse. I reached into my fanny pack, took out a piece of candy to suck on and get a sugar high, handed her one, then asked her if she was okay, and she barely nodded. Paramedics tended to people who had overheated and broken down. One guy was bleeding from his rear. That wasn't my business. We heard that two people had had heart attacks a few miles back. All of the drama was typical.

Livvy asked, "Tommie, did you come by my house last night or early this morning?"

Tommie spat, wiped her mouth. "If you're asking, then you already know the answer."

Livvy said, "Jesus, Tommie. You said that you were in bed by ten. Why did you lie?"

"You said the same thing, Livvy. You were in bed, but I guess you should've been more specific."

I said, "What is the issue between you two? What was going on at your house, Livvy?"

Tommie said, "Worry about your house, Frankie."

Livvy said, "Tommie, you came by my crib in the middle of the night."

"I came by your house, Livvy. Had my headphones on when I came in, so I didn't hear you before I saw you."

I said, "Somebody want to tell me what's going on?"

Tommie said, "Do you want to tell Livvy what's going on with you, Frankie?"

Livvy asked, "What's going on with Frankie?"

I said, "Want to tell Livvy what's going on with you, Tommie?"

Livvy asked, "What's going on with you, Tommie?"

"I know you don't want to start a question-asking party, Livvy."

The last mile was ten kinds of hell, but we smelled the Pacific Ocean and that seawater called me. About one hundred yards out we kicked it hard, huffed and puffed, gave it all we had, and took it down to a sub-eight-minute-mile pace. I was at the right end, Livvy was next to me, and Tommie was next to Livvy. We held hands and raised them up high. We crossed the finish line like we had won the damn race. Our photo would make us look like champions. We had conquered 26 miles and 385 yards in four hours and six minutes. While I took deep breaths and felt like crying because we had done it again, I hugged Livvy. Beta-endorphins danced around in my head and gave me that sensation of calmness. Livvy was in pain. As exhausted as Livvy was, you would think she had run the entire race. Tommie limped around like she was auditioning for *The Walking Dead* and kept cringing and making butt-ugly faces. Those 42 kilometers had messed her up. She took her cellular out. I knew she was back to her anger and calling Blue. Trash day at her house. Hands on hips, a Mylar blanket over my shoulders to keep my body heat from escaping, I inhaled lungfuls of salty air and limped around on throbbing muscles and numb feet. Livvy walked with us. She saw Dr. Debra and Dr. Shelby and went to congratulate them.

Sweating profusely, panting, I asked Tommie, "Who are you looking for?"

Tommie marched through the hundreds

of aching and chafed people, found her way over to Beale Streets. I watched them. Something intense was going on. She wiped sweat from her brow, then pulled a note out of her fanny pack and handed it to him. She put the note in his sweaty hands, held his hands, and looked in his eyes, her expression very somber, very serious. She was talking fast. His excited grin went away; his expression of happiness turned into confusion. He tried to say something, but Tommie shook her head. He tried to hold on to her fingers, but she pulled away, lowered her head, and as she was talking she backed up. She shook her head like she was done talking and left him standing there. He called her name. She didn't look back. He looked stunned and she looked incredibly sad. He walked after her, but she turned, jogged away, sensed he was chasing her and held up her hand, and that rejection, that body language, told him not to follow her. That was a good-bye, done in public. He watched her five-foot-ten frame move through the exhausted and jubilant crowd.

Eyes down, maybe not feeling good about herself, Tommie came to me. She came and stood by me to feel protected. I knew her. She came to me like I was her mother.

I asked, "How long have you been cheating on Blue, Tommie?"

"A relationship is like a marathon. It can start off rough, but you have to warm up. You have to find the right pace. Not every mile is going to be easy. Sometimes you have to get your second wind and refocus. It's not always going to feel good. It's about how bad you want it. You have to be committed."

"Save the Easter speech and poetry for a fool. How many times did you sleep with that young guy, Tommie?"

"I need my family."

"That many times. Why would you do that, Tommie?"

"Family is all that matters in the end, Frankie."

Not far away, Beale Streets leaned against a rail and read the pages of whatever Tommie had given him. An incredulous look was plastered on his face, an expression similar to the one I had when a woman called me and told me she was married to the man I was engaged to and trying to procreate with.

In a firm yet angered and worried voice I asked, "What's in the letter?"

"It's an A and B matter, so C your way out. I don't press you about Franklin, your car getting jacked up, your business being attacked. You have your secrets. I have mine.

Learn where to draw the line, Frankie. It's not your business."

I reached and pulled her hair like I was trying to take a handful out by the roots.

She screamed.

I asked, "How long have you been seeing that guy?"

"It's over. I did some hard thinking while I ran. I know what I want to fight for."

"How long?"

"It's. Over. Let me go, Frankie. Have you lost your mind?"

"No, but you have definitely lost yours." I let her sweaty hair free. "We're going to need that note back."

We moved on, limped by people who had come from all over the world and heard at least fifty languages.

At the friends and family meet-up area, we saw Blue and his daughter.

Tommie was shocked to see Blue. Monica ran to Tommie, called her Mommy loud enough for the world to hear. People around them laughed at the display of love. Tommie switched modes, became joy and smiles. Tommie and Mo kissed each other and laughed like the world was made of cotton candy.

Beale Streets stood to the side, all five foot eleven inches of him, with a thirty-two-inch waist and severe Abercrombie & Fitch model looks, only now the man with the badass Afro owned a bad-tempered expression, like rejection had given him viral meningitis. He raised his head in degrees.

He saw Tommie with her family.

Beale looked like he walked into a temple, didn't like what was going on, and was ready to start flipping over tables.

I hoped he wouldn't.

I hoped he knew better.

Tommie kissed Blue on his lips. Beale saw her tongue Blue. The twentysomething man looked through the swelling crowd of overachievers, glowered toward Tommie and the man she was engaged to marry. Tommie hugged Blue, his back to us, while she made curt eye contact with Beale Streets, swallowed like she felt trapped, then diverted her attention, took Blue's hand in her right hand, held Monica's hand in her left. She held Blue's hand tight, then kissed him again and again and again, each kiss a message to Beale. That was a statement as powerful as whatever was in that long letter.

His Dear John letter in his sweaty hands, wearing one of the Mylar warmers over his shoulders, Beale Streets was pissed. He was outraged. He moved through the crowd, his pace as if the run had caused him no pain whatsoever, and directed himself toward Tommie and her family.

I was heading to cut the young buck off, but Livvy was already jogging in that direction.

Livvy said, "What's going on? What did you do to upset my sister?"

I added, "Walk away, Beale Streets. Take your pretty eyes and put them on someone new."

Livvy tilted her head. "I was at his event with Tommie. Wait. Tommie's creeping with this guy? I knew something was going on."

I waved her away. "I got this, Livvy. Go keep Blue and Tommie away from this."

Livvy asked Beale, "Is that why your ex did that drive-by singing and bloodied her knees? Is that why the mean girl walked up and had words with Tommie? Was that performance for Tommie and you?"

Beale responded. "I guess you don't know. I'm in love with Tommie and Tommie is in love with me."

I said, "No you're not. Don't even fool yourself into thinking like that."

"You don't know the truth. We're blissfully in love. She knows she loves me. She was with me late last night. Well, more like the early hours of this morning. She was with me, in my bed, before she went to your

403

house, Frankie. We made love before she went to your house. She's moving in with me *today.* That is what she told me *after we made love.*"

"Don't lie on my sister like that."

"We made love. Ask her."

I said, "Look over my shoulder and you can see who Tommie is in love with, Beale Streets."

Livvy said, "Walk away, Beale Streets. Blue will beat your ass and my husband will help him."

I said, "He'll crucify you, right here, in public."

Livvy continued, "So if you know what's good for you, drop the letter, then walk away, forget about my little sister."

I said, "Don't make new enemies today."

Livvy added, "This is the wrong family to mess with."

My cellular vibrated. It was on my right arm. I didn't bother to look at it, not now.

One crisis at a time was all I could handle.

I said, "Before you walk away, Beale, like my sister just told you, whatever Tommie gave you, I need it back right now."

He shook his head. "This is from Tommie to me, and this matter is between Tommie and me."

"I want the note that she gave you and I

want that note right now."

He shook his head, then smiled. "Sorry, my sisters, and no disrespect, but I don't know you. Tommie talks about both of you all the time, told me about your false engagement, Frankie. And Livvy, or Olivia, she has told me a lot about you as well. It feels like I know both of you, but I know I don't."

Then I heard a voice over the music and international chatter. "Beale Streets? Is that you over there with the McBrooms? Tommie, it's Beale Streets. Let's go over and tell our favorite writer hello."

It was Blue's voice. All conversation ended and everyone tensed and looked in his direction.

He came up behind us; Mo was holding Tommie's hand, and they were a few steps behind Blue.

Livvy took a step back, but I took a step closer to Beale Streets, put my hand on Pretty Eyes's shoulder, and gave him a smile that dared him to fuck up my sister's relationship, here, now, in public.

Blue extended his hand and Beale Streets extended his. Blue was muscular, another LL Cool J. Beale Streets was toned but not as powerful. There was a twenty-year age difference between the men.

Blue said, "Beale Streets, remember my fiancée, Tommie? I bought her your book when it first came out. She's read it two or three dozen times. She's as big a fan as I am. We were at your event."

Beale nodded, said, "Tommie."

Blue said, "How is Tanya Obayomi? I see her at the gym. The conversation is always about you."

"I've moved on, so there is no need to converse regarding me and her."

"She asks me for advice on how to get you to come back to her."

"My energies are elsewhere. I am focused on someone else now."

Beale Streets stared at Tommie, mouth open, the note bouncing against his leg. Beale Streets and Blue looked like they could pass for brothers. Beale was a younger version of Blue, with no child.

Blue said, "And this is the princess of the castle. Say hello to Mr. Streets, Monica. He's a writer like Daddy and Mommy. He's one of the best writers in America."

Mo said, "Good afternoon, Mr. Streets. *Hola, cómo está usted, si usted habla español.* You're older than me so I have to use *usted* to show respect, unless you tell me it's okay to *tuteo* with you."

We laughed at Monica. Tony had been

teaching her Spanish since the day he met her.

Beale cleared his throat and said, "Nice to meet you, Monica. You're a beautiful little girl."

Monica said, "The pleasure to meet you is all mine, Mr. Streets."

"Tommie is your mother?"

"She's better than my mother. She makes sure I have food every day and makes sure I have everything I need. She cares about me and never ignores me. When my daddy marries her I'm going to adopt Tommie to be my real mother and me and Daddy are changing our last names to McBroom."

Everyone laughed.

Tommie said, "We're a happy family, Beale. We have speed bumps, but we're very happy."

Then there was silence. Awkward silence with Beale holding the pages of whatever Tommie had given him in his hand, his body language telling me he was two seconds from reading it all out loud.

I said, "Y'all keep going. Livvy, I see Tony over there looking for you. He's with a tall Asian woman. Anyway, I was chatting with Beale and now I need some space, people. I know my lips are dry and cracking, but all of y'all are happy couples and I'm single and trying to get my flirt on over here."

Blue took Tommie's hand, and they headed away, the Santa Monica breeze cool on our faces. Tommie glanced back at me, but not at Beale Streets. She was scared.

I said, "Maybe I came at you too direct, too strong, and for that I will apologize. Now, I'm asking politely, will you please give me whatever correspondence Tommie gave you, Beale?"

"With all due respect, Frankie, this correspondence belongs to me."

" 'Miss McBroom' to you."

"I love Tommie and Tommie is in love with me, not Blue. She loves me. I won't embarrass her out here, but let me tell you this truth. She's had enough of him. He's using her and has no intention of giving her what she deserves. He had a vasectomy in order not to get her pregnant. I would give her the world."

What I saw in Beale Streets's pretty eyes was profound, love and obsession swimming together.

Then I saw Tony and the tall Asian woman. She was as tall as Tommie. She was dressed casually. Jeans and flats, a UK flag on her sweatshirt, a SANTA MONICA hoodie dangling in her hands. I guess she'd bought that on the boardwalk. They were laughing, heading toward Livvy. She hugged both of them. My suspicion that Tony had gone creeping down baby-making Cheaters Row again went away.

I walked away from Beale Streets, went over, and they introduced me to the Asian woman. She was a doctor from the UK. Her accent made her hard to understand, so that ended the conversation.

Tommie didn't come over, wasn't interested in meeting the Asian lady.

I felt a chill and looked for Franklin again. As I walked through the crowd, someone followed me.

"Frankie McBroom?"

I turned around to see whose unfamiliar voice had called my full name like I owed him money.

I saw him, saw his smile, and said, "Daniel."

He handed me a blue Gatorade.

I asked, "Why are you giving me Gatorade? What's the significance?"

"You said you'd want a sports drink when you were done. It's what they're giving out."

I looked around, noticed a hundred runners carrying the same sports drink.

I accepted, opened it, and took a long chug, replenished before I told him thanks.

Beale Streets was still there, off to the side,

rereading whatever Tommie had given him.

People came over to him, tried to start conversations, but he brushed them all away.

He was dealing with heartache. An abrupt heartache that had blindsided him.

Tommie clung to Blue like she was afraid. She was scared but was playing it off.

Blue smiled, but his eyes frowned. Tommie held his hand, but he didn't hold hers back.

They might be breaking up after all, only it wouldn't be Tommie leaving Blue.

While Daniel was excited and talking, I cut him off, asked him to excuse me for a moment. I checked my phone before sending Driver a text. He called right away and the news he had scared me.

He said, "Okay, the social security number you gave me for Franklin and the one on the military papers seeking divorce are different social security numbers. He's lied to either you or the government."

"What else is there to lie about?"

"He has a felony theft from 2004."

"He's a felon? Franklin Carruthers, the man I was falsely engaged to, is a felon?"

"I'm not done. Actually I'm only at the top of his rap sheet."

"Jesus. How many offenses does he have?"

"He has one from '04, another from '05, forgery from '06, felony forgery from '07, and a bail-jumping charge from 2008."

"Why didn't anyone come after him, like in the movies?"

"Maybe he fell through a crack. All I can say is it looks like he got himself a fake social and changed — well, modified — his last name. Somewhere along the line he found seed money to start his business. He's living the life but hasn't shared any of his wealth with his wife. He's a one-percenter and she's in the military, drawing a salary that next to his would look like the taxes on a welfare check, if there were taxes on welfare checks."

"What is his real last name?"

"It's spelled C-a-r-o-t-h-e-r-s and pronounced the same way as C-a-r-r-u-t-h-e-r-s. He did a minor makeover, grew dreadlocks, and reinvented himself. He's not from Alabama. He was born in Houston, grew up in one of the six wards, then moved to Oklahoma. When things got too hot with the law, he gave himself a new state, Alabama. The only thing the same is the Southern accent. If he hadn't married his wife using his new identity, the one that made him a bona fide 'Bama man, he never would have needed a divorce to marry you. He could've just walked away from that old life and been your husband."

I was speechless. I was humiliated. I had introduced that con man to my family and friends. I had traveled the world with him. Had planned a wedding, and was trying to make a baby with him. I was numb. Couldn't think, could barely speak.

Driver said, "Take a deep breath. We have more things to discuss before we hang up."

"Okay."

"Did he have access to your personal information?"

"He was with me day and night, lived at my home, had access to my entire life."

"You told me that you saw him while you were running today?"

"He could've hit me in the back of the head, that's how close he was to me at one point."

"Are you safe, Miss McBroom?"

I told Driver that I was with my family, with other men who could protect me, so I was cool.

We ended the call.

I took a deep breath and with mixed feelings gave my attention back to Daniel.

I tried to fake the funk, but the anxiety was insurmountable and pretending wasn't my style.

I said, "Let me be honest. This isn't going

to happen. My life is complicated at the moment."

"So you're not single."

"I am. But I have to resolve a major issue before you and I can go any farther. And after it's resolved, I don't think I can see you. I don't think I will be able to see anyone, not romantically. Don't take it personally, Daniel. It's my mess."

"What happened?"

"That's not up for discussion."

"May I ask what the odds are of you calling me again?"

I said, "Thanks for the Gatorade. Vodka mixed with Jack Daniels would've been better, but I won't complain."

Monica ran over. She gave me the tightest hug and told me she was proud of me. I waved good-bye to Daniel, walked away holding Mo's hand.

"Auntie, you're *awesome.* You and Mommy ran the entire marathon and never stopped."

Monica was pure love. She was like Tommie, and that almost made me wish I had a kid. Almost. The damn kid had stolen all our hearts. In my mind she was already a McBroom.

Seconds later, Rosemary Paige weaved through the crowd and sprinted over to me in a hurry.

She pulled me to the side and spoke with urgency, her concern nothing to do with real estate.

She said, "Frankie McBroom. Hurry and come with me. Someone vandalized your car. They carved *bitch* and *whore* in the paint, broke out all of your windows, and flattened all of your tires."

"No, no, no, no, no."

"I hate to be the one to bring you the bad news."

"I don't believe he did this again. I don't believe he's treating me like this."

"You know who did it?"

"I know who did it."

Panic gave me an adrenaline rush. Franklin had found and attacked my car because of last night. I didn't want Mo and Livvy to see that, didn't want Tony and Blue to know. That made my heart pump and without pause I left with Rosemary Paige, running to get to her car so she could hurry me back to mine.

Around the same time I was hurrying off with Rosemary Paige, Driver was receiving his information on Franklin's wife.

The woman he had married, then tried to dump to marry me, had also become a thief. The car with the Texas plates wasn't hers.

She had driven back and forth, had gone from San Antonio to LA twice, had driven fourteen hundred miles one way, no doubt wearing a diaper to reduce potty stops, in order to track me down, had found me, then gone back to the base before finally going AWOL.

Driver knew exactly where she was and was calling me as he tried to rush to pick me up. The GPS on the car she had stolen from a friend in the military, a friend who was still deployed in the Middle East, showed she was already in Los Angles. Her maiden name was Phyllis Rosemary Paige.

I didn't see that coming.

It was hidden in plain sight and I never saw it coming.

As I jogged away with Rosemary Paige, Mo sprinted behind us.

I heard her calling out for me over the celebration and its rumble. She zigzagged through the crowd and caught up.

Mo thought I was going to the bathroom and needed to go real bad, so Tommie had sent her to go with me. I looked back and saw Tommie, waved at her, saw that things now looked tense between her and Blue, assumed that Beale Streets had created damage, and if things were going to be said, I preferred that Monica not be there to witness or hear those words, so I grabbed Mo's hand and hurried her along.

Even in the midst of my most trying moment, I was still their big sister, still had responsibilities, and I was doing my best to protect my siblings, doing what I could to make sure my family was okay, but I felt our world falling apart.

TOMMIE

Beale Streets. My friend. Read this. Please read every word.

Pardon the blotches on the page. Ink runs when mixed with salty water. I'm crying.

I'm engaged and now I know how a cheating woman feels. I hate the feeling, but true love is so strong. I should feel like a queen with Blue as my leader, not a pauper. I want to marry him, wanted to marry him long before we had even kissed the first time, because he's a great guy, he's humble and hardworking, and he would be a great husband, but the things that he brought with him, his leftovers, have left me in a state the opposite of bliss. We have issues that love might not be able to erase or mend. I'm confused. I'm afraid. After all we've shared, I don't want you to think badly of me.

I hope to have the courage to give you this ridiculous letter that reads like a manifesto.

I want to look you in your eyes, be a woman, not a coward who sends a text or tweets, or sends a message on Facebook, to tell you that we are done, that this is over. I will tell you, then go back to my life. Tonight I will be in bed in the modest three-bedroom home that I share with Blue. We have a home, not a house. We have love in every room; we have the sounds of joy and pain.

We are family.

I will sleep with my back to him and he will snuggle up against me.

He will mold his beautiful body against mine as he has done since we started our journey.

I will wear a T-shirt and no bottoms. He will touch me, feel that skin, and understand the signal.

He will pull me to him and kiss me, give me his tongue, then pull my just-put-on T over my head.

He will go down the hallway to check on Mo, then come back, ease our door closed, and turn the lock. He will want me and I will never tell him no, because I always want him. I want him to always want me. I have never stopped wanting him. I wouldn't know how to breathe if he stopped wanting me.

It is the intrusion of his ex that has set me on the wrong path.

We will try to be quiet, and I don't mind.

Love doesn't need to shout to be heard.

Love is most powerful as soft whispers and softer moans.

I will make sure he has an orgasm. If he wants another, I will please him again. When we're done, I'll get up and unlock the door, pull on a T-shirt, then tiptoe down the hallway and check on Mo again.

By the time I make it back, he will have pulled his boxers back on.

We will once again cuddle. No talking. Eyes closed. Hearts beating next to each other.

He will fall asleep first and I will lie there with my eyes open, wondering what my life would have been if I had never met him. I will wonder why he was the man I fell in love with at that time of my life.

I will wonder why I love him now.

I will wonder what he sees in me.

I will wonder what would have happened if he had never moved into the apartment across the street from mine, if I had never developed a crush on him after watching him be so good with his daughter. Maybe I thought that he was the type, that if we had a child, he would be good to our child too.

But we did meet.

I pursued him.

I have to remember that I was the anxious one in this relationship.

This was my choice.

I promised him that I could handle anything that came my way.

I promised my sisters that I could handle this the way our mother handled all of us.

I had thought that by now we'd be an official family, that he and I would have made at least one beautiful child together. He didn't live up to what he had promised. Maybe my expectations were too high.

It can be a horrible thing to expect so much from someone else.

It can be so unfair, asking them to commit to our own selfish needs.

Maybe the unhappiness isn't about Angela.

It could be about me not getting what I want.

Maybe I am behaving like a spoiled brat.

Maybe this is my way of throwing a temper tantrum.

Maybe it's about that other definite thing that happened between Blue and me that made things indefinite. Maybe the vasectomy is the root of my anger. That was the first time I felt the enormous weight of that emotion called betrayal. It was debilitating. Not every betrayal is about someone having sex with another. When we don't get what we want, when we feel swindled, misdirected, that is disloyalty as well. I had been loyal to Blue in all ways. I had been honest, up front, considerate, and loyal. I was ride or die. I was his virgin whore. Sexual betrayal is the effect, the cause deeper than the roots of a cottonwood tree.

Now, day and night, I stare at the elephant in the room.

Our elephant is bold but has no balls.

I still wondered if he had a vasectomy because he was seeing someone else.

There was no proof. I looked high and low, went through all of his accounts and receipts.

Nothing.

It confused me that he would do that for no reason. Or maybe he didn't trust me and felt the need to simply outsmart me. It left me feeling emotionally dismantled.

I had played our relationship out in my mind, from our wedding to our first child.

A woman can plan. A woman thinks she needs a man for nothing in this world but soon realizes she is wrong. The same way every black-owned business has to acquire goods from a white distributor, women have to do business with men, be it professional or personal, to achieve too many of our goals.

They have the goods.

I guess I could say Blue kept his goods from ever being shipped from the warehouse.

I wonder if I really want to have a baby or if it's just because he took that option off the table.

I wonder if he was trying to force me to turn to another man in order to fulfill my dreams.

You have said many things that hurt me, but I have to thank you for the truth.

I didn't like feeling deceived. But he is still there with me, in love with me. Supporting me in all I do. If I had become pregnant, then I suppose he would have felt trapped. I will try to refocus on the commitment I have made to him and his daughter, will make love to him, will comb her hair, will make us breakfast, as she calls me Mommy, as Blue calls me his future wife. I want this.

When I am angry at Blue, when I feel that bottomless disappointment, then I feel fear, and in those moments I have to be careful, have to not seek you out as the remedy, because that is not a cure, only a poison.

Sex is more than physical and the act of exchanging energy in that manner is different for a man than it is for a woman. Men penetrate women, take corporeal shape inside of us, and we surround you, envelop you, feel the intrusion into our physical bodies. You touch our spirits.

A man enters a woman and for that duration he is inside of her in many ways.

Therefore a man becomes part of her in all ways.

Man throbs. Woman feels.

She feels him as he fills her up.

A man moves inside a woman.

You took up residence inside of me.

You were part of me.

You lived inside of me.

I held you captive inside of me and I did not want to let go.

We were one, without beginning, without end. A man can feel a woman, but he puts his energy of life inside her. Whether you're on your back with me on top of you, or if you're behind, or on top of me, you'll never comprehend what a woman feels. You control her and only feel pleasure. A woman feels pain and pleasure caused by a man, and the man only feels pleasure. A woman feels more.

The imprint does not fade when the sex is over.

The shape of you has changed the shape of me.

I can't allow two men to live within me.

I can't keep changing shapes mentally, physically, and emotionally.

I can't be a mother to Monica and a lover to you as you are a lover to me.

I can't have the seed from two men battling for victory inside of me.

But there can be no battle. Not when one is unarmed.

If you won, then I would gain what I think I desire but lose everything my heart wants.

I can't be on my back with you between my legs, sucking on my neck, my ear, my tongue, arousing me as I hold your erection, guiding it inside of me again, starting what I won't want to end.

For me the connection between love and sex and orgasm is strong.

I've always led my sex life with restraint.

I am an artist, a liberal, but I am not a libertine.

I am not a liar, yet I have become both.

You are a beautiful dream that I run to when the sun is high. You are my daydream. You are the light that I bring to my darkness. I have to abandon all daydreams and

424

face the truth.

I hope that you are still reading.

I hope the blotches, the tears, haven't washed away my words.

This has to end.

Eventually Blue will suspect.

I think he already does.

He doesn't suspect you.

He suspects that someone is distracting me.

I was getting to the point where I didn't care.

I was almost at the point where I wanted him to find out.

Eventually he will see your fingerprints on my skin, smell you on my breath, or taste you on my tongue. Or worse, I will become too emotional and want him to find out. I will sabotage myself.

I can't come back to your bed, your floor, your wall, your chair, your stairs, your shower. Coming back to fall into that liberating madness with you again and again will do nothing more than destroy my future. Or destroy the future of an innocent child who loves me so much. Destroying her would destroy me. I love that child more than anything in the world. More than I could ever love you. More than I love Blue. Mo needs me the way I needed Frankie and

Livvy's mother. That little girl was born of another woman, but I am her mother on this earth. I am her role model. Having her in my life gives me purpose.

You were unhappy, a man who longed to know his real parents.

I was in a state of rage I didn't know how to deal with.

We both were in search of our identities.

We both wanted to know who we really are.

We filled empty spaces for one another.

We gave each other a place to put our rage.

We can't control our lives, so we tried to control each other.

When one person is heartbroken and the other is unhappy, misery is the common enemy. When unhappiness meets misery, it is easy to fall in love for the wrong reasons.

Letting that love go is hard. Love comes fast but fades slowly, slowly, slowly. I am fighting gravity. Scared tears roll down my disingenuous face. It is the pain from my excoriated heart. Remembering you inside me. Many rooms. Countless positions. I am hiding from those sensations and stirred emotions in the bathroom of my home, a coward with insomnia due to childish chaos. Existing between come-stained sheets in my mind. I exist between here and there.

Between greed and hunger. Between the taste and smell of you and the taste and smell of him. Between happiness and misery. Between lie and truth.

I exist in this space for the last time. You have existed in my space for the last time.

I have chosen and the choice was not an easy one. I wrote Blue a farewell letter before I began to pen this one. But that letter will not be delivered. I did not choose you, Beale. I am sorry.

Tears fall as I write these simple words.

I am sorry.

Never meant to *heart* you.

Never meant to *hurt* you either, because I *heart* you so much.

I can say that now that it is over. I heart you.

I heart you so much, and yet not enough at the same time. I could never heart you the way I heart Blue. I would never leave Blue to be with you, but if we were together, despite the chance to have a better life, despite all of your trappings of success, even if we were married with children, I would leave you for Blue in the beat of a broken heart. Each day I would live to catch a glimpse of him again, to have him see me, to have him welcome me. If he wanted, I would have an affair with him. My heart would explode and you would become insignificant. I would leave you and abandon the children to be with him again.

I would leave all you have and choose to be poor with him.

That's love, Beale. That's real love. That's beyond choosing what feels good at the moment.

I've been hurt before. Physically and mentally abused by my first boyfriend. That violence was my secret. That pain I felt, I would never wish that on anyone. If I have hurt your heart, forgive me.

Forgive me.

If not now, then in your own time, in your own way.

Just forgive me.

I have to go back to the family I love.

I will go back to our arguments, because those are our arguments.

I will go stand by Blue and face the dawn, each time ready to fight at his side.

It has never been my goal in life to heart someone and then hurt them like this.

I want you to find your parents, if that is what will give you your peace.

I want you to try again with Tanya Obayomi, if I was the cause of your rejecting her.

She loves you. I know she does. It's impossible not to love you. She bloodied her knees for you. She sang for you, from her soul. She made herself look stupid in the name of love, and that is love.

I want you to be happy. Let us both thrive on happiness, not pain.

I am a happy person. I used to be the happiest person I knew.

I want to find a way back to being her again, but only for Blue.

This is my first step.

Saying good-bye to you is the necessary first step.

With each word I pray that you own the emotional maturity to understand.

If I had owned emotional maturity, this never would have commenced.

I take the fault for all of this. I take the blame.

I write this much partly because I am scared. This letter has been partly me debating between my needs, my fantasies, stability, and curiosity. You are my secret. You felt right, but you are my wrong. I need you to not reveal yourself. I need you to be my friend. If you love me as you say, be my ally, my second self, not a false friend gathering ammunition and waiting for my weakest moment to start firing secrets.

This is Tommie McBroom, at her weakest

moment.

This is Tommie McBroom, as terrified as she has ever been in her life.

This had to end for you.

For me, this has ended.

We're done.

We're done.

We're done.

This is good-bye from your confused muse, who now has profound clarity.

This is a parting farewell from your eclectic, bohemian, bourgeois friend.

Tommie McBroom

FRANKIE

Once I was inside Rosemary Paige's sports car, she sped us along the 10 eastbound toward downtown LA. Monica fell asleep in the back. She had had a long night. Music was on low, Alice Smith covering Cee Lo's "Fool for You" on repeat, but I hadn't noticed the song of obsession.

Rosemary Paige said, "You're an amazing woman, Frankie McBroom."

"You're in the wrong lane. We need to merge to the left to get on the 101 North."

She didn't merge onto the 101 North to head back toward Dodger Stadium.

I said, "What is this, some kind of a joke?"

"It should be obvious, Frankie Mc-Broom."

"You need to get over and take the next exit."

My phone buzzed at that moment and I looked at the text message. It was a photo from Driver. He had verified a photo of

Franklin's wife on social media. That was when I knew I was in the car with Phyllis Rosemary Paige. Something showed on my face, some realization, because that was when she reached under her seat and took out a military-issued gun.

In a tone of complete disbelief I said, "You're Franklin's wife."

Gun resting in her lap, Rosemary Paige reached underneath her seat again and that time she pulled out a bloodied knife.

She whispered, "Think about the kid, Frankie."

My voice filled with fear and anger. "What are your intentions, Mrs. Carruthers?"

"I really wanted this to be between you and me at the end."

Eyes on her, I moved away from her. "You're Franklin's wife."

"I am the real Mrs. Carruthers, not the one who wants to be."

"Why are you driving east on the 10? Nothing beyond downtown but cows, smog, and gangs."

"Mexico. This ends south of the border. I complete my personal mission."

"This is kidnapping. You are kidnapping a minor and me. Look, I am not with you willingly and I demand that you stop and let me and Monica out of your fancy red

Dodge Charger at the next exit."

"You have a nice home, Frankie. I liked the smaller one better, but the larger one is nice."

"It was you. You broke into my homes."

"I want you to know that any time I wanted to I could've hurt you and you never would have seen it coming. I dressed as you dress, even wore your lingerie, ate in your kitchen, slept in your bed during the day, took showers, lived in your house pretty much right under your nose."

"You put on my underwear?"

"Only the brand-new stuff. Victoria's Secret is expensive. I'm not gross. I had to dress like you, get into your mind and try to understand what Franklin saw in you that he didn't see in me.

"Your home laptop isn't password protected. I know you stopped e-mailing him and I know he's never stopped e-mailing you. I read every love e-mail he sent you. That hurt my heart. He never sent me one love e-mail. I am his wife, and I was overseas fighting for his freedom, and not one love note."

"I have no control over that."

"I was inside your home the night you went on a date and kissed a handsome guy good night at the front door. I was on the other side of the door watching you and him make out. You and Daniel."

"I don't believe you. My alarm was on. It was always on."

"Believe it, Frankie. I know all of your secrets. I went into your special room. The one at your first house, you were in that room with Franklin, doing things with my husband. You're a piece of work."

"You broke into my home over and over, and now you're chastising my personal life?"

"You sleep with my husband, insult me, and have the nerve to look disgusted?"

"This is not the way to handle this, Mrs. Carruthers."

"I saw the GoPro that Franklin had at his house. I saw what you and he did together."

"Jesus."

"No matter how many times you called his name, there was no Jesus in what you did with my husband. I really wished that I hadn't sat there in his bedroom and pushed play and seen what I saw."

"Gatorade and flowers. You sat at my dining room table sipping Gatorade and holding flowers."

"Gifts from Franklin's home. I had a little fun. When I first found where he lived, when I bypassed his security and went inside his home, I saw your things there. That pissed me off. I brought some of them back to you, that's all. I moved a few things that belonged to him from your house back to his."

"You were in my home last night. You were inside of my home waiting."

"I was in your home when Tommie came over. I was going to have it out with you then, after I knew that you had gone to be with Franklin. I followed him when he went to meet you. He had no idea. He went up the hill, to a place lovers meet after-hours, and I eased up the winding hill behind him with my lights off. I was angry, was going to surprise the two of you. But I saw him talking to a guy. I put my car in neutral and coasted backward down the hill; then I went to your home and waited for you and Franklin."

"How did you get past my alarm system? That system is new. It's the best they make."

"That's classified information. You're a civilian and not privy to how the military operates."

"What do you want from me? I am not at fault here. What have I ever done to you?"

"Franklin. Let's talk about Franklin. Let's have a little girl-talk session on this road trip."

"I have nothing to do with him, and you

know I don't. I want nothing to do with him."

"He fixated on your billboards. He saw your face on bus stops. You were his movie star."

"I have no idea what you're talking about. I sell real estate. People draw mustaches on my images at bus stops. My picture is where people sit and fart while waiting on a smelly Metro bus."

"You were the ideal woman. I don't see the attraction, but beauty is in the eye of the beholder."

"I never went after your husband. We met by accident, Mrs. Carruthers."

"No, it wasn't an accident. It was orchestrated. Step by step, bit by bit, it was orchestrated."

"I didn't go after your husband. I had no idea he was married, not until you called me."

"You were so disrespectful."

"You weren't exactly friendly yourself."

"Look in the glove compartment."

"Is there a bomb in there?"

"I don't hurt children."

I put my fingers on the glove compartment, clicked it open, saw that the inside was jammed with photos. She told me to take all of them out. I did. There were over a thousand snapshots.

All were images of me. It was my life, captured on film.

I asked, "How long have you been following me?"

"I *never* followed you — well, not until recently. I drove across America, came and met you when I had a weekend furlough. I drove day and night from San Antonio to LA and back just because I wanted to look in your eyes and try to understand what was so special about you, Miss Frankie McBroom."

"I don't understand these photos. You've been photographing me since I met Franklin?"

"You're seeing this all wrong. I am not the bad guy here. Franklin took those photos."

I looked at the images, confused, outraged, unable to think clearly.

She said, "He had fixated on you."

"Why are you lying?"

"He had followed you and photographed you."

"I met him by chance when I was at my PO box collecting my mail."

"No, it was calculated. He had spied on you and saw where you collected your mail, and then he rented a mailbox at the same place on La Tijera Boulevard so he'd have a reason to run into you."

I couldn't remember that day, couldn't focus with the blade of a knife pointed at me as she drove sixty-five miles per hour with a loaded gun resting in her lap, the business end aimed toward me. All I remembered, with any clarity, was back then I had the Christmas blues and had run into Franklin.

"He was married to me and obsessed with you. Isn't that just wonderful?"

"For all I know you took these."

"I was deployed. I was tracking terrorists. I was stalking the big game."

"I had no idea, Rosemary Paige."

"Mrs. Carruthers."

"Apologies. I had no idea, Mrs. Carruthers. This is the truth. I investigated him and found out this morning that he had filed for divorce and had tried to file before we ever went out."

"He filed when he started to pursue you, Frankie. Don't you understand this? He filed when he saw you and began to fantasize about you and lose interest in me. He filed while he stalked you."

"After I found out about you, I didn't want him. You heard me put him out of my home."

"He didn't care. He wanted you and

438

wouldn't stop until you said yes, knew eventually you would take him back."

"I have no control over him begging, but I'd never take him back. I will be more than happy to file an order of protection and have it illegal for him to contact me, if that will make you feel better. Just pull into a police station."

"He prefers you to me. That hurts. He changed my life, told me he loved me, and this hurts."

"I have no control over that."

"My parents disowned me because of him."

"How did you meet?"

"I haven't seen or talked to my sisters. I envy what you have with your siblings. I sat and watched you, Tommie, and Livvy. Livvy was lucky. The night I followed her, the night I observed her, the apartment she went to, I had assumed that was her home. I was rushing and careless when I set it on fire."

"You did what?"

"Then the home I had followed Tommie to, I thought it was hers, but then I realized she was having an affair with Beale Streets. I followed her home. If she didn't have a daughter, I would have tossed a firebomb through her front window one night and burned her home to the ground too."

"You're joking."

"I don't harm children, not here in America. Children here are misguided, but they aren't threats, not like overseas."

"You've being following my sisters?"

"*Observing.* Tommie's sweet, and I like her, but she's a mess. It's always the nice ones who do you wrong in the end. Blue is an excellent teacher. Tony, they respect him at his job. I haven't quite figured out the Asian woman that he and Livvy have befriended. She's a doctor, so I think it's a professional friendship. Monica has so much energy when she's at school. The teachers love her."

"You followed my entire family?"

"I studied my enemy and looked for her weakest points."

"I am not your enemy, Mrs. Carruthers."

"You are and you know you are."

"I have never been your enemy. Franklin is the enemy. If anything, we have a common enemy. We should be sipping wine and girl talking about him, comparing notes and dates. We should be trying to figure out how he played us so well."

"I met Franklin online. My parents said the Internet was the devil's tool, but I found a way to connect with a world that they didn't want me to have any part of. My parents were right. They were right. I should've listened to them. I should have stayed in Pennsylvania where I was respected and valued."

"You sound like you have family values. Why would you do things to my family? They have done nothing to harm you."

"Afghanistan. Iraq. Doesn't matter where. Sometimes, even with the best-laid plans, there will be collateral damage."

"Please. Let Monica out of the car."

"You brought her along, Frankie. Whatever happens, it's your fault. This was to be where we ended our race. Our final marathon."

We passed an overhead digital sign. An Amber Alert had been issued. That meant every electronic billboard on every freeway was lit up with the same information. On the digital display was Monica's grinning photo and full name, with the make and model and plates for the car we were in. As we passed cars I saw people look at us, then back at the Amber Alert, then raise their phones and start dialing 911. I saw that people were trying to be brave and follow us as they reported they had seen us, probably with hopes of having their faces on the news as heroes when this nightmare ended.

Rosemary Paige noticed we were getting a lot of attention.

She grinned as if she was amused. "How did they find us?"

I said nothing.

She finally looked up from the traffic and saw the electronic billboard, saw the Amber Alert.

"How do they know, Frankie?"

"That's classified information."

"That's your last time being snarky."

"You can dish it out, but you can't take it."

"Let me see your phone."

I handed it to her.

She saw it was on. GPS was on.

Driver was on the other end.

I said, "He's heard our entire conversation, Rosemary Paige. The authorities know everything."

She dropped my phone out of the window, let it bounce, break, be run over by other vehicles.

I said, "Please, let Monica go."

"You will regret that."

"That's all I ask."

"You are so going to regret that."

"She has nothing to do with this."

It happened so fast, in the blink of an eye. She stabbed me.

Mrs. Carruthers growled and stabbed me viciously in my shoulder.

At first there was no pain at all. My body went into shock. It felt like a cruel prank, then I saw blood, realized that that bitch really had stabbed me. A dull throbbing kicked in and the pain tried to overtake my senses. Pain arrived, sharp and intense. I gritted my teeth, but there was nothing I could do. She had the knife. We were going eighty miles per hour now. She drove extremely fast but was very controlled, methodical.

My pain became great; she had stabbed me down to my bone.

I opened my mouth to cry out, but there was no sound. I struggled to breathe.

She gritted her teeth and said, "Scream and I will do the same to the child."

"Bleeding. I'm bleeding. I'm bleeding."

"I know."

"You stabbed me. You fucking stabbed me."

"Language, Frankie McBroom. Language. And show me some respect."

I was wide-eyed; blood rivered from my wound. What kept me alive flowed from me, but nothing mattered except getting Monica out of this car. Her life mattered more than mine.

That psycopath sang along with Alice Smith as she took curves and transitioned to other freeways at the speed of a rocket. She rode treacherously close to big rigs. That scared me more than the knife wound. She took over the HOV lane and then was moving at one hundred miles an hour through a cluster of big rigs. When traffic bottlenecked, she sped down the shoulder, a dangerous lane where cars could be broken down or there could be debris that could cause a tire to blow and the car to flip at that pace. Several miles later she merged back into regular traffic, a smirk on her face, convinced she had gotten away.

Monica woke up. "Auntie? Why are we going so fast?"

"Monica, everything is okay. I need you to keep your eyes closed."

She could tell we were in trouble, knew that she had woken up in my hell.

Monica cried, revealed her terror, and I knew she saw my blood dripping.

I looked back at her and forced a smile. "Monica, just sit there and be quiet and Auntie will do her best to make sure you're okay. Mo Mo bo bo, banana fanna fo fo."

Tears poured and she said nothing. She had awakened from a dream into a nightmare.

Soon one single highway patrol car followed us, was directly behind us, at least four car lengths. He followed us for three miles, less than three minutes, before another California Highway Patrol unit came down the ramp and entered the freeway, looked at the car. I put a bloodied hand up to the window so he could see. He saw Monica in the backseat, saw a terrified child who was crying but saying nothing, then looked at the driver. They backed off, slowed to the pace of the CHP behind us, blocked that lane.

She asked, "What was your time?"

"What?"

"The marathon. Your time. I allowed you to run, allowed you to finish your last run. Your time?"

"Does it matter?"

"Are you being flippant?"

"Let the child out of the car. If you have

an issue with me, let it be between us."

"LAPD is following us."

"CHP, not LAPD."

"They have turned on the flashing lights."

"Let Monica out of the car. Let her run back to the police."

"You're in no position to make demands."

"Be reasonable. You're a soldier. You don't do this to innocent children."

"There is a Starbucks coffee cup in the cup holder in the back. Get it."

"Are you going to poison me?"

"Get it. Don't make me ask you again."

I reached back and touched Monica on the knee, whispered that Auntie was sorry, told her it was okay to cry, that I wanted to cry too, and I eased the Starbucks cup from the cup holder.

Through tight lips Rosemary Paige commanded, "Open it."

Inside the cup was a detached penis with *boegroes* surgically inserted under the foreskin.

I dropped the cup and tried to get away from the detached member. Mrs. Carruthers forced me to touch it. Mo saw my expression of terror and screamed. Mrs. Carruthers yelled, demanded quiet.

She said, "I couldn't pretend anymore.

This covert operation, I was tired of spying."

My voice shook as I made my redundant plea. "Let Monica go."

"I apologize for the negative things I said about the kid. I didn't mean it when I called her a half breed and said she looks like a little yellow monkey with ugly hair. I was just writing things to get to you, that's all. I have a lot of black friends. I married a black man. I'm not racist. She's a wonderful child. Precocious and amazing. I mean that from my heart."

"Prove you're sorry. Let my niece go."

"Watch your voice."

"Rosemary Paige . . . Mrs. Carruthers . . . you can stop before this goes too far."

"Understand, I have to complete my mission. When you dedicate yourself to something, you don't bail just because it's not in your favor anymore. You have to stay committed to the mission statement."

"You don't have to do this, Mrs. Carruthers. Franklin is not worth all of this."

She stabbed my leg. I screamed in pain, a level of pain I had never known.

She was beyond her point of no return. I was as powerless as Monica.

She said, "Frankie and Frankie. Frankie and Frankie. Frankie and Frankie."

She had nothing to lose now.

She had risked it all. The gun was in her lap. The bloodied blade was in her right hand.

She said, "Try it and next time it will cut your throat. Just try and take it from me."

She was trained to torture and kill. I was trained to talk shit and sell houses and make money.

Flashing lights and sirens added to the roar of the engine, a sound that barely muffled Monica's whimpering and asking for her mommy and daddy to save her and her auntie from the bogeywoman.

The loud croaking noise, that *weee onngg weee onngg,* the high-pitched sound from a dozen sirens, those wails and their overlapping and alternating pitches, that warble that screamed terror, and the speed of this madwoman, my being injured, all of this was too much to wake up to. Mo trembled and cried. It hurt, but I reached back and held Monica's hand. My hand was bloodied, but she held my fingers.

She said, "Auntie, I went to the bathroom on myself."

"It's okay, Monica. It's okay. I think I did too. This will be our little secret, okay?"

"I want my mommy." She had awakened from a soft dream, found herself in a horrible nightmare, and struggled to talk between stifled sobs and hitched breaths. "I want my mommy and my daddy."

There was no way out of this. I should have seen this coming. I had been fooled again.

If I had inhaled hard enough I would have been able to smell the smoke from a fire at least fifty miles away.

Franklin's home in Blair Hills was ablaze, was burning to the ground. Franklin was inside.

While I was still running the marathon, she had dealt with Franklin in the most horrific way imaginable.

I had no idea if my house was still standing.

That home had no importance to me now.

Mrs. Carruthers was polite, took the Starbucks cup from me, then threw it out the window as she drove.

Mrs. Carruthers asked, "What's the penalty for littering here in California?"

In severe pain, hand clamped down on my wound, sweat draining from my face, I looked in the side-view mirror at the police. They were there but could do nothing for us. Monica had put her face in her lap, her eyes covered with her hands. She was hyperventilating. She could barely breathe.

Mrs. Carruthers said, "Be glad the kid is in the car. What was in the cup, well, I was going to make you suck on what you had loved until Tijuana. I'm sure he'd've liked that. He liked that so much when you were in Africa and Italy. I swear that was the plan, cock-sucking bitch. Be glad the little girl is here."

I whispered, "Please. I will do whatever you want me to do, just let Monica out of the car."

"You called me crazy. You had no idea what my life had been like, and you called me crazy."

"I'm sorry for that. I was upset. You didn't exactly make a favorable first impression."

"You have no idea how many of my friends have died for a pointless war. I needed the money to support my husband and I went to war when I was young and stupid. America and the military-industrial complex can both go to hell. America spends more money on the military than a dozen countries combined. I lost my husband to you because they allowed it to happen. They have more ongoing conflicts and wars in the world than any other country, and every time I came home and tried to be a wife they sent me right back. You never would have stolen my husband from me if the government hadn't been complicit."

"I'm sorry you had to go through all of that. I really am."

"The thing that's the most insulting is if I had died in the middle of all of this, he would still be my husband and would have gotten over four hundred thousand dollars. He wanted the divorce when I was home, when I was safe, but when I was deployed, when I was dodging bombs, he was hoping to get a big payday. Frankie McBroom, Franklin was more complicated than you can imagine. He conned me. Married me. Got me to join the army. I think that's what he did. My death would have been his gold mine."

She cranked up the volume and Alice Smith sang loud enough to drown all screams.

Rejected by family. Betrayed by man and country.

She had been hoodwinked. She had been bamboozled.

Her logic was as flawed as her rage was bottomless.

She was losing control. In my mind she had lost control a long time ago. In order to do the things she'd done she'd lost the plot months ago, maybe years ago.

There was no traffic in front of us, just

dozens of highway patrol cars following as both police and a pair of news helicopters flew overhead and played this moment live for Los Angeles.

She exited the freeway and sped down the ramp.

Surface streets were twice as dangerous for a high-speed chase.

The muscle car did over sixty where the speed limit was twenty-five miles per hour. She broke through stop signs and endangered pedestrians. People were diving out of the way to keep from being run over. She ran red-lit intersections as she fled with Monica and me as her hostages.

She hopped back on the freeway. The lunatic stabbed me again. Monica shrieked and cried.

Mrs. Carruthers snapped, *"Shut up, shut up, shut up."*

She was breaking down.

I was in horrific pain, the world foggy now, and in my agony I raised my right hand and rubbed my bloodied fingers on the passenger-side window. I painted the window with my own blood. The news choppers were close enough, and I knew with those telescoping lenses they could see my crimson window, would broadcast the bloodied handprint in the window to the rest of Los Angeles. This was real breaking news. People would love a tale about ruthless betrayal and bloodthirsty vengeance. When we passed under bridges, people were on top, had gathered to watch the way the roaches had come to watch O. J. Simpson back in the day. On the opposite side of the freeway, in northbound traffic, they had all seen the choppers in the sky and now the traffic was starting to get congested with looky-loos.

Southbound freeway entrances had been systematically blocked as the high-speed chase continued, and with no cars being allowed to merge into the pursuit, it became just us and open highway in front of us, again going over one hundred miles an hour as she stomped the accelerator to the floor.

LIVVY

Within minutes Livvy's phone rang.

It was Panther.

Livvy was surprised but happy to hear her Southern voice, suddenly ecstatic.

Until she heard what Panther had to say.

Panther told her that she had horrible news.

She said that Frankie McBroom and Monica had been kidnapped.

Livvy asked her if it was a joke.

Panther told her it wasn't.

Livvy said that was impossible, because her sister was with her; then Livvy went pale as she searched the crowd.

She couldn't find Frankie.

She didn't see Monica anymore.

She saw Tommie and Blue off to the side, deep in conversation, one that had both of them close to tears, too close to their own truths.

Livvy hurried in their direction, still sure

that this had to be some sort of McBroom prank.

Tommie's phone rang.

Blue's phone rang.

It was the same news, breaking news on KCAL 9.

There was another deadly high-speed pursuit in the car-chase capital of the country. Monica was in the car. Frankie was in the car. They all looked at the high-tech LA Marathon race monitors, the high-speed chase now playing where the repeat of the race had played moments before. Word had spread over social media that one of the marathoners had been taken hostage, had been taken from the finish line. They caught the car chase as they were passing the 605. They stood and watched the red muscle car speed across four Southern California freeways. The news clocked them at one hundred miles per hour when they entered the Long Beach area. Thirty minutes went by and it felt like a year on the planet Neptune. The speeding car moved between big rigs and vanished for a second, the longest second God ever made.

Tommie screamed. Blue held her and he cried out in agony for his daughter.

As everyone held their breath the driver reappeared and left the big rigs behind like they were all parked at a truck stop in Barstow. Something flew out of the car, out the driver's-side window.

In a voice of outrage and terror Blue barked, "Is that Franklin?"

Tommie said, "He's been stalking her. He's been stalking her since they broke up."

Tommie told them about the notebook of love letters, told them Frankie had gone to see him last night and threw his engagement ring in his face, told them that Franklin Carruthers had been breaking into Frankie's house and that was why she had moved all of a sudden, and he had broken into her new home and left flowers, and had stolen Frankie's underwear and left a giant vibrator on her bed last night.

The newscaster said the car with the kidnapped child was moving at incredible speeds and that this chase showed the driver had no intention of stopping. Over and over they said they were sure this one would end in a crash, in injuries, in fatalities. Officers followed but weren't going to try to stop a car moving at such a high rate of speed, not with a pit maneuver, not by dropping spikes, especially with a little girl inside being held hostage.

Then they had more information. They posted Monica's photo, her full name, and

456

no one knew the source. They posted Frankie's professional image from her Facebook profile. They posted the profile image of Phyllis Rosemary Stoltzfus-Carruthers's Facebook page as well.

Tommie shouted, "That's Rosemary Paige. What the hell? I saw her talking to Frankie and Monica a few minutes ago."

Livvy said, "Her surname is Carruthers. She's Franklin's wife? This makes no sense."

Tony asked, "Is she a hostage too? Did Franklin take all of them?"

Blue's cellular rang and he hurried to answer.

It was Monica's mother.

She was already at LAX, ready to board a plane to get to her next Beyoncé concert in China, had been watching television, and the breaking news had stopped her from eating her Chick-fil-A long enough to call and see what kind of madness had erupted since the madness she'd left behind.

They watched the pursuit, barely breathing, clinging to each other, mumbling prayers, and living in absolute disbelief, begging for it to end. Moments later the news reported that Franklin Carruthers had been located in Culver City. His home in Blair Hills had been burned. Franklin had been found in his garage. He had been murdered.

One of the helicopters broadcast an extreme close-up of the fleeing car. The passenger-side window was covered in redness, had been smeared in blood.

Matter-of-factly the chisel-chinned broadcaster turned to his Botoxed and enhanced cohost and said that at this point they had to apologize for that last graphic image, but they were broadcasting live. For the sake of journalism, they had to be honest; it seemed that the driver was on a murderous rampage that already included Franklin Carruthers. Therefore, without any communication as she fled southbound on the 5 into Chula Vista, they didn't know whether the two hostages in the car had already been slaughtered.

FRANKIE

Going over one hundred miles an hour, Mrs. Carruthers stomped the accelerator to the floor. I knew that a car like the one we were trapped in, it could fly past one hundred sixty miles per hour.

That was if she had the proper tires. The wrong tires wouldn't be able to take the heat.

The wrong tires would explode, and the rest would be left up to gravity, friction, and God.

I bled a river. Monica cried an ocean.

I thought about what had been in the Starbucks cup.

Franklin's wife was crazy.

She was insane.

Then the unexpected happened.

The car stalled like it had vapor lock, sped up again, then slowed down.

For five seconds it felt like it wasn't getting any gas.

The car had run smoothly up until that moment.

It stuttered like it was starving for better fuel. My eyes had been closed as I held Mo's hand, that arm wounded and in incredible pain. I opened my eyes and tears from the pain fell before I could see through a sort of fog. Mrs. Carruthers hadn't taken her foot off the accelerator, but the car slowed down.

For a second I thought she was slowing to push me out the door or make me jump.

The car slowed, became jerky, coughed like it was getting sick, and refused to accelerate again.

There was a downhill slope and we rode that way, no engine, all gravity, coasted until we were on a bridge; then the freeway was flat. We were no longer in motion. Behind us the flashing lights stopped.

She put the knife on the floor at her left side, away from me, and shifted into neutral.

She tried to start the car again, again, again, again, again.

I set free a painful chuckle and with much irony said, "I guess somebody has a bad fuel pump."

"No, no, no. Gas, gas, there has to be enough gas in the tank . . . has to be . . . has to be."

Jaw tight, I took a breath, ached, put my hand on the car door, let my fingers grip the lock.

I snapped, "Get out of the car, Mo. When I open the door, push my seat forward, get out, and run to the police."

Mrs. Carruthers pushed a button, made the two doors lock before the confused child could respond.

I said, "Mo, when I let my seat up to let you out of the back, I want you to hurry and get out."

"No, Frankie. She gets out on my side, not your side. You let her out, you might try something, and I would not appreciate that. This is how we're going to do this. You get out first, Frankie. You get out and come around the car to me. Come to me and I'll open my door and let her go. I'll let her walk to the police after I get out. I need you on this side, by my door, and after I get out she can walk toward the police."

"You want me to be your shield. You want her to walk because you know they won't shoot while she is heading toward them. Don't do this, Mrs. Carruthers. Please, don't."

"I'm not giving up. God didn't bring me this far to fail."

"Let Mo out first."

461

"You come to me first. Then I will let her go after I am out of the car, while you are here with me."

"If the car starts when I get out, you'll leave with Mo."

"I won't leave you, Frankie. This is between me and you."

"Pinky promise?"

She nodded. "Then we're in this together."

"We're simpatico. We're a two-member sorority."

"I need you to hurry."

I said, "Monica."

"Yes, Auntie."

"Be brave."

"Yes, Auntie."

"I'm going to get out of the car and I'm coming around to the other side. When this nice lady has gotten out, she's going to let you go to the police. I want you to walk toward them and don't look back. You're going home."

"I'm not going if you're not going."

"Do what I say, Monica."

"Okay."

"You're going home."

Mrs. Carruthers said, "Going home. That's what they tell us at the end of our tour. We're going home."

"Why does that make you chuckle?"

"I have no home to go to. You stole that from me, Frankie. Only one home left for me and you."

I knew where this was going. I knew what she meant.

I told Monica, "When you get to them they will take you home. Tell Tommie, Blue, Livvy, and Tony I love them, okay?"

"Okay, Auntie. I'll be brave."

"I love you, Monica."

"I love you, Auntie."

It was hard to do, but again I said, "Mo mo bo bo, banana fanna fo fo."

She cried. "Frankie Frankie bo bankie."

"I can't go with you, Mo. But Auntie will always be with you."

I opened the door with my bloodied right hand and swung my feet around, pausing with the pain, the sweat dripping from my forehead more than it had during the marathon. I didn't know where I was in the world, but I knew we hadn't made it to Mexico. We were north of San Diego, as far as I could tell. My vision focused and I saw officers were behind their cars, behind their car doors, guns aimed. It took me a moment, helicopters still flying overhead, apartments in the distance, the air cool on my dehydrated skin as I hobbled inch by inch to the other side of the car, to Mrs. Carruthers's car door.

This would be my last Sunday on top of soil.

Afternoon sun on my head, I had run my last race.

Mrs. Carruthers let her window down. The car still had power. She continued trying to make the engine turn over. She had lied to me. She would've left me in the middle of the freeway and driven away with Monica if it had.

That made me angry.

Hardly able to breathe, I panted, light-headed, and said, "Let Monica get out, as you promised."

"Try to run to the police, I'll shoot you."

"Does it look like I can run anywhere?"

"Try me. I will shoot you in front of the kid."

"That's evil."

"Franklin was evil."

"He saw you as the evil one in the union."

"I *never* abandoned him. I *never* cheated on him. I was a faithful wife. I loved him the way I loved God and country."

She showed me a nervous grin.

The grin went away, left severe anger behind.

The bloodied knife rested in her lap, the

gun in her hand.

She had terrified me, had become my terrorist, but I didn't back down, couldn't back down, not until Mo was okay.

I said, "Look behind you. Police. News. People are watching from the other side of the freeway. This is a spectacle. Is Franklin worth it? Would he have done this for your love?"

Her eyes began to tear, and I saw the innocence that used to be inside of her, saw the innocent little girl who grew up in Pennsylvania and was given the core values that centered around the Son of God, a man born of a virgin, who then died three decades later for humanity's sins, and was bodily resurrected from the dead. But her world was not like mine. I bet she had thought life back there in the heart of Lancaster's Amish Country was too mundane and wanted to escape her bubble and be part of the world I had grown up in.

She was a long way from where she had started.

She swallowed and clenched her teeth.

Mrs. Carruthers leaned forward in her seat as Monica squeezed, crawled out. When Monica's feet were out, as soon as her body had cleared the seat, I saw what I needed to do, saw what I *had* to do. I couldn't hesitate.

I *didn't* hesitate. Before Rosemary Paige realized what was going on, I threw my weight
toward the space that had been left open
one second too long, jammed my body like
I was trying to squeeze into the backseat.
Monica was out. Nothing mattered after she
was free. I yelled for her to run as hard as
she could.

She was confused.

I shouted for Monica to run.

She took off toward the police.

I tried to use my weight to wedge the seat
against Mrs. Carruthers, to push her into
the steering wheel, would have smashed
every bone in her body if I could. She was
strong. She had trained and carried
weighted bags for miles in the military. She
had strength; I had adrenaline. I was bleeding, dizzy, but determined. Halfway in and
halfway out of the car, I called for the police
to come quick. I could barely breathe, so I
knew no one heard me over all of the noise.
I was ready for Franklin's wife to shoot me
for not honoring the deal, but that deal had
been made under duress, so as far as I was
concerned, there was no fucking deal. She
grunted, got her position, and pushed her
seat back against me, and that pressed
against where she had stabbed me. I
screamed, saw the world turn bright red,

then backed away from the pain. She found enough space to twist her body. She struck me in my wounded arm and pushed back against me again, made the seat push against that fiery wound. Blood. There was so much of my blood. My legs refused to support me. I wanted to flee like Monica had done, wanted to run so hard and fast my feet would kick my backside with each stride. I took a step and the pain consumed me. I collapsed to the freeway. I fell like a rock dropping from the clouds. It felt like minutes had gone by, but only two or three seconds had passed since Monica had escaped toward those sworn to protect and serve. Mrs. Carruthers was out of the car in a flash, and I expected her to grab me by my short hair, force me back to my feet, hold me by my neck with the blade at my throat or with the business end of the gun aimed at my head, and make me her human shield. But with guns on her, with me flat out on the ground, I guess her fight-or-flight kicked in.

She took off running with her weapons in her hands.

In my mind she moved like a kangaroo, each step putting her thirty feet away. She was fast. Police moved by me with their guns drawn. Stabbed, skin abraded with road rash from the fall, I looked up and saw Monica was near the police.

Seemed like they were a thousand miles away.

That was all I needed to see.

I was done trying to be strong.

Helicopters remained in the sky. I tried to raise my hand and wave, but I didn't have the strength to lift a finger. I couldn't feel anything. I didn't want to, but I closed my eyes.

I'd lost a lot of blood. Then there was a pain in my chest.

It was hard to breathe. I was suffocating.

The world became my merry-go-round.

I was spun into darkness.

Then the world was bright.

I heard Monica's voice again. She had dashed back to me, had outrun the yells of the police. Ambulance sirens warbled in the distance.

"Auntie, I'm not going to leave you."

"I told you to run to safety."

"I'm not going to leave you. We're family."

"Obey me, Monica. I need you to run back to the police so they can get you to Blue and Tommie."

"You saved me. I'll save you now. I'll

protect you. I'm being brave."

"Look . . . stand your brave ass up and wave at the helicopters. Stand up and wave so Mommy and Daddy will know you're okay."

She did what I asked her to do but only waved for a couple of seconds.

Law enforcement called for her to come back to them, but she refused, tried to attend to me.

Her pained expression intensified. "I want you to be okay, Auntie, because you are very special. You are special to Mommy. You taught me how to play Monopoly and I win every time. Please be okay."

"You're stubborn. You're as stubborn as a McBroom, you know that?"

"I know. When Mommy and Daddy marry, Daddy can be a McBroom too."

As her little hands held my bloodied hand, I swallowed and closed my eyes.

"Frankie Frankie bo bankie. Don't die, Auntie. Please don't die."

I couldn't respond to her. Her voice faded, was swallowed by the pandemonium. In between blinks, officers were around me, like they had magically appeared, and were taking her away.

She was taken away, rescued kicking and screaming my name. They had to pry her hands away. She wanted to stay with me. There were shouting voices and many sirens warbled and warbled and warbled. Before the next blink ended, that entire ruckus faded too. I closed my eyes. No more blinking. I walked into the bright light. Dressed in white, I went on a journey to see my deceased momma and my daddy. With invisible wings on my back, I floated over the scene. I saw what had happened.

In that short span of time, an instant that felt like an eternity, Rosemary Paige had sprinted to the edge of the freeway. She jumped from the twenty-foot bridge, and the news helicopters stayed with her every desperate move. She dropped, fell badly, didn't have her balance, and she broke her left leg. She was down and within seconds three officers surrounded her with their guns drawn. She held her gun, screamed at them as they barked at her, was seconds from being double popped, but pushed her gun away and put her hands on top of her head. The lunatic surrendered.

With the world watching the tragedy unfold, it was all over but the crying.

It was time for black suits, black ties, black dresses, for McBrooms and Wimberleys to stand with friends and strangers. It was time for all to meet on Crenshaw Boulevard at

Angelus Funeral Home and shed tears as they stood over my coffin.

On the asphalt, underneath the warmth of the sun, helicopters overhead, I died.

LIVVY

Livvy woke after sunrise and saw the time. She cried. She remembered the funeral and cried softly. Tommie had cried the hardest. She always cried the hardest. Tony woke up a moment later.

Livvy ran her fingers through her short haircut, yawned, said, "Didn't mean to wake you."

"It's fine. You okay?"

"No. Sad. I feel incredibly sad. We have to go to the graveyard. I don't like death. I hate death."

"I know it's hard. I'm here for you."

"Christmastime without her. I'm going to cry all day. I'm going to cry, cry, cry."

"I know. I know you miss her."

"Tommie is going to cry too. I have to —"

Tony moved behind her, put his hand on her belly.

He said, "Look at that little bump. You're showing."

"I'm going to be so fat. I'm going to be short and chunky and turn into a ball."

"Before I bounce you and shoot a three-pointer, are you sure it's mine?"

"Don't start."

"I've already beat one paternity suit. You plan on serving me papers in front of everyone?"

"Asshole. But the look on your face when you were served, that was priceless."

They laughed. Enough time had passed where the tragedy could be made fun of.

She whispered, "I love you, Tony."

"I love you so much, Olivia."

"I'm scared. We're no longer going to be DINKS — Double Income, No Kids."

"You're going to be a great slave master. I mean mother. You will be a great mother."

Things had changed. After that day that had felt like the worst day in her life, things had changed. Dr. Ashley was around for a little while, but soon it was time for her to go. Livvy had made peace with knowing that Carpe was no more, that Panther existed but what they had would never be again.

She had tried to re-create what was impossible to re-create. She couldn't do this anymore. She couldn't keep trying to return to that world.

She had been to Ashley Li what Panther

had been to her, and Tony had been to Dr. Ashley what Carpe had been to Livvy. In the end, Dr. Ashley had her sabbatical, had her fun, and when it was done, when that season ended, she went back across the pond. She went back to be with the man who had broken her heart. Livvy understood, even if she didn't agree. She hadn't heard from Ashley.

It was fine. Ashley Li had her own issues and would have to deal with them in her own way. She was attached to Livvy, to Tony, and would have sought permanent residence in America to remain in a ménage à trois, to help Livvy through that difficult period of her marriage by working at UCLA Medical Center while remaining engaged in a domestic arrangement with Livvy and Tony. But it wasn't what Livvy wanted, not for her marriage; maybe with Carpe and Panther, but not in her marriage, not in her home. Livvy had had her last adventure and had found closure. Not all at once, but gradually. Not completely, but enough to move on. Ashley had had her awakening and took her new predilections back across the pond, smile wide, her anklet sparkling, her high heels clacking.

A woman who had sweet secrets had the best smile.

Olivia had given Dr. Ashley a pair of heels.

She had bought her Welsh friend and brilliant lover a pair of Blahniks, the same style, same color, identical to her most prized heels. Livvy had gifted her companion, the betrayed woman who had learned to fly again, with Lucite and leather T-strap Manolo Blahniks, had their final intimate moments, a sensual celebration, then sent Dr. Ashley on another adventure.

Livvy had been a healer.

Pay it forward.

Always pay it forward.

Soon Livvy had wanted Tony again, only him.

She was able to be with him again.

The river had settled, its course moving in a normal direction. The new earthquake had made things adjust.

Being pregnant changed everything.

It gave her a new focus.

She had new priorities.

Tony asked, "Can you handle going to the grave today?"

"I have to go. I have to go to the cemetery."

Tony headed for the shower.

Livvy picked up her cellular and called her sister.

She asked Tommie, "Should we swing by

and pick you up?"

"Blue is going to drive me."

"Whoa. That's major. You're talking again?"

"We've been talking quite a bit."

"You've seen him since you moved out?"

"We went away together for the weekend to see if we could sort things out."

"And? You're his BAE again? You're his Before Anyone Else, or is it over for real?"

"We'll talk. And *stop* trying to sound hip. You sound *stupid* when you do that, Livvy."

They ended the call so Tommie could get ready for the trip to the cemetery. Blue was back in her life.

Livvy smiled, almost started crying happy tears.

She went to the glass shower door, undressed, then joined Tony. He began washing her body and she became aroused. She leaned back into him and he washed her breasts, touched her nipples. Since the pregnancy, she was aroused more easily, was aroused all the time, morning dew all day long.

She said, "Can't get me pregnant now, but feel free to give it your best shot."

"Get ready for my sweetness. It's about to come. Turn around and taste the rainbow."

"Will you stop being silly and stop imitating that damn Skittles orgasm commercial?"

They laughed, kissed, and joined, then for a few moments made love under the warm waters.

As they made love, more tears rained and she told Tony, "Thanks for being patient with me."

After she dressed, Livvy picked up an *Essence* magazine from the stack on her nightstand. Beale Streets was on the cover. The magazine had spotlighted his marriage to Tanya Obayomi, now Mrs. Tanya Obayomi-Streets, a glamorous Nigerian and highly intelligent woman with an MBA, a woman who was also an actress and a singer, and now by many, with her fame-by-marriage, touted as a renaissance woman. After the LA Marathon, after Tommie had given him the note, there had been a sudden engagement, one spurred by rejection, one that seemed to be out of spite, then a quick marriage in the Hamptons, his adoptive parents at his side, his adoptive brothers and sisters in the wedding party along with Tanya Obayomi's family. Aside from being America's East Coast meets Africa's West Coast, it looked like postracial perfection, if there were such a thing as postracial, if there were such a thing as perfection. It was the anti-*Black-ish,* anti-*Empire,* anti-*Power,* anti-*Scandal,* anti-*The Haves and the Have Nots,* anti-*The Real Housewives of Atlanta,* anti-*Being Mary Jane,* and anti-*Love & Hip Hop* crowd. They were the higher thinkers, the overachievers, the leaders with few followers, the ones who dined with Obama and held benefits for sick babies in underdeveloped nations, the ones who openly chastised all media that used sex, money, drugs, violence, deceit, and drama to line their pockets but ignored that most of their fortunes had come from exploitation of their fellow man. The twentysomething polyglot Beale Streets and his barely twentysomething bilingual bride, his singing and acting Mensa member, they looked handsome together, as if they'd overcome an unseen barrier. Livvy had glanced over the article. Beale Streets was still trying to find his birth parents to settle his issues.

Livvy was still amazed at how much he looked like a younger, less muscular, more learned version of Blue. He could have passed for Monica's father or her older brother. Blue didn't find that humorous.

A copy of the farewell note that Tommie had given him had ended up in Blue's hands.

Beale claimed he had no knowledge of

how it happened. The original good-bye letter had been left in his home, with his files. Only one person had been inside his mansion. Tanya Obayomi had been the one. No one cared. They had had insurmountable issues at that moment. The McBroom clan had had greater problems. The world had watched Frankie McBroom fighting for her life and dying on the freeway.

The high-speed pursuit had lasted over an hour and traversed many southbound freeways and just as many counties. The blood. The dying. The death. She died live on air, in front of all of Los Angeles.

Her live death trended on Twitter. It was posted on YouTube.

Livvy had stood next to Tony and watched her sister die. Tommie had stood next to Blue, in agony, terrified and in prayer. It had been a horrible day in Santa Monica. That day in March had been the worst day.

She had needed Tony to get through those rough days. She had clung to him. They had stood united, one heartbeat. Tragedy had brought them back together, as disasters caused families to reunite.

She was going to become a mommy.

Olivia McBroom-Barrera was carrying the next generation of the McBrooms.

Livvy pulled on flat shoes, then gathered

her Lucite and leather T-strap Manolo Blahniks, the shoes that had been her emotional favorite; wiped away tears for Carpe, for the first lover she'd ever had die; and she boxed the Blahniks, went downstairs, went outside, put the Blahniks in the curbside trash can as she waved at neighbors, and without looking back went into her living room and stood in front of the Christmas tree. She smiled. She felt like she had a real marriage now. She had evolved. Next year there would be too many gifts for her baby under their tree. New memories would now replace old.

Livvy gazed at the gifts for the living. She wiped away tears and regarded yuletide gifts bought as offerings for the dead. Soon Tony was next to her, wiping away her tears. It was time to go visit those who had gone to heaven's waiting room.

LIVVY

It had rained the day before and that coolness remained in the desert city's winter air. Livvy and Tony arrived at Inglewood Park Cemetery first. The first stop, the McBroom tradition, was the McBrooms' parents' graves. No McBroom would lie while being touched by the spirits of their predeceased loved ones. They would give honor to other deceased family members before they left.

Tony said, "Bernard and Betty Jean Mc-Broom. *Estamos aquí. Ya estamos aquí.*"

Livvy said, "Mom and Dad. Merry Christmas. And stop speaking in Spanish, Tony."

Tony said, "Betty Jean, *mi madre,* you're finally going to be a grandmother."

Livvy slapped Tony's arm. "I was supposed to break the good news."

"You think she doesn't already know? You think they don't already know?"

"Mom and Dad, we're pregnant. Dad, I know, you think that a man and woman saying 'we're pregnant' sounds *dumb,* especially since only one of us will have swollen feet, but we're having a baby."

Tony opened up two folding chairs and they sat facing the tombstones. Livvy put a flower down for each parent. She looked across the grave sites and saw Blue's Nissan pulling up, arriving CP Time.

Blue tooted his horn as he passed in search of a place to park.

Tony and Livvy waved, then went back to holding hands.

Livvy said, "You loaned him the money?"

"It wasn't a loan. Gave it to him a few months ago."

"After Frankie . . ."

"About a month after."

"Did he have the procedure done?"

"You will have to ask him."

She asked, "Do you miss Dr. Ashley? She was totally enamored of you."

"Intelligent woman. We had some very intense conversations regarding our fields."

"Did you fall in love with her?"

Tony asked, "Did you want me to fall in love with her?"

"I'm not sure. In the beginning, honestly, I think I did."

"It felt like you did at one point."

Livvy nudged him. "You fell in love with her."

"I was becoming attached, but I felt she was more attached to you."

"I expected that one day I'd come home and find out you were gone to London for good."

"Same here."

Livvy said, "I didn't want you gone, but I was afraid to be with you again."

"Why?"

"Was too afraid of being hurt again. Kept thinking about you and the girl you cheated with."

"I will never let you down again, Livvy. You're my Betty Jean and I want to be your Bernard."

"A ninety-nine-year-old man divorced his wife of over seventy years when he found out she'd had an affair eighty years ago. I don't want to have our child and find out you strayed again decades from now."

"I will be a better husband and the best father."

Livvy spoke of Dr. Ashley. "She was our bridge over troubled waters. And we were her friends in a time of need. What do you think we should do now, Tony? After the baby, should we go see her?"

"We should let it fade."

"Good answer, Tony."

"It's the only answer, as far as I am concerned."

"I need to be sure that we're back on track."

"For the sake of the baby, I need to know you want to be here with us, Olivia."

"There is no other place I want to be."

"Livvy? Are we okay? Am I going to end up being a single dad like Blue used to be?"

She laughed. "I'm fine, Tony. We're fine. *Todo bien.*"

"No more Spanish at the grave site. Daddy hates Spanish."

They laughed a little, better friends now than they had been at the start, a stronger couple.

Tommie eased out of Blue's car and side-by-side they walked toward the grave site, flowers and small tokens in their hands. Livvy put her hand on her belly, held Tony's hand, hoped that tragedy would never befall them. Just as Tommie and Blue made it to them and they all hugged, a Maserati pulled into the cemetery and parked right away. The passenger door opened and Monica hopped out of the car, flowers in one hand, gifts in the other. She ran across the graves to get to Blue and Tommie.

Frankie eased out of her ride, grabbed her

metal crutches, limped, and took her time getting to her family. They watched her struggle. Halfway to them, Frankie stood up and held the crutches high in each hand. She danced a jig, then gave the world two thumbs up as she walked a Tyra Bank's killing-it-on-the-runway walk.

Everyone laughed, then stood up and applauded the woman who had died on the side of the road, then been brought back to life in the back of an ambulance as it sped toward the hospital.

Livvy noticed Tommie and Blue. They were holding hands. As they stood at the grave site, they revealed their secret. Tommie wore a wedding ring. Blue wore a wedding ring.

They had eloped.

Tommie had purchased a simple wedding dress online. Monica had gotten to wear her beautiful white dress.

They'd driven to Vegas a week ago, the three of them.

Tommie was radiant.

She said that she had another announcement to make.

Her next announcement answered the question of whether Blue had had the procedure.

Tommie

"Blue?"

"Yeah, Tommie?"

"They're mad because we eloped."

"What did you expect?"

"We can invite them to our next forty-nine weddings."

"You're serious about getting married in every state?"

"Dead serious."

"Then we better start saving."

Christmas morning in Los Angeles. It was the only morning when there was no horrific traffic, and that lasted about three hours. When the three hours was up, everyone was in their car and traffic on every freeway was worse than rush hour on a three-day-weekend Friday when there was a torrential downpour. We made it back to our area. When we turned on Edgehill, I saw that Angela was parked out in front of our home, in her car waiting on us. She hadn't called.

I said, "Mo, your mother is here. You haven't seen her on Christmas in years."

Mo didn't sound too thrilled as she said, "Angela is here at our house?"

"Mo, never call your mother by her first name."

Blue said, "Your mother probably has your Christmas presents, Mo."

I asked, "Did you know Angela was coming by our home today, Blue?"

He shook his head, then told Monica, "Santa probably left some of yours with her."

"Santa Claus is not real. I'm a big girl now. I know you buy all the presents, Daddy."

I said, "Really, Mo?"

"You buy them too, Mommy."

"Thank you very much, little girl."

"When are you going to start calling me a big girl?"

"Well, excuse me, big girl."

"I'm not a little girl anymore. Give me some respect."

We laughed.

Blue said, "Well, let's pretend that you still like Santa, just for this year."

"Dad, if Angela has presents, you know

Angela bought them from the store like you do."

"I order online."

I said, "Monica, when we get out, call her *Mother*. Or *Mommy*."

"But you're Mommy."

"Don't argue with me, Mo. Don't make Angela feel bad."

When Monica had been kidnapped, while the news waited for her to be reunited with her family, Angela had dropped her trip and been brought to the hospital while we waited on Monica and Frankie. Monica told everyone I was her everyday mother, that her real mother was never around, never rode her bike with her, never called, was always gone to have fun with Beyoncé.

She told them I was her mother.

She had said that live on air, and that went out to the world.

As we cried and were in shock from what had happened, those were Mo's words.

Angela was hurt by that. The vicious things people said online devastated her.

She had to shut down her Facebook and Twitter behind all of the mean comments.

Mo asked, "Okay, but can I call her Angela when I am with you and Daddy, Mommy?"

"Ask Daddy, then ask me again to see if I

agree with his answer."

"Daddy, can I —"

"That's between you and my wife."

I said, "Your wife."

"That's what I said."

"I love the way it sounds when you say that."

"I love saying it."

We parked and Angela hurried out of her car before we could open our doors. She was in a short skirt and high heels, a long leather coat over it all, extensions in her hair, and she looked like a backup dancer for her idol. Her hair blew like she had her own personal wind machine. Monica ran to her, hugged her, did that more out of rote than true affection. Angela spoke to Blue, nodded at me, then took three boxes from the backseat of her car. She had also brought Monica a bicycle and a flat-screen television.

Monica said to Angela, "Guess what, Mommy?"

"What's that, Monica?"

"I'm going to have a little brother or sister, but I hope it's a sister because then I would be the older sister like Frankie is and the next one will be like Livvy; then she can have another, like Mommy."

I said, "Mommy Tommie. Call me

Mommy Tommie so it won't be confusing."

She said, "I hope she will be like Mommy Tommie and I can be the boss, like Frankie."

Angela looked at me, made direct eye contact for the first time, sought confirmation.

I nodded.

She said, "Wow. You're pregnant."

She looked at my left hand, then saw Blue was wearing a golden wedding band.

She asked him, "You're married?"

He nodded.

She asked, "When did that happen?"

Blue said, "We eloped. Mo went with us. We just decided to do the damn thing."

I asked, "Did you want an invitation, Angela?"

And just like that, Angela's mouth began to quiver and she started to cry.

I didn't expect that. I really didn't expect that. She didn't congratulate us. Just looked sad.

Blue carried Monica's presents inside, and I asked Monica to help him.

When they were gone, I faced Angela.

This moment was long overdue.

I asked, "What's the issue?"

"There is no issue."

"There has always been an issue. What is

it about me that you dislike so much?"

"Why are you always so disrespectful to me?"

"I've never been disrespectful to you, Angela."

"From the start. I used to come to Blue's apartment and you never spoke to me. You used to walk right by me and you never said hello. You just looked me up and down. You've always been so mean."

I took a second. "Were you hoping he would come back to you?"

"No. Of course not. I did for a while, but I'm not like you. You're really good at this. You're good with Blue; you're good with Mo. What Blue and I had, it's not like this. It wasn't on this level. It wasn't an everyday thing either. But I got pregnant and he told me to keep it and told me he would raise her, because he knew I didn't have what it takes. I try to be her mother the best I can, but we never really connect. I'm not patient, not all day and all night. I don't like kids' movies, but I try. I get angry over little things and I snap at her the way my mother used to snap at me, because that's all I know. I tell her I love her and she responds that she loves me, but she never tells me first, so that sort of hurts. I know she doesn't like me, Tommie. I know that. And

491

it hurts knowing that no matter how hard I try, she doesn't like me."

"She loves you."

"She tolerates me. When I'm with her, it's like she's forced to be with me."

"You're her mother. All you have to do is show up, Angela, and don't do it begrudgingly."

"She loves you, Tommie. I see it in your blogs. You have a thousand pictures of her with you and her smile is genuine, and on the few photos she has taken with me, her smile is always forced. It's like watching you blog about how I am losing my daughter. I know it's too late. I know that it is, and it hurts. I have lost my daughter and it feels like you're my mother and you're taking her away from me to give to someone else. It hurts. I can't go through this again, not with a daughter, not with my daughter, but I'm not any better at it this time than when I was younger. She doesn't call me. I stopped calling for a while, waited to see if she was going to call me, if she was going to miss me, and that call never came. I feel like she wants me to vanish, like it would be a relief to her if I died because then she wouldn't have to deal with me. So I just go away and do my thing because I know she couldn't care less one way or another."

"Wow."

"Shit. Now I'm crying in front of you. I promised I wasn't going to cry in front of you."

"Well, I'm crying too."

A moment passed, and as she wiped tears from her eyes, I wiped tears from mine.

I cleared my throat and said, "Angela."

"What, Tommie?"

"We're family."

"I know you are."

"No, *we're* family. You and I are family. We're not friends, because people get to choose their friends, but they don't get to choose their neighbors or their family. I didn't choose you, but you are part of my family. You're Monica's mother. Her true mother. I am her earth mother. We are all connected."

"I have no idea what *earth mother* means."

"The point is this: We are family. We will both be at Monica's wedding. We will both be at her graduation. We will both chase boys away when she starts liking them — well, at least I know I will. We have to do better than this. We have to work together at some point. I can't fight you every time I see you."

A moment passed. A very uncomfortable

moment. This was our first civilized conversation.

I said, "Look, Angela, maybe it is me. I need to feel loved, same as you need to feel loved."

"Everyone wants to feel like someone likes them. That's the reason you blog. You do it for the attention. You do it because you want everyone to agree with you and think you're all high and mighty."

"I'm sorry for all of that. I apologize."

"Sure. Yeah, right."

"I'm serious. I just apologized to you and I think you're blowing it off."

"Wow. Okay. You were serious?"

"I'm serious. Maybe I went too far. I apologize."

"I accept your apology."

"You're not good with social graces, are you?"

"I guess not. I mean, I'm not a debutante. I don't know which silverware to use."

"Let's back this up a little. People say they're married, you're supposed to congratulate them."

"Congratulations. I'm glad Blue found someone who is good to him and my daughter."

"Does that trouble you?"

"It caught me off guard. Thought it wasn't

going to happen. I was speechless."

"Okay. Now I am waiting on your apology for being rude to me on multiple occasions."

"Are you taking the blogs down?"

"Nope. But I will be kinder to you, if we can make that possible."

"Okay."

"Or you can stop reading my pages. Why are you on my blog? Are you following me?"

"You're a good writer. I can't write like you can. I feel everything you say, and it hurts. The words you use, they are pretty, and sometimes I have to use a dictionary, but I can feel everything you feel."

"Apology. I'm waiting."

"Sure. I apologize. If you mean yours, then I mean it."

"Come here for a moment."

"For what?"

"Come here."

I called Monica and she came running back out. I had Monica get between us while Angela and I got down on our haunches. Monica was as surprised as her mother. I took out my phone and we all smiled and took a round of selfies. Each time we changed positions. I actually touched Angela, put my arm around her like she was my sister. It was hard to do. It wasn't much, but it was a start for both of us.

Angela hugged Monica and said she was getting ready to leave.

I asked, "Where are you going?"

"Back home."

"You have plans?"

"I don't have any plans. Just came to drop off the presents."

"You're dressed like you had plans."

"I thought everybody over here would be dressed up and I didn't want to show up looking like a bum, that's all. I'll go back home and pull on some sweats and make me a sandwich or something."

I said, "Why don't you stay over here and kick it with Monica for a while."

"Really?"

"Yeah. Open her presents with her. Just don't get drunk and paint the walls."

"Okay. This is weird and just got weirder. You don't want me in your house."

"I know. Even Scrooge took a break for Christmas. We can be mean to each other again after New Year's if that makes you feel better. But let's have a cease-fire for at least forty-eight hours."

"Thanks for inviting me into your home."

"As opposed to you showing up uninvited."

496

"I guess I will come in for a few minutes."

"We have plenty of food. You should kick off your high heels and stay for dinner."

"You're pushing it. Are you being phony?"

"I'm serious."

"Why?"

"You've already puked, showered, and used the toilet, so you might as well sit at the dinner table."

"Wow. You're not serious."

"I am serious. Stay and break bread with your daughter. She needs to see you and Blue interact when people aren't angry and screaming and acting like fools. She needs this. We'll do it for Monica."

"I don't want to intrude."

"You've already basically spent the night here."

"I woke up here that time, and, yeah, that was embarrassing."

"You called Blue to come get you in the middle of the night. That disturbed me back then."

"Tommie, to be honest, I don't remember calling him. That's how drunk I was. I thought I had called someone else, this other guy. Blue pulled up and the rest was a blur until I woke up here. That was so damn embarrassing that I couldn't wait to get on a plane and leave here. I want to leave now."

"Are you invited to Hova and Beyoncé's swank penthouse or an Illuminati meeting or something?"

"No, I'm not. I could go to the movies, or go walk on Venice Beach, or drive PCH awhile."

"Well, it's Christmas. Don't run away just to be alone in a crowd. I'm serious. It's okay to stay here and spend the day with Monica. We're going to eat, drink, open gifts, play dominoes, watch movies, and be lazy for a while."

"It's exciting over here. This is why I never take Mo with me. She gets bored with me."

Monica looked at her and smiled. "Stay, Mommy. Mommy Tommie is a real good cook."

"I can't cook. I know that. The kitchen gives me the heebie-jeebies. I have a phobia, I think."

Surprised, I said, "You can't cook? You're afraid of cooking?"

"Never learned. I either overcook or undercook, and I get afraid I'm going to cut or burn myself, or leave a pot on and accidentally almost burn down the house again, or the oven will explode. When I try — if I try — what I make never looks like it does on the box. For me, figuring out a recipe is like being in a science class."

"How do you eat?"

"I eat out. Unless people invite me over to eat, I just eat out, or eat leftovers."

"Every meal?"

"Well, yeah. I make sandwiches, but I don't cook. That's why I don't keep Mo so long."

"You don't do potlucks?"

"I'm the one who brings the paper plates and plastic forks and sodas and napkins."

Then I saw what I hadn't seen before. She hadn't had a good mother herself.

Monica said, "I know you love to eat out, Mommy. Not you, Mommy Tommie, but you, Mommy-Mommy. That's why you always give me fast food. But we have real food in this house. Let me show you."

Angela held Monica's hand, and Mo held her hand, and mother and child headed inside.

I called out, "Angela."

"What's up, Tommie?"

"Merry Christmas."

She smiled at me for the first time ever. "Merry Christmas to you too, Tommie."

"You ever give Mo back rides?"

"Well, no."

"She likes back rides. She's growing fast. Let her ride your back before she gets too big to carry."

It was awkward, like Angela had no idea how to do it, but Monica got on her mother's back. That excited Monica. Angela had never given Mo a back ride. That was sad. It was time to change that for the better. I guessed that Angela hadn't had a father in her life either. I understood her aloofness, her lack of social graces that made her seem like a bitch. She hadn't had stability and had no idea how to offer stability. She partied like she was still a teenager. I bet her mother had done the same. Throw a kid a cold bologna sandwich, then go party all night. Angela needed better friends. She needed sisters in her life. She needed somebody to be nice to her for a change.

I stayed outside, in my driveway. I was alone with my thoughts. I waved at Vince and Dana Brown, did the same for their happy children, told all to have a merry Christmas. My head was high. Maybe I was better than Angela. That was how I felt. It was petty. But I was allowed to have my petty moments.

I was better than her and I had the ring that signified I was the ruler of my mini kingdom.

All she had was tits and an ample ass, a wannabe Beyoncé booty. A blow job could only get a woman so far. The way to a man's heart was still through his stomach. A man needed to eat three times a day, and I guess coochie wasn't filling. At least hers wasn't. I laughed at myself, that joke so damn crude and funny to me.

Love rose from within my body.

I loved Mo.

I wanted Monica to love her birth mother too.

We would have to work on that.

I wanted my child to love me as much as Mo loved me.

I sighed. Everything had changed back in March.

I looked off into the distance, in the direction of Beale Streets's mansion, an estate that was miles away.

Feeling a little sad, I leaned against Blue's car, my hand on my belly, afraid yet smiling. I had made the right choice.

I wiped away tears.

TOMMIE

I stayed outside, enjoyed the eighty-degree weather. Livvy and Tony arrived first.

Tony hugged me, kissed my cheek, then went inside to get a beer and watch the game.

Livvy leaned against the car, a look on her face that said something was on her mind.

I told Livvy, "Mo's mother is inside."

"Why is she inside your home?"

"I invited her to stay for dinner."

"Are you going to poison her like they did the king on *Game of Thrones*?"

"Not today."

"Friends close. Enemies closer."

"I need you and Frankie to be nice to her. Not a phony nice, a real nice."

"You're married. Blue's your husband. You want to rub it in her face."

"I got the ring. Bow down before the queen."

"You're too much."

"She didn't know me and Blue were back together. She dressed up super sexy for Blue, has on sky-high heels and a skirt so short I can read her lips when she jiggles her ass. Well, Angela just had her bubble of hope burst when she saw we were back together and now we're husband and wife."

"And you let her in your house?"

"Mo's got my back. She'll tell me everything that happens."

"Why are you outside all by yourself?"

"Livvy, something she said, I ignored it when she said it because I didn't want to know."

"What?"

"Monica isn't her first child."

"She said that?"

"Not directly. She slipped and said she had a baby before Monica."

"With Blue?"

"Before Blue. But I think Blue knows. I think he's protected her secret. I think that's why he put up with her, because he knows what she's been through. I swear she said she had had another child."

"With whom?"

"She didn't slip and say and I didn't ask. Sounds like her mother forced her to put her first child up for adoption. She let that slip. I was flabbergasted. We changed the subject, but that blew me away."

"When did she have the first kid?"

"Sounds like she was in high school, maybe before. Said her mother had issues with it. I know she grew up in San Bernardino, and that is the Mississippi of California. At least, people seem to think it is."

"Over two decades ago? Her kid would be an adult."

"She had a boy. She slipped and said it was a boy."

"Her son would be a grown man."

I thought about how Blue had been obsessed with Beale Streets, how he had learned all about him, how he had taken me to meet him downtown at the library. Blue was more than interested in Beale. Blue had been researching Beale. I had mistaken that *research* for adulation. I swallowed, tried to connect dots. Monica and Beale had similar features. Like father and daughter. Like brother and sister.

Blue was Angela's type. The men she had taken her photos with online, the ones I assumed she had hooked up with, from what I remembered seeing on her pages, they were all physically fit, all in the same ethnic and complexion genre as Blue. I shook my head as if I were trying to erase those thoughts.

Livvy asked, "What are you thinking about?"

"Beale Streets. Not gonna lie, he flashes in my mind from time to time."

"Is Blue past that letter you handed Beale? Is he past the disappointment and anger?"

"He says he is. It broke him down. We were all devastated. It came at a horrible time."

"But is he okay? A man is never past betrayal, Tommie. How is it affecting him?"

"I see it in his face from time to time, the pain, in his jaw, but he says he forgives me."

"That was some letter, Tommie. I cried for you and for Blue. Your relationship had been our role model, Tommie. You had surpassed both Frankie and me. We prayed for the two of you to reconcile."

"That letter to Beale was my heart. Beale knows I had written a good-bye letter to each of them, then I shredded the one I had written to Blue. And since Blue saw the letter, he knows I had written a good-bye letter to him as well."

"He knows more than you wanted him to ever know."

"He knows everything. I was that close to leaving Blue. But my love for him is greater. I couldn't lie to myself or to Beale. Blue read it, and I had to own what I had done and felt."

"I can't get over the fact that you'd written a good-bye letter to Blue."

"Yes. And it was twice as long as the one I gave Beale, maybe three times as long. But I felt that I had to write a letter to Monica too. I owed her that much. And . . . and I couldn't do it. It was impossible. That morning before the race, I had sat in Frankie's kitchen and tried to write that note."

"You were going to break up with Monica, too."

"While I ran the race I tried to think of what I could tell Monica, and while I ran I knew where I needed to be."

"I worried about you."

"Blue saw all I had written to Beale. Knew I was about to leave him. I had to move out, but not because of the tension."

"But you never told Blue why. You just let him assume."

"No, I never told him why I moved out for a while. Never will. I had to be gone. He had snuck away to do something, and I guess I did the same, only what we did were polar opposites. I didn't see Blue, but I picked up Monica from school, fed her, and she spent most nights with me, except for that week."

"The week you were sick."

"Told her I had the flu. Blue was working and I called Angela. I called her and told her I was sick, and Blue was working and we needed her to woman-up, to pick up her daughter from school for the week, needed her to up her game and be mommy for at least five days. She surprised me when she just said okay, then went and picked up Monica. She kept her that week. Had to be the worst week of Monica's life."

As I stared off into the distance, Livvy put her hand on mine. She knew me. She knew about the letter. They all knew. But only Livvy knew it all. Only Livvy knew that I had been pregnant back in March. I had been pregnant with Beale Streets's child. That had been a hard choice.

I would never be proud of myself for that. It would haunt me all of my days. The same way something haunted Angela. We both had ghosts. We had pains we'd never intended to mention aloud.

Blue had reissued weapons to his sailors. I had left him awhile, went and stayed in Jackie Summers's empty apartment on Stocker and Degnan, had left because I had to decide what I was going to do. Going back to Beale wasn't an option. Blue came to see me. Said he needed me. Said Monica needed me. We'd had an emotional night, in Jackie Summers's apartment, while Mo was with Angela. Now I was pregnant with Blue's child. I had gotten what I had asked for. I had my heart's desire.

The road had been winding and with many potholes.

The cost had been great.

Livvy said, "The only way your marriage will work is if you let Beale go."

"He's moved and moved on."

"You have to do the same."

"I have moved on. I'm married. I'm happy."

"The shoes he bought you."

"Those boots and T-shirts and trinkets are boxed up in the back of my closet."

"You have to let go all the way. Mementos are designed to awaken memories. You wake memories, you awaken desires."

"I have let go. I wouldn't have done what I did if I didn't want to let go all the way."

"You have to let go of everything symbolic. Lose the shoes."

"They're just shoes."

"Shoes are never just shoes. Didn't you learn that watching *The Wizard of Oz*?"

"I know. I want to forget about him. I do great most days. Then there are these moments."

"It hits you all of a sudden. It might start with a dream. A delicious dream. And you wake up tingling. Wet from what you couldn't control. You miss him more than you ever thought possible, then wear those boots, wear them while you're with Blue, and you start to want that old love back."

"Stop it, Livvy."

"Learn from my mistakes. Don't do to Blue what I did to Tony. We have gone through hell."

"That's your version of taking Tony through hell? Your hell has air-conditioning and lemonade."

"Stop it."

"What was going on with you and Tony? I had to scrub my eyeballs with bleach."

"Stop. It."

"Y'all couldn't find a black girl to play your games with or what? You know sisters get down like that nowadays. They do everything white people do. Why didn't you get a brother, have two guys? Wait, Frankie did that freaky mess in Cancún."

"Whatever. Joke about it, but we have gone through hell and come out the other side."

"Are you bi?"

"Don't deflect."

"You didn't answer. That's cool. We need

509

diversity in our family. I bought you a rainbow flag and a box of Skittles for Christmas."

"Will you stop joking?"

"Joking about the Skittles, but I did buy you a flag."

"Look, my point is that I wasn't nice and it was rough on Tony after he cheated. And if I open my present and see a flag, I will beat your butt from here to Barstow."

"Tony deserved whatever you did back then. Keep it real. Say he didn't and I will pull your ear like Momma used to do."

"Blue is a good man, Tommie. He's always been the kind of man you need in your life."

"I know."

"Let Beale out of your heart. Blue deserves better. He deserves the best."

"I have let Beale go. We're no longer friends on Facebook and I don't follow him on Twitter. No text messages. Nothing."

"Get him out of your heart. That's the way this works in the long run. Leaving him there, it will rattle you. It will be like an earthquake that comes and changes the direction the river flows. Leftover love can be strong and can be as powerful as the New Madrid earthquake in 1812 that made the Mississippi flow backward. Things can change us, and it might not be possible to ever change back to who we were."

"Beale's married to Tanya Obayomi. I'm married to Blue."

Livvy whispered, "Things that can't go on forever don't."

"Why are you over here getting all deep on me? God, you are sounding like Momma. Are you channeling Momma?"

"You keep thinking about his life, that moment you decided, and what could've been your life."

"Are you going to give me front-yard therapy on Jesus's faux birthday?"

Livvy was serious. "You made the right choice. I need you to accept that you made the right choice. You did what was best for you at the moment. That's the best we can do, Tommie."

"I made a choice, but I can never say it was the right choice. I will never know that."

"I know."

I said, "Two roads diverged in the woods, and I could not travel both."

"I have a few words for you. Words written by Lewis B. Smedes. I memorized it to recite it to you."

"Let's get it over with, Sister Reverend Livvy McBroom-Barrera. When you're done, I will pass the collection plate."

" 'Forgiving does not erase the bitter past.

A healed memory is not a deleted memory. Instead, forgiving what we cannot forget creates a new way to remember. We change the memory of our past into a hope for our future.' " She rubbed her nose. "It's not the best performance, but you get the point."

I nodded. "A memory, even when healed, is never deleted. That's deep, Livvy."

"That is the hell Tony and I have endured. There was no air-conditioning, no lemonade. It was a journey through bitterness, through memories that were our open wounds. I've escaped from the past. We drank from a bitter cup of pleasure, but now things are sweet again. Not as sweet as they were at the start, but I can no longer taste the bitterness. We're husband and wife as husband and wife should be."

We were silent for a while, waved at Latino neighbors, waved at my new white neighbors, taking in the neighborhood, this moment, this day of peace.

Christmas music kicked on in my small home.

Monica ran outside with her mother, Tony, and Blue. They all waved at us as they went to Angela's car. She opened the trunk and they took out paper plates, plastic utensils, sodas, and napkins. Blue, Angela, and Tony went back inside.

Mo ran to us and told us to come inside so we could open more presents.

She asked, "Do we have an extra present for my other mommy, Mommy?"

"We sure do. I have an extra box of perfume and a new scarf all wrapped up in pink boxes."

"Can I give those to her? Please, please, please, please, please?"

"You sure can. We'll get a card from the dresser and you can sign it for her with the gifts."

"Call Auntie Frankie and make sure she's okay. I'm really getting worried, Mommy."

"Why, little girl? You just saw her. Something happen I need to know about?"

"I just hope Auntie Frankie didn't get in the car with another stranger. Sometimes she does things not so smart."

Livvy and I laughed like we were going insane. Monica was serious. It really wasn't funny, but the way Monica said it, we laughed until we cried. Monica ran back to get her mother a card and presents. Livvy and I followed. As we headed across the lawn, Frankie pulled up in her Maserati. I hated the pretentiousness of that car, and she knew that. I shook my fist at her, shouted at her for once again showing up on CP Time.

Livvy's voice cracked when she said, "We almost lost her, Tommie."

"I know. Franklin. His wife. That was a horrible day for everyone we've ever touched. Don't start crying, Livvy. If you start crying, I'll start crying and it will become a cry party."

"Just don't start doing any haikus. I hate haikus. Dumbest poetry I've ever heard in my life."

"Livvy is a freak. One day I will tell Frankie. Lets girls eat coochie."

"Stop it. This is not funny."

"Never knew you felt that way about Asian cuisine."

"Don't judge me until you've walked in my shoes."

"I'm telling Frankie about your Chinese food."

"If you tell Frankie, swear to God, I'll kick your butt."

"At least you were in the boss position, sitting on face like you were running the show. I do hope you like the flag I bought you."

"Did you buy me a flag? Don't make me hate you."

"It was a colorful scarf, but I just told Mo to give it to her mom. I'll find something to give you to go with the Skittles."

She bumped up against me, then we jumped silly and danced the Bump in honor of our pending baby bumps.

We waited on our oldest sister to finish chatting with my neighbors across the street.

I said, "Livvy."

"What, Tommie?"

I looked down. "You're still wearing that anklet."

"It's on my left ankle."

"Not good enough."

She squatted and took it off.

She asked, "Feel better?"

"Your nasty baby can't play with my baby."

"Your baby will be as sneaky as you are."

We laughed and pushed on each other, pinched each other, chased each other across my lawn, acted like we were young girls again, then stopped and pretended to be Celie and Nettie, played patty-cake and did the lines from *The Color Purple.*

Frankie came up to us and said, "How are my favorite pregnant MILFs in training doing?"

Livvy turned to me and said, "Did you hear what this cougar called us?"

I said, "Cougar with a bleached valve trying to crack jokes on two innocent pregnant women."

Frankie said, "And don't expect me to babysit all those crying babies at the same time either."

Frankie pushed me out of the way, played patty-cake with Livvy. Then I pushed Livvy out of the way so I could play patty-cake with Frankie. We hugged, laughed, rubbed each other's flat bellies, and cracked jokes for a couple of minutes. Frankie made jokes about who would gain the most weight, me or Livvy. Laughter came from inside. Mo was having fun. Soon the men called for us to come inside and bless the food. We took our yuletide joy inside my home. This area was my neighborhood, and the people inside my home were my community. We went to have fun, stand in a circle, hold hands, give thanks, break bread, open gifts, and once again be family.

ACKNOWLEDGMENTS

Greetings and salutations from Little England, a.k.a. Bimshire, a.k.a. Reaper-ville.

Okay, it's Carolyn's only son, a.k.a. Virginia Jerry's grandson from down on Kansas Street in South Memphis. Well, I'm in the Caribbean today. As the sun beats down and the beige fan rattles, pull up a seat, grab a Vitamalt — my treat, or a Banks if you prefer — and sip along with me as we take care of a little housekeeping. Oh, before I get started, the day's off to a great start. I just read the first review for *One Night* and it was given five umbrellas. Cool beans. Hope you all checked it out.

So, we're back with the McBroom sisters, some years later, not as long as the time between when *Naughty or Nice* was released and when *Naughtier Than Nice* will be released. I shortened it quite a bit. I didn't want Mo to be a teenager yet; for Tommie to be engaged that long could have happened but didn't feel right.

The good thing with fiction is that we get to manipulate time, and weather too, like they did once upon a time on *General Hospital.* Okay, I did manipulate the weather in a few books . . . blame GH.

I looked at *Naughty or Nice,* at the endings for the McBroom sisters, and played what-if once again. What if you get what you ask for? What if it doesn't go as you expected? Frankie had the softer story in the first novel, so I decided to give her a meatier role, and the opposite for Livvy. I wanted hers to be important to her, but not on the level it was in the first novel. Everybody can't be the star.

And Tommie . . . well . . . the most innocent of the bunch . . . sorry, Tommie! Love ya!

When I was working on this project I realized that many of the characters from the previous novels lived in the same area. Since quite a few had been joggers or runners, it wasn't a stretch for them to all be in the same running club.

Yeah, I know. That's so Southern Cali.

But that's Southern Cali to the bone.

Now, let's get down to business. No man is an island and no writer does it alone. Let me give shout-outs to my crew.

I want to thank my editor, Denise Roy, for helping me sort this one out, as she has done with quite a few novels up to this point. You're amazing. You make me shine and I thank you for that.

Special thanks to my amazing copy editor, Aja Pollock. Outstanding work! Thanks for putting the polish on the shine.

Emily Brock! I have to say thanks to you and the crew in publicity back at the ranch. I'm finishing this one as you are getting the tour together for *One Night,* and I want to thank you in advance.

Sara Camilli! My agent, my second mother, thanks for helping me try to get back in order.

Quiana Victoria Nicholson, Queen of the Haikus, thanks for assisting Tommie Mc-Broom.

To my peeps in LA at the Planer Group, Carl and Tammy, thanks for the support as I stayed on the move and made it to the other side of a very interesting journey. You guys are awesome^10.

To my wonderful readers, both newbies and non-newbies, thanks for the reposts, for the retweets, thanks for tagging me whenever you had a copy of my work nearby, and thanks for carrying the novels all around the world. I love to see how a novel travels, where it goes, and I've seen photos in many places I would love to visit. So many countries, so little time, but I will do my best to make many more trips abroad, and the new people I meet will all be reflected between the pages, as usual.

It's time to run to Chefette and grab a snack pack, so I'll start to wrap it up.

The Dickster is about to leave the crib. *Dickster.* Cracks me up. Sounds like I should be a villain on *The Flash.* Thanks for that nickname again, Rebel Glam LOL. We will see if it sticks.

In case I was rushing and forgot anybody, it wasn't on purpose. Here's your chance to make sure everyone who picks up your copy knows your invaluable contribution to the project. I want to thank _____ because while I was sick, they brought me soup, gave me rides to the doctor, and reviewed every page to make sure this book was the bomb. _____ had meetings with the McBrooms, washed my bicycle, and made me cup after cup of green tea. They are the best of the best of the best. If you're their boss, give 'em a raise.

Peace, love, and big smiles from a lifetime member of '06. I need some ice, ice, baby.

Hasta luego! See ya when I see ya!

Eric Jerome Dickey

Thursday, January 20, 2015, 3:47 P.M. Latitude: 13°7'0" N. Longitude: 59°29'0" W. Elevation: 36 m. Levi's, blue T, bald with a thin beard, dreadlocks on the shelf in the garage next to the glue gun.

Oh, if you're still reading, there is a little bit more with the McBrooms. See the next page.

FRANKIE

Beyond being hoodwinked. No longer bamboozled. The pain from being betrayed gone but not forgotten. I no longer felt bottomless rage. Hair much longer and in a funky-yet-professional natural style, gun in hand, I patrolled my home, the lights on my Christmas tree blinking in the living room. I checked each window, each door, did that with my security guard. A Rottweiler walked at my heels, was on patrol with me. Just like me, she was a mean bitch when it was time. A stalker could outsmart an alarm, but a Rottweiler was better than anything made by ADT. I went to the master bedroom, undressed, and prepared to shower. I looked at my arm and my leg, inspected where I'd been stabbed. My keloidal scars were ugly. A couple rounds of plastic surgery would make them hard to detect.

I showered, and while I did, I felt absolutely nervous. It was the eve of New Year's

Eve and I tried to stop it, but that day in March played in my mind. When her stolen car had started giving her trouble, I thought that maybe debris was in the fuel line, or there was a problem with the vacuum pipes and hoses, or with the wiring. She had run out of gas. That was it. The authorities told me the car's fuel gauge was inoperative and she had simply run out of gas. If not for the chase, she could have stopped at a pump, pumped gas as she kept Monica as a hostage by her side, and only God knows which way the wind would have blown after that. The bitch had run out of gas.

She had executed her psychological torture perfectly, but her exit strategy had been faulty.

My cellular hummed with a text. It was from the man called Driver. He wished me a belated merry Christmas and a happy New Year. I wished him the same, then thanked him again for saving my life.

I almost became emotional. I would have done anything for Driver. I really would. I waited to see if he would send a follow-up text, but there was none. He had saved me, but most important he had saved Monica. He had broken his policy and stuck around after the sirens came on and saved both of us.

I looked at the clock and dressed, sprayed on perfume, inspected myself a dozen and a half times.

I was as nervous as a sixteen-year-old preparing for her coming-out party.

Daniel arrived a few minutes before nine P.M. He was always a few minutes early.

My Rottweiler followed my command and went to the back door and sat quietly.

When the door to the garage whirred and eased open Daniel parked inside, took the middle slot. My cars were parked on opposite sides. I wanted him inside so no one would see his ride in front of my home. Mrs. Carruthers and her husband had been buried in separate cemeteries, all of that done months ago, but her harassment had done its mental damage. Didn't need any more acid on cars, not ever.

Daniel came toward me, smiling, a Christmas present in his hand.

I said, "You made it here fast."

"This is for you, Frankie McBroom."

"You bought me a present?"

"Merry belated Christmas."

He handed me the beautiful, small box, then kissed me right away, and that surprised me.

"Behave. Let me open my present."

He had bought me a Pandora bracelet. It

was amazing.

I said, "Daniel Madison."

"I hope it's not inappropriate."

"I wasn't expecting anything."

"It has trinkets for a runner and a home to symbolize real estate."

"The charms are beautiful."

"Glad you're smiling. I had hoped you would like the present."

"I love it. Thank you so much. I will cherish this gift. I always wanted one."

He helped me put it on and we kissed again.

He asked, "Want to go out to dinner?"

"No."

"Thought you wanted to go to Post and Beam and hang out?"

"We've had enough dinners. We've had enough drinks. Let's chill."

"You sure?"

"Look at me. Take a close look at me."

I had on black shorts that were sweet on my ass and a long-sleeve top sheer enough to show the sexy bra underneath. I was dressed provocatively, like a strong female character in the complicated-women movies, when Greta Garbo, Barbara Stanwyck, and Norma Shearer were the boss queens, before the Hays Code shut all of that down and muted a woman's point of view on love, life, and self-truth. I wasn't a vamp or a victim of love, but I was the chairman of the board and channeled Jean Harlow in my attitude. I was a smart and confident woman who refused to be stifled by events in my past, and I was at home and didn't feel the need to hide my sexy. Excluding my flats, but including the matching thong, I had on four pieces of clothing, clothes easy to remove when that moment of intimacy arrived. I was dressed the way a woman dressed when she wanted to be undressed.

Daniel held a jacket in his hands, but he had on straight-leg jeans and a T-shirt. His T hugged his chest, made his build stand out. Daniel was more handsome now than when I had met him three seasons ago. We'd spent some time together after the March madness had died down. We had dated, taken long drives up into wine country, but we weren't a couple. We had kissed many times, had become kissing buddies, and had had countless conversations, from intellectual foreplay to silly talks.

He had visited me in the hospital a few times, had brought me lunch from Chin Chin when I complained about the bland hospital food. He'd been very delicate with me. He had slowed it down, and now I thought I was ready to take it to an adult level. I was nervous, again trembling like a virgin. In my head Betty Wright was singing "Tonight Is the Night." I was ready to be baptized in affection, born again.

He didn't have to become my man, but Frankie needed to get her groove back.

I went to the back door and gave my dog the command to chill out while Auntie Frankie went to handle her business but if someone tried to get into the house from the back, to have herself a good late-night snack. She barked twice and complied.

As my heart raced and my desire did an anxious dance, I took a breath to calm myself while I gave Daniel a perfunctory tour of my home, starting with the patio in the back. After the formal dining area and the informal dining area, I paused long enough to pour us a glass of wine. We chatted, finished the glass, gave knowing smiles, and then we headed toward the stairs, shared a kiss or two along the way. We made our way up the stairs to the bedrooms. He noticed the double dead bolts on one of the bedroom doors.

He asked, "What's in there? Government secrets?"

I used the keys to unlock the door. The once well-appointed room made for fun and fantasies was empty. Everything had been cleared out. Franklin's wife had touched my things when she violated my space. I'd replaced my toilets, scrubbed my tub, and trashed all of my lingerie as well.

He asked, "Why do you keep the door to an empty room locked?"

"I'm locking certain memories inside."

"Should I ask?"

"No, you shouldn't."

He followed my Marlene Dietrich sashay down the hallway. Mirrors were on both ends so I could always see what was behind me, as mirrors were all over my home so I could see behind me at all times. I saw his eyes on my bottom, watching the mesmerizing movements of the booty. Lights came on. I had installed upgraded lights with motion detectors. They came on whenever someone walked the hallway.

I was afraid of a ghost. Mrs. Carruthers was dead, but I still felt like she was following me.

I thought about my DBV. The doctors said I had experienced a DBV — deathbed vision.

Rosemary Paige didn't jump from the bridge.

Mo never ran back to me to look over me.

Those things didn't happen.

The officers would never let a freed hostage return to danger. Once Mo ran toward the officers, they whisked her off to safety as the world applauded.

They applauded her and watched my bloodied body in the middle of the freeway. I had lost blood and had created my own fantasy world. Maybe as I lay there dying, I just didn't want to be alone.

No one wants to die alone. In the end, no one wants to be alone.

They explained that a DBV is what the dying experience just before their true death occurs, when the body is shutting down, when the eyes start to shut off and create that bright light. Some people imagined they saw loved ones. Others imagined they saw family who had died long ago. Some saw celebrities coming to take them home.

As I had bled and slipped into cardiac arrest, I had seen Monica.

When Franklin's wife had gotten out of the car and tried to escape on foot, she had found herself surrounded, and they had shouted for her to drop the knife, to drop the gun, but she turned, paused, argued with them as they screamed orders to drop the weapons. Then the woman who had murdered her husband raised her gun. She didn't have to. She was trained, and her type of training scared law enforcement, half of them former military. It had to be hard to point a gun at one of your own. She had tours of duty under her belt. On that day in March when insanity had shut down the 5 freeway, she had raised her unloaded gun. They opened fire. She made them shoot her. She was ready to go home. The soldier had grown tired of fighting for a country she felt didn't love her, for a man who no longer desired her, was weary from a never-ending combat, and wanted to go to her final home. I wondered if she died thinking Franklin was worth it or wishing she could go back in time and undo the moment she had met him online.

I wondered if she saw him, if he was part of her DBV.

I wished I had the power to undo the moment I had met Franklin at the post office.

That would have saved him, saved her, saved me, saved all of us from that experience.

I wished I had the power not to be the one Franklin had seen and who had inspired his infatuation.

I was fine now. I was fine.

There was no one left to stalk me.

I had to say that out loud ten times a day.

The Carrutherses were in purgatory stalking and arguing with each other. If God took a page from a play by Sartre and left them trapped in a small, windowless room together for eternity, a room with no exit, it would be fine by me.

Daniel asked, "You sure you're up for company this evening?"

His words brought me back to him, and I lost all interest in being afraid, didn't care about any lunatics or ghosts. I turned to him and expressed corners of my sexuality in my eyes, in my voice, in the way I touched my mane. Sexual playfulness was in my body language. Double entendres were on my mind, and I didn't want to shut down this part of me abruptly, as I had done each time we'd been together.

I wanted to explore and be explored, wanted to have adult time and mature thoughts.

I was modern and intelligent, but I wasn't perfect.

We all have a blind side.

I regarded Daniel, and with a diminishing smile, I stopped our fun as if I were stopping time.

I asked, "Are you still single? Before we go on, I need to know you're single."

"I am single, Frankie."

"But?"

"Since I met you, I have dated other

people. Nothing serious. I didn't run off and get married."

"You've had premarital sex with other people."

"I have had a few encounters. Only with one woman."

"With anyone I know? Is it ongoing? What's the status on that?"

"No one you know. It was off and on for three months. That ended a couple of months ago."

I grinned, relieved that I wasn't his obsession. I asked, "But no girlfriend at the moment?"

"No girlfriend at the moment. I'm single, and I woke up like this. And you?"

"Follow me."

"Where to?"

"I wanted to surprise you. I went on Sepulveda and got you a Christmas present."

"Really?"

"You might get an unexpected belated Christmas present for being a good boy."

"Might?"

"Let me show you the rest of the house."

"This is an amazing property, Frankie. The mirrors make it seem that much larger."

The tour ended at the master bedroom. My heartbeat sped up. My palms dampened.

Daniel's eyes took in the gorgeous room and its colorful walls. King-size bed. Beige carpet. Recessed lighting. Sitting area with sofa and love seat. Cushions were on the floor. The balcony faced the back of a hill, so no one could see inside my boudoir. I opened the French doors and we went out on the balcony.

"Now, Daniel, before we go to the next step, we have to do some legal housekeeping."

"Okay."

"We need to take care of the legalities of intimacy."

"What legalities of intimacy?"

"My invisible attorney is here and I need you to sign my invisible consent forms."

"Which type of consent forms?"

"Pre-sex agreement and post-sex agreement, both nondisclosures."

"You're serious?"

"What happens here at Frankie's playhouse, it stays at Frankie's playhouse."

"Tell me more about this contract I will need to sign."

"What you do to Frankie and what Frankie does to you are not up for discussion with any third party. It will be for our memories, but not for posting on any social network or texting or any other outlet.

Nothing is to be discussed with anyone, out of respect, until the other party is deceased."

"Wow. That's pretty intense."

"It's not negotiable. Sign and stay or we can move to the front of the house and be kissing buddies."

"Tell your invisible attorney that will be no problem. I brought my own invisible ink."

"The main rule about sex with Frankie is you don't talk about sex with Frankie with anyone, ever."

"Understood. Anything else?"

"Now for the most important part of the contract."

"Which is?"

I kissed his lips. "Check box number five if you plan on making me have an orgasm."

"Checked eight times."

"We'll see, shit talker."

"Is it okay to spend the night? Should I check that box?"

"Only if you're going to be a man at work. You have to put me to sleep to earn your sleep."

"Consider the box checked."

I took his hand, led him back inside, beyond the sitting area, to the bed, which had fresh linens, and we stood at the foot of the bed and kissed again, that long and dizzying kiss the signing of the contract.

I said, "You kiss my neck like you want to take my clothes off."

"You kiss me like you want me to show you my birthday suit."

If he had come into my home like that, all hot and bothered and ready to go, tonight I would have been turned on by that energy, would've been ready and willing, and we never would have made it out of the garage. He seduced me, kissed my face, my neck, pulled my top away, licked my breasts, sucked my nipples, kissed the scars of my shoulder, kissed the mark on my thigh, undressed me, pulled away the rest of my clothing, then kissed my skin as it was exposed. My vagina was on display. It sparkled. It was a work of art.

He said, "Wow. That looks amazing."

I blushed a little and exhaled. "Stopped by my sister's spa and got vajazzled for you."

"For me?"

"No one else is going to see it but you. Like?"

"This is going to be the best Christmas present ever."

"Happy belated Christmas. Now get naked. I want to watch you strip to your birthday suit."

He undressed himself without rushing.

With each button undone, with each piece of clothing removed, I sat and watched him wear his amazing birthday suit. He had a nice tool. A handsome cock. There hadn't been any augmentation. There hadn't been any trips to Suriname; there were no *boegroes.*

I appreciated that.

He motioned for me to open my legs wider, so he could get a better view of the decorations that surrounded his present. He was confident, and this was his gift, so I did what he asked.

From one Christmas to the next I had existed without experiencing passion on this level. It felt like it had been longer. It felt like it had been forever and a day. Trying to hide my rising desire and tension, I took a deep breath and pulled the new sheets back. I threw all but one pillow to the carpet.

We were nude, standing before a bed that had fresh sheets over a new mattress.

Moments from now he would be inside me.

First time with a new lover, the anticipation was powerful.

He sucked my ear, massaged my breasts, and whispered, "Want to go out on New Year's Eve?"

I moaned. "Really? You're going to ask me

that now?"

"They say who you spend New Year's with is who you'll be with the rest of the year."

"I know."

"The way you spend New Year's Eve determines how the year will go."

"Slow your roll. Let's see how this evening goes first."

He was a man on fire, his craving powerful but not obsessive. He lifted me, placed me on the edge of the bed. Daniel sucked my toes, kissed my feet, kissed up my legs, worked his tongue north, kissed my scars, kissed where I had been stabbed, kissed that spot a dozen times, moved north again, his journey unhurried, then paused in the middle. I fell into a warm heaven. Famished, I reciprocated his kindness and generosity. I did a sweet Shemar on his Moore, did a little Morris on his Chestnuts.

Soon the handsome man who had a crush on me positioned himself between anxious thighs, both of us breathing heavily. My pre-orgasmic shudders and elongated sighs intensified when he touched engorged lips with the slope of his erection. I cooed, spoke in murmurs and whispers. He woke up slumbering nerves. We were skin to skin, eye to eye, inhaling and exhaling, as I sucked his bottom lip. We sucked tongues like they were coated with honey and cream. He rested on me, did a slow grind where wetness bloomed. I couldn't take it anymore. He rose up on his elbows, adjusted himself. He was ready. I tensed. He went gently into my secrets bit by bit and I whined, held on to him, and eased into my soft hallelujah song. He filled me. We'd only started and I was impressed, knew that I would want to experience this passion again. It was stunning from the top. Kisses were gems of perfection. His stroke was powerful yet not rushed. More intense than forceful. Unhurried yet measured. Strong and poignant. I tried to maintain the façade of coolness, tried to control the fire, but his rhythm was as deeply moving as he was moving deeply. It was exquisite. When that sensual side of me broke free, when my back bowed again and my hands clutched sheets, my fantasies of being with the man only known by the moniker Driver again went away. The way Daniel pleased me, it was a damn shame I had shut down the houghmagandy room. He might motivate me to start it up anew. This was how I wanted to spend my next New Year's Eve. This New Year's Eve at midnight, as fireworks went off all over the City of Angels, and as my phone would ring with the pregnant McBrooms and Monica and Blue and Tony calling to wish me a happy New Year, Daniel would be stroking me . . . doing an Idris on my Elba like this . . . just . . . like . . . like . . . this.

ABOUT THE AUTHOR

Eric Jerome Dickey is the *New York Times* bestselling author of twenty-two novels, and is also the author of a six-issue miniseries of graphic novels for Marvel Entertainment, featuring Storm (*X-Men*) and the Black Panther. He also penned the original story for the film *Cappuccino,* directed by Craig Ross Jr. Originally from Memphis, Tennessee, Dickey is a graduate of the University of Memphis, where he pledged Alpha Phi Alpha, and also attended UCLA. Dickey now lives on the road and rests in whatever hotel will have him.